CUPCAKES AND KISSES IN MICKLEWICK BAY

ELIZA J SCOTT

Storm

This is a work of fiction. Names, characters, businesses, places, events and incidents are either the products of the author's imagination or used in a fictitious manner. Any resemblance to actual persons, living or dead, or actual events is purely coincidental.

Copyright © Eliza J Scott, 2025

The moral right of the author has been asserted.

All rights reserved. No part of this book may be reproduced or used in any manner without the prior written permission of the copyright owner. This prohibition includes, but is not limited to, any reproduction or use for the purpose of training artificial intelligence technologies or systems.

To request permissions, contact the publisher at rights@stormpublishing.co

Ebook ISBN: 978-1-83700-026-5
Paperback ISBN: 978-1-83700-027-2

Cover design: Rose Cooper
Cover images: Shutterstock

Published by Storm Publishing.
For further information, visit:
www.stormpublishing.co

ALSO BY ELIZA J SCOTT

Welcome to Micklewick Bay Series

The Little Bookshop by the Sea
Summer Days at Clifftop Cottage
Finding Love in Micklewick Bay
Christmas at the Little Bookshop by the Sea

Life on the Moors Series

The Letter – Kitty's Story
The Talisman – Molly's Story
The Secret – Violet's Story
A Christmas Kiss
A Christmas Wedding at the Castle
A Cosy Countryside Christmas
Sunny Skies and Summer Kisses
A Cosy Christmas with the Village Vet

Heartshaped Series

Tell That to My Heart

To my family xxx

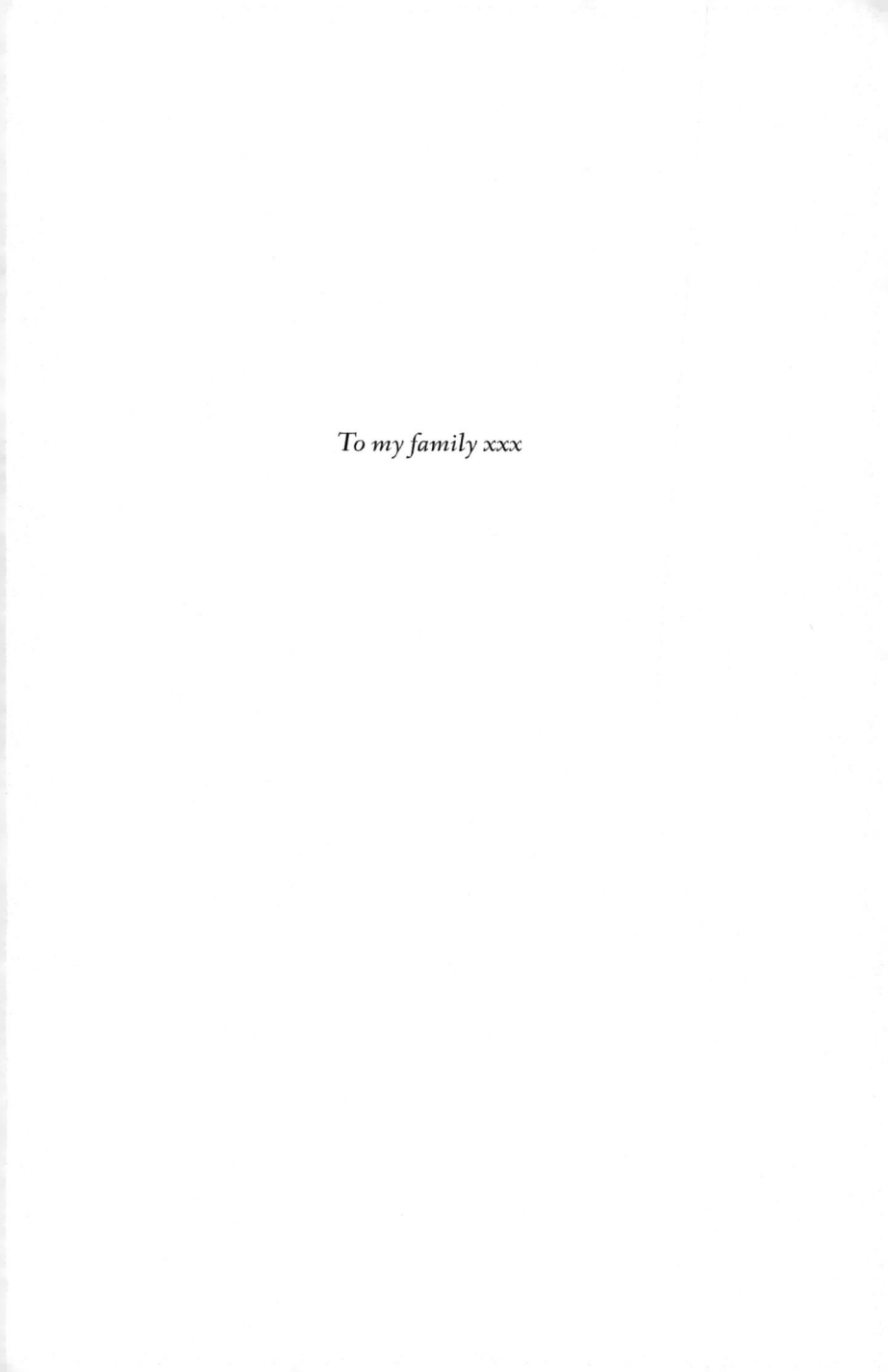

ONE

THE FIRST FRIDAY IN JUNE

'Finished!' Jasmine Ingilby said, puffing out a sigh of relief. Setting down the fine paintbrush she'd been using to dust iridescent powder over the cake she'd spent most of the day decorating, she took a step back, running a critical eye over her handiwork. The brief had been, well... brief: three-tier Victoria sponge to celebrate a pearl wedding anniversary. But Jasmine had been okay with that; she enjoyed being given a free rein, allowing her creative side to take the lead.

'Just do what you think, Jazz,' Ali Harrington had said when she'd called to place the order. 'After seeing the wedding cake you made for Kendra and Tom Wilson, I know I can trust you to come up with something totally awesome – those sugar paste flowers were *amazing*! They looked so realistic.'

The feedback had given Jasmine a thrill; not only had she been in her element decorating the cake Ali referred to, but she'd also gained a considerable number of new customers off the back of it. Her diary was now bulging for the rest of the year with orders trickling into the next. She had no idea how she was going to fit them all into her already hectic schedule, but she'd do it even if it meant working into the early hours and getting up at the crack of dawn. After all, it wouldn't be the first time.

And now, a month after Ali's phone call, she was standing in the tiny kitchen of her little home, surveying the end result, the cloyingly sweet smell of sugar paste and icing sugar hanging in the air.

The three-tiered confection was a study of understated elegance, decorated in ivory-coloured fondant icing and topped with a cluster of delicate roses in a matching shade of sugar paste. The top and bottom tiers were edged with cream ribbon, while the middle one was trimmed with a string of faux pearls. Jasmine had spent an age making the individual roses, using her cake-decorating tools to curl the petals in order to create a realistic effect. The final touch had been to add a soft pearl-like shimmer of iridescent powder in a nod to the anniversary for which it had been commissioned. Jasmine smiled. Usually self-critical, she was pleased with her creation. And, after Ali's feedback about the Wilson's wedding cake, she felt sure Ali and her family would be happy with her interpretation of the brief.

Her own parents' ruby wedding anniversary was a couple of months away and Jasmine planned to make something similar for them but with elements in a rich red trim referencing the red stone that symbolised the fortieth celebration. Though she was going to trim theirs with sugar paste "lace" using the confectioner's mats she'd recently invested in. The equipment would punch the intricate design into the sugar paste, creating a delicate vintage lace effect which she could then affix to the base layer of fondant icing. Jasmine couldn't wait to try it.

Her green eyes flicked to the clock on the wall, its face glaring back at her accusatorially, making her heart lurch. It was twenty past seven. 'Yikes! How the bloomin' 'eck has it got to that time?'

She was late, of course – when *wasn't* Jasmine late? It came with the territory of being a single mum to two lively children while juggling two part-time jobs and her growing celebration cake-baking business. And though she thrived on being busy, and regularly found herself wishing there were more hours in the day, there were times when she felt she was – to quote her mum – in danger of catching herself coming back. She fell into bed exhausted every night, sleep pulling her under as soon as her head hit the pillow, and before she knew it, the six a.m. alarm was rousing her with its ear-splitting screech the following morning. Much as her body cried out for an extra hour's sleep, Jasmine resisted the temptation to snuggle back under the duvet. Instead, she'd heave herself out of bed so she could catch up on her jobs around the house, throw a load of laundry into the washing machine, or even make a start on the sugar paste elements of whichever celebration cake she was currently working on. Whatever it was that was screaming out as a priority at that time, was given her full attention. It was the only way she could keep on top of everything.

But since her cake decorating business had taken off, Jasmine had found herself becoming perennially late, this evening being a prime example. It wasn't because she was unorganised – the opposite was, in fact, the case, with her slew of lists and planners – it was more that she was a perfectionist, tweaking her creations until they satisfied her exacting standards. Losing track of time had, frustratingly, become a hazard of her life recently and she'd been racking her brains to figure out a way around it. Thus far, she'd had limited success.

In an ideal world, Jasmine wouldn't be constantly under pressure to keep things running smoothly, wouldn't be dashing from one job to another to make sure there was enough money to pay the bills and to make sure her children got what they needed. And she wouldn't be wracked with the guilt that constantly ate away at her, telling her she wasn't giving her children enough attention, which was the worst part of it all, especially since she'd noticed that her daughter, Chloe, had been quieter than usual recently, which she hadn't been able to get to the bottom of yet. Not having to deal with all of that would be the dream. But, maybe, after the phone call she'd received earlier, there was a faint chance it might be more than just a dream – not that Jasmine wanted to build her hopes up too much; she was nothing if not cautious in that regard.

But right now, at twenty past seven on a Friday evening, Jasmine should have been sitting in The Jolly Sailors pub with her friends, glass of wine in hand as they all caught up with what had gone on since their last get-together a week earlier. In those few precious hours, she allowed herself to switch off, slip out of "mum mode", not to mention "work mode", push her never-ending list of jobs to the back of her mind, and relax with her closest friends – her 'me time' as they called it. As a rule, Florrie from their friendship group would stop off at Jasmine's house on Rosemary Terrace and scoop Jasmine up on her way to the Jolly, but knowing she would be running late, Jasmine had texted her friend earlier and explained about the cake, telling Florrie to make her own way down to the pub, adding that she'd join them as soon as she could. She knew they'd understand.

'No worries, flower. And don't go stressing yourself out, rushing around like a headless chicken; just get there when you can,' Florrie had said in her reply, which, Jasmine had thought at the time, was easier said than done.

Would there ever be a time when she wasn't running around like a headless chicken? Jasmine wondered. The way things had been going recently, it was hard to imagine. Next week was a classic example. Not only did she have an extra couple of hours working for Spick 'n' Sparkle, the cleaning company owned by her friend Stella's mum, but she was also covering two shifts for a colleague at the bakery in town on top of her own. Then there was the celebration cakes she needed to bake and ice. The reminder triggered a squeeze of stress in her chest. Before she let it take hold, Jasmine pulled herself up and drew in a deep breath.

'Right, it's Friday night, fretting about next week isn't going to help or make a difference. You need to get your backside into gear and get down to the Jolly with your friends!' she remonstrated with herself, relieved not to have a tardy babysitter to contend with – something that had, disappointingly, become increasingly regular – thanks to Zak and Chloe having a sleepover at her parents that night.

Feeling instantly brighter, she quickly washed her hands before separating the tiers of the cake and carefully placing them into boxes ready for collection first thing in the morning. That done, she whipped off her apron and shoved it into the washing machine before rushing upstairs where she wriggled out of her cake-making clothes. Much as she'd love nothing better than to jump in the shower, time was against her, so she gave herself a quick squirt of deodorant instead, then changed into a clean pair of cargo trousers, teaming them with a yellow and white striped T-shirt. She didn't have time to look in the mirror; the couple of coats of mascara she'd applied that morning would have to suffice, and she wasn't going to give the state of her dyed-red pixie crop a second thought after all the icing sugar and sparkles that had been floating around the kitchen. If she sparkled like a Christmas bauble, it was too bad!

'Ignorance is bliss and all that,' she muttered to herself, knowing her friends would take her as they found her.

Racing downstairs, Jasmine grabbed her phone and her keys, stuffing them into her bag, which she slung over her shoulder cross-body style. She slipped her feet into her battered Converse plimsols then reached for her green utility jacket. Seconds later, the front door closed behind her with a slam. Standing on the doorstep, she puffed out her cheeks, squinting in the bright evening sunshine.

Sucking in a deep breath, she set off, hurrying along the

street of two-up, two-down terraced houses, unzipping her bag and rummaging for her sunglasses, warm air rushing over her skin. If she put her best foot forward, she could get to the Jolly in twenty minutes, provided she didn't melt into a sweaty puddle beforehand, that is. She had so much to share with her friends and was eager to get their opinion on a couple of things. Her heart fluttered at the thought.

It wasn't until she was striding along the top promenade of Micklewick Bay on the North Yorkshire Coast, her feet pounding over the flagstone pavement, that Jasmine's thoughts had steadied sufficiently to allow herself time to process her day, and in particular, *that* phone call. Excitement fizzed through her as she replayed the conversation in her mind. *Oh, my days!* She could hardly believe it – she'd actually had to pinch herself several times to prove she hadn't been dreaming or hallucinating! Things had suddenly taken off with her celebration cake-baking business in a way she could only ever have dreamt of and, much as she didn't want to tempt fate or jinx herself, she hoped it was a sign that her life was about to turn a corner. And boy, did it feel good. She'd sent her friends a brief text earlier, hinting that she had something big to tell them. Their enthusiastic replies suggested their interest had been thoroughly piqued and she couldn't wait to share the details with them.

She gave in to the smile that had started tugging at her mouth. It didn't matter one jot to Jasmine that her hair was sticky with icing sugar or that sunlight glinted off the edible glitter that had found its way to the tip of her nose and the dusting that decorated her left eyebrow. It was par for the course. Nothing could dampen her spirits tonight – not even her former in-laws, and that was saying something. She elbowed the recent toxic encounter with them out of her mind before it had a chance to take root. It wasn't as if anything she ever said to Gary and Alice Forster made any difference and their latest accusation, of her still hanging on to some of Bart's stuff, was just the latest in a long line of hassle she'd had with them. But Jasmine wasn't going to give their spite and negativity the tiniest bit of headspace, especially tonight. Tonight was all about positive vibes only.

She strode on, arms swinging, as the mellow evening sun shone down from a clear blue sky. The town was still bustling with day-trippers and locals making the most of the fine weather. Upping her pace, she glanced to her left, taking in the stunning vista that stretched out before her. A handful of fishing boats bobbed about on the waves that sparkled in the sunshine where seagulls dipped and dived, their cries carrying over the water. But what dominated the view was the precipitous range of cliffs that held the North Sea at bay along this stretch of the North Yorkshire coastline. Taking centre stage was the rugged broad shoulders of the iconic Thorncliffe that loomed over the cove where the higgledy-piggledy cottages of Old Micklewick huddled close together, and the Jolly sat stoically facing out to sea. The beach below swept around in a dramatic arc of golden sand, reaching all the way along to where work on the new marina was underway, transforming the fortunes of the once tired part of town. The skeletal shapes of industrial Teesside further up the coast seemed incongruous juxtaposed against such an idyllic seaside scene. Jasmine loved her hometown and couldn't imagine living anywhere else, not least because her family and best friends were here; after her children, they were what mattered most in her life and she loved them all dearly.

She soon reached Skitey Bank, the steep road that wound its way down to the bottom prom and the beach beyond, and hurried along it, almost tripping over her own feet in her haste – despite its steep ratio, it was far easier than the alternative of tripping down the uneven range of one hundred and ninety-nine steps. She'd taken a tumble down them several times before in her rush to get to the Jolly. The extra traffic snaking up and down the bank was a reflection of the beautiful weather the seaside town had been blessed with that week.

Beads of sweat prickled her brow as she scurried by boats and the precariously stacked lobster pots by the sea wall, weaving her way through clusters of people ambling along at a leisurely pace, the hush of the tide idly lapping at the shore in the background. Up ahead, the characterful, whitewashed building that was the Jolly came into view, triggering a wave of relief that her destination was within reach. Even from here she could see the outside seating area was heaving with customers, with every table taken.

As she drew closer, the jaunty sound of a fiddle floated towards her, accompanied by the familiar tones of the folk band that played there every Friday. It was joined by the tempting smell of fish and chips that wafted under her nose, making her stomach growl, reminding her she'd only had a banana for her lunch which seemed like an age ago. Jasmine had found that the sweet scent of the sugar paste and icing sugar took the edge off her appetite while she was busy cake-decorating, and she had to make a concerted effort to remind herself to grab something quick to eat just to keep from flagging.

Stepping inside the pub, she wasn't in the least bit surprised to be met with a wall of people. It was always a popular spot, in no small part because of landlady Mandy's fish and chips which were legendary and had recently won an award for being the best in town – from the corner of her eye, Jasmine had caught the chalkboard on the wall outside proclaiming the very same.

The ancient pub was oozing with character, with its thick, uneven walls, the low ceiling supported by smoke-darkened oak beams, the wide inglenook fireplace and the repurposed hurricane lamps that cast their soft light around the room. It was no wonder people were tempted back.

A loud, cackling laugh rang out above the folk music and conversation. Jasmine instantly recognised it as belonging to

Lobster Harry. When he wasn't out to sea in his ancient trawler, the grizzle-faced fisherman was as much a fixture in the pub as the old ship's bell that hung above the bar.

As she pushed her way through the throng of warm bodies towards the table where her group of friends gathered and put the world to rights every Friday evening, she caught the eye of Ando Taylor. She groaned inwardly as he gave her an exaggerated flirty wink. He was a harmless soul who was regarded as something of a local character, though he was known to stray into the realms of silliness when he was on the wrong side of a few pints of beer. His penchant for skateboarding, and his youthful garb of ripped jeans, battered leather jacket, brightly coloured trainers, topped off with a baseball cap worn back-to-front, belied the fact he was well into his forties. He'd been showing an increasing amount of interest in Jasmine over recent months but, much to her irritation and no matter how many times she turned him down, he remained undeterred. She gave him a tight smile and continued her way across the bar, hoping he wouldn't trouble her tonight.

It was Maggie who spotted her first, her face lighting up with a smile as she gave an enthusiastic wave, causing the others to turn and follow suit.

Jasmine smiled back, her heart lifting; it was always so good to see her pals.

'Jazz, you made it, flower!' Florrie said when Jasmine reached the table. She pushed her tortoiseshell glasses up her nose and grabbed her friend's hand, giving it a squeeze.

'Hiya, lasses,' said Jasmine.

'Yay! So glad you're here, Jasmine.' Lark beamed a warm smile at her, making her pale green eyes crinkle.

'Oh, you look all hot and bothered, petal. Park your bum and catch your breath.' Maggie's smile was dampened by the faint hint of a troubled expression. Jasmine inwardly berated herself for not running a smudge of concealer over the dark circles that seemed to have become a permanent fixture beneath her eyes these last couple of months; her haste to leave the house meant she hadn't given it a second thought. She knew her friends' concern for her had been growing with all the extra hours she'd been working and she didn't want to worry them, especially tonight when she had exciting news to share. She didn't want anything to take the edge off that.

'I agree, you do look all of a fluster, Jazz,' said Stella, reaching for the bottle of Pinot Grigio chilling in the wine bucket and filling the spare glass. Though she smiled, the look in Stella's eyes betrayed that her thoughts were straying down the same path as Maggie's.

Jasmine draped her jacket over the back of the seat at the head of the table before flopping into it. She blew out a long breath, feeling her heart rate begin to settle. She inhaled slowly, the familiar soothing scent of the essential oils Lark doused herself in tickling her nostrils and overpowering any perfume the others were wearing. 'Tell you what, hot and bothered, and all of a fluster, doesn't even begin to cover it. I'm shattered and I'm absolutely sweltering. And I don't even want to think about the horrors taking place inside my plimsols after the race I had to get here.' She gave an exaggerated shudder, making everyone laugh.

'Can't say I'd be keen to give that too much thought, either,' Maggie said dryly, hitching an amused eyebrow at her.

'Yeah, me neither.' Stella pulled a faux horrified face.

Jasmine grinned, giving her T-shirt a quick waft in a bid to cool herself down. 'I was that engrossed in the cake I was decorating, I completely lost track of time – mind, it's fair to say I had a phone call that didn't exactly help. Meant I've had a right bloomin' rush on to get here. That said, you can trust me when I say, wild horses couldn't keep me away from our Friday night get-togethers. They're what keeps me sane.'

'There you go, get a mouthful of that.' Stella smiled kindly.

She was sitting on the settle to Jasmine's left and slid the glass of freshly poured wine towards her. As ever, Stella was looking effortlessly sophisticated in a simple linen halter-neck dress, its shade of blue complementing her ice-blue eyes and glossy, blonde hair that she'd tied back into a sleek, low ponytail. Her cool, unapproachable exterior and straight-talking nature belied her warm personality and sharp sense of humour, and the fact that she was very much a woman's woman.

'Thanks, Stells.' Jasmine took a sip, the crisp, cool citrussy notes making her tastebuds dance. 'Mmm. That's nice.' She was already beginning to feel the benefit of the cooler temperature of the pub, its thick, centuries-old walls doing a sterling job of keeping the heat of the sun at bay.

'So, come on then, spill the tea, missus. We've all been dying to know what you meant in that text you sent us this afternoon,' said Maggie, who was sitting on the other side of Stella. She'd exuded a happy glow ever since she and husband Bear had become parents to much-longed-for baby Lucia last Christmas, and Jasmine noted the recent bout of sunny weather appeared to have lifted her naturally olive skin, adding to the effect. Maggie was looking colourful in a short-sleeved empire-line dress in a light cotton fabric that was splashed with bright pink flowers on a yellow background. She'd piled her shiny, dark curls up on top of her head, fixing them in place with a turquoise-coloured scarf. To Jasmine's mind, Maggie could carry off bold, clashing colours like nobody else she knew.

'Yes, come on, Jazz, we've been trying to guess what it could be,' said Florrie, who was looking all fresh and cool in a white blouse with short, puffed sleeves, making Jasmine feel even more of a hot and sweaty mess in contrast. 'We've been coming up with all sorts of suggestions.'

'Mm. Knowing you lot, I dread to think what they'd be.' Jasmine rolled her eyes jokingly.

'My suggestion was that you'd got a cake order for the new

people who've moved into the big house on the cliff above the marina, then you'd be able to satisfy our curiosity, and tell us who they are,' said Lark. She owned and ran Lark's Vintage Bazaar in the town's Victoria Square. It was an enchantingly eclectic store that sold an array of vintage clothing and accessories, alongside a selection of crystals and a range of essential oils Lark mixed herself. She flicked her wavy blonde hair over her shoulder, sending her armful of bangles jangling – a sound as synonymous with Lark as the aroma of the aforementioned essential oils that wafted in a fragrant cloud around her. She was rocking her usual other-worldly vibe in a floaty Indian cotton sundress in muted shades of pinks and blues, shot through with fine silver thread that glittered under the lamplight.

'I should probably warn you, our Lark's is the tamest suggestion.' Stella gave Jasmine a loaded look.

'It is,' agreed Maggie, giving a mischievous grin before taking a glug of her fizzy orange juice. Since she was still breastfeeding, she was steering clear of alcohol.

'That's because our Lark doesn't let herself get carried away like the rest of you,' said Jasmine, glancing around at her friends, before taking another sip from her glass. 'I'm not sure I want to know what you came up with.'

'Mine was that you had a mystery man lined up and had agreed to go on a date with him.' Maggie waggled her eyebrows at her.

Jasmine almost choked on her mouthful of wine. It was worse than she'd imagined. 'You what? You must be bloomin' joking!' Her horrified expression made them all hoot with laughter.

'What a face,' said Lark, chuckling into her glass.

'When d'you reckon I've had the chance to meet a man, mystery or otherwise?' Jasmine shot them a look that said she thought they'd truly lost the plot.

'Ah, well, I've heard cake decorating can throw you into the path of all sorts of eligible young gentlemen,' said Florrie.

'"Eligible young gentlemen?" Have you been having Jane Austen readings at the bookshop or something?' Florrie co-owned The Happy Hartes Bookshop with her boyfriend, Ed. 'You need to step away from the romance novels, flower. My life couldn't be any further removed from that particular genre if it tried. Come to think of it, I'm not sure what genre my pathetic excuse for a love life would fit into.'

'Horror?' said Stella.

'Tragedy?' offered Maggie.

'How about comedy?' suggested Lark. 'Sorry if that sounds mean, it's not meant to.' She pulled an apologetic face.

'Crime?' added Florrie.

'No need to apologise, Lark. And I reckon it's all of the above, though Mags's suggestion probably fits the bill best,' said Jasmine. 'But having a tragic love life suits me just fine.' They all laughed heartily at that.

'I know we're only messing about, Jazz, but in all honesty, it would be lovely to see you in a relationship. You've been on your own for too long,' said Lark. 'You need someone to love you, someone who has your back and will support you; someone you can share your hopes and dreams with.'

'Couldn't agree more,' Maggie chipped in. 'And, let me tell you, there's nothing better than snuggling up together on the sofa of an evening, even if it is just for an hour.'

Jasmine swept her gaze around her friends to see the others nodding in agreement. She shot them a look of disbelief. 'You lot have either hit the wine early or you've completely lost the plot. Even if I wanted a relationship – which I *don't* – I haven't got time for one, never mind a spare hour for a snuggle on the sofa. Trust me, if I had any spare time, I'd spend it catching up on some sleep. *On my own.*'

'So, I'm guessing that my suggestion, which was that you'd

finally been tempted – a.k.a. "worn down" – by Ando's offer of an evening dining on past-their-best pickled eggs washed down with a glass or two of his homebrew wasn't the exciting news you were going to share?' said Stella.

Jasmine gave her friend a "really?" look. 'Trust me, Stells, it's so wide of the mark, you couldn't even see it with a pair of super-strength binoculars on a clear, cloud-free day.'

'Ah.' Stella's mouth quirked in amusement. 'But, in fairness to us, that's what you get if you dangle a little piece of juicy information in front of us; our imaginations go into overdrive.'

'Tell me about it.' Jasmine grinned, shaking her head. 'But having said that, you lot know full well that never, *ever*, in a million years would I be tempted by Ando's tragic weekly offers. Nope, lasses, I'm afraid you're way, *way* off track with those suggestions.'

Much as she was making light of it, there was a tiny part of Jasmine that could warm to having someone to share her life with. She missed having cuddles, missed curling up on the sofa like Maggie spoke of. But she wasn't prepared to entertain the notion any further. For more than the reasons she'd given her friends, she was determined to remain single.

'In that case, will you *please* just put us out of our misery?' Florrie said pleadingly, pulling Jasmine out of her musings.

'Okay,' said Jasmine, just as her stomach gave a loud rumble. 'But first, can we order our food? I'm famished!' She gave an apologetic smile as they all let out a collective groan.

'I'll see to it.' Florrie pushed herself up. 'Usual order: fish and chips with all the trimmings, lasses?'

A chorus of agreement followed.

'No sharing any of your news until I get back, okay, Jazz?'

'Wouldn't dream of it.' Jasmine laughed.

The women had been best friends since primary school, with the exception of Maggie, whom Florrie had met at university in York. Having moved to Micklewick Bay to live with then boyfriend Bear Marsay, Maggie had been welcomed into the group wholeheartedly. Despite their different personalities, they all shared the same values. It was these qualities that added balance to the friendship, with Stella's feistiness and Jasmine's quick temper being softened by Lark's more gentle nature and Florrie's altruistic ability to see all sides of an argument; she regularly played devil's advocate. Maggie appeared to be a mix of all of them.

Ten minutes later, Florrie returned. 'Right then, that's the food ordered.' She slid back along the settle next to Lark where she looked at Jasmine expectantly.

'Yep, come on, Jazz, let's hear your news,' said Stella.

A smile started to spread across Jasmine's face as she brought the phone call back to mind. 'I still can't believe it,' she said, a wave of excitement rushing through her. 'And it's actually got something to do with you, Mags.'

'*Me?*' Maggie said, her dark brows shooting up in question.

Jasmine nodded. 'Yep, you.'

TWO

'So, like I said in my text, I was left a rather interesting message on my mobile this afternoon – it was actually from a number I'd ignored on account of it being one I didn't recognise; thought it might be some scammer trying to get my bank details or the weirdo who doesn't say anything.'

'You're still getting those funny phone calls?' asked Florrie.

'Yep, though they've eased off a bit recently, and the silent ones have stopped completely, thank goodness – might have something to do with the fact I mentioned them to Bart's parents when they were giving me grief the other day. I didn't directly accuse them, just threw in that I'd been getting them, saying I had enough on my plate without them giving me earache. Said that I was going to contact the police, get "whoever it is" stopped that way.'

'Ooh, they wouldn't like that.' Florrie chuckled.

'Good for you, Jazz,' said Stella.

'You should've seen the look on their faces; kind of gave away that they were the perpetrators.'

'Yeah, why doesn't that surprise me?' said Maggie.

Over the last few weeks, Jasmine had received a slew of

calls from unfamiliar or withheld numbers. When she'd answered, she was met with either an eerie silence or someone alleging to be from her bank or trying to sell her something. She found both varieties irritating though the silent calls had begun to make her feel uneasy, sending a spike of anxiety through her whenever her phone rang. It was why she'd come to the decision not to answer any numbers that weren't in her contact list or whose identity was withheld. If anyone genuinely wanted to reach her, she figured they'd leave a message and she'd get back to them if necessary.

'Anyroad' – Jasmine pushed thoughts of the Forsters out of her mind – 'so, there I was, busy icing the Harrington's anniversary cake, lost in my thoughts, trying to work out how I was going to manage everything I've got going on next, when my mobile started ringing. As I mentioned earlier, it was an unfamiliar number, so I let the call ring out, see if whoever it was left a message. And from the little ping that followed, they evidently did...' Jasmine paused, glancing around at them, a mysterious smile on her face.

'Ooh, the intrigue,' Florrie said, chuckling.

'Talk about keeping us in suspense, Jazz!' said Stella.

'Just trying to add a little drama.' Jasmine grinned at them.

The friends listened as she explained how she'd continued decorating the anniversary cake, the phone call slipping from her mind until an hour later when she took a break to make a cup of tea and ease the crick in her shoulders.

'Imagine my surprise when I hear Lady Caro Hammondely's plummy tones travelling down the phone line, saying she has something she'd like to run by me concerning a new venture at Danskelfe Castle, and asking if I'd call back!'

'How exciting, Jazz!' Lark exclaimed, her eyes wide.

'I'm guessing it was the real Lady Caro and not one of your scammy calls,' said Stella in her familiar dry tone, setting the friends off laughing.

'I'll be honest, I did stop and wonder about it for a minute or two, what with all the warnings you hear that scammers are using more elaborate methods to con people.'

'It's always good to be cautious,' said Maggie.

'Exactly.' Jasmine paused to take a sip of her wine. 'So, my next thought was that she'd got the wrong number.'

'But, going by how excited you sounded in your earlier text, and the enormous smile on your fizzog when you walked in, am I right in assuming the call was genuine, and that Lady Caro had meant to call you?' asked Florrie.

'Aye, it was definitely genuine, and definitely me Lady Caro wanted to speak to.' Jasmine nodded, a wide smile spreading over her face once more. 'When I called her back, the first thing she mentioned was how we'd met at the sleigh ride and how Mags had "added a little excitement to proceedings", as she put it. There's no way a scammer would know details like that.'

'Good point,' said Stella, her eyebrows twitching in amusement as she scooped up her glass of wine. 'It was definitely a memorable experience, for lots of reasons.'

Stella wasn't wrong, thought Jasmine, as her mind flicked back to the day in question. None of them had expected it to end quite as dramatically as it had.

Christmas was just around the corner when the group of friends – partners and Jasmine's children included – had visited Danskelfe Castle having booked a sleigh ride, which had been a fantastically festive experience that had exceeded all their expectations. They'd been enjoying some post-sleigh ride refreshments when a heavily pregnant Maggie had surprised them all by going into labour and ended up being rushed to Middleton-le-Moors hospital by none other than Lady Caro herself. It was fair to say, it had been an unexpected and dramatic way to end the day, but the end result had been an adorable little bundle in the form of baby Lucia – or Lucy, as Maggie and Bear referred to her.

Jasmine's gaze swept over her friends, four sets of eyes looking at her, eager to hear her news.

'So, what was Lady Caro's reason for calling you?' asked Lark.

'Would you believe she had a business proposition for me?' The prospect still felt unreal to Jasmine, even more so saying it out loud.

'A business proposition?' Florrie sat up straight and pushed her glasses up her nose.

'Ahh, I think I know where this is going.' Catching Jasmine's eye, Maggie gave an enigmatic smile.

'Long story short,' said Jasmine, 'as you all already know, Danskelfe Castle has become a popular wedding venue, but Lady Caro said they're wanting to take their wedding packages to the "next level", as she put it. She told me they're keen to offer something exclusive and not simply offer the wedding service and reception afterwards.'

Florrie sucked air between her teeth. 'Sounds pricey. I've heard their weddings are pretty expensive as it is.'

'Doesn't seem to put folk off though; I hear they get booked up really quickly,' said Stella, turning back to Jasmine. 'Sorry for interrupting, Jazz.'

'No worries. So, the next thing Lady Caro says is that they've decided to offer a wedding planning service, which was the reason she contacted me – apparently, it's something a lot of couples have been asking about. But honestly, my heart nearly stopped, I thought I must've heard wrong! *Wedding planning? Me?* I told her I didn't have the foggiest idea about wedding planning, that Bart and me had never got around to getting married and that the closest I'd ever got to a wedding was my brother's, and Maggie and Bear's. Mind, you'll be relieved to know I somehow managed to keep it to myself that love and mush and happy-ever-afters are my idea of hell!' she said, giggling.

In fact, Jasmine would go as far as to say, if she had to pick what she considered to be her worst job, it would be a close-run thing between a wedding planner or a chiropodist. *Ew!* The idea of having to handle other people's feet made her shudder – and quite possibly had the edge on its competition.

'I mean, can you imagine me pandering to a fussy bride?'

'Er, that would be a no, Jazz,' Maggie said matter-of-factly. It was no secret between the friends that Jasmine's own personal experience had hardened her heart to the concept of love. She frequently referred to it as "far-fetched-nonsense" or "a load of old claptrap", and she'd professed enough times that she was never going to give it the time of day again. Bart Forster had made sure of that.

'So what did Lady Caro say?' asked Lark.

'After she'd finished hooting with laughter, she told me it wasn't wedding planning she wanted me for, but my wedding cakes. She said you, Mags' – Jasmine nodded in Maggie's direction – 'had told her all about them last time you were dropping some of your Danskelfe bears off. So I owe you a massive thank you.'

Maggie had her own cottage business designing and making bespoke teddy bears out of recycled luxury wool and Lady Caro had commissioned her to make some for the lodges in the Danskelfe Castle grounds as well as a bride and groom set for the bridal suite. She'd recently delivered an order for a new range of lodges in the castle grounds, which was when Lady Caro had broached the subject of wedding cakes.

'You're very welcome, flower,' said Maggie. 'Lady Caro just mentioned in passing that a couple at one of their recent weddings had the "most magnificent creation". From her description, I thought it sounded like the one you'd made for Kendra and Tom Wilson, with it having five tiers and hand-painted sugar-paste flowers tumbling down the side. Turns out it was the Wilson's cake. Lady Caro said everyone was totally blown away by it, describing it as a work of art and wanting to know whose handiwork it was.'

'Ooh, I'm not surprised. That one was so dreamy,' Lark said wistfully. 'If I ever get married, that's exactly the sort of wedding cake I'd like.'

'We'll be sure to let Nate know.' Stella gave an impish grin, making Lark shake her head.

Nate was Lark's friend who owned a successful upcycling business on Endeavour Road. He'd been sweet on Lark for as long as her friends could remember, but for reasons none of them could quite understand, she'd kept him firmly in the friend zone.

Maggie picked up what she'd been saying. 'I pointed Lady Caro in the direction of your Instagram page, too. She was really impressed, so it was nowt to do with me really, your amazing cakes speak for themselves.'

Jasmine felt her face grow hot at the compliment. The cake she'd created for the Wilson's wedding had been one of her favourites, one that she'd felt showcased her cake-decorating skills to their best advantage. She'd gained a whole heap of orders off the back of it. She'd pushed herself with the amount of work involved, staying up until the early hours until she was happy with every tiny detail. The end result hadn't only served to prove her efforts had been worth it, they'd also confirmed that cake decorating – particularly wedding cakes – were what she'd love to do full-time given the choice. *If only*, she'd thought at the time.

'So, the upshot is that Lady Caro wondered if I'd be interested in being their go-to wedding cake maker and provide all the cakes for their weddings as part of the planning services package. She gave me a brief low-down of her ideas but then suggested I pop over to Danskelfe Castle to have a proper chat so we can iron out the details. Said she'd show me round the place while I was there so I could get a feel for what they're after.'

That had sent a thrill running through Jasmine, though a spike of concern had followed hot on its heels, momentarily tempering her excitement, as her thoughts had gone to her diary and her already jam-packed schedule. She couldn't even begin to think how she was going to fit in such a meeting over the next couple of weeks; it seemed every single second of every single day was accounted for. But come hell or high water, Jasmine was determined to do just that. After all, it wasn't every day you got a business proposition from somewhere like Danskelfe Castle and something told her it could be an opportunity that was too good to turn down. If she had a guaranteed, regular income from this new venture, then there was a chance she could give up one of her other jobs and concentrate on her passion of baking and decorating cakes. The thought had triggered a flutter of excitement in her stomach.

Jasmine went on to explain how Lady Caro had told her that the number of bookings for weddings had increased, such that they were having to turn couples away, which was far from ideal, especially when they were eager to build on their success in that department. Lady Caro had said that it was after a brainstorming session that offering an in-house wedding planning service was settled upon. This discussion had also led on to considering the option of hosting weddings on a smaller scale, using one of the less grand rooms at the castle. That way they could offer packages with a lower budget, making it more affordable and, hopefully, increase their appeal to couples who wouldn't be able to stretch to the more expensive alternative. They still intended to keep the more lavish option, having the capacity to run both size weddings on the same day, so that wouldn't be a problem.

'It would mean I'd need to have two wedding cakes ready at the same time,' said Jasmine, 'but if I cut down on my hours cleaning or at the bakery, then that should be totally manageable. I suggested offering a small-ish range of designs to choose from, that way I'd be able to make a load of sugar paste decorations and elements in advance and in bulk, which seemed to go down well. I also mentioned offering slight variations with the colour scheme if the couples wanted something more unique to them. Things like different coloured ribbons and trims, cake stands; small things that wouldn't be time consuming to implement.' Jasmine could feel her enthusiasm for Lady Caro's proposal building by the minute.

'That sounds genius, Jazz!' said Florrie. 'At last, your cakes are getting the recognition they deserve.'

'Yeah, it's about time, they're awesome, everyone says so.' Lark beamed at her.

'Thanks.' Jasmine felt her cheeks flame at the praise; she'd never been good at taking compliments, but it didn't stop her heart from surging with fondness for her friend.

'So, have you organised a day to pop over there?' asked Maggie.

'I just need to see if I can do a bit of re-jigging with my shifts, but I'm hoping to get across sometime next week.'

'If you need a companion for moral support, I'd be happy to oblige.' Florrie gave a jokingly hopeful smile.

In truth, Jasmine's heart had sunk when Lady Caro had told her the only time she was free the following week was Tuesday morning at around eleven o'clock. It was when Jasmine had a shift cleaning. Lady Caro had given the impression that she was eager to get started as soon as possible with the wedding planning service, and Jasmine didn't want to risk delaying the meeting in case it caused her to look elsewhere for a cake maker. She desperately didn't want that to happen, so had made the excuse that she'd need to check her diary – which wasn't to hand – and get back to her to confirm the meeting. She'd been relieved by Lady Caro's breezy reply in the affirmative.

As soon as the call ended, Jasmine had reached for the calendar she kept on the wall by the fridge. One glance at next week told her what she'd already suspected; she was working every day, with Tuesday morning blocked out by a session cleaning for Stella's mum. Cancelling it wasn't an option for several reasons, the first being that she prided herself on being reliable and didn't want to let Alice down and have to find a replacement, the second was that the client was Hilda Jenkins. Jasmine had grown fond of Hilda and knew her elderly friend looked forward to her shifts. For Hilda, the session wasn't just about having her house cleaned, it was about looking forward to having some company and a bit of a chat. Jasmine didn't want to disappoint her. And there was also the reason that Jasmine simply needed the money. The balance for a week-long sports activity Zak had been eager to sign up for that ran in the summer holidays was due in a fortnight and her finances were already stretched to the limit.

Her son had bounded through the door after school last month, bursting with enthusiasm. 'Please can I go, Mum? *Please*. All my friends are going. They reckon some famous footballer's going to do a day's coaching. It'll be dead mint! Please say yes,' he'd said, thrusting the leaflet into her hand. Jasmine had struggled to hide her shock as her eyes landed on the price. *How much?* She'd steadied herself, her brain doing a quick calculation of how many extra shifts she'd need to do to cover the cost. She didn't have the heart to quash her son's happiness and tell him she couldn't afford it, especially since her finances had meant he couldn't go on the trip to Edinburgh last April. The edge had been taken off her guilt for that one by the knowledge that he wasn't the only one of his friends not going. But she could see how excited Zak was about the summer sports camp and had told him he could go.

On top of that, her ancient little car had developed a reluctance to start recently and much as she kept trying to tell herself it was just one of the vehicle's quirks and that it would be okay, her gut told her otherwise. And then there was the rattling sound that emanated from the bowels of the engine without warning as she drove along. It would grow alarmingly loud before seemingly running out of steam and puttering to a stop. Jasmine was uncomfortable with the attention it attracted, and that it made people stop and stare. There was no denying a trip to the local garage was on the cards, and that was never cheap.

Sitting there in the pub, Jasmine put that particular collection of worries out of her mind. She'd called Lady Caro back later that afternoon, confirming their appointment in the hope that she could swap her cleaning shift with her mum who also worked for Spick 'n' Sparkle. To say Lady Caro was thrilled would be an understatement.

'That's me all caught up on my news,' Jasmine said, feeling she'd hogged the conversation for long enough.

'Well cheers to our Jazz and her future success as a professional wedding cake designer.' Stella raised her wine glass and the others followed suit.

'Cheers to our Jazz!' they chorused, making Jasmine's cheeks burn bright.

'So what's new with everyone else?' she said.

'Been a pretty quiet week for me,' said Lark. 'Though I did hear that the new owners have moved into Njord's View.'

The art deco-style property located in an enviable spot on the cliffs had undergone an extensive refurbishment project that had taken months but now stood proud looking down on the newly built marina, its vast windows glinting in the sunshine. The identity of the new owners had generated much speculation in the town, but no one had put a name to them yet. It would seem that was about to change. Jasmine felt her curiosity spring to life.

'Really?' Maggie looked suitably intrigued. 'I'd heard the scaffolding had been taken down and work was finished on it.'

'And rumour has it the man who owns it is pretty hot to trot,' said Stella, waggling her eyebrows. 'Not sure if he has a partner though.'

'Just as well you're spoken for, then, Stells.' Maggie's eyes twinkled mischievously, making Stella laugh.

'He'll have half a dozen partners and a sordid past by the time the local gossips get to work,' chuckled Florrie.

'Maybe he'll take a shine to our Jazz.' Stella sent a cheeky grin Jasmine's way.

'Not even remotely funny, Stells.' Jasmine pinned her with a stern stare.

'Joking aside, flower, we'd love to see you with someone. You've been on your own too long, you've forgotten how lovely it feels to have someone to share the weight of your worries and concerns, not to mention your workload. It feels good to be with someone who has your back – I know all of us here have your back and would do anything for you, but it's not the same.' Florrie's words took Jasmine by surprise. She felt a lump forming in her throat.

'Here, here,' said Maggie, the others making sounds of agreement.

'Get knotted, you lot.' Jasmine grabbed her glass and hid her face behind it.

THREE
SATURDAY

'Mum! Mum! I've been invited to a party!' Zak burst through the front door of eighteen Rosemary Terrace, landing in the kitchen on a waft of warm summer air and a wave of enthusiasm, his football tucked under his arm.

Jasmine, who'd been feeding a load of laundry into the washing machine, straightened and turned to look at her son. She couldn't help but smile at the expression on his face, the smattering of freckles that grazed his nose and cheeks lending him an adorably mischievous appearance. 'Morning, Zak, lovey, a party, eh? That sounds exciting. Whose is it?' She was used to her son's boundless energy and enthusiasm, but this morning, from the way he was dancing from foot to foot, it appeared to have been cranked up a notch or two. She headed over to him, throwing her arm around his shoulders and pressing a kiss to the side of his head. It crossed her mind that if his recent growing spurt continued, it wouldn't be long before he was towering over her.

'*Mum*,' he grumbled, wriggling free of her embrace and scrubbing at the spot where her kiss had landed, making her laugh. 'He's called Connor and he's really cool. He's in my class and he's mad on football like me and his party has a football theme – he said I can wear my Micklewick Lions football strip – *and* he's going to the sports week in the summer holidays. He's just moved here. I'm his best mate and he's mine. It's his party next weekend and it's going to be at his house. It's that massive one on the cliffs.'

Jasmine struggled to keep up with Zak's words as they tumbled out in an effusive torrent. He beamed a smile then proceeded to bounce his ball several times, earning himself a pointed look from his mum.

'Not inside, Zak,' she said, her mind going back to the last time he'd bounced his football in the kitchen and the devastation that had followed. He'd whacked the ball with such force, it had ricocheted off the fridge and flown across the table, where a newly decorated birthday cake sat. She'd looked on in disbelief as the fondant replica of a pair of red designer high-heeled shoes in croc leather she'd painstakingly spent hours to perfect was skimmed off, ending up in a ruined heap on the floor. If that wasn't bad enough, the cake was due for collection in just over an hour.

Jasmine's frazzled nerves had been soothed once she'd realised there was enough leftover sugar paste from the fondant shoes to allow her to hurriedly create a new, albeit slightly smaller, pair. She'd been inordinately relieved when the cake was collected and had left her house. The customer had been delighted with it and in blissful ignorance of the drama that had unfolded an hour beforehand. Disaster may have been averted in that particular instance, but it wasn't something Jasmine was eager to repeat. Ali Harrington had yet to call to collect her parents' anniversary cake, which was sitting in three boxes on the worktop beside where Zak was standing and had been bouncing his ball seconds earlier. She didn't fancy that cake suffering a similar fate, nor the prospect of having to explain to Ali why it wasn't ready.

'Soz, Mum. I forgot.' Zak ceased his bouncing and treated her to a sheepish grin that made her heart melt.

'So, what day and time is this party then?' Jasmine's mind quickly segued to her calendar, just as Chloe skipped in, followed by Heather whose hands were full of her grandchildren's backpacks and a variety of other bags. 'Hi there.' Jasmine smiled, glancing between her daughter and her mum. She held her arm out for Chloe, who skuttled across for a cuddle. She absently pressed a kiss to the top of Chloe's strawberry-blonde head, glad to see her daughter's mood seemed brighter today. Jasmine hoped to get the chance to have a word with her mum when the kids were out of earshot, see if Chloe had let slip about anything that could be bothering her.

'Now then, lovey.' Heather smiled warmly. 'I should warn you, a certain someone's very excited.' She nodded towards Zak.

'So I see.'

'He's been talking about the party *all* the time, Mummy. It's been party this, and party that,' said Chloe, shaking her head with a weariness that was way beyond her seven years.

Jasmine caught her mother's eye and the pair exchanged an amused look.

Zak grinned broadly. 'The party's next Saturday, in the afternoon, can't remember the exact time. The invitation's in my school bag, but Connor says I can get there early if I want. And he says I can stay over, but you have to call and say it's okay with you. There's a phone number on the invitation. And guess what? His house even has a cinema and a swimming pool. How *awesome* is that?'

'That's very awesome, Zak.' Her thoughts went back to the conversation with her friends the previous evening, and their curiosity about the owner.

She peered at her calendar, noting she had a ten-year-old boy's football-themed birthday cake to have ready for next Saturday morning. She fleetingly wondered if it was for Zak's new friend – Jasmine recalled not recognising the name – Osborne – when the order had been placed and had assumed it was for a family out of town. Her next thought was that she had a shift from twelve till four at the bakery that same day. 'I'll need to know the time you can be dropped off, but I can't see a problem getting you there.'

'Cool!' Zak beamed at her.

'Right then, rascals, can you take your stuff upstairs, please?' She didn't want the house to look messy when Ali called to collect her parents' cake.

She watched as they gathered their bags and headed into the hallway, the sound of Zak thundering up the stairs in his usual way following seconds later. She listened, waiting for the familiar sounds of them going into their respective bedrooms, before turning to her mother. 'Thanks for having the kids again, Mum, I really appreciate it.'

'No problem, lovey, they were good as gold, as always.' She set the children's bags down by the back door. 'Your dad and me'd be happy to help out getting Zak to and from the party next Saturday, if you're stuck.'

Jasmine groaned inwardly. She already needed to ask her mum if she'd be able to cover her shift on Tuesday so she could make her meeting with Lady Caro at Danskelfe Castle and felt uncomfortable asking for more help.

As if sensing her daughter's hesitation, Heather said, 'Wouldn't mind an excuse to have a sneaky peek around that particular property. Mind, I've been hearing all sorts of rumours about the new owner, ranging from him being a famous artist, to a sports celebrity to a lottery winner – oh, and an opera singer. Someone even reckons he's a spy for MI5.' Heather chuckled.

Jasmine laughed. 'Wowzers, that's some wild mix. Whatever it turns out they do for a living, they've generated a load of interest, so let's hope it doesn't disappoint the gossipmongers.

Though, I daresay, after Zak's been to the party we'll be a bit more enlightened.'

'Or even more confused,' said Heather, making them both chuckle. 'So, did you enjoy yourself with the lasses last night?'

'I did, thanks, we had a laugh.'

'Good.'

Jasmine inched closer to her mum, lowering her voice. 'Very quickly, before the kids come back downstairs, I've been meaning to ask if you've noticed anything different about Chloe? She hasn't been herself this last couple of weeks, seems to have lost her sparkle a bit. I know she's not naturally as exuberant as Zak, but she's been quieter than usual. It's been worrying me.'

'You beat me to it, flower, I was going to mention something once they were out of the way, but I did notice she seemed to have something on her mind, wasn't her usual chatty self – your dad picked up on it, too. I asked her if she was okay, and tried some subtle questions to see if they'd reveal anything, but it just made her clam up so I thought it best to stop. But I did get the feeling it was something to do with school. The name Nina cropped up a couple of times and not in a way that made me think Chloe was fond of her, more like she was bothering her. Didn't catch this Nina's surname though.'

Jasmine's heart twisted. 'Poor little Chloe. I had a feeling it was something to do with school, not that she's mentioned anyone in particular to me. She complained of having a tummy ache a couple of times last week, tried to convince me she was too poorly to go to school but I could tell it wasn't genuine.'

'Ah, bless her, that's a shame. Sounds like this Nina girl's the root of the problem if she's trying to get out of going to school,' said Heather. She looked thoughtful for a moment. 'Zak might have a better idea about it. You could maybe try asking him a few discreet questions.'

'Yeah, that was my next plan.'

Their conversation was interrupted by an urgent knocking at the door, startling them both.

'Bloomin' 'eck!' said Jasmine.

'Oh, my days! Who on earth's that?' Heather pressed her hand to her chest.

'It's probably Ali Harrington come to collect her parents' anniversary cake.'

'Talk about having a knock like a policeman.'

'S'probably cos she's running late,' said Jasmine, on her way to answer the door.

'I'm so sorry I'm late, Jasmine. I hope I haven't spoilt your plans,' Ali said, out of breath and looking slightly dishevelled.

'Come in, and there's no need to apologise, I had no plans to be anywhere this morning,' said Jasmine. 'Is everything okay?'

'Long story, but it's been one of those mornings. Grandad went AWOL from the care home; had us all searching everywhere for him. Poor Mum was frantic with worry.'

Jasmine recalled hearing that Ali's maternal grandfather suffered from dementia. 'You poor things, I hope he's okay. Did you manage to find him?'

'We did, thank goodness. He'd taken a wander down to the bottom prom and had been trying to persuade Ando Taylor to teach him how to skateboard, of all things. It was Ando who kindly contacted Mum, told her Grandad was with him.'

'Blimey, that's quite a morning you've all had.'

'Aye, just a bit.' Ali smiled as she rolled her eyes.

It crossed Jasmine's mind that Ando may be a bit daft when he'd had a drink or two, but, ultimately, he had a good heart. It still wasn't enough to make her want to spend an evening with him, sharing his jar of pickled eggs and "Gut Rot" homebrew, though. She couldn't imagine anything would ever tempt her to do that.

'The cake's just through here. I hope you like it.' Jasmine led the way to the kitchen.

'I have every faith in you, Jazz. I know it'll be awesome without even looking at it.'

Since Ali was running so late, she declined Jasmine's offer of unboxing all the tiers of the cake so she could take a peek at each one, and was happy to just see the top one decorated with the roses.

'Oh, my God, that's stunning, Jazz! You're so talented. Have you thought about giving up your other jobs and focusing on this full time? I reckon you'd be inundated with orders.'

'That'd be the dream,' Jasmine said, the praise making her cheeks flush as her thoughts went to her meeting with Lady Caro, though she didn't want to jinx it by saying anything to Ali. 'So, here are the instructions of how to put the cake together – it's very straightforward – and here's a bit of edible glue to keep the tiers in place. It's best to do it once you're at the venue, that way you don't risk it getting damaged en route.'

'Thanks, Jazz, you've thought of everything. Right, I'd best dash.'

'Time for a cuppa, Mum?' Jasmine asked once Ali had gone.

'Aye, a quick one, lovey. Your dad's going to whisk me over to York this afternoon and I need to get changed.'

'How nice.' Jasmine reached for the kettle as her mum headed over to the small table.

'Did you see, there's another house gone up for sale out there?' asked Heather.

'What, on this street?'

'Mm-hm. Number twelve's got a For Sale sign on it.'

'I reckon over half the street must've gone on the market this year.' Jasmine hoped her landlord wouldn't be tempted to jump on the bandwagon and sell this place; affordable rental houses were hard to come by in Micklewick Bay.

'And you'll never guess what else I've just spotted,' Heather said, her green eyes, so like her daughter's, dancing with the news she was about to share. 'It's going to cause a right load of gossip and speculation, I can tell you.'

'What is?' Jasmine looked up, thoughts of Lady Caro's offer slipping to the back of her mind.

'Go on, have a guess.'

'Er, someone's painted the station building bright blue with pink stripes.'

'Granted, that would generate a bit of gossip.' Heather chuckled. 'But nope, you're way off.'

'In that case, you're going to have to enlighten me.' That her brain had been wrestling with so many other thoughts, meant conjuring up random guesses felt nigh on impossible to Jasmine right now.

'Well,' said Heather, hooking her bag over the back of a dining chair, 'as I was driving by the Micklewick Majestic this morning, I noticed there was a sold sign fixed to the gatepost; it was hard to miss actually.'

'No way?' This was news. The Micklewick Majestic was a once grand hotel that had been known as the jewel in Micklewick Bay's crown until recent years when its owner's fortunes had taken a turn for the worse. The imposing Victorian building had stood empty, falling further and further into disrepair as the years went by, ending up a pathetic and forlorn shadow of its former self.

'Yes way.' Heather nodded.

'It's been on the market for that long, I'd actually forgotten about it.' The For Sale sign had long since succumbed to the wind blowing in from the North Sea and now lay in several pieces on the ground.

'Aye, I know what you mean. Mind, whoever's bought it has their work cut out for them.'

'You're not kidding, especially if the exterior is anything to go by. Last time I passed the place, it looked as if the grounds were being used as a local dumping site.'

'I think they have been.'

Despite her mum's news, Jasmine's thoughts quickly switched back to the phone call from Lady Caro and the dilemma it posed of how she was going to squeeze in a meeting with her.

'Ooh, this looks interesting.' Jasmine turned to see her mum admiring the latest sugar paste decoration she'd been working on while she was waiting for the kids to land back. Her open sketchbook was beside it, showing her design of a fondant cruise ship set on a vibrant blue sea, complete with white, frothy waves and dolphins cavorting amongst them. She'd enjoyed thinking up the design and had even included a small sandy island with a palm tree.

'It's for a client from out of town who's stipulated a cruise ship design. It's not due till next week, but I thought I'd make a start on the elements now.'

'You're so creative, lovey.'

'Thanks.' Jasmine gave a distracted sigh.

'Everything okay, lovey?' her mum asked, a frown furrowing her brow.

'Yeah, it is, it's great actually.' She flashed her a smile. 'Well, it would be if it wasn't for one thing.'

'Oh?'

Jasmine recounted the details of the phone call from Lady Caro as her mother sipped her tea.

'Oh, sweetheart, that's wonderful news!' Heather pressed her hand to her chest. 'I'm so proud of you, and your dad will be, too, when he hears about it.'

'Thanks, Mum. My mind's been racing with ideas for cakes since the call. It's all I've been able to think about.' Jasmine sat back in her seat. Though talking about it had set excitement coursing through her veins again, it was tempered by the concern of whether her increasingly busy schedule was sustainable. She puffed out another sigh.

'So what's the thing that's bothering you?'

'Lady Caro's asked if I can pop over there for a visit to discuss things further. She suggested Tuesday morning, but the only trouble is I've got a cleaning shift for then – it's Hilda, who I can't let down. And the rest of the week's manic, and Lady Caro says she's busy anyway. I haven't got a clue how I could possibly squeeze anything else in, never mind driving over to Danskelfe Castle. I don't have a minute to spare, not to mention the half day the meeting will probably take.' What Jasmine didn't say was that another concern had started to nibble away at the edges of her mind. Lady Caro had sounded so keen to get cracking with the wedding planning service, Jasmine's worries that she'd offer the cake contract to someone else had been growing. It didn't help that there was a cake decorator near Middleton-le-Moors whose creations Jasmine couldn't help but admire.

'I really hate to ask, Mum, especially with all you do for me already, but—'

Heather didn't miss a beat. 'Simple solution, flower: I'll cover your shift for you. I've known Hilda all my life, we get along like a house on fire. And it's not as if it'd be the first time I've cleaned for her. I know I'll be a poor second, but we both know she'll understand, especially where your cakes are concerned – she's always singing their praises.'

'Are you sure, Mum? I know you're already really busy as it is.' Guilt crawled over her. Heather also worked for Alice as well as caring for an elderly neighbour.

'Of course I'm sure. I'm not doing anything else on Tuesday morning, and even if I was, I'm never so busy that I can't help out my super-talented daughter when an amazing business opportunity comes her way.'

'Not sure about the super-talented bit.'

'Well, I am. Lady Caro hasn't contacted you for no reason. This could be too good an opportunity to pass up, Jasmine lovey. You never know, it could even mean you have the chance to give up your other jobs and focus on your cake decorating business full time. You've said numerous times that would be the dream.' Heather dipped her head, looking directly into her daughter's eyes. 'It's none of my business, but if you want my advice, you should grasp the opportunity with both hands, or at the very least hear what Lady Caro has to say.'

'But—'

'No buts, it's sorted. I'll cover your shift – you've helped me out in the past. Alice won't mind as long as someone's doing it, and Hilda will be just fine. I'll fill her in on all the local gossip.'

Jasmine took a moment to mull over her mother's offer. Her words about the possibility of being able to treat her cake decorating business as a full-time job filled her mind and made her pulse gallop. It really would be a dream come true. And if her mum's prediction proved right, the meeting with Lady Caro could potentially result in an increase in her earnings in the long term. Jasmine gnawed on her bottom lip. Much as she could do with the money she'd earn from Tuesday's shift, Jasmine told herself she should look on the meeting as an investment.

But then there was the fact that she was relying on her mum to help her out again. Her parents were always stepping in to look after the kids, whether it be picking them up from school or ferrying them to their various after school and weekend activities when Jasmine was working or pushed for time with a celebration cake to get finished. She didn't know how she'd manage without them. The thought that they'd start to think she was taking advantage always lurked at the back of her mind, not that they'd ever given her the slightest hint that was the case, but all the same, it didn't stop her from fretting about it. And it didn't help her guilt that her older brother, Jonathan, and his wife, Flic, had never asked them to look after their two boys.

'And if you're worried about losing the earnings from the

shift, then you can keep them.' Heather's voice snapped her out of her musings.

'Definitely not! It's bad enough that you're covering it for me without giving me your wages, Mum. I'm not a charity case,' Jasmine said vehemently, her cheeks flushing pink. Much as she appreciated her mum's gesture came from a good place, it didn't stop her feeling a spike of annoyance. Her pride would never let her accept any financial help from her parents, not that it stopped them from offering on a regular basis. It made her resentful of her position at times.

'Since when has accepting help from your own mother been charity?' Heather asked softly.

'It's enough that you'd be getting me out of a tricky situation and covering my shift. If you're sure, I'll take you up on your offer, but I'm not taking money from you.' Jasmine shot her mum a look that told her she wasn't open to any further negotiation on the matter.

'You've always had a stubborn streak.' Heather rolled her eyes and shook her head affectionately.

'Can't think where I get it from,' Jasmine said jokingly, her irritation all but forgotten.

'Hmm. I reckon it must be your dad.' A smile tugged at the corners of Heather's mouth.

'You reckon?' Jasmine giggled. Stubborn was the last thing her easy-going dad could be described as. 'Anyroad, thanks, Mum, I honestly don't know what I'd do without you. I'll call Alice, let her know, and Hilda, too.' Relief that that particular problem was sorted washed over her, its strength taking her by surprise.

'Hey, I'm just chuffed I can help, especially when an opportunity that's too good to miss is concerned.' Heather smiled fondly at her. 'Particularly if that opportunity could make life easier for you. Don't think your dad and me haven't noticed how tired you've been looking recently, petal. You need to cut yourself a bit of slack before you run yourself into the ground.'

'I'm fine, Mum, honest. At lot of things seem to have come at once, that's all.' Jasmine didn't want her parents to start worrying about her. They'd done enough of that after Bart died. Then, their concerned expressions had just about torn her heart in two. Though, if she was being completely honest with herself, she'd noticed the usual feeling of tiredness that hit her by the end of the day had felt more like exhaustion recently, and it had been getting harder to drag herself out of bed when the alarm went off in the morning. 'And don't forget I was out with the lasses last night, which as you know, getting together with them is the perfect switch-off for me.' Jasmine beamed at her mum, hoping to convince her.

'Aye, and I'm glad to hear it. And while we're on the subject, your dad and me were saying just the other day we hope your Friday nights out is something your work commitments don't sneak into. You need a break and a bit of wind-down time with your friends. It's important, especially now you seem to be working all hours.'

'The only thing that bothers me—'

'And before you say it, your dad and me love having the kids and they love staying with us.'

'Thanks, Mum.' Jasmine smiled, her heart filling with love for her parents. It was true, Zak and Chloe loved spending time with their grandparents, heading out to the countryside for walks, or down to the beach crabbing and paddling, or even just spending time at their home, helping her mum bake, or her dad with odd jobs around the house and in the garden. Both grandparents and grandchildren seemed to thrive on the time they spent together which warmed Jasmine's heart – and went some considerable way to assuaging her guilt.

The relationship couldn't be more different to the one Zak and Chloe had with Bart's parents. After their son's death,

Alice and Gary Forster had shunned Jasmine and Zak – Jasmine had been pregnant with Chloe at the time – saying they wanted nothing to do with any of them, that seeing them only served to remind them of the wonderful son they'd lost. Jasmine had struggled to get her head around such logic. The passage of time hadn't made it any easier, nor helped to explain their lack of contact with her children.

But, right now, she had more pressing matters on her mind, not least the worry that her daughter was potentially being bullied at school. The thought made Jasmine's blood run cold. Her children took priority over everything else and she was determined to get to the bottom of whatever it was that was bothering Chloe.

It was a couple of hours later, when she was preparing a quick picnic for her and the kids to have down on the beach, that a text from her mum landed. Jasmine reached for her phone and quickly scanned the message.

Her heart froze. 'No!' she gasped, pressing her hand to her mouth.

> Hi Jasmine, thought I should warn you, but I've just heard the dreaded Jason Scragg's moved to town with his family. He has a son called Bruce who's Zak's age and a daughter called Nina who's Chloe's age. Made me wonder if she's the girl who Chloe was talking about. Sorry to dump this on you, flower. Try not to let it spoil your picnic xxx

The surname glaring back at Jasmine made her blood run cold. It was quickly followed by a tight squeeze in her chest.

No! She clamped her hand to her forehead, her breathing shallow. *It couldn't be! Why was he back? Had he returned to seek vengeance? And, if so, why had he waited for so long?*

FOUR

'Please don't tell me they're back.' Mere mention of the Scragg family had the power to trigger a wave of painful emotions and resurrect a slew of unwelcome memories from over twenty years ago. And it wasn't just Jasmine who felt this way towards them. The town had heaved a collective sigh of relief when the troublesome Scraggs had upped sticks and moved out of the area.

She swallowed, and drew in a steadying breath, taking a moment to calm herself and marshal her thoughts. She didn't want the kids to rush in and see her knocked off-kilter like this. They'd know something was wrong straight away and she didn't want anything to spoil their picnic, particularly since the Scraggs were the cause.

It felt like a lifetime ago that she and Jason Scragg had come to blows. Scraggo – as he was known then – was an inveterate bully who'd strutted around the school like some sort of juvenile gangster, with his mini-henchmen by his side, instilling fear into the other pupils with his menacing ways. Looking at it from this vantage point, and with a greater understanding of his family circumstances, Jasmine could see that Scraggo's behaviour had stemmed from the fact that it was himself, and what was going on in his own unsettled home life, that he was unhappy with. His subconscious way of dealing with his situation had been to project those feelings and frustrations onto someone else. Someone he viewed as weaker than him. Someone who was unlikely to fight back. Someone who would allow him to vent the unhappiness that had churned around inside him without the risk of consequences. And someone who had nobody at home to contact school and fight his corner. Jason Scragg had found the perfect candidate in little Max Grainger.

And he'd made the lad's life a living hell.

Jasmine's jaw tightened and her heart pounded as memories crowded her mind, each one jostling for prominence. An image of Max and the hurt in his eyes loomed as clear and vivid as if it had happened only yesterday, resurrecting the intense feelings of anger and injustice Scraggo's actions had created all those years ago. She could fully understand why her nine-year-old self had reacted the way she had at the time, and even now, she didn't regret it one little bit. And though an understanding that had come with maturity had allowed her to scrape together a modicum of sympathy for the bully and his family circumstances, it didn't mean she viewed it as an excuse for his hideous behaviour. She still considered it unforgivable. It took a certain sort of person, whatever their age, to treat another as cruelly as he'd treated Max. History was not going to repeat itself with the next generation of Scraggs. And if this Nina Scragg thought for even the tiniest of seconds she was going to get away with making her daughter's life a misery, then she had another thing coming. She'd picked on the wrong child.

She was determined to nip this new generation Scragg problem in the bud before it had a chance to escalate. There was no way Chloe was going to suffer in the way Max Grainger had. Of that, Jasmine was certain. She'd do some surreptitious questioning when they were having their picnic on the beach later that afternoon. She'd also have a quiet word with Zak, see if he could shed any light on things. Then she'd call school first thing on Monday morning, armed with the details, and make them aware of the situation.

In the meantime, she only hoped she didn't clap eyes on Jason Scragg in town; the urge to give him a piece of her mind was going to be hard to resist. She knew she had to deal with him and his toxic progeny through the proper channels, and that meant going through school.

Jasmine added more sand to the castle-shaped bucket and firmed it down with the small spade, the sound of children's laughter in the background, the screech of a herring gull as it wheeled overhead. She and the children had found themselves a decent patch on the beach, not far from the pier whose gangly limbs towered over everyone as it stretched its way out to sea, and marked their spot with their beach towels. To the right of them, the cliffs stood proud in the distance, Maggie and Bear's whitewashed cottage perched atop Thorncliffe and glinting in the sun. While to the left was the new marina that was under construction.

Adjusting her sunglasses, Jasmine's eyes surreptitiously flicked to her daughter who was sorting through the shells she'd carefully collected. Chloe was looking adorable in her favourite pink flowery shorts and unicorn T-shirt. Zak had tasked them with building "the most awesome" sandcastle on the beach and had issued instructions that they should take it seriously. He'd started on the moat and had gathered bits of wood to make a drawbridge. Jasmine noted his face was bright red, his forehead covered in beads of sweat. She handed him his insulated bottle of water decorated in superheroes. 'You need to keep hydrated,

Zaky. You too, Chlo.' She handed Chloe hers. Since the text from her mum, all Jasmine had been able to think about was the Scraggs, her emotions veering from boiling rage to pity for Chloe. It had been a battle to keep her feelings hidden, but somehow she'd managed.

'So how're things going with the seaside project you and Sophie have been working on in class, Chlo?' Jasmine asked, being careful to keep her tone light and casual as she tipped her bucket upside down, lifting it up to reveal a perfect sandcastle. She figured bringing Sophie up in conversation and using the topic of the collage would be a good way of subtly broaching the subject of school since it was something Chloe had been excited about. She'd been paired with Sophie Stanhope, her best friend, to make a picture of the beach using recycled bits and bobs. Both girls had been bubbling with enthusiastic plans for their design.

Chloe's face was shiny from the sunblock Jasmine had slathered over her in a bid to protect her fair skin. The little girl pushed her strawberry-blonde hair back, knocking her sunhat skew-whiff in the process, though she seemed not to notice. 'We had to start it again because it got... We just needed to do it again.' She gave a half-smile, a shadow of sadness darkening her expression, before quickly turning her attention back to her shells. Her shoulders heaved with a sigh.

It wasn't the reaction Jasmine had expected. She felt her anger spike. She instinctively knew one of the Scraggs had something to do with it. Her gaze slid to Zak whose non-verbals were telling her that he knew the reason the collage needed to be redone, but she resisted the urge to ask him in front of Chloe.

She'd managed to have a brief word with her son earlier when they were at home. He'd nipped in from the backyard where he'd been patiently trying to teach Chloe how to spin a football on the tip of her finger, and Jasmine had seized the opportunity. In the few short minutes she'd quizzed him, she'd learnt that Nina Scragg had recently turned her attention onto Chloe, as had Bruce Scragg with Zak. He said he had no idea what had brought this about, but Zak had assured his mum that he could handle Bruce, who was in his class. As if hearing him say that wasn't bad enough, Jasmine had been beside herself when her son had told her he'd recently had to step in when he'd caught Nina teasing Chloe and calling her names. 'I wanted to tell you, Mum. Honest. But Chlo made me promise not to in case you got in touch with school and it made things worse. Please don't let on I've said owt.'

'I won't, son, but you've done the right thing in telling me.' Jasmine had given his shoulder a reassuring squeeze. Her stomach had churned and her cheeks burned with anger at the thought of her children being on the receiving end of the Scragg siblings' nastiness.

'So what was Nina Scragg saying to Chlo?' Jasmine had asked, injecting a forced calmness into her voice as she braced herself for what she was about to hear.

Zak's gaze had fallen to his trainers. 'She was just being mean, that's all.'

'Didn't you at least get some idea of what she said?' Much as Jasmine had felt desperate to push her son to tell her everything he knew, experience had told her she needed to tread gently if she was to get a hint of what the girl had been saying.

'It was something about...' He'd started to shuffle awkwardly, still reluctant to give her eye contact.

'Something about what, lovey?' Jasmine had asked gently.

'I think it was about Chlo not having a dad.' His cheeks had flamed. 'Her stupid brother's been saying the same sort of stuff to me as well, but I just tell him to get lost.'

'I see.' A tidal wave of rage had surged through Jasmine, her hands balling into fists, making her knuckles blanche. It had been a battle to stop herself from seeking out Jason Scragg and telling him to sort his children out or else she would.

'You won't go up to school about it, will you, Mum? Promise?' Zak had pleaded.

Jasmine had taken a deep breath, using every ounce of strength to quash her blazing anger. 'Don't worry, Zak, I won't. I'll find a way to get it sorted.' She'd been reluctant to make promises she knew she was going to have to break, but she hadn't wanted to put the dampeners on her son's weekend by having him worry that she'd be seen going into the headteacher's office by his classmates.

And now, here on the beach, seeing how the light had dimmed in Chloe's eyes, Jasmine decided she wouldn't push her daughter any further for now. There was no way she was going to let thoughts of the Scragg family dominate her children's day. As hard as she worked, Jasmine always made sure she kept a chunk of the weekend free to devote solely to her children, and she didn't want that precious time to be tainted by the likes of the Scraggs. She'd deal with them next week; it would at least give her time to figure out how best to tackle the problem, and for the initial heat of her anger to cool. Now was the time to take Chloe's mind off them.

'Tell you what, how about we try to build a really tall sandcastle?' Jasmine said, injecting a cheerfulness into her voice she didn't feel. 'We could each fill our buckets with sand, and pile them one on top of the other, see how high we can make it. What do you think, kids?'

'Yeah! That sounds dead cool! We can keep going till it collapses.' Zak responded with his usual enthusiasm. He didn't waste a moment and immediately started shovelling sand into his bucket, sending it flying everywhere.

'What d'you reckon, Chlo?' Jasmine peered over at her daughter. 'How many buckets do you think we'll manage before it all comes tumbling down?'

A smile spread over Chloe's face, sending relief rushing through Jasmine. 'I reckon four buckets,' Chloe said, her familiar cheerful tone returning.

'Right, let's get cracking. Then, when we've done that, we can go and get some ice creams. Sound good?'

Both children cheered. Happiness was restored.

FIVE
MONDAY

Jasmine was almost done steam cleaning the floor in the generously proportioned kitchen of one of Spick 'n' Sparkle's clients. It was the new property she'd been given after Enid had died. Her mind had been lost in thoughts of her elderly friend, lingering on happy memories of their chats together, when her mobile started ringing, pulling her out of her musings. For most of the morning, her mind had been turning over what she was going to say at the meeting she'd arranged with Chloe's teacher, Mrs Butterfield, after school this coming Wednesday. She'd need to keep a lid on her temper, speak calmly and rationally. In other words, the opposite to how she was feeling. She'd already spoken to her mum, asked if she could pick the kids up for her, that way it would avoid alerting them to her visit to the school.

She turned the steam cleaner off and wiped the sweat from her brow with the back of her hand, then reached for her phone in the pocket of her jeans. Her pulse took off at a gallop when she saw Micklewick Bay Junior School's number looking back at her. Why was someone from school calling her? Her mind went into overdrive, her first thoughts going to Chloe and her problems with the Scragg girl.

Sucking in a fortifying breath, and reminding herself to keep calm, Jasmine accepted the call. 'Hello.'

'Hi, Jasmine, it's Charlotte Scholes, Mrs Armistead's PA again.' Jasmine had spoken to her only that morning when she'd called to organise a meeting with Chloe's teacher. She knew Charlotte, from working with her mother, Chris, at the bakery. The young woman popped in from time to time, and Jasmine had found her upbeat and friendly.

'Oh, hi, Charlotte. Is everything okay?' Jasmine hoped she wasn't calling to rearrange the appointment. With her calendar being as jam-packed as it was, she didn't know where she'd be able to squeeze it in at any other time that week.

'I'm calling on behalf of Zak's teacher, Mrs Hebbelthwaite. There's been a bit of an incident involving Zak and another child and Mrs Hebbelthwaite has asked if you could make an appointment to have a chat with her and the headteacher about it. She suggested tomorrow morning at ten thirty, if that's any good? I'm conscious you mentioned you were busy from our earlier phone call.'

Jasmine gasped audibly, her thoughts whirring. 'What kind of incident? Is Zak okay?' She could feel her pulse whooshing in her ears as panic squeezed in her chest.

'Zak's fine, but Mrs Hebbelthwaite is keen to get this matter sorted out, which is why she suggested a meeting for tomorrow,' the PA said kindly.

Jasmine's stomach was churning – she was eager to get it sorted, too. 'Right, yeah, 'course. I understand.' She pushed her fingers into her pixie crop, leaving her fringe standing on end. 'The only thing is, I have an appointment tomorrow morning and I'm not sure how long it's going to take but there's a chance it could run well into the afternoon. Is there any chance I could speak to Mrs Hebbelthwaite after school today? Or, if that's no good, how about after school on Wednesday since I'll already be there?' A feeling in her gut told her the two matters were connected. A joint meeting would avoid the need to cancel her trip to Danskelfe Castle at short notice – not that she wouldn't do it if necessary, her kids were always her priority.

'I'm really sorry, Jasmine, but as headteacher, Mrs Armistead has stressed she wants to be involved in the meeting, too, and unfortunately, looking at her diary, I can see she isn't free either of those times.' Charlotte sounded genuinely apologetic.

Jasmine's shoulders slumped further as the turmoil inside her cranked up several notches. The plates she always seemed to be spinning threatened to come crashing to the ground at any moment. 'Can I ask, does this have anything to do with the Scraggs?'

The pause the PA took before answering told Jasmine everything she needed to know. 'All I can say right now is that Zak's been involved in a fight with another pupil.'

'A *fight?*' Dread pooled in Jasmine's stomach. This was worse than she'd initially thought. Zak had never been in a fight before, and she'd never previously been called up to school to discuss his behaviour. 'You did say he's okay, didn't you? He hasn't been injured?' If the child from the new generation of Scraggs was anything like his father, he'd have no qualms about unleashing his aggression and spite.

'Both pupils are fine,' Charlotte said calmly. 'But Mrs Armistead is keen to speak to the parents from both sides so the situation can be resolved as quickly as possible.'

'Of course,' said Jasmine. Mrs Armistead wasn't the only one. Jasmine wished she could rush up to school and see her son right now, make sure he really was okay. She rubbed her forehead with her fingertips, wrestling with the thought of rearranging her meeting with Lady Caro. 'Just give me a second to bring up the calendar on my phone.'

Before she had a chance to put the call on speaker phone, Charlotte spoke. 'Listen, Jasmine, leave it with me. I'll have a word with the headteacher and see if she can squeeze in a quick meeting straight after school today before the other commitment she has in her diary. You did say you were free then, didn't you?' she said, compassion evident in her voice.

'Yes, yes, I am. That would be brilliant, thanks, Charlotte.' It would give her time to finish up here and head home, change out of her work jeans and Spick 'n' Sparkle T-shirt and tidy herself up before heading to the school.

'Okay, I can't make any promises, but, like I said, leave it with me. I'll get back to you as soon as I know.'

'Thank you.' Jasmine mentally crossed her fingers, hoping Charlotte would come back with a yes.

Sitting in the reception area outside the headteacher's office, Jasmine absently glanced around the walls that were decorated with an array of the pupils' brightly coloured artwork. It projected an air of positivity and cheerfulness, so at odds with her current mood. She switched her attention to her hands in her lap where her fingers were twisting in knots. Her right leg jigged up and down as it always did when she was feeling unsettled or anxious. The two hours since the PA's call confirming the meeting had felt more like ten. She wished she'd been able to see Zak straight after school, to make sure he was okay, to hug him close. Little Chloe, too. But she reminded herself that speaking to Mrs Armistead and Chloe's teacher was a priority and whatever had been going on with the dreaded Scraggs needed putting right without a moment's delay. She couldn't even begin to imagine what her friends would have to say when she told them that the once most despised family in Micklewick Bay had returned.

'Mrs Armistead won't be long.' A voice broke into her thoughts and Jasmine looked up to see Charlotte smiling kindly at her.

She offered a weak smile in return.

Moments later, the door facing her opened and Mrs Armistead appeared, smiling. She was smartly dressed in a light blue trouser suit and crisp white blouse, its lace collar softening the look. Her fair hair was cut into a blunt bob. Jasmine would put her in her late forties. 'Sorry to keep you waiting, Miss Ingilby, would you like to come in?' the headteacher said in her usual friendly, but at the same time, no-nonsense manner.

'That's okay. Thank you for seeing me at such short notice.' Jasmine stepped into the bright, neat office where Fay Butterfield, Chloe's teacher, was sitting in one of the chairs at the side of a large desk. Beside her was Mrs Hebbelthwaite who was Zak's teacher. Both greeted her with a warm smile which went a small way to allaying her nerves.

'Hello, Miss Ingilby,' Mrs Butterfield said.

'Hello there,' said Mrs Hebbelthwaite.

'Hi.' Jasmine forced her mouth into a smile.

Despite the myriad feelings currently running riot inside her, Jasmine noted the neatness of the room – the row of filing cabinets on one wall, the bookcase on another, potted plants and watercolours blurring the hard edges of the space. Her eyes settled briefly on the desk where a notebook and pen were set out along with a couple of framed photographs and a pot of pens.

'Please take a seat,' Mrs Armistead said, indicating to the brace of chairs in front of the desk as she herself slipped round to the other side where she settled herself in a large leather chair.

Jasmine sat down and glanced between the three women, her heart hammering.

'So, Mrs Butterfield tells me you'd made an appointment to see her before Charlotte contacted you earlier today,' the headteacher said.

'That's right, yes.' Jasmine nodded, her breathing short.

'Okay. In that case, I think it would be best if we start with the reason you wanted to speak to Mrs Butterfield, and we can take things from there.' Mrs Armistead placed her elbows on the table. She threaded her fingers together before resting her chin on them. It was an easy posture, with no hint of defensiveness, that told Jasmine the headteacher was ready to listen, was open to hear what she had to say. So different from Mr Trousdale – or Troutface Trousdale as he was known by the pupils – who'd been headteacher in her day. He'd been strict, had zero personality and had run the school with a rod of iron. He never smiled and his face was permanently set in a sour expression. Even the teachers had jumped to attention whenever he walked into the classroom. On the day he retired, it was as if the old school building had breathed a sigh of relief. Being approachable and the owner of a positive outlook meant that Julie Armistead was everything Richard Trousdale was not.

Jasmine was thankful she was dealing with her and not the former head today.

Inhaling a calming breath through her mouth, Jasmine reminded herself once more to keep her emotions in check – she wanted to be sure her concerns were taken seriously, that she didn't give the impression she was an overly protective, hysterical mother who thought her children were perfect and could do no wrong. She went on to explain how Chloe had become quiet and withdrawn over the last couple of weeks, and how she'd been reluctant to go to school on a morning. 'It's not like her at all, she usually loves school. I've never had any trouble getting her here.' Jasmine then told them what Zak had shared with her. The three women listened intently throughout, expressions of concern occasionally flashing in their eyes, though no one passed comment.

'I'm sorry to hear Chloe's been feeling unhappy about coming to school, that's not what we want at all,' said Mrs

Armistead, leaning back in her seat when Jasmine had finished speaking. 'We want our children to feel happy and safe here.' She turned to Chloe's teacher. 'Mrs Butterfield, have you noticed any recent changes in Chloe?'

Fay Butterfield cleared her throat. 'Yes, I have, actually. I was going to contact you myself, Miss Ingilby, but you beat me to it. Both Miss Unthank – I'm sure you'll know she's one of our teaching assistants – and myself have picked up on it. Chloe's a popular, well-liked pupil, with a sunny, cheerful nature. And though she's one of our quieter students, she always throws herself wholeheartedly into whatever she's been tasked with, which is why it's been so easy to spot the recent change in her.'

'Right,' said Jasmine, a spike of concern shooting through her. 'And what do you think has been responsible for these changes you've noticed?'

'Well...' Mrs Butterfield's eyes flicked briefly to the headteacher. 'There have been a few occasions where we've had to address a situation – the damage to Chloe and Sophie's beach collage you mentioned being an example. Nina Scragg had been caught spoiling it by other pupils. And there was an occasion when paint had been thrown over a model Chloe was making as part of our seaside project. It transpired Nina was responsible for that, too.' Mrs Butterfield paused, as if choosing her words with care. 'And then there's also the element of verbal unkindness, which, from what you've just said, you're evidently already aware of, and which we have spoken to Nina about. We've made it very clear that it's not at all acceptable.'

'I can assure you, Miss Ingilby, we stress to all of our pupils that unkindness is not tolerated at our school,' Mrs Armistead interjected, her expression now grave.

Jasmine felt her heart rate gather speed. 'What's the...' She took a moment as she searched for the right word. 'What's the subject of this verbal unkindness?' She pressed her lips together in order to stop her anger from spilling over, simultaneously bracing herself for what she was about to hear.

Mrs Butterfield shuffled awkwardly in her seat and cleared her throat again. 'Unfortunately, it's about Chloe's father, or rather that... that he... um... passed away.'

Pain seared through Jasmine and her eyes burnt with unexpected tears – it was rare for her to show that she was hurt, even rarer for her to cry. *Poor little Chloe.* She blinked quickly, clenching her jaw in order to keep her rampaging emotions in check. Though Zak had hinted at this, having it confirmed by Chloe's teacher somehow made it infinitely worse. She swallowed down the lump that was now clogging her throat. 'That's worse than unkind, it's cruel. What sort of child uses the loss of a parent against another?' She swept her gaze between the sympathetic faces looking back at her.

'We can fully appreciate why this will have caused Chloe – and yourself – distress, which is why we'll be speaking to Nina Scragg's parents. Not that I want to diminish the levity of what Nina said – it truly is terrible – but I honestly think she won't have fully understood the impact of her words,' said Mrs Armistead.

Oh, if she's anything like her toxic father she'll have understood and meant every nasty little word of it. 'So what happens now?' Jasmine asked, keeping her thoughts to herself and choosing not to comment on the headteacher's observation.

'Well, that leads us on to why we wanted to speak to you about Zak,' said Liz Hebbelthwaite. Zak's teacher went on to explain how over the lunchtime break, Zak and Bruce Scragg had got into a physical fight and had to be separated by the playground monitors.

Jasmine listened, her mouth falling open as she took in the details. 'But that doesn't sound like Zak at all – I know that's what all parents say, but, honestly, he's never done anything like that before. He must've been provoked.' She willed them with all her might to believe her.

Mrs Hebbelthwaite nodded. 'We're very aware that's out of character for Zak. He usually adopts the role of peacekeeper, uses his humour to help diffuse arguments and disagreements amongst his peers. Which is why we were so surprised to find him involved in something like this.'

That his teachers appeared to know him well had a calming effect on Jasmine. 'He mentioned to me over the weekend that he'd been having trouble with the Scragg boy. Said he'd been making fun of him not having a dad.' Her eyes swept over the three faces, hoping to read their expressions, her heart aching for her son. She was relieved to see compassion reflected back at her. 'Zak told me it didn't bother him, but I could see it did, though not to the extent that things would become physical between them. Do you know who started the fight?' *Please, please say it wasn't Zak.*

'According to the pupils who witnessed it, Bruce pushed Zak a couple of times, knocking him over, which was when Zak retaliated but, luckily, the playground monitors got involved before things could escalate.'

Jasmine nodded, relief washing over her to hear that Zak hadn't been the instigator. 'So what happens now? Is Zak in trouble?'

'Well, of course we don't condone the fact he was involved in a fight, but that we've addressed the situation with you is enough to satisfy the procedures we have in place at school.'

Jasmine nodded. 'And what about the Scragg boy, seeing as he was the one who started it? Surely he can't be allowed to get away with what he said to Zak, nor what his sister's said and done to Chloe.' Jasmine could feel her indignation rising.

'Miss Ingilby, you can rest assured that both Bruce and Nina Scragg will be dealt with accordingly,' the headteacher said, holding eye contact with Jasmine. 'It might simply be a matter that they're taking time to settle in; after all, they haven't been at the school for long. Going forward, we'll be sure to monitor the situation closely.'

'Good.' Jasmine mustered up a smile of relief. She hoped there'd be nothing further to monitor after the two Scragg children and their parents had been spoken to, but she had a horrible feeling that wouldn't be the end of it.

SIX

Jasmine hurried away from the school, head down, mind whirling. The fingers of stress had a firm grip on her, making her oblivious to all around her. She didn't see the large, fluffy black dog lolloping towards her until it was too late and she found herself flying over the top of it, landing with a thud in an unceremonious heap on the pavement. Shock had done a sterling job of numbing her senses – but, unfortunately, not her knees which were now throbbing after making contact with the unforgiving York paving stones – and she was only half aware of a voice calling in the background.

'Ouch!' She pulled a face as she went to push herself up, but her legs were too shaky. Tears stung her eyes and she fought to keep them under control. Of all the times for this to happen, when she was desperate to get back home to her children. Before she had a chance to process another thought, the black dog pushed its face into hers, delivering a slobbery sweep of its tongue across her cheek. 'Arghh!' She scrunched up her nose. If the pungent odour of the great lolloping hound's breath was anything to go by, it had recently eaten something containing rotting fish.

'Ernest! Stop! Now!' called a man's voice. 'Ernest! Heel!' The sound of shoes pounding over pavement and heavy breathing grew closer.

Jasmine tried to get to her feet a second time, but the dog nudged his wet nose at her, its whiskers tickling her face and making her lurch backwards. *Flaming heck! That breath!*

Soon she became aware of someone standing beside her, a concerned voice asking if she was okay. 'I hope you're not hurt. Can I help you up?'

'Um... I... I'm—' Before she had a chance to get her words out and tell him she didn't need any help, Jasmine found herself being very gently lifted to her feet.

'I really must apologise about Ernest, he's a bit too enthusiastic for his own good. He's absolutely harmless, just thinks everyone's his friend,' explained the man.

'No harm done.' She hurriedly dashed away her tears, hoping the stranger hadn't noticed. In truth, though her knees were singing out with pain, it was her pride that had taken the worst of the battering. She felt acutely embarrassed at falling over such a large dog – *how had she missed him?* – especially when there was a witness to her clumsiness. 'It was my fault.' She glanced across at Ernest whose tail was wagging vigorously. She could swear he looked pleased with his efforts and, despite herself, she couldn't help but give a watery smile.

'You sure you're okay?' the man asked again.

Jasmine nodded. 'Yes, thanks.' She just wanted to remove herself from this excruciating situation and get back home to Zak and Chloe.

'Unfortunately, Ernest managed to wriggle out of his collar, and tear off on an adventure before I could stop him. He's a good lad most of the time, aren't you, fella?' The stranger ruffled the dog's floppy ears which was received with great delight. Ernest offered his paw, which brought another smile to Jasmine's face.

She switched her gaze from Ernest to the man, their eyes meeting. Jasmine gave a loud gasp, suddenly struck by an overwhelming sense of déjà vu. Judging by the stranger's expression, he clearly felt something, too.

'Jingilby?' The man's face broke out into a smile that revealed even, white teeth.

She stood rooted to the spot, her mouth hanging open, her mind racing. She rubbed her fingertips over her brow, trying to make sense of the situation. It had been a lifetime ago since anyone had used that name. And there'd only ever been one person who'd done so and he'd left town over twenty years ago: little Max Grainger. He'd been a childhood friend – in fact, the pair of them had been so close they were more like siblings. They'd also been in the same class at Micklewick Bay Primary School.

The Jingilby nickname had come about when Max Grainger had spotted her name on a typed list lying on their teacher's desk in the classroom, the typo in her surname making him roar with laughter: J ingilby. 'Look, Jazz, they've called you Jingilby!' he'd said, blending her initial with her surname. 'I like it! It sounds happy, just like you. I'm going to call you Jingilby forever now.'

Jasmine hadn't minded in the slightest; she'd liked the sound of it, too. Interestingly, the nickname failed to catch on with her other friends who stuck with Jazz, leaving only Max who called her Jingilby, which to her somehow felt right.

It couldn't be! She took a second, scrutinising the man's face. *Oh, my days. It is!* Now she looked more closely, the happy twinkle in those hazel eyes, the freckles splashed across his nose and cheeks, could only belong to one person.

'Max? Max Grainger?' She looked on as his smile grew wider. His eyes sparkled and sent her hurtling back to over twenty years ago. The wave of happiness that flooded her chest took her by surprise. 'Is it really you?'

'Yup, it's really me, Jingilby.' He laughed, his eyes dancing just as she remembered. 'And I'd recognise those mischievous eyes and fiery hair anywhere. Boy, is it good to see you.'

'It's good to see you, too.' She could barely believe this tall, broad-shouldered man was the same little Max Grainger who'd been involved in such a huge chunk of her childhood.

They looked at one another for several moments, laughing in disbelief. Ernest looked between them, his tail sweeping over the pavement.

Max was the first to speak. 'I'd hug you, only I'd worry I'd hurt you after your tumble. You sure you're okay?'

Jasmine rolled her eyes and shook her head. 'Yeah, that wasn't my finest hour, but I'm fine.' She was relieved to find the pain had started to subside. 'My mind was elsewhere, which was why I didn't spot Ernest.'

'I'm not sure it would've made a difference if you had, he moves pretty quickly when he sets his mind to it, so you wouldn't have had much of a chance to put your brakes on.'

'In that case, I don't feel so clumsy then.'

'So, how've you been? You look well. How're your parents? Sorry for all the questions,' said Max. They both laughed at that.

'That's okay. I've got just as many for you, once I get my head round the fact you're actually here in Micklewick Bay.' She was just about to ask where he was staying when their attention was taken by the sound of his phone ringing.

'Sorry, Jingilby, I'm expecting an important call, I'd better check who it is.' He pulled an apologetic face as he reached into the back pocket of his jeans and retrieved his phone.

'Hey, no problem.' Jasmine watched as he swiped the screen, a frown crumpling his brow. She took the opportunity to check her own phone and was shocked to see a slew of missed calls and texts from her mum's number, her mind flying to her kids. She hoped everything was okay there. She felt her mood deflate.

'I really should take this call, Jingilby.' Max's voice brought her back into the moment.

'And I need to get back home.' She pressed her mouth into a smile.

'Oh, okay.' He sounded disappointed. 'It'd be good to meet up sometime,' he said, his finger poised to accept the call.

'Yeah, definitely. My parents still live in the same house, so you could always call and see them. I could meet you there.'

'Sounds perfect.' He gave her a warm smile, raising his hand in a wave. She waved back before turning away and heading in the direction of her car, her head spinning. As she strode on, she was struck by a thought that sent a chill running up her spine: did Max know about Jason Scragg being in town?

Once in the close confines of her car – which she'd parked well away from school to ensure her children wouldn't spot it and realise where she was – Jasmine scrubbed her face with her hands, her mind turning over the details of the meeting. She'd decided to tackle thoughts of Max later, especially since seeing him again so unexpectedly hadn't sunk in properly yet.

How had it got to this with the Scragg children? Was she to blame? Had she got so busy her children felt they couldn't come to her, tell her of their worries and concerns? She really hoped not; they'd always shared everything with her. The reason Jasmine worked so hard was for her kids, so she could afford to give them what they wanted, make sure they had the same as their friends, that they didn't do without. Had they subconsciously picked up that she felt permanently exhausted? A worse thought crossed her mind: had it tainted the quality time she set aside to spend with them, meaning they didn't enjoy it as much? If this was the case, how had she not noticed? Granted she had felt more tired recently, but she'd still savoured every moment she spent with Zak and Chloe. They were her world, her reason for getting up in the morning. She'd hate for them to feel she was too busy for them. Guilt churned in her stomach and made her face prickle. It would be inordinately unfair if her reason for juggling so many jobs had been to the detriment of Zak and Chloe's well-being.

'Ugh!' She threw her head back in frustration, just as a knock at the driver's window almost made her jump out of her skin.

'Jeez!' She pressed her hand to her chest as she turned to see Stella peering in at her.

'You okay, Jazz?' Stella asked, her pale blue eyes brimming with concern.

Jasmine wound down her window. 'Flippin' 'eck, Stells, you frightened the life out of me!'

'Sorry, flower, but you were chuntering away to yourself and you looked so stressed out, I just wanted to make sure you were okay.' She was dressed in her workwear of a neatly tailored black trouser suit and crisp white blouse, a designer handbag over her shoulder. Her glossy blonde hair was swept back into a neat French pleat.

Jasmine puffed out her cheeks and released a noisy sigh. 'I wish I could say I was, but I was called up to school; problems with the kids. You'll never guess who's back.'

'Who?'

'Jason Scragg.' Jasmine watched as Stella's face paled. 'And he's brought his kids with him.'

'You're kidding me.'

Jasmine shook her head. 'Wish I was.'

'Two ticks.' Stella hurried round to the passenger side of the car, her high heels clicking over the pavement. She climbed in beside Jasmine, twisting round to face her friend and filling the small space with her clean, crisp perfume. 'Tell me everything, leave nothing out.'

Jasmine heaved another sigh. 'I'll just text my mum, tell her not to worry, that I'll be back soon.'

That done, she proceeded to recount the contents of the meeting at school to Stella.

Her friend screwed up her face. 'Hideous little brats!' She'd never made a secret of her dislike of children – the exception being Zak and Chloe, with the recent addition to that exclusive list being Maggie and Bear's baby Lucia. Career-driven, Stella was the first to admit she didn't have a maternal bone in her body and, consequently, children didn't feature in her future. 'Mind, shocked as I am to hear Scraggo's back in town, it doesn't surprise me that his offspring are as obnoxious as their father,' she said distastefully.

'Yeah, same here.' Jasmine nodded sadly.

'I know you'll be worrying that it's going to be a case of history repeating itself, but from my perspective, I can assure you it looks very different,' Stella said in her usual no-nonsense manner. 'For starters, school are fully aware of the situation and have assured you they'll deal with it, which is a far cry from our day when the teachers seemed to turn a blind eye to what that worm Scraggo was doing. Old Troutface Trousdale was a complete waste of space as far as student well-being and bullying was concerned, especially when it came to the Scragg family. If he spent as much time being an effective headteacher as he did twitching that irritating moustache of his, then Micklewick Bay Primary would've been one of the best schools in the area.'

They both chuckled at the memory, each giving a quick burst of the "Troutface Mouth Wiggle" in the way they used to as pupils.

'In all seriousness, looking back, I actually think Troutface was scared of Scraggo's father.'

Jasmine nodded; her friend had a point. 'I reckon you could actually be right there.'

'Hmm. I've developed a nose for these things.' Stella's work as a criminal barrister meant she encountered a whole host of unsavoury characters and relationship dynamics. It afforded her an insight into how they operated and had enabled her to finetune her senses. Her gut feeling concerning situations were rarely wrong. 'And don't forget poor little Max Grainger had no one at home to stick up for him. Zak and Chloe have you, and heaven help anyone who takes you on, Jazz! Jeez! You're like a lioness protecting her cubs, ready to tear the throat out of anyone who hurts or upsets them! Fierce doesn't remotely cover it.' They both laughed heartily at that.

'I completely hold my hands up at that, but in my defence, apart from my mum and dad, I'm the only one they've got, which is why I'm so protective of them.'

'Jazz, trust me when I say, there's no "only" about it where you're concerned. You're the most amazing mother, Zak and Chloe are a credit to you. I don't think I've seen kids more loved or better cared for than those two – and little Lucy's included in that now, too. And don't forget, I kind of know where you're coming from with your family dynamics; it was the same for me growing up, with it being just me and my mum.'

'True.' Jasmine nodded. Stella had grown up in a single parent family with Alice, her mum, grafting all hours. She'd set up Spick 'n' Sparkle so she could make a better life for her and her daughter. Stella hadn't met her father until recently, though what she'd seen hadn't made her regret his lack of involvement in her life. But the key difference between Stella's and Zak and Chloe's situation was that Stella's father hadn't died in tragic circumstances as Bart had. The hope or possibility that she'd be able to connect with her father at some point hadn't been snatched away as it had with Jasmine's children.

'And I think there's a *teeny-tiny* factor we're forgetting about.' Amusement danced in Stella's eyes.

'What's that, then?' Jasmine asked.

'Er, don't tell me it's slipped your mind how you whooped Scraggo's arse in front of pretty much the whole school? I doubt very much *he's* forgotten. It's the stuff of legend; gave you superhero status for a considerable length of time afterwards.' Stella gave a throaty giggle.

'I hadn't forgotten about that.' Jasmine smiled sheepishly. In truth, it hadn't been far from her mind since her mum had sent the text mentioning the Scragg name. 'But we were kids then, and much as I could willingly throttle his little brats right now, I can hardly do to them what I did to him! I'd end up in court with you defending me, and correct me if I'm wrong, but I reckon the judge and jury wouldn't be too sympathetic to my cause.'

'You know I don't defend, Jazz,' Stella said dryly, a smile hitching up the corners of her mouth.

'Thanks!' Jasmine shot her a look of faux hurt. She and the rest of their friends were all aware that though Stella was a criminal barrister, her practice was exclusively prosecution; she refused to represent the sort of "scrotes" as she called the defendants involved in her cases, which were predominantly gaslighters, wife beaters and drug dealers.

'I'm only joking, and anyway, I didn't mean that. I just mean he'll be wary, that's all. Trust me on this, Jazz, Scraggo won't want his kids to attract your attention.'

'Which leads me very nicely on to telling you about someone I ran into just before I got to my car.'

'Ooh, I'm intrigued. Who is it?'

'Max Grainger.'

Stella paused, as if allowing Jasmine's words to sink in.

'Max Grainger, as in the little Max Grainger we've just been discussing.'

'The very one.'

'Wow! I wonder what he's doing back in town. You don't think it's got anything to do with Scraggo and his return, do you?'

'I'm not sure, we didn't get much of a chance to talk, so I've no idea if he's here to stay or just on a fleeting visit.'

'And how did he look?'

'Well, he's grown – a lot! Still has the same sort of happy-go-lucky smile and twinkly eyes, but he must be over six feet tall and has filled out a heck of a lot – there's no trace of the skinny little kid he used to be. And though he was dressed casually, he looked smart, too.'

'Not that you paid much attention, of course.' Stella chuckled.

Jasmine gave her friend an "I'm really not in the mood for that" look. 'All I'm saying is that he looked like he'd done okay for himself.'

'Which is what we'd all hoped for him,' Stella said.

'Exactly.' Now Jasmine thought about it, it was good to think Max's life had turned out well for him. She found herself hoping he'd be true to his word and call in on her parents, knowing how much they'd love to have a catch-up with him.

'And going back to what you said about you and your parents being *all* the kids have, I'm afraid I'm going to have to pull you up about that,' Stella said, interrupting her thoughts.

'Oh?'

'Slightly hurt that I have to remind you, but hey...' Stella gave a shrug, feigning offence before fixing her with a smile. 'I'm only teasing,' she said, nudging Jasmine with her shoulder. 'But joking aside, I don't want you to forget that Zak and Chloe – and you – have got us, your best friends, and we love you. You only have to holler if you need anything, no matter what it is, and we'll be there for you, day or night.'

Not for the first time that day Jasmine felt her throat constrict and tears burn her eyes. She blinked quickly, hoping her friend hadn't noticed. Jasmine didn't do emotion in front of anyone, not even her best pals. 'Thanks, Stells, I'm here for you, too,' she said, her voice tight.

SEVEN

The chat in her car with Stella had helped settle Jasmine's emotions such that she felt sufficiently calm to head to her parents' house without the risk of her anger and indignation bursting out of her in front of her children. Desperate to get her kids home, she gave her mum a hurried and abridged version of what had been discussed in the meeting at school, telling her she'd go into greater detail later. 'Oh, my days, sounds like a horrible case of déjà vu!' Heather said.

'And you and Dad might want to prepare yourselves for a surprise visitor.' Jasmine deliberately saved telling her mum about Max until she'd shared what had happened up at school.

'A surprise visitor? Please don't tell me that Scraggo's threatened to call here?' Heather's outraged expression made Jasmine laugh.

'No way! Don't go worrying about that, he wouldn't dare.'
'Good.' That seemed to pacify Heather. 'Who then?'
'Max.'
'Max who? Surely not little Max Grainger?'
'Little Max Grainger.' Jasmine nodded.
'How... I mean... Oh, it'll be lovely to see him.' Jasmine

watched as her mum's face softened. 'But how do you know? Have you seen him?'

Jasmine explained how she'd bumped into him and the conversation that had ensued, which had Heather chuckling heartily.

'And how're your knees?'

'Much better, thanks.'

Heather's face was wreathed in smiles. 'Your dad'll be over the moon when I tell him – about Max, not your knees, flower.'

Jasmine knew her parents would be thrilled to see Max, he'd been a permanent fixture at their house when he and Jasmine were children.

Max Grainger had lived diagonally opposite Jasmine and her family on Arkleby Terrace, a street of sturdily built authority houses that boasted generously proportioned gardens. Most of them were now privately owned, as was the case with Jasmine's home. Max lived at number nine, she at number eight. They were in the same year at school and had known each other all their lives, with Max being a regular fixture in the Ingilby residence. Though they weren't related, Max had always addressed Jasmine's parents as Auntie Heather and Uncle Steve.

Though money was often tight at number eight, love and affection flowed freely, as did laughter and happiness. Jasmine and Jonathan never felt they were doing without, rather they were taught to value and appreciate what they had. There were always hot meals on the table, and Heather prided herself on her laundry skills, ensuring her family's clothes were clean and perfectly pressed. Bus driver Steve, in what he jokingly used to refer to as his role of "hunter-gatherer" grew soft fruit and vegetables in a patch at the bottom of the garden, his green fingers supplying the family with an abundance of fresh produce – Jasmine and Jonathan would be tasked with picking the berries for which they were rewarded. Both Jasmine's parents instilled the importance of good manners and kindness in their children. And though their respective family circumstances meant neither Heather nor Steve had gone to university, they were keen to encourage their children to follow their heart, telling them that they'd support whatever choices they made. They had a strong work ethic, fitting in extra shifts around their children in order to save money for family holidays, Christmas and birthdays. Keen to instil the value of money in their offspring, Jasmine and Jonathan were given weekly tasks in order to earn their pocket money.

All of this meant that both Ingilby children grew up feeling loved, valued and with a strong sense of their place in the world.

It couldn't have been more different for little Max Grainger just a stone's throw away on the other side of the road.

Max had no memory of his mother. He'd been just eighteen months old when she'd walked out after a blazing row with his father. When it had become local knowledge, Heather had offered to look after Max while Bazza *supposedly* went out to work. Everyone knew he was unable to hang on to a job for more than a week and spent most of his time in the pub, wasting what little money he had. It would be fair to say he'd taken advantage of Heather's kindness on multiple occasions. Little Max spent so much time with the Ingilby's he and Jasmine had grown up almost like siblings.

As Max had grown older, his father's irritability had increased, which seemed to coincide with his drinking habit; there didn't seem to be a day when Bazza wasn't drunk. He started accusing Heather of interfering, saying she was spying on him and reporting back to school and Social Services, who'd begun circling around number nine. Of course, Heather hadn't reported anything to anyone, of which she'd eventually manage to convince him. Instead, she'd kept a close eye on little Max. But Bazza's explosive outbursts had meant she'd had to tread carefully around him in order to avoid his displeasure which he'd barked with such viciousness, she'd become scared of him. Heather had told Jasmine when she was older that she'd felt torn at times, thinking that Bazza didn't deserve his son, whom she described as an adorable, loving little boy. She and Steve had dropped subtle hints to Max's grandfather when they'd encountered him on his rare visits, but it would appear that Bazza had convinced Jimmy he was managing fine, especially with the Ingilby's helping out the way they did. 'Seemed, despite all his yelling and accusations that I was a busybody, I served a purpose in his mind after all.'

Heather also told her that it was obvious to others who lived close by that Bazza wasn't parenting Max as he should, but they were too fearful of reprisals to say anything or take action. She herself had been reluctant to report him and be responsible for the little lad being taken into care. She'd added that the one saving grace was that he didn't physically hurt his son. If he had, then Heather and Steve wouldn't have hesitated to involve the authorities. Instead, they'd made sure Max was welcome at their home any time, day or night. The open invitation meant he had access to a hot meal whenever he wanted, and had a chance to get warmed through in the colder months.

On the nights he slept over, sharing Jonathan's room, Heather would surreptitiously gather up Max's clothes and give them a whizz around the washing machine, repairing any holes and rips where possible. Anything she deemed beyond saving she got rid of and replaced with something similar of her son's. And he'd loved the luxury of having a deep bath, filled with bubbles, spending ages playing with a collection of Jonathan's old plastic toys they'd hung on to. And he'd been over the moon when Jonathan had said he could have the Micklewick Lion's football kit he'd grown out of. Max had worn it non-stop for a week and told Jasmine he'd even slept in it. Since then, Heather was sure to pass on any of the clothes her son had outgrown, which Max had declared to be "mint". It helped that Bazza didn't seem to notice. It was the same when his son returned to number nine with his wild curls tamed courtesy of Heather's scissors.

To say Bazza Grainger was a cold-hearted, selfish man would be an understatement. It was obvious to all he put his own needs before his young son. He made no secret that he didn't want a job, and any he'd had, he'd been sacked from for a litany of offences, including drinking, stealing and being abusive to his bosses or their customers, or not bothering to turn up. He'd essentially made himself unemployable. He seemed to forget – or not to care – how all of this would affect his son.

EIGHT

Once back at Rosemary Terrace, Jasmine had sat Zak and Chloe down at the kitchen table and spoke calmly, telling them about her chat with their teachers. Zak's face had fallen at first, but once he'd realised his mum wasn't angry, his regret for retaliating with Bruce Scragg had been as tangible as Chloe's relief at getting her worries off her chest. 'I want you both to know that you can tell me *anything*, even if you think you've done something wrong – *especially* if you've done something wrong. It's always best to get things out in the open rather than keeping it to yourself and worrying about it,' Jasmine had said. 'Worries have a horrible habit of somehow getting bigger if you do that. I've always told you I won't be angry with you for being honest with me, and have I ever been cross with you for telling the truth?'

'No, Mum,' Zak said, shaking his head.

'No, Mummy,' Chloe said. Their serious expressions made Jasmine's heart ache with love for her children.

She reached for their hands, giving them each a squeeze. 'And the last thing I want is for you to bottle up your worries. I'm your mum, and a mum's job is to be there for her children.

I'm on your side, kids, I always will be, no matter what. And, much as I don't approve of you getting into a fight with that Scragg lad, Zak lovey, I can completely understand why you did it. But in future, I think it's probably best if you do all you can to ignore him, which I appreciate is easier said than done. But the chances are, if he doesn't get a reaction out of you, he'll soon leave you alone. He's a bully and bullies need something to fuel their nasty behaviour. And if you feel you can't tell your teachers about what he's been doing, you can always tell me. I'll make sure it's sorted.' She held back from saying she had a far worse story to tell of what she'd done to Bruce Scragg's father when she was Zak's age. She'd save that for another day when they were older; she didn't want to be accused of setting a bad example, or for Zak to copy what she'd done – Heaven forbid! But she still didn't regret what she'd done.

With that particular topic dealt with, she hugged them both close, doing all she could to quell her growing concerns at the return of the Scragg family to Micklewick Bay. She knew the trouble with them was far from over. In truth, she feared it had only just begun, but she couldn't let her children sense that.

Pushing her doubts out of the way with a hefty shove, she gave a wide smile and said, 'Right then, you two monsters, how about we head into town and grab a pizza from Pepe & Chiara's for tea?'

'Yay! Takeaway pizza!' said Chloe, a beam brightening her face.

'Cool!' said Zak. 'Am I allowed a Pepe's Super-Special Meat Feast, Mum?'

'Course you are, lovey.'

'And can we share a margherita like we usually do, Mummy?'

'Sure can, Chlo. And some cheesy garlic bread, if you both fancy?'

Zak and Chloe cheered at that.

Getting a takeaway was usually reserved for special treats or weekends, but Jasmine reasoned with the difficult time her kids had been having recently, they deserved a little something to buoy their spirits. If a Pepe & Chiara's pizza takeaway served that purpose, then she was going to seize it with both hands and worry about the cost later.

'Right then, what are we waiting for?' She jumped up and grabbed her bag. 'Last one to get their shoes on is a rotten egg!' Giggling, she raced out of the kitchen and into the hall where their outdoor shoes were lined up by the front door.

Chloe let out an excitable squeal and shot after her mum, while Zak leapt to his feet, squawking as he tripped over the table leg, losing valuable seconds. 'Mum, you cheated!' Laughing hard, he threw himself down the tiny hallway and pushed his feet into his trainers, beating his mum but coming second to his little sister.

'Mum's a rotten egg! Mum's a rotten egg!' Zak sang, Chloe joining in and giggling as the pair danced a victory jig.

'Argh! How did that happen when I got here first?' Jasmine said, laughing hard and thinking how good it was to see merriment dancing across her children's faces.

'It's cos you took too long tying your laces, Mum. You should've used skill like me; I just pushed my feet in my trainers,' said Zak with a guffaw.

'I reckon you're right, Zak.' Jasmine didn't let on that she'd been deliberately slow at fastening her laces. She'd let Chloe win, thinking it would further boost her daughter's mood and, judging by her smiles, it appeared to have done just that.

Once in the car, it took the key a couple of turns in the ignition before the vehicle coughed itself into action, reminding Jasmine she needed to book it into the garage for a long overdue check-over. Her fears for the potential cost had meant she'd held off up to now, but this latest trouble in getting it started was becoming increasingly regular. She knew ignoring it wasn't going to solve the problem, and she was conscious it should feature highly on her list of priorities – especially since it was due its MOT next month, which was something she couldn't afford for it to fail – but with so many other things to contend with, and concern as to the potential cost, it had kept slipping further down the list.

What made matters worse was that she needed her car to get around to her cleaning jobs. Alice had a couple of Spick 'n' Sparkle work vans, but they were already being used by staff who didn't have their own transport – those who used their own vehicles were given a fuel allowance by Alice. Jasmine didn't even want to think about the potential loss of shifts while her car was in the garage getting fixed – if, indeed, it was repairable. That thought sent an anxious shiver running through her. *Don't even go there!* she told herself. *That's a worry for another day.* Her head was feeling as though it was ready to burst with so many thoughts that needed her attention. There was barely any room to cram another one in there.

Along with the worries about the Scragg family, at the back of her mind guilt was blooming along with the growing concern that something about her job commitments needed to change. Her parents were a good second to her as far as childcare was concerned, but recent events concerning the Scragg children meant Jasmine felt she needed to be more hands-on with Zak and Chloe. She stifled a sigh, suddenly feeling the weight of being a single parent, not wanting to alert them of her internal battles. She only hoped this meeting with Lady Caro tomorrow would provide the solution she needed.

But, right now, she was going to give her children her undivided attention. There was going to be none of this spreading herself too thinly, or getting distracted by her commitments, or letting her worries cloud her mood this evening. She was going to make sure they enjoyed themselves. Something at the back of her mind told her it would do her good, too.

Once in town, she parked up on Endeavour Road and they made their way along the pavement to Pepe & Chiara's. Chloe slipped her hand into Jasmine's and skipped along happily beside her while Zak raced ahead in his usual carefree way. It was good to see both children behaving more like themselves again.

She only hoped it would last.

She found her mind wandering to Max, wondering if she'd bump into him again. It would be good to hear his story, find out what he'd been up to since he'd left Micklewick Bay. She hoped his adult life hadn't been as tempestuous as his early childhood. If anyone deserved to have a peaceful, settled life, it was Max Grainger.

NINE

TWENTY-FIVE YEARS AGO

Jasmine knew Jason Scragg was trouble the moment she first set eyes on him in the playground of Micklewick Bay Primary School. She'd been in a huddle, chatting with Stella, Florrie and Lark, when his arrogant swagger had caught their attention as he made his way around, appraising the other children, a menacing gleam in his eye. Even at such a young age, his body language exuded a sinister vibe, sending out a clear message: he wasn't to be messed with. He'd only just arrived at the school and yet already he was flanked by a couple of "henchmen" in the form of Tyrone Hornsby and Decker Dixon; two of the school's hard-knock lads, as they walked slowly around the playground, side by side. Such posturing meant they were given a wide berth by the other pupils, particularly the younger ones, though Jasmine couldn't help but think it made them look slightly ridiculous. Rumours abounded about him being expelled from two previous schools, which was why he'd ended up in Micklewick Bay.

It wasn't long before Scraggo made his presence felt on a more personal level, particularly with those he'd singled out as being easy to intimidate. He'd taken up residence in a corner of the playground that was tucked out of view from the playtime supervisors. Like some sort of juvenile gangster, he'd send Tyrone and Decker to seek out the latest "victim" he'd picked off, telling the unsuspecting pupil that Scraggo wanted a word. Everyone soon came to learn that it was more than a "word" the bully was after. It invariably meant the handing over of pocket money, sweets or anything that had caught his eye. The undercurrent of fear he generated thanks to the threats of what he'd do if he found out anyone had "spragged" on him, meant no one dared tell the teachers or playground supervisors. Particularly so, Max Grainger.

Once Scraggo had her friend on his radar, it was as if he'd made it his mission to make the younger boy's life a misery at every opportunity. He mocked him mercilessly for having dirty, scruffy clothes, and for having shoes with holes in. He took great pleasure in telling Max he smelt like a rubbish bin, which had led to him thinking up the cruel nickname: "Rubbish". 'Urgh! Rubbish, you stink! Doesn't your mum wash your clothes?' he'd mocked, his face twisted into a spiteful sneer. 'Oh, yeah, I forgot, you don't have one. She ran off with another fella, didn't she, Rubbish?'

'No, she didn't!' Max had cried.

'Yeah, well, where is she then, Rubbish? If she'd cared about you, she'd have stayed, wouldn't she?' Scraggo had said, barging past Max and knocking him with his shoulder.

When this had been reported back to Jasmine, her heart had ached for her friend; the thought of how much it would've hurt him was almost unbearable. If she'd seen Scraggo at that moment, such was her rage, she'd have had no qualms about giving him a piece of her mind and to heck with the consequences. She knew her mum did her best to wash Max's clothes whenever she had the opportunity, but it didn't stop the smell of number nine lingering once he'd gone back there; it was ingrained in his clothes and the very fabric of Max's home.

Jasmine had ventured inside her friend's house only once when Bazza Grainger was at the pub, and she'd been shocked at the chaos – not to mention the smell. Carrier bags, clothes and a variety of junk were strewn around everywhere, making it difficult for her to navigate her way across the floor without standing on something. Unwashed dishes were piled in the sink, spilling out onto every available worktop, and the wallpaper was peeling from the walls. She'd never seen anywhere like it. If she didn't know better, she'd have thought the place had been ransacked. Not that she said anything to Max; it wasn't his fault, and there was no way she'd hurt his feelings.

The situation intensified when Scraggo had picked up on Max not having a coat after the younger lad had arrived at school one morning soaked to the skin, rain dripping from his curls and down his face. He, along with Tyrone and Decker, had pounced on him in the toilets where he was trying to dry himself off with the paper hand towels, taunting him mercilessly, saying his dad was a layabout who spent all his time in the pub. That he was a "cheapskate" who'd rather spend money on beer than his son. And they'd refused to believe Max when he'd said he'd lost his coat. To this day, Jasmine was sure they'd had something to do with it.

Word of what had happened to Max soon filtered to Jasmine and her friends. And as soon as she'd got home that night, Jasmine told her mum about it. Heather had immediately dug out one of the coats Jonathan had outgrown, which she'd set aside for Max to wear in a year or two's time. She'd given it to Max when he called over for his tea that evening, telling him she'd been having a sort out and asking if could do her a favour and take it off her hands. Max had been delighted with his new coat.

But his happiness was to be short-lived.

Two days later, Max had been distraught once more when it had gone missing from his coat peg at school. After a frantic search, Jasmine, with the help of Stella, Florrie and Lark, had found it slashed and stuffed down one of the girls' toilets. And if that wasn't enough, it had been daubed with paint.

Though he'd tried to hide it, pretending it didn't matter, it was clear that Max was heartbroken.

Despite the headmaster being given the names of the suspected perpetrators, Mr Trousdale did nothing, which had enraged Jasmine. She realised then that the rumours about Mr Trousdale being scared of Jason Scragg's father were very probably true.

The headmaster's lack of action meant Jason Scragg's bullying campaign continued, with Max hiding what was happening from Jasmine as much as he could. But she'd noticed how he dragged his feet on the walk to school, not to mention the notes stuck to the back of his jumper with the word "Rubbish" scrawled across. It had been the same with his PE bag, which he'd found on the floor next to his coat peg, the contents strewn far and wide and, judging by the footprints, they'd been given a thorough stamping on. Adding insult to injury, his name on the inside of his bag had been scribbled out and the word "Rubbish" written in its place.

Despite Max's efforts at hiding it, word soon got round the other pupils at Micklewick Bay Primary School, resulting in them keeping him at arm's length in order to avoid attracting Jason Scragg's attention. No one wanted to be tarred with the same brush as Max Grainger and suffer the consequences.

Which was what had prompted Jasmine to take action. She knew it could lead to her getting into serious trouble with school and her parents, but she felt so strongly about what Scraggo and his pathetic henchmen were doing to Max, she was prepared to risk it.

. . .

By the end of the week, she'd formed a plan and was ready to put it into action as soon as the moment presented itself.

It was the mocking voices and cry of, 'Leave me alone!' that caught the attention of Jasmine and her friends that Friday when they'd barely left the school gates.

Jasmine looked on in disbelief as her brain processed the scene before her: Max was covered in rubbish. *How did that happen?* Her gaze moved to the figure standing beside him, her jaw tightening as her eyes landed on Scraggo. She took in the upturned bin in his hands and cruel sneer on his face, realisation hitting her. 'No!'

Scraggo threw the bin to the ground, the clatter echoing around the street, as he and his cronies started laughing and jeering at Max. In the next moment, he gave Max a hefty shove, knocking him to the ground. 'Urgh! You really are rubbish now, aren't you, *Rubbish?*' He loomed over Max, sniggering as other pupils gathered round them.

A burning rage exploded in Jasmine's chest. Much as she hadn't wanted anything as horrible and humiliating as this to happen to Max, she'd been waiting for an opportunity to exact revenge on her friend's behalf. And now was the perfect time.

Seeing Max struggle to his feet, fighting back tears, snapped her into action. She stormed her way over to Scraggo who was making a big show of encouraging the onlooking pupils to mock her friend.

'Leave him alone! Just leave him alone!' she roared, fury propelling her as she hurtled towards him, her backpack swinging from side to side on her back. The cries of her friends telling her to be careful falling on stony ground behind her, she felt utterly fearless.

Scraggo, along with everyone watching, turned to face her. 'Or what?' he asked, mockingly, before shoving Max again.

'Or you'll be sorry, that's what!'

'Oh, yeah?' He threw an amused look in the direction of his

two friends, before swaggering towards her, an arrogant smile curling his top lip. 'How d'you reckon I'm gonna be sorry, then? You're nowt but a weedy girl.'

Jasmine landed in front of him, her nostrils flaring, her face burning with anger. He gave her a hard shove to the shoulder and she staggered backwards. 'Come on then, show me how I'm gonna be sorry.' A gasp ran around the group of pupils who'd been watching events unfold, tension suddenly filling the air as he reached for her.

'Get your hands off me!' she yelled as he took hold of her shoulders.

'Argghhh!' Before Scraggo had a chance to utter another word his legs were whipped from beneath him and he hit the floor with a resounding thud, air huffing from his lungs.

'That's how.' Jasmine made a show of dusting her hands off. 'And what was that you were saying about me being a weedy girl?' She wriggled her backpack from her shoulders and reached inside. 'And this is for what you did to Max's coat.' She squeezed hard on the bottle of red paint she'd brought from home, covering Scraggo's coat and school trousers. 'How's that for a taste of your own medicine, you loser?'

'Gerroff! You're crazy! Gerroff!' Scraggo yelled, rolling around and covering his face with his arms to avoid the paint, but Jasmine's aim was too good and she wouldn't be satisfied until she'd emptied the bottle on him.

Hoots of laughter registered in her ears, along with the voices of Stella, Florrie and Lark who'd started clapping and cheering. Cries of 'Whoop! Whoop!' and 'Go, Jazz!' filled the air as the rest of the onlooking pupils joined in.

Scraggo staggered to his feet, his coat spattered with paint, the laughter and jeers growing louder. With his cheeks flushed with embarrassment, he grappled for his schoolbag and made a hasty retreat.

'You okay, Max?' Jasmine asked softly as she helped brush the rubbish from his clothes.

He nodded, still dazed. 'Yeah.'

'Did he hurt you?' Her eyes went to the graze on his chin; she'd take him back to her house so her mum could clean it up for him. Thoughts of her mum sent a dart of panic shooting through her; Jasmine knew she wasn't going to be pleased once she'd heard what her daughter had done.

'Not really. There's this, though.' He pulled his top lip taut, revealing a chip in one of his front teeth.

What she saw chased all worries of her mother from her mind, though she tried to hide her shock, not wanting to cause Max any further distress. 'Don't worry, that can be mended.' She pushed up a smile. 'D'you remember when our Jonathan chipped his tooth?'

Max nodded.

'Well, the dentist did something to it – can't remember what it was exactly – but now you can't even tell his tooth was broken. It's that good, I can never remember which tooth it is. My mum and dad'll sort it out for you like they did for Jonathan.'

Max swallowed and peered up at her. 'Thanks, Jingilby,' he said in a small voice.

'What for?'

'For... what you just did... stopped Scraggo from—'

She jumped in, not wanting him to feel embarrassed or awkward. 'You'd have done the same for me.'

They grinned at one another. 'Not sure I'd have thought to squirt him with paint, but that was *epic*. You looked totally fearless.' They both started to laugh hard at that.

Despite her laughter, lurking at the back of her mind was the thought that she was going to be in serious trouble with school and her parents for what she'd done, but she didn't care.

If it meant Scraggo left her friend alone, any amount of telling-off and detention would be worth it.

Back at home, Heather Ingilby listened in disbelief as Jasmine and Max recounted what had happened outside school. Jasmine watched the mixture of emotions crossing her mum's face as she'd dabbed gently at Max's grazed chin, sticking plasters to his bleeding fingers.

'Well, let's hope that's the end of his bullying, lovey,' she said calmly. 'It's disgraceful it got as bad as it did. That Mr Trousdale has a lot to answer for. And, much as I can understand you wanting to stick up for little Max, your dad and me don't condone you using physical force or fighting, young lady.'

'Scraggo pushed me first, and it was that hard he nearly knocked me over,' Jasmine said defensively.

'I understand that, but you need to be careful, especially where that family's concerned. You could've ended up seriously hurt. I don't want to hear of you doing anything like that again, is that clear?'

'Yes, Mum.' Jasmine nodded, feeling suitably chastened.

The following week, the office at school had been bombarded by a plethora of complaints from parents all concerned about the reports they'd been hearing concerning the Scragg boy's bullying behaviour. Many had threatened to remove their child or children from the school unless Mr Trousdale took action, which had sent the headmaster into a tailspin.

A week later, Jason Scragg was no longer a pupil at Micklewick Bay Primary School, though no one knew the exact details why. It later transpired that the family had left town.

Almost instantly, Max's smiles had returned – albeit slightly altered by his chipped tooth – along with his usual sunny disposition. Little did they know it was to be short-lived thanks to a visit by the police to his home.

TEN

PRESENT DAY – MONDAY

That night, Jasmine lay in bed. Max Grainger had slipped into her thoughts, keeping sleep at bay. She recalled the day he'd burst into their kitchen, sobbing his heart out. The pain in his eyes had haunted her for months afterwards. It had been etched in her mind, the memories still vivid whenever she hauled them out, not that she'd done that for a long time.

Her mum had abandoned whatever it was she was stirring in a pan on the oven and rushed over to him, pulling him into a hug where he'd proceeded to sob uncontrollably.

Jasmine had hardly ever seen Max cry and on the rare occasions she had, it was nothing like the tears she'd witnessed then. Max was always cheerful and upbeat, and rarely without a smile. But that day, his usually twinkly hazel eyes were puffy and red, and his nose was streaming. It had been obvious he'd been crying for a long time and she'd known instantly something bad must've happened, either with his father or Jason Scragg.

Jasmine's stomach clenched at the memory. She'd always been protective of Max when they were younger, with him having no one to stick up for him at home.

When he'd finally stopped crying enough for her mum to ask if he could tell her what had got him so upset, he'd said, in between sobs, that it was "everything". Jasmine couldn't recall ever seeing anyone look so utterly defeated, which even as a child, had felt wrong; he was too young to look like that. It was as if every ounce of energy and spirit had been sucked out of him, a stark contrast to the usual lively, happy-go-lucky boy who bounced around on a wave of joie de vivre, despite his family circumstances.

Even one of her mum's "cure-all" hot chocolates hadn't tempted him that day, nor the prospect of dunking one of Jasmine's freshly baked extra-chocolatey cookies into it. It was something both she and Max used to enjoy doing whenever she'd made a batch with her mum. Indeed, Jasmine's family used to joke Max had a sixth sense for when they'd been baking since he'd always appear in the kitchen when the first batch of cakes or cookies were lifted from the oven. Not that there was any wonder since the young lad was always ravenous; making sure his son was properly fed wasn't exactly high on Bazza Grainger's list of priorities.

Jasmine gazed into the darkness of her tiny bedroom, her heart twisting as she recalled Max's reply to her mum when she'd asked what she could do to help make things better. His words still rang in her ears:

'You c-can't... f-fix it, Auntie... Heath...er. My d–dad's... been p-put in... p–prison. The p–police took h–him. I've... r–run... away. Th-they d-don't know wh-where... I... am.'

At the time, Jasmine remembered thinking she must've misunderstood, or heard wrong. Surely the police hadn't put his dad in prison? Max was only nine years old – same as her. The police wouldn't leave him on his own with no one to look after him, would they? That was the sort of thing that happened on the television, not in real life.

She'd never seen her mum turn as pale as she did that day;

she'd clearly been stunned, too, though she'd stayed calm, no doubt for Max's sake while she worked out what to do. She'd watched her mother's expression morph from shock to concern as Heather Ingilby switched into coping mode, just as she did whenever she was faced with a tricky situation. Relief had washed over Jasmine, knowing her mum would get this sorted for Max, of that she was certain. Jasmine had grown up with the belief that, between them, her mum and dad could fix anything.

Heather had sat Max down at the table, taking the seat beside him and asked him how he knew the police had taken his dad.

'I s-saw them. I s-saw it hap... happen,' had been Max's answer.

Jasmine had felt sick just hearing that, but to have witnessed it must've been absolutely terrifying. It had explained why Max was so upset.

Reliving the memory had sent Jasmine's pulse thudding, even more so when she recalled what Max had shared after her mum had asked him to tell them what had happened.

Jasmine and her mum had listened intently as Max went on to describe how he'd been in the back garden of his home while his dad was crashed out on the sofa in the living room when he'd heard a commotion. Amongst the unfamiliar raised voices, he heard his father shouting angrily, along with the sound of furniture crashing about, and the loud barking of a dog. He'd crept into the kitchen to hear a police officer telling his dad he was under arrest on suspicion of stealing a car and dealing drugs. They'd started a search of the house using a police sniffer dog which was when Max had fled and raced through the back garden gate. Finding no one at home at Jasmine's house, he'd run and run until his legs were tired and he was overcome by a stitch in his side. He'd ended up near the local allotments and had hidden behind a shed until he felt brave enough to head to the Ingilby's.

'Please don't make me go back home, Auntie Heather. I'll be scared the policemen will come back,' he'd said, panic in his eyes. 'Please can I stay here? Please can I live with you and Uncle Steve?' he'd asked pleadingly.

The mere memory of the desperation in his voice still had the power to make Jasmine's stomach churn. She closed her eyes, the image of him jumping up and flinging his arms around her mum and burying his head into her neck filling her mind along with the ensuing conversation:

'*Please, please*, Auntie Heather. I promise I'll be good. Please let me live with you. You always make me feel so happy when I'm here. And everyone always thinks I'm Jingilby and Jonathan's brother cos we've got nearly the same colour hair and we've all got loads of freckles. You and Uncle Steve could adopt me. You could be my new mum and dad.'

'Ooh, sweetheart.' Heather had wrapped her arms around him, her bottom lip quivering as she'd blinked back tears. 'I wish it was as—'

'*Please*, Mum, *please* can Max live here?' Jasmine had asked, suddenly brightening and taking up her friend's plight. 'He can share with Jonathan.' She'd thought it was the perfect solution since Max had idolised her brother who was two years their senior and they were as mad on football as one another.

Her mum had remained noncommittal, saying they'd have to contact his grandad who lived over Harrogate way before any decisions were made.

They'd met Jimmy Grainger a few times and Jasmine's parents had always found him pleasant. Jasmine had overheard them discussing him and Bazza after one of Jimmy's visits, wondering how on earth such a decent man could have produced a wastrel, layabout of a son, her dad declaring Bazza to be a "right bad apple, if ever there was one".

Heather had managed to track down Jimmy Grainger's phone number and brought him up to speed with the situation regarding his son and grandson. Jimmy had been shocked to hear that things had got so bad that his son had ended up in prison and had gone on to explain how Barry, to give Bazza his proper name, had gone off the rails once he'd met Max's mum, Martina, severing all ties with his parents. His mother had gone to her grave believing her son hated her.

They ended the phone call agreeing that Max should stay at the Ingilby's overnight and Jimmy would travel from his home in Harrogate the following day.

True to his word, Jimmy arrived just after eleven o'clock that Sunday morning, with Max eyeing him warily; being very young the last time he'd seen his grandfather, he'd had little recollection of him.

Jimmy had spoken to his grandson kindly, asking him questions about the things he liked, such as his favourite food – Auntie Heather's Sunday dinners and Jingilby's double-chocolate cookies – and if he was keen on sport. Max's eyes had brightened on hearing his grandad was an avid football supporter.

Jimmy had listened as Steve and Heather had sung Max's praises, telling him he was a bright kid, and keen to learn, that he just needed a bit of stability in his life for him to reach his full potential.

'Well, I'm his grandad, and it's time I stepped up to the plate. I need to make sure that potential doesn't go to waste,' Jimmy had said.

After lunch, Steve had accompanied him to number nine where they'd gathered Max's pitifully small amount of belongings together and placed them in the boot of Jimmy's car, while Heather stayed with the children.

Jasmine and Max had watched from the front window, her stomach curdling at the thought of her best friend being taken all the way to Harrogate. She'd never been there before and it felt like it was at the other side of the world.

With the car packed, Jimmy had declared it was time to leave. 'Come on then, lad, it's time we were off, then we can get you settled in your new home.'

New home! Panic had clawed at Jasmine's insides, her eyes burning with tears.

Max had leapt to his feet and thrown himself at Heather, his eyes filling with a mix of sorrow and uncertainty. 'Can't I stay with you, Auntie Heather?' he'd whispered, his voice wavering. 'Please?'

'Not right now, lovey,' Heather had said, her voice choked. 'You need to go with your grandad, but you're welcome to come and visit us any time you like. Don't ever forget that, little love.'

'And you can play football with me and my mates,' Jonathan had said when he'd come in from the back garden.

'And we can come and see you in Harrogate.' Steve had squeezed Max's shoulder, injecting a bright tone to his voice that hadn't been remotely convincing. 'It's a lovely spot.' Jasmine had never seen her dad cry before, and had been startled to see him swipe tears from his cheeks. It appeared to act as a catalyst to her own tears and, like a dam bursting, they'd started streaming down her face.

She'd run over to her mum and Max, wrapping her arms around them both as she'd sobbed uncontrollably.

'Come on, now.' Heather's voice had been thick with emotion. 'Any more tears and your dad's going to have to get a mop and bucket and swill this place out.' She'd forced a smile as she began prising Max's fingers from her.

'Thank you both for everything.' Jimmy's face had been wreathed in concern. 'We'll keep in touch.'

'Aye, you do that,' Steve had said.

Jasmine and Max had stood looking at one another through puffy, bloodshot eyes. 'You've been the best friend ever, Jingilby.'

'So have you, Max.' Jasmine's voice had been no more than a whisper. Somehow, she'd managed to dredge up a smile.

In the next moment, his skinny arms had wrapped themselves around her, and he was practically squeezing the air from her lungs.

'Thank you for sticking up for me,' he'd said, releasing her and giving a snotty sniff.

'S'okay.' She'd barely been able to speak, her throat was so tight.

'Bye,' he'd said.

'Bye, Max.'

Jasmine had watched in disbelief as he'd slipped his hand into his grandad's and headed down the path, her heart ready to burst with sadness.

They were almost at the gate when Max had stopped and turned, pulling his shoulders back and fixing her with a determined gaze. 'When I grow up, I'm gonna be a millionaire with a really fast car and I'm gonna drive back to Micklewick Bay and marry you, Jingilby!'

'Don't be so daft, Max.' Jasmine had felt her cheeks burn crimson as a round of 'Ahhs' had gone up, followed by a ripple of laughter and a teasing whistle from Jonathan. But she hadn't been able to stop herself from smiling through her embarrassment.

'Ey up, flower, how's that for a proposal?' Her dad had chuckled, giving her a nudge.

'Aye, well, there's nowt like having a bit of ambition, lad.' Jimmy Grainger had smiled down fondly at his grandson before throwing Jasmine an amused wink.

She'd switched her gaze back to Max. The smile he'd mustered was enough to trigger his dimples, along with the faintest hint of a twinkle in his tear-stained eyes.

She'd smiled back at him before he'd turned and walked away.

It was to be the last Jasmine would see of Max Grainger for over two decades and now, she couldn't help but wonder what sort of path his life had followed. And what had brought him back to Micklewick Bay.

ELEVEN

Tuesday morning found Jasmine fizzing with nervous energy thanks to her upcoming meeting with Lady Caro. Once she'd dropped Zak and Chloe off at school, she hurried back home where she rushed round, loading a pile of clothes into the machine ready to set away on her return. The client who'd ordered the cruise ship birthday cake had been and gone – another satisfied customer, who'd declared Jasmine's design stunning.

Keeping busy had kept her mind occupied rather than sitting around allowing her anxiety to bloom while she waited until it was time to get ready for her appointment at Danskelfe Castle.

Uncertain of what to wear to meet a member of the aristocracy – and with a wardrobe that was distinctly casual – Jasmine opted for her newest pair of green cargos, teaming them with a white shirt. She eschewed her favourite Converse for a pair of chunky brown leather sandals on the grounds that her faithful plimsols were now on the shabby side. She gave her eyelashes a quick sweep of mascara followed by a smudge of green eyeliner on her lower lids. After running her fingers through her hair –

that was, for once, free of all traces of edible glitter and the stickiness of icing sugar! – all that was left to do was scoop up the folder of photos she'd gathered together of her cake commissions so she'd have something to show Lady Caro, and she was good to go.

Once in the car, she threw the folder onto the passenger seat beside her then dropped her bag into the footwell, a background thrum of nervous anticipation running through her. She pushed the key into the ignition and turned. A reluctant 'pfft' followed. Jasmine's heart lurched. She repeated her actions a further three times before the old banger spluttered indignantly to life and proceeded to kangaroo hop to the end of the road.

She'd almost reached the junction by the Micklewick Majestic Hotel when the car juddered dramatically before grinding to an abrupt halt and thrusting her forward.

'No! Don't do this to me. Not today, of all days!' Jasmine tried the ignition several times, but the car refused to come back to life.

She put her head in her hands as panic rushed through her. She wasn't going to be able to get to Danskelfe; she'd have to cancel her meeting with Lady Caro after all. She groaned and flopped back in her seat just as the noisy beeping of a car horn sounded behind her, making her jump and reminding her she was in the middle of the road. 'I haven't stopped here on purpose!' she said, throwing her hands up frustratedly as the driver swerved round her.

Gathering her thoughts, she drew in a slow breath. 'Just calm your jets, Jasmine. Don't give up so easy. You need to think straight, there's bound to be a solution,' she said out loud. Her mind started running through any other options of getting to Danskelfe. She ruled out a lift from her mum straight away since she was covering her shift with Spick 'n' Sparkle, and her dad was out of the equation since he was working a shift on the buses. Gnawing on her bottom lip, the next idea to come up was the possibility of catching a train to Danskelfe; Jasmine knew there was a stop at the nearby village of Lytell Stangdale but she wasn't so sure there was one at Danskelfe itself. Getting the train timetable up on her phone revealed that even if there had been a stop at Danskelfe, the station was miles away from the castle. And besides, the next one in that direction wasn't until early afternoon and would involve a change at Middleton-le-Moors. As for taking the bus there, that would involve a lengthy journey with numerous changes 'Ugh! That's no good, it'd be tomorrow by the time I got there!'

She massaged her temples where she could feel a headache brewing, at a loss for what to do next.

Just as she was considering calling Lady Caro to rearrange their meeting, a succession of beeps from a car horn pulled her out of her thoughts. 'Jeez!' She glanced in her rear-view mirror, her eyes locking with local wide-boy, Dick Swales – or Dodgy Dick as he was known in town – smirking at her from his fancy four-wheel drive. 'All right, all right! I'm not sitting here for the fun of it, you know!' She turned the key in the ignition again, but was met with nothing. Just as she expected, the car behind beeped again. 'Argh!' Jasmine opened her door and climbed out just as Dodgy Dick manoeuvred his vehicle around hers, before driving off, Wendy, his bouffant-haired wife, treating her to a mocking smile.

Jasmine couldn't dislike the slippery businessman and his wife any more if she tried. They'd been pestering Florrie and Ed to sell the bookshop to them with the intention of converting it into a hair salon and beautician's. It hadn't gone down well when their offer had been refused and a campaign of intimidation had followed until Dick and Wendy finally got the message, which had taken some considerable time. Since then, all friends of the bookshop owners' were treated with the same disdain by Dodgy Dick and his wife. Not that Jasmine could give two hoots.

With the shiny four-wheel drive disappearing around the corner, she turned her attention back to her predicament. She needed to find a solution, and fast.

'Morning, Jazz, you okay?' Florrie's voice interrupted her musings.

Jasmine turned to see her friend standing alongside Ed who had their black Labrador, Gerty, on the end of a lead.

'Hiya, Jasmine. Looked like you were miles away just then.' Ed grinned at her, brushing his dark, floppy fringe off his face.

'Oh, yeah, hi.' Jasmine gave a small smile. 'My car's finally given up on me.' Gerty nudged her knee and she bent to ruffle the Labrador's ears. 'Now then, lass.'

'But aren't you supposed to be heading over to Danskelfe for a meeting with Lady Caro later this morning?' asked Florrie, looking slightly alarmed.

'I am.' Jasmine rubbed her brow with her fingertips. 'I was just trying to work out how I could get there but neither the bus nor the train'll get to that part of the moors on time. I'll have to cancel.' The thought made her heart slump.

'*What?*' said Ed.

'No way should you cancel, Jazz! You've been looking forward to this meeting,' said Florrie.

'I don't have a choice, everyone's busy or at work.'

Florrie pushed up the sleeve of her cardigan and checked her watch. 'Right, what time do you need to be there?'

'Eleven o'clock. Why?'

'I can take you.' Florrie nudged her glasses up her nose.

'But what about the bookshop?'

'Leah's in first thing, and I can call my mum, ask her if she can pop in a bit earlier; she won't mind, she'll be happy to help, especially once she hears the reason. And it's not as if we have any events on or school visits today. Ed'll still be able to crack on with the window displays. I do believe a hammock is going to be included in one of them, isn't that right, Ed?'

'If I tell you that, it'll completely spoil the surprise.' The window displays were always hidden behind a thick curtain, and only revealed once they were fully complete.

'I'd better warn you, if a hammock is included, I make no apologies if I'm tempted to climb in it,' said Jasmine.

'We'd have no problem with that, Jazz,' said Ed.

'As long as you don't snore,' added Florrie.

''Fraid I can't guarantee that.'

Ed's displays in the double-fronted bookshop's windows had become legendary in the town, with each one declared better than the last. Florrie's partner had previously worked as an artist and dressing the windows had allowed him to set his creative talents free. It had also generated a huge amount of interest for the bookshop, thus increasing their trade.

'So, is it a yes for the offer of a lift?' asked Florrie, bringing the subject back to Jasmine's current predicament.

Jasmine glanced between Florrie and Ed, her friend's suggestion running through her mind. 'But—'

'No buts. And don't forget I did tell you on Friday, if you wanted any company to just holler.' Florrie grinned, hitching her eyebrows.

'Looks like I've got some company, then.'

'Fab!' Florrie beamed at her.

'First, I reckon we need to get your car out of the middle of the road,' said Ed, watching a driver slow down, craning her neck as she drove by Jasmine's abandoned vehicle. 'And if you leave the key with me, I can get in touch with the garage for you, if you like? Get them to collect it.'

'Um...' Concern for the potential cost of getting her car fixed was jostling for priority with being late for Lady Caro.

'Come on, let's get cracking, missus.' Florrie patted Jasmine's arm, breaking in to her thoughts. 'You get in and release the handbrake, we'll push.' She headed to the rear of the car where Ed had positioned himself, while Gerty looked on from where he'd hooked her lead over the railings of the Micklewick Majestic.

'Thanks for this, Florrie.' Jasmine pushed her sunglasses back and gazed out of the window as they took the turn for the moors, following the road sign that directed them to the villages of Lytell Stangdale, Arkleby and Danskelfe. A clear blue sky spread out before them, with the undulating moorland and verdant green fields drenched in sunshine beyond. She released a sigh. The background thrum of stress had shrunk back to its familiar level and now only a trace of her earlier headache lingered. She could cope with that.

'Hey, it's no problem at all, flower. I haven't exactly made a secret of the fact that I've been desperate for an excuse to head back to Danskelfe Castle since our sleigh ride at Christmas.' She flashed Jasmine a smile, her brown eyes hidden behind her prescription sunglasses.

Jasmine smiled back. Florrie had been so taken with their Christmas visit there she'd been keen to get the friends together for another visit.

'I know it might sound daft – and I really don't want to tempt fate, which I know doesn't sound like the sort of thing cynical old me would say – but I've got a good feeling in my bones about this meeting,' said Jasmine.

Florrie slowed the car to allow a couple of the free-roaming sheep and their lambs the North Yorkshire Moors were known for to amble their way across the road. 'It doesn't sound daft at all, it's exactly what Lark was saying yesterday morning when she popped into the bookshop. And we all know Lark's usually right about these things. Anyroad, it's not just you and Lark; we all think it, too.'

Hearing that sent a buzz of excitement reverberating through Jasmine. 'It would be so amazing to get the contract. I honestly think it would make a massive difference to the kids and me.'

'No more rushing round like a headless chicken,' said Florrie.

'You've no idea how good that would be.'

She'd lain awake until the early hours the previous night, her mind running over just how much Lady Caro's offer could change things for her and the children – when her worries about the Scragg family, or Max's reappearance weren't occupying it. It had the potential to free up some time and allow her to focus on what she loved doing as a way of earning enough money to provide for the kids and pay the bills, which was a concept she hadn't dreamt possible for herself. The more she thought about the offer, the more she'd found herself desperately wanting it. Jasmine knew it was why she felt so apprehensive today. It had been a long time since she'd let herself get excited about anything and, she had to admit, there was something quite pleasant about the occasional bursts of anticipation that pushed through her whenever it popped into her thoughts.

She checked her folder again, making sure it was all in order. After everything that had been happening with Zak and Chloe, she'd found herself distracted and had kept having to reassure herself that the photos she'd brought were her best ones and not some random images she'd quickly scrabbled together. She could easily show Lady Caro the photos she had on her phone, but Jasmine had felt the need to take something physical. She'd considered asking Lady Caro for her personal email so she could send a selection of her best photos beforehand, but Jasmine hadn't wanted to appear pushy. Plus, she'd be the first to admit she was a technophobe and didn't have the first clue about putting the images into files or folders, or whatever you called them, rather than bombarding Lady Caro with a multitude of individual attachments – she was only just getting the hang of Instagram!

Jasmine knew Florrie would have happily helped her, but with time being tight it meant she'd had to settle for the photos she'd printed out and occasionally used to show customers. She'd made time to draft some costings of a selection of her cakes to show Lady Caro which had taken longer than she'd expected. Her eyes skimmed over the figures. Putting them together had made her realise with what she charged per cake, her profit margins were quite small, and that was without taking into account the amount of work she put into them. But she'd been keen to be competitive and keep her prices low in order to attract custom. After all, some of the celebration cakes available at the supermarkets were quite professional-looking these days. Jasmine told herself it would be just as easy to pop one in a trolley while doing the weekly food shop, so she had to do something to make hers stand out and be more appealing.

She huffed out a sigh.

'Is everything all right, Jazz?' Florrie pulled her eyes away from the road, snatching a look at her. 'You're not worried about the meeting, are you? I have no doubt it'll go well. Don't forget, it was Lady Caro who called you, not the other way round.' To the outside world, Jasmine gave off an air of confidence, but her oldest friends knew that beneath her tough veneer of self-assuredness, she was prone to worrying, doubting herself and her decisions. Particularly so since Bart had died. That, together with the events that took place on the run-up to his death, had shot her confidence to pieces.

'It's not that... well, maybe it is a little bit. I can't tell you how badly I want her to like my ideas and the photos of my cakes.'

'She'll love them, Jazz, like everyone does.'

'I hope so.' She paused for a moment. 'But that's not the only thing that's bothering me.'

'I thought there was something else. Do you want to talk about it?'

Jasmine heaved another sigh. 'There's been a bit of a situation with the kids and I've had to have a meeting at school with the teachers; the head was there, too.'

'Goodness, sounds serious. Are Zak and Chloe okay?'

'They're fine – at least, I hope they will be.' Thoughts of Jason Scragg and his son made her stomach twist. 'You remember Jason Scragg – aka Scraggo – don't you?' she said.

'Now that name's a blast from the past. Not sure any of us could ever forget him. Why?' Florrie said, her voice loaded with dread.

'Well, it would seem he's back in Micklewick Bay and he's got a couple of kids in tow who, unfortunately, are the same age as my two, and let's just say they've been making their presence felt.'

'No way!'

''Fraid so. I had a brief chat with Stella about it last night – she saw me just after I'd been to school. I was going to tell you, but didn't want to mention anything until after the meeting with Lady Caro in case it affected my mood and she picked up on it. I don't want to risk her thinking I'm not interested or underwhelmed by her offer. Seems I can't keep it to myself though.'

'Knowing you as I do, Jazz, I reckon you're better off talking about it – bottling it up has never worked well as far as you're concerned.'

Jasmine knew Florrie was referring to her relationship with Bart and the problems that had troubled it throughout. They'd grown increasingly worse until their partnership could only be described as dysfunctional. Jasmine hadn't wanted to burden her friends by talking about it, or be disloyal to Bart, but it had taken its toll, with her becoming withdrawn and moody. She'd even begun to distance herself from her friends, fearful that they'd drag the truth out of her. It was something she'd sworn never to repeat, and the reason she'd remained single since Bart's death.

'Yeah, you're right.' Jasmine went on to give a brief rundown of what had gone on with the Scragg children, her friend listening quietly beside her.

When she was done, she blew out a noisy breath, feeling unexpectedly relieved to have shared it.

'Well, it sounds like you can take comfort from the fact that the school are onto it and it won't get out of hand like it did in our day. I've heard good things about Mrs Armistead, she's a way better headteacher than Old Troutface ever was. I'm sure Zak and Chloe'll be okay.'

'Yeah, I did come away from the meeting having confidence in her and their teachers.'

'Good.'

'I still can't believe Scraggo's back in the town, though.'

Florrie stole a look at her, a mischievous smile spreading across her face. 'I reckon he'll be hoping you don't see *red* if you know what I mean?'

'See red?' Jasmine's brow crumpled. 'Oh, you're referring to *that.*' She caught Florrie's eye and they both spluttered with laughter at the memory of her covering Scraggo's coat with red poster paint.

'I'll see more than bloomin' red if his kids bother Zak and Chloe anymore.'

'That, Jazz, I don't doubt for a minute,' said Florrie. A beat passed. 'I wonder whatever happened to little Max Grainger? Scraggo used to make his life a misery.'

'It's funny you should say that.' Jasmine had been waiting for a convenient point in their conversation to introduce the subject of Max.

'Oh?' Florrie briefly took her eyes off the road and stole a look at Jasmine. 'Do I sense you have news?'

'You do. I actually saw him last night. It was only brief, but I get the feeling he's done well for himself. His clothes looked quite stylish – not that I know much about stuff like that – but he looked "well-groomed", I think is the expression.'

'Ooh, tell all.'

'Let's just say, he got a classic reminder of me at my most elegant best.' She flashed Florrie a wide smile as she shared the details of how they'd run into one another, Florrie spluttering with laughter as Jasmine described her ungainly tumble over Ernest.

'I wonder if he's here for good, or just a quick visit?' said Florrie, slowing down at a set of temporary traffic lights where roadworks were taking place.

'Didn't get the chance to ask. I daresay we'll find out if he drops in on my parents.'

'It'd be nice to have a catch-up with him. I remember him as a sweet lad, always so upbeat despite his circumstances.'

'He was.' Jasmine's thoughts drifted to the times they'd played together, his worse-for-wear clothes and wild curls. 'I hope he's had a happy life, heaven knows he deserves it.'

'I wonder if he'll run into Scraggo?' said Florrie. The traffic lights switched to green and she pressed down on the accelerator.

'I wonder.' From the glimpse she'd had of Max, she'd noted an impressive set of biceps under his short-sleeved shirt. She guessed he'd be pretty good at looking after himself now. The small, skinny kid had long gone.

TWELVE

'Oh, look, there's Danskelfe Castle up ahead!' Jasmine sat up straighter in her seat, her eyes roving over the imposing building, a flag fluttering from one of its turrets. It appeared to rise from the precipitous crag it had been built upon, which afforded it an ethereal quality. On a cloudy day, Jasmine could imagine it would appear quite foreboding.

'Wow! Imagine getting married there,' said Florrie.

'Don't fancy it for you and Ed, do you?'

'Much as I think it would be fabulous, I'm more of a low-key lass. I think Ed and me'll stick to our plans for a small do in Micklewick Bay, that's more our vibe.'

Ed had surprised Florrie with a proposal last Christmas Eve and, with all the work and plans they had for the bookshop, including the conversion of the upstairs flat to a tearoom, they'd decided to wait until next year to get married. That way, they'd be able to give it their full attention.

'Hmm, maybe. I could see Stella getting hitched there, though, couldn't you?'

'Definitely! Mind, there's a slight problem with that: Alex would need to propose first.'

'True,' said Jasmine. 'Maybe we could get Ed to have a word with him, give him a nudge in the right direction.'

'Maybe we should.' They exchanged conspiratorial smiles.

'I never thought we'd be talking about our Stells getting married.' Florrie laughed.

'Yeah, I know what you mean. I'd love to make her wedding cake, I'd do something elegant, understated and sophisticated, just like her.' The thought of being the wedding cake creator and supplier for an upmarket venue like Danskelfe Castle was mind-blowing for Jasmine and she sent a silent prayer heavenward, hoping with all her heart the meeting would go well.

'Yikes!' Florrie slammed on the brakes as a pheasant shot out in front of them, its colourful feathers glowing in the sunshine. 'Daft bird appeared out of nowhere,' she exclaimed as it raced off into the bracken, cackling angrily.

'Hazards of the country roads, I expect.' Jasmine's heart was thudding after the emergency stop.

'Aye, that and the free-roaming sheep. They have no road sense.'

Before long, the car was rattling over the former drawbridge and nosing its way into the courtyard of Danskelfe Castle – as per Lady Caro's instructions, rather than using the public car park – parking up alongside a brace of four-wheel drives, including the new-style Land Rover Defender that had been used to transport Maggie to hospital when she'd surprised everyone by going into labour with baby Lucy.

They'd just climbed out of the car when the great oak door to the castle was thrown open and Lady Caro stepped out. She was an image of countryside chic in a pale blue polo shirt, the collar turned up, and a pair of well-cut jeans and expensive-looking suede loafers. She was closely followed by a trio of waggy-tailed Labradors that spilled out onto the age-worn flagstones, apparently thrilled to greet their visitors.

'Jasmine, darling, welcome. It's so wonderful to see you.'

Lady Caro's cut-glass accent bounced around the ancient walls. She rested her hands on Jasmine's shoulders and delivered a noisy kiss to each cheek, her chestnut ponytail swinging from side to side. 'Mwah, mwah.'

'Hi, Lady Caro, I'm so sorry we're a bit late but—'

'It's Caro, and there's absolutely no need to apologise, darling. I've just finished a Zoom meeting and hadn't noticed the time.' She waved Jasmine's concerns away with a manicured hand.

What a relief!

Lady Caro turned to Florrie, smiling warmly. 'Hello there, you look awfully familiar, have we met before?'

'We have,' said Florrie, holding out her hand. 'I'm Florrie Appleton, I was part of the infamous sleigh ride party with Jasmine and Maggie.'

Lady Caro gave a hoot of laughter. 'Infamous is very much the right word!' She ignored Florrie's outstretched hand, instead greeting her in the same way she had Jasmine. 'Welcome, darling, it's lovely to see you again.'

'Actually, the reason Florrie's here is because my car broke down; Florrie came to the rescue and brought me – it's never happened before, I'm going to get it booked in at the garage as soon as I get back,' Jasmine added hastily. She wasn't sure if Lady Caro would be expecting her to personally deliver the wedding cakes to the castle and didn't want her car problems to put her off or give her cause for concern. *Worry about getting it fixed later, Jazz. Focus on Lady Caro now. Enjoy this moment and don't forget to smile!*

'Well, I for one am jolly glad you were able to come to Jasmine's assistance.' Caro smiled before turning to Jasmine. 'I've been very much looking forward to picking up where we left off with our chat the other day! I can't wait to hear what you have in mind for our weddings.'

'I've come prepared.' Jasmine waved the folder in her hands

and gave a smile, hoping her suggestions would live up to Lady Caro's expectations.

'Excellent.' Lady Caro clasped her hands together before swinging round on her heel. 'Right then, ladies, come this way.'

The two friends followed Lady Caro and her gaggle of dogs into the castle, Jasmine peering up at the elaborate coat of arms above the door as she stepped inside.

She heard Florrie gasp beside her. 'Oh, wow! This is so beautiful,' she said as they glanced around, taking in the thick stone walls and age-darkened beams.

'Just a bit,' said Jasmine, her presence there suddenly feeling very surreal. She was almost tempted to pinch herself to make sure she wasn't dreaming.

They trotted along, keeping pace with Lady Caro's long, determined strides, the sound of the Labradors' claws clicking over the old flagstone floor. They passed ancient suits of armour and dark oak coffers, some of which were bedecked with elegant floral arrangements in antique vases, the fragrance of the blooms filling the air along with a tang of woodsmoke and the unmistakable aroma exuded by ancient stone walls. While gilt-framed portraits of formidable-looking Hammondely forebears and opulent tapestries adorned the walls.

'You have a wonderful home, Lady Caro,' said Florrie.

'Please call me Caro, and yes, it's not a bad old shack. Bit draughty in the winter, and the upkeep is eye-wateringly expensive, which is why we're always thinking up new ways to diversify and keep the old gal in the style to which she's become accustomed – I should probably clarify that when I say "old gal" I'm referring to the castle and not my mother.' She gave another of her hoots of laughter, while Jasmine and Florrie laughed politely. Word had reached Micklewick Bay that Lady Davinia was a bit of a dragon, not that they wanted to let on to her daughter that they knew.

Lady Caro came to a halt in front of a solid oak door. 'Welcome to the engine room, ladies.'

'Right, first things first: tea.' Lady Caro set about making a pot as they chatted about everything from the recent spell of warm weather to the handmade bears Maggie had made for the castle's holiday lodges. Lady Caro's office could only be described as impressive. A large, mullioned window dominated one wall, offering spectacular views of Danskelfe Dale, while a partner's desk sat at the opposite end of the room to a large stone inglenook fireplace. As with the hallway, vast family portraits adorned the walls. 'They're not my personal choice for in here, particularly the one of Marmaduke, the fourth earl, and his rather penetrating gaze that seems to follow you everywhere, but we've got nowhere else to hang them, so they've had to stay put. I had thought about sticking a blindfold on old Marms, but my father advised me against it in case it damaged the paint, and since he's still the boss here, I have to do as I'm told.' Her dry sense of humour and relaxed attitude put Jasmine and Florrie instantly at ease.

'Right then, let's get down to business,' Lady Caro said, once she'd made tea. 'I'm desperately excited to hear your suggestions and ideas, so fire away, Jasmine.'

Jasmine's heart leapt. *Here goes!*

She started by elaborating on their phone conversation of the previous week, using the photos of the cakes she'd brought with her, explaining the most suitable designs, her reasons for them, and the costings as she went along. 'The more expensive cake can be more elaborate, with more tiers, more elements, the cheaper one less so, though we can still make them look special. And there's a degree of flexibility in the designs with regard to accent colours, i.e. the ribbon around the base, the colours of the flowers, etcetera, not to mention whether the cake's fruit or sponge – if you'd like to go ahead, I can let you have some cake samples to taste.' Jasmine had hoped to be able to bring some with her today, but with everything that had been going on, she hadn't had the time to make any.

Lady Caro sat back in her seat. 'I love it! Your suggestions are perfect, and exactly what we're looking for, darling. I suppose you did your training at some super-duper patisserie school?'

'Um... no.' Jasmine's voice faltered and she stole a look at Florrie. 'My mum taught me to bake and I'm self-taught as far as the decorating's concerned. I started off making and decorating birthday cakes for my own children, then people began asking if I'd make cakes for them. Just seemed to snowball from there.'

'Jazz's built up an amazing reputation in and around Micklewick Bay,' said Florrie. 'I heard a couple singing her praises in the bookshop on Saturday. One referred to her as the "go-to cake lady", the other one said she'd never seen or tasted a cake as fabulous as the one Jazz had made for her friend's little boy. We're all very proud of her.'

Jasmine gulped, feeling heat rise in her face. 'Thanks, Florrie.' Though she felt uncomfortable hearing such praise, she felt a flood of love for her friend.

'No need to be so coy, Jasmine. The ladies in the shop are right. And, in the spirit of being honest, I've had a few sneaky tastes of some of the cakes you've made for the couples having their weddings here and they're utterly sublime. The sponge cakes are as light as air, and the fruit cakes so rich and delicious.'

Jasmine couldn't help but beam. 'I'm so pleased you liked them.'

'Which is why I'd like to offer you a contract to be the Danskelfe Castle wedding cake supplier. And not only that, but also to supply cupcakes and the likes for our corporate events.' Lady Caro beamed back at her. 'Before you accept, I need to tell you that I heard how much you charge for your cakes and from these costings...'

Jasmine's heart sank. *Uh-oh! I should've known it was too good to be true.* She went to speak but Lady Caro jumped in.

'In all honesty, darling, I can't accept these terms.'

'Oh.' Jasmine's face fell and she sensed Florrie tense beside her.

'Goodness me, don't look so mortified, it's good news! What I wanted to say was that you sell yourself way too short. I've had a look at other wedding cake designers whose cakes aren't in your league but cost three times as much.'

'We've always told Jazz she doesn't charge enough,' Florrie chipped in.

'I completely agree. Which is why I think we can offer you considerably more than you're probably expecting per cake while still making a decent profit ourselves. Much as we're keen to make money, we like to encourage loyalty from our suppliers and show we value them; we want to keep the best for ourselves. With that in mind, these would be our terms...'

Jasmine's eyes widened in disbelief as Lady Caro went on to state the amount they'd offer her per cake. She did a quick mental calculation; if she delivered two wedding cakes per week, which is what Lady Caro had implied, then it would mean there was a chance she could give up at least one of her jobs, and reduce the hours of the other. In turn, that would mean she'd be at home more, and be able to fit decorating the cakes around Zak and Chloe. She blinked, letting it all sink in. This could be the break she and the kids needed, and would mean she could top up her earnings by still making cakes locally in Micklewick Bay.

'You don't have to answer right now, if you'd rather not. Go home, have a think about it and let me know as soon as you've made a decision.'

Lady Caro's words cut through Jasmine's thoughts. She looked across at Florrie who was smiling happily at her.

'I don't need to think any more about it, Lady Car... I mean, Caro. I've thought loads about it since our call. Thank you so much for your amazing offer, I'd love to accept it.'

'That's fantastic, darling! I'm beyond delighted!' Lady Caro clapped her hands enthusiastically. 'I think this calls for a celebratory cup of tea, then I'll give you a quick look around the castle, show you where the ceremonies take place.'

'So, do you have an idea of when you'd like to get started with the wedding packages?' Jasmine asked, before it slipped her mind.

'Good question. Well, we're hoping to be able to offer the smaller packages pretty soon. We put out a few feelers to test the water as regards to time and from the feedback we've been getting, it could be as soon as a couple of months.'

'Wow! That's quick,' said Florrie, her eyebrows shooting up.

'I know, it would seem people are rather keen.' She turned to Jasmine. 'In the meantime, I wonder if I could place a personal order? A birthday cake for my father.'

'Of course, I'd love to make a cake for your dad. Do you think he'd like one in the theme of the castle, or would he prefer a more formal style?'

'I think he'd be utterly enraptured with a castle-themed cake.'

'Fabulous.' Jasmine's mind had already started whirring with ideas.

'That's what I think they call a successful trip.' Florrie beamed at Jasmine as they waved Lady Caro goodbye from the car and headed out of the courtyard.

'Oh, my days! Did that really just happen?' Jasmine looked back at Florrie in disbelief. 'Please tell me it wasn't a dream and

I'm going to wake up and find myself having to do more shifts at the bakery or take on more cleaning jobs.'

'Jazz, flower, it wasn't a dream, it was all very real. You deserve some good news like this. Now, just sit back and let it all sink in.'

Jasmine was quite happy to do just that when her mobile phone pinged, heralding the arrival of a text. Her first thought was to hope it wasn't from school.

She fished it from her bag, tapping on the screen to see a message from her mum.

She opened it, her stomach clenching as she read.

> Jasmine, how come there's a For Sale sign on your house??? xxx

THIRTEEN

'What?' Jasmine scrunched up her nose. Her first thought was that her mum must be mistaken. The little houses on Rosemary Terrace were packed in like sardines, maybe the For Sale sign was on number twenty next door. After all, their front doors were side by side and if the sign was placed between them, then it could very easily confuse people. She massaged her brow with her fingertips.

'Everything okay?' asked Florrie.

'Um... I think so,' said Jasmine, distracted as she tapped out a quick reply to her mum. She pressed "send", just as the signal bars shrank from four to none. 'Bugger!'

Aware of her friend casting a concerned glance her way, Jasmine recounted the message from her mum.

'Surely it must be next door, Jazz. That house has been empty for a while. It would make sense if the owner put it up for sale. I mean, it's not as if you've heard anything from your landlord about your place, have you?'

'Not about that, no.'

'Well, there you are. He's legally obliged to give you notice if he wants to sell the property unoccupied,' Florrie said. 'And, more importantly, if he was going to advertise it for sale, he'd have to let you know the estate agents would be calling round to take photos and measure up, wouldn't he? And since that hasn't happened, I reckon you can stop worrying, and get back to basking in the fabulous news of your new business venture.'

Jasmine felt reassured by Florrie's logic. 'Yeah, I s'pose you're right.' She reasoned that since Micklewick Mansions Estate Agents were also the letting agents for her home it would suggest they'd have given her notice if her tenancy agreement was coming to an end. And they'd also inform her if her home was being put on the market, especially if people were to be shown around while she still lived there. At least, she hoped they would.

'Good. Now sit back, enjoy the scenery and stop fretting.'

'Yes, ma'am.' Jasmine chuckled at Florrie's friendly-bossy tone.

But as they drove on, a doubt started running through her mind. Though her landlord hadn't given her notice of his intention to sell eighteen Rosemary Terrace, he had been in touch a couple of weeks ago, telling her he was sending someone round to inspect the property, make sure it was in a good state of repair, which was completely out of character. She usually had to hound him to get things fixed, and even then there was no guarantee it would happen. The reason he'd given was that he'd had his fingers burnt when another of his properties had been trashed by a tenant who'd done a runner owing several months' rent.

Though Jasmine had understood her landlord's reasons, she hadn't been too thrilled that the only time such an inspection could take place was when she was at work. Despite being permanently busy, she kept a tidy home, and knowing he would have no issues in that regard, she'd reluctantly agreed to the visit. Since she'd had no feedback, she'd assumed everything was okay. But now, after her mum's text, it crossed her mind that he might have had an ulterior motive for the inspection. The worst of it was that she wouldn't put it past him not to be upfront. She'd always found him slippery and reluctant to make eye contact. And he hadn't exactly been quick to respond to any problems, like when the radiator in the bathroom had started leaking last winter. She'd managed to turn it off, but it had meant having a shower was a freezing prospect in a room with such fridge-like temperatures.

As for the other problems with the property he was responsible for, like the rotting windows which Jasmine had done her best to hide with regular applications of paint, the missing roof tiles which were the reason for the damp patch on the ceiling in Zak's bedroom to name but a few, they seemed to get ignored, despite informing Micklewick Mansions of them on a regular basis. She'd heard it was the same with most of her landlord's other rental properties. But what gave her concerns extra weight was the fact that Don Carswell, the head estate agent, was also her landlord's brother, and if rumours were to be believed, they were as dodgy as one another.

She swallowed down the ball of stress that had lodged in her throat. It sometimes felt that no matter how hard she tried, her life didn't get any easier. It was exhausting having the sole responsibility of keeping everything running smoothly. Much as she hated to admit it to herself, she did feel the green-eyed monster occasionally rear its ugly head at the mums waiting at the school gates, talking about what a great help their partners were. But now wasn't the time to dwell on that. She needed to focus on getting back home, so she could check for herself that the For Sale sign was for next door.

Jasmine pushed the key into the front door of her home, a puzzled expression on her face. She'd had a good look at the "For Sale" sign and, from the way it had been positioned so centrally between the two houses, it was impossible to tell if it was advertising her home or the one next door.

Kicking her sandals off and scooping up the handful of post on the doormat, she rushed to the kitchen, hooked her bag over the back of a chair and grabbed her laptop. Once it had booted up, she clicked on the Micklewick Mansions website and hastily typed "Rosemary Terrace" in the search bar. Scrolling through the list of properties it threw up, her heart lurched when an image caught her eye. The page seemed to take forever to load, and she jigged her leg impatiently, a sense of doom mushrooming.

'Oh, my god!' She pressed her hand to her mouth.

Looking back at her were photos of her home, with hers and the children's belongings for all to see.

A mix of anger and anxiety whirled like a tornado inside her. None of it made sense. Why had the letting agents not told her? Why did they think it was okay to send someone round to take photographs when she wasn't in? And worse, how was this going to affect Zak and Chloe? Moving house was unsettling. With what had been going on with the Scraggs, they were already dealing with enough.

She snatched up her phone and called the Micklewick Mansions' number, asking the receptionist to put her through to Don Carswell. On hearing the identity of the caller, the receptionist immediately declared he was out of the office and would be for the rest of the day.

But Jasmine knew a fob-off when she heard one. She reached for her bag then gathered up the handful of newly delivered letters – she could scan over those as she headed into town, see if there was anything from the estate agents, though she very much doubted it. Don Carswell may be too much of a coward to speak to her, but she needed an explanation. There was no way she was going to take this underhanded, unprofessional treatment lying down. She was going to wipe the floor with him.

And then, she'd have to set to with the task of finding her and the kids somewhere new to live. A wave of exhaustion went head-to-head with the rage boiling inside her.

Before she'd even set foot inside Micklewick Mansion's office, her worst fears had been confirmed by the photos for all to see in the window advertising her home. She'd stormed through the door, taking Don Carswell by surprise as he was sipping his coffee and engaged in what appeared to be flirty banter with the receptionist. Jasmine tore a strip off him before he had a chance to speak; she had no time for his smarmy excuses. She accused him of being deceptive and unprofessional before stomping out of the office and slamming the door behind her.

Out on the street, Jasmine's chest was heaving and her stomach was churning. She couldn't remember a time when she'd been this worked up; it was as if everything was piling on top of her, threatening to extinguish the good news of her Danskelfe Castle contract. Tension was making her head feel like it was ready to explode, sending her stress shooting out geyser-like. She bit down on her bottom lip – there was no way she could head home feeling like this. She had a fairy-themed birthday cake to start on when she got back, and she didn't want to channel negative vibes into it. She needed to take a minute to let her emotions calm down; she couldn't think straight at the moment, with what felt like a cyclone raging around her mind.

Deciding a head-clearing walk along the top prom would probably help, she made her way through the streets until she reached the top of Skitey Bank. Before long, she found herself sitting on the wooden bench that Florrie and Ed had funded in memory of his grandparents, Bernard and Dinah Harte – they'd also been Florrie's much-beloved bosses at The Happy Hartes

Bookshop. Her heart was still pounding, but she figured that probably had as much to do with the pace she'd walked to get there as it was the stress of finding out she'd be losing her home.

She rubbed her hands vigorously over her face. 'Ugh!' Why was it when something good happened, something had to take the shine off it? she wondered. Her life had worked that way for so long she'd almost got used to it, plodding on, dealing with whatever was thrown at her, accepting it without question, not thinking too deeply about it. It wasn't as if she asked for a lot; as long as her children were happy and healthy, and were warm and well-fed, that was enough for her. She felt blessed that she had such a wonderfully supportive family and the best group of friends anyone could wish for. She knew they'd have her back whatever the problem; they were as good as family to one another. But she couldn't help but think that somewhere along the way she'd lost her identity, which was why Lady Caro's offer meant so much to her. Maybe the old Jasmine, the one before her dysfunctional relationship with Bart had taken its toll, would resurface and her spirited personality would be allowed to shine. *Don't get carried away. Baby steps and all that.* But now wasn't the time to dwell on that.

Her next thought was that she should ask Stella about her legal rights regarding what had happened with her home. She visualised what her friend would have to say to Don Carswell, taking pleasure in imagining her words wiping the smarmy smile off his face. Stella was the queen of scathing put-downs. What she'd give to see that!

But then again, Jasmine reasoned with herself, did she really want all the extra hassle of lodging a complaint? She had enough to contend with right now, and she had a feeling the grief that would come with it could quite possibly tip her over the edge. She wanted to focus her energy on making sure Jason Scragg's obnoxious kids got the message to leave Zak and Chloe alone, wanted to make sure her children knew that she wasn't too preoccupied with any other concerns for them to talk to her or share their worries. Was it too much to ask that their life be on an even keel for a while?

She looked out to sea where the sun was dancing lightly over the waves, her gaze absently skimming over the little fishing boats that chugged their way over the water, seagulls circling above. The murmur of the sea was still audible up here on the top prom, a soothing, rhythmic sound. Her eyes moved along, landing on the pod of surfers in their glossy black wetsuits this side of the pier. They were out in force today. In the distance, to the right, Thorncliffe was basking in the sunshine, as were the patchwork of fields that belonged to Clifftop Farm.

Something caught her attention on the bottom prom, and she watched as a figure threw a skateboard to the ground before making a great show of jumping aboard and propelling himself forward at an alarming speed, narrowly missing holidaymakers ambling along. Jasmine watched with morbid fascination as the skateboarder attempted some elaborate manoeuvre which resulted in his skateboard flying off in the direction of the beach while he collided with a sandwich board advertising the local surf school. She winced, momentarily distracted from her worries, as he tumbled head-first over the board with an almighty clatter. It must've hurt if the sound of the impact from the top prom was anything to go by. In that moment, she knew it could only be one person: Ando Taylor.

The sound of a motorbike roaring by on the road behind her pulled her thoughts away from Ando and back to the reason for her sitting on the bench. She was considering heading back home when she remembered the letters in her bag. Unzipping it, she reached inside, wondering if she'd find an official letter from Micklewick Mansions.

The first piece of correspondence was a receipt from the football summer holiday activity week that Zak had enrolled on.

A small smile fluttered on her lips at the thought of how much her son was looking forward to it, especially with his new friend.

The next was a leaflet advertising incontinence pants. *Who chooses where to send these ads?* 'I might wear belly-whackers but I'm not quite ready for those just yet,' she said aloud, setting it down on the bench beside her.

Another envelope contained bumpf from one of the companies she bought her cake decorating supplies from. She'd look at that later.

She eyed the remaining piece of post. Something about it sent a ripple of unease running through her. *Oh, what now?*

She slid her finger under the flap and eased out the thick piece of folded paper, dread pumping through her as she opened it out. Her eyes landed on the letterhead: Parker-Conley Legal.

Her first thought was that it was a letter regarding her official notice to quit Rosemary Terrace. But as she read down the neatly typed rows of words, she realised it was something far worse.

She was being threatened with legal action.

FOURTEEN

She reread the letter, tears blurring her eyes, myriad emotions tearing at her insides. 'Not this again!' she cried, turning the head of a man walking his dog nearby.

Stuffing the letters into her bag, she scrambled to her feet, tears spilling onto her cheeks. It felt as if she'd been hit with one thing after another with no chance to recover in between. She was punch-drunk with it all. She walked on, down Skitey Bank and towards the Jolly, passing the boats and lobster pots, with no thought as to where she was going.

Soon she found herself wandering blindly around the ancient, cobbled streets of Old Micklewick in amongst the higgledy-piggledy cottages, tears pouring down her face.

'Are you okay, lovey?' a woman asked kindly.

Unable to form a single word, Jasmine nodded and walked on. She had no idea why she'd come to this part of town, all she knew was her home was the last place she wanted to be right now. She turned onto the little row of independent shops on Mariner Street that was bustling with people, a seagull screeching from one of the stout chimney pots. The sweet smell of fudge hung in the air, the heady scent of kippers being smoked further along.

She dragged her hand over her face and sniffed.

'Jazz, flower, whatever's wrong?' Lark appeared before her in a cloud of essential oils, her bracelets jangling as she took hold of Jasmine's arms. She was dressed in her usual boho style of floaty white top with wide lace straps, trimmed with mirrored beads, and a pair of harem pants, while Turkish-style shoes adorned her feet. Her long blonde waves hung loose over her shoulders.

'What's happened? Are you okay?' The concern in Lark's pale green eyes was enough to set Jasmine's tears off again.

'Oh, Lark, it's t-too m-much... it's all j-just too m-much. I-I c-can't do th-this any m-more.' Jasmine buried her head in her friend's neck and sobbed.

'Oh, lovey, everything's going to be all right, I promise.' Lark guided her to a quiet corner, smoothing her hand over Jasmine's hair. 'Why don't we go back to my cottage? You can tell me all about what's got you so upset and we can see how we can put it right.'

'Ok-kay.' Jasmine allowed Lark to lead her along the twists and turns of the street and down onto Smugglers Row, a mismatched huddle of small cottages with red pantile roofs. It was like stepping into another world.

Painted a delicate shade of pale pink, with its aged door made of wide planks of natural oak wood upon which hung a wreath constructed of white shells, Seashell Cottage couldn't have looked more achingly sweet if it tried. Stepping into a tiny, tiled vestibule area, Jasmine was enveloped by the heady aroma of lavender and rose geranium essential oils, a fragrance she associated with her friend's home. After kicking off their shoes, she followed Lark into the characterful living room whose Georgian sash window looked directly out onto the street. Privacy was afforded by the profusion of flowers in the window box outside and the lines of jewel-coloured beads that hung down from a wooden pole that Lark had made herself. The beads caught the sunshine, sending kaleidoscopic rainbow splashes around the room, adding to the enchanted feel of the space.

'Right, lovey, you plonk yourself down there while I make us some tea.' She directed Jasmine to a small, squishy sofa covered with an old patchwork quilt and set with an array of brightly coloured plump cushions, handing her a box of tissues. Just like the rest of the tiny cottage, this room was filled with reclaimed furniture and accessories, all with their own unique history and story to tell. A large mirror with a decorative painted frame sat above a small inglenook, a log burner nestled within. Either side of the fireplace were built-in cupboards and shelves where Lark displayed her treasures along with a variety of crystals. Underfoot was a sisal carpet strewn with a couple of hand-woven rugs in sumptuous berry shades. A vibrant hand-stitched wall-hanging Lark had picked up in France on a sourcing trip with Nate adorned the wall by the door. Though the proportions of the room were small, Lark had been careful to ensure every bit of available space had been put to good use. To some it might feel cluttered, but Jasmine found its distinct hippy vibe soothing. It was Lark Harker to a "T".

'Here you go, get that down you.' Lark padded into the room, handing Jasmine a chunky mug of what smelt like a bunch of dried weeds.

'Th–thanks, Lark.' Though her tears had ceased, her eyes were red and swollen, and her shoulders still gave the occasional shudder.

Lark set her own mug down on the coffee table before them then curled herself into the armchair next to her friend, flicking her blonde waves over her shoulders. 'So, what's happened, flower?' She reached for Jasmine's hand, smoothing it with her fingers. 'It's not like you to get so upset.'

Jasmine felt her throat tighten. She shook her head and closed her eyes, tears escaping through her lashes.

'S'okay, Jazz, take your time. You can tell me when you're ready.'

Jasmine dabbed at her eyes. 'It's everything, Lark.' Her voice wavered. 'It's all got too much. It's been hard enough making sure there's enough money for everything, that the kids have got all they need, keeping track of when I'm meant to be working and where. But now there's all this... I don't have enough hands for the balls I need to keep in the air.' She stifled a sob, looking at her friend through puffy eyes. The last time she'd cried like this had been when she'd heard Bart had died. She'd always been strong, but that had toughened her veneer even more so.

'Oh, sweetheart, it's no wonder everything's got on top of you. The lasses and me have been worried sick about you for a while now. The only time you seem to stop to catch your breath is our Friday nights at the Jolly or the occasional reading at the bookshop. You're heading for burnout, if you haven't already reached it. It might not seem it right now, but it's good that you're having a cry and giving in to your emotions.' She gave Jasmine's hand a squeeze. 'So, was the meeting at Danskelfe Castle not what you hoped it would be?'

'It was the opposite.' Jasmine took a sip of her tea and pulled a face at the bitter flavour that filled her mouth, making Lark giggle. 'What the bloomin' 'eck is this?'

'It's camomile tea, known for its calming properties. I gather you're not a fan.' Lark chuckled some more.

'Tastes like my dad's compost heap.'

'And we all know of the benefits of homemade compost, so drink up and let it work its magic; you'll get used to the taste soon enough.' Lark grinned at her. 'So, you know the old saying about a problem shared?'

'Yes.' Jasmine tried another sip of her tea; it wasn't getting any better.

'Good, then why don't you tell me exactly what it is that's got you so upset?'

'Shouldn't you be at the shop? I don't want to take up your time if you're busy.'

'Busy is the last thing I am when one of my besties has just been sobbing her heart out. The shop can wait. Right now, nothing's more important than being here with you, Jazz. And besides, I'd never settle if I left you like this, so fire away. Tell me all...'

Lark listened as Jasmine told her everything from Scraggo arriving back in town with his children – she'd looked horrified at hearing that – to the meeting with Lady Caro at Danskelfe Castle – Lark had clapped her hands together and squealed with delight – to learning that her home had been put on the market. She'd also repeated what she'd told Florrie about running into Max which had been greeted with one of Lark's mysterious looks.

'But then I got this.' She fished the letter out of her bag and handed it to Lark. Jasmine watched as she read it, her friend's face morphing from interest to utter disbelief and then to disgust.

'What kind of people do that sort of thing?' She hurriedly placed the letter on the table as if she couldn't wait to get it out of her hands.

'Bart's parents, that's who,' Jasmine said sadly. She picked up the letter and read it again.

Dear Ms Ingilby,

Re: Items belonging to Mr Bart Forster

. . .

We act on behalf of Mr and Mrs Gary Forster.

Our clients have instructed us to contact you in relation to several items of jewellery that belonged to their deceased son, Mr Bart Forster. Mr and Mrs Forster believe that you have these items in your possession.

Our clients have informed us that despite asking that you return the jewellery on numerous occasions, you have persistently ignored their requests. As you and Mr Bart Forster never married, the items, which we are advised are family heirlooms and of some considerable value, form part of Bart Forster's estate and, therefore, should be handed back to his parents, in particular his father, as his named next of kin.

The pieces of jewellery include:

- *1 carat solitaire diamond ring set in 22ct gold*
- *Sapphire and diamond earrings*
- *22ct gold charm bracelet*
- *White gold necklace with three diamond pendant*

We would advise that the items listed above should be deposited with us as soon as possible, failing which our clients will have no choice but to instigate legal proceedings in order to retrieve them.

Yours sincerely,
David Parker-Conley
Solicitor

The contents sent Jasmine's heart plummeting all over again.

'I can't believe they're still banging on about their stuff, you've told them a million times you don't have it.' Lark looked at her askance.

'Yeah, but it's the Forsters we're dealing with. You know what they're like.'

'Yeah, I do, lovey. And much as I don't like to think badly of them, especially when they're Zak and Chloe's flesh and blood, I honestly think you really are all better off without them, especially that Gary Forster, he's a right nasty piece of work,' Lark said vehemently. 'I mean, that ring they mention in the letter was the one Bart gave you as an engagement ring, wasn't it?'

'Aye, it was.' Jasmine sighed. It was unusual to hear Lark make negative comments about anyone. She tried another sip of her tea and fought against pulling a face.

'So even if you still had it, it should legally be yours.'

Their eyes met; they were clearly both thinking the same thing. 'Provided he hadn't taken it without them knowing,' Jasmine said. 'And I can't imagine them ever admitting he'd done anything wrong, never mind accepting it. You know what they were like about him.'

'Don't we just! He really was their golden boy and they were totally blind to his failings.'

'Which was why they blamed me for everything that went wrong for him.'

'Hmm.'

A heavy sigh escaped Jasmine's mouth. 'I haven't got the energy to fight them, Lark.' She looked at her friend through weary eyes. She didn't have the energy to do anything, least of all get excited about her Danskelfe Castle news. She just wanted to hide under her duvet and escape all her problems, hoping they'd go away. 'They're never going to believe I haven't got their stuff. And even if I had, I'd have given it to them years ago to get them off my back if nothing else.'

'I know you would, flower.'

'What am I going to do?' Jasmine's bottom lip wobbled.

Lark sat upright in her chair. 'I'll tell you exactly what we're going to do. After you've drunk your tea' – she flashed Jasmine a wide smile – 'I'll make us a bite to eat – no arguments, you haven't been eating properly recently which will've been contributing to you feeling rubbish – then I'll contact Stells, tell her about the letter, get her legal take on it. How does that sound?'

'Sounds good.' Jasmine mustered up a watery smile. 'Thanks for being such a good friend, Lark. I don't know what I'd have done if you hadn't found me.'

'You were guided to me, flower; I was meant to be in Old Micklewick this afternoon, meant to find you, and meant to get some camomile tea down you.'

'Compost heap juice, you mean.'

'Mmm. I beg to differ!'

They grinned at one another before Lark wrapped her arms around Jasmine and squeezed her tight, her bracelets jingling away. 'It's going to be all right, Jazz. I promise. Please trust me on this. You might not think so right now, but the rest of the year is going to be awesome for you.' She released Jasmine from her embrace and took a step back, her hands resting on her friend's shoulders. 'And when have I ever been wrong about these things?'

'Can't remember you ever being wrong, Lark.' It was true – whenever Lark had one of her feelings or premonitions about something, she was invariably right. Though Stella and Jasmine gently teased her about it from time to time, the group of friends had learnt to trust her otherworldly instincts.

An hour later, Jasmine was feeling much better. Lark had helped shape her worries into a manageable size which had been a huge weight off her shoulders. On top of that, Stella had called back from a room tucked away in the court building at

York, full of fury about the Forsters. Lark had switched it to FaceTime, and the pair had peered at their friend dressed in her courtroom gear of black robes and white horsehair wig covering her blonde hair which was tied back into a ponytail. She made for an intimidating sight.

'S'cuse the get-up but I've just come straight from a trial. I spotted your message and wanted to call straight away. So, what's been going on?'

Jasmine had brought her up to speed with the details.

'Despicable bullies! They're just trying to intimidate you by going through a lawyer, but don't let them,' she'd said, her bold, no-nonsense tone filling the small living room. 'If you like, I can call round tonight after the kids have gone to bed, help you draft a letter. The Forsters want putting very firmly in their place and to finally accept that their son wasn't the little angel they hold him out to be. I'm sorry he passed away, I can't imagine what it must have been like for them to lose a child, but they need to stop clinging on to this sort of negativity. It does no one any good. And, deep down, I'm sure they know you haven't got those things.'

'I agree,' Lark had said. 'It's as if by stirring up trouble, it somehow keeps his memory alive. They don't seem to realise that by acting the way they do, they're not just hurting other people, they're hurting themselves, too. I'd feel sorry for them if it wasn't for the fact they're always so unkind to our Jazz.'

'It's the way they are, Lark; they seem to feed off each other's nastiness. Anyway, Jazz, there's always the option of using a solicitor to send a letter on your behalf, of course,' Stella had added. 'Thinking about it, receiving a reply with a solicitor's letterhead might have a better effect than one directly from you – no offence. Might give them the shake-up they need, make them stop hounding you.'

'None taken, Stells, I appreciate your advice.' Jasmine had reached the point where she was prepared to do whatever it took. 'They can come and search the house, I've got nothing to hide, and they won't find any of that stuff hidden away. In fact, I wish they would, then they might leave—'

'Stop right there, Jazz.' Stella's authoritative voice had spliced through her words. 'Do not, under any circumstances, suggest that to them or their lawyer. Knowing the Forsters, they'd be round before you could catch your breath, rummaging through your stuff, helping themselves to whatever they wanted.'

Stella's stern tone had sent a spike of alarm through Jasmine. 'You don't have to worry about that, Stells. It was just said tongue-in-cheek. I wouldn't let them over the doorstep.'

'Good. And don't forget there's the option of making an appointment with old Maurice Cuthbert at Cuthbert, Asquith & Co. They offer a free initial half hour there. I doubt he'll tell you anything different to what I've just said, but at least if you decide to go ahead and instruct a solicitor to act on your behalf, you're already there and can set the wheels in motion, get things moving.'

'True,' Jasmine had said, Stella's words running around her mind.

'Oh, and Jazz, try not to worry, I'm sure this'll get sorted quickly. It's just the Forsters' latest way of creating another fuss around themselves, keep that in mind. They're all bluff and bluster.'

'Let's hope so.' Jasmine had offered up a smile.

'Right, I'm going to have to dash, I've got a conference with the CPS in five minutes. But if you need me, just leave a message and I'll get back to you as soon as I'm free. As I said, I'm happy to drop by this evening if you need a hand drafting that letter.'

'Thanks, Stells. Good luck with your case. See you later.'

'Bye, Stells.' Lark and Jasmine had waved at their friend until she'd disappeared from the tiny screen on Lark's phone.

'Feeling better?' Lark had asked, turning to Jasmine.

'I am actually. Thanks for being so supportive.' Jasmine had thrown her arms around her friend and planted a kiss on her cheek in a most un-Jasmine-like display of affection. Though the traces of her earlier headache had still lingered, and her eyes had felt puffy, the talk with her friends had left her feeling inexorably relieved.

'Hey, no worries at all. You've done the same for me over the years; we've all been there for each other, always will be. Anyroad, how about another calming cup of camomile tea?'

'Lovely as the offer is, I'm fine for stewed compost right now, thanks.' Jasmine had pulled a face.

'Rude!' Lark had said, chuckling.

'Looking at the time, I reckon I'd best head back home. I've eaten such a big chunk into your afternoon, I daresay you've got a load of stuff to catch up on, and I've got a birthday cake to bake and a conked-out car to track down.'

'You haven't eaten a chunk into my afternoon at all, but I think I'll head back into town with you. Nate said he'd drop by later to discuss our next sourcing trip.'

'"*Sourcing trip*", eh?' Jasmine had put finger quotes around the words, nudging Lark with her shoulder. 'Is that what you're calling it these days?'

Lark had rolled her eyes good-naturedly as she'd swiftly changed the subject. 'These are for you, they're good for tackling stress.' She'd handed Jasmine a small silk purse containing two crystals. 'One's rose quartz to help with your stress levels, the other's onyx which is for protection. I've programmed them for you, all you need to do is keep them close and give them a rinse under the tap every now and then. And this is a rollerball containing lavender and scented geranium essential oils. Whenever you feel your stress levels rising, just roll it over your temples and your wrists, it'll help bring them down. And this room spray contains the same mix, it can be used as a pillow mist, too; should help you sleep better.'

'Oh, thank you, that's so kind, flower.' Jasmine never ceased to be amazed by Lark's thoughtful nature. 'I actually feel so much calmer for spending time here. Whatever it is you do, it's working. Don't suppose you fancy a lodger?' She grinned at her friend, savouring the lighter feeling.

With the sun beating down on them, and the aroma of seaweed hanging in the air, the two friends made their way along the bottom prom to the one hundred and ninety-nine steps that gave access to the top prom and town. They chatted away about the lack of affordable rental property in Micklewick Bay, the sound of the waves idly lapping against the shore in the background.

They were deep in conversation when a Land Rover pulled up beside them and Bear leant out of the window. 'Now then, lasses. Need a lift?' Maggie's husband was built like a brick proverbial, his bushy beard and wild shock of chin-length wavy hair lending him a Viking-like appearance. However, his striking looks belied the fact that he was a gentle giant, even more since he'd become a dad.

'Thanks, Bear, that'd be great.' Jasmine leapt at the chance.

'Thanks, Bear.' Lark beamed at him.

The two women climbed into the rear of the vehicle, settling themselves down onto the benches.

'So how come you're down here? I thought vehicles weren't allowed this far along the bottom prom,' asked Jasmine.

'I've just been having a look at the roof of one of the beach huts. The new owner said it had been leaking; wants me to fix it for her.'

'Fair enough.'

As Bear indicated to pull out, Jasmine could feel the weight of Lark's gaze opposite. She gave her a quizzical look. 'What's up?'

A mysterious smile twitched at the corners of her friend's mouth. 'I can't shake the feeling that Max Grainger is going to feature heavily in your life again.'

Jasmine gave an easy-going roll of her eyes, hoping Bear hadn't heard – he'd no doubt report back to Maggie who'd give her a right grilling about it. 'Don't get yourself carried away, flower. You just concentrate on you and Nate.' She flashed Lark a wide smile which was enough to stop her friend from pursuing her "feeling".

FIFTEEN
FRIDAY

The rest of the week passed in a blur, with Jasmine spending any spare moment she had trawling the internet and checking shop windows and noticeboards in town for adverts in her search for a new home before they were due to leave Rosemary Terrace. The only place that had seemed suitable, and not too far from where they were currently living, had apparently been snapped up a couple of hours before she'd rung to book a viewing. It had been a struggle to hide her disappointment. If the lack of suitable or affordable property was anything to go by, her house hunting was bound to take more than the couple of weeks she was hoping for. Eager to help out, her parents had told her she and the kids could move in with them if necessary, but, as kind as the offer was, Jasmine would rather find somewhere of their own and get Zak and Chloe settled without having to go through the upheaval of packing up and moving home an extra time. Plus, if they ended up at her parents, it would mean the children would have to share a room, which she doubted would go down well. The potential for niggles and arguments wasn't at all appealing, but at least her parents' offer had taken the pressure off if she was unable to find somewhere to move to in time.

At Rosemary Terrace, Jasmine had taken the tiny box room, giving Chloe the bigger front bedroom while Zak had the room in the converted loft space, which he loved and referred to as his "man cave" which tickled Jasmine. Since she only used her bedroom for sleeping and housing her small collection of clothes – which she kept on a tiny rail as there was insufficient room for a wardrobe – Jasmine reasoned she didn't need much space. But Zak and Chloe sometimes played in their rooms as well as having sleepovers with their friends, so it felt only right that they should have the more spacious bedrooms.

The Scragg situation at school seemed to have calmed down, for which she was inordinately relieved, especially since Chloe seemed so much happier and more like her cheerful self. Zak had reverted to his boisterous ways, enthusing about his new friend Connor and his football-themed birthday party that coming Saturday.

It was one less thing to worry about. *If only everything could be fixed so easily*, she thought.

Stella had called round at Rosemary Terrace on Tuesday evening armed with a bunch of flowers for Jasmine and a tub of raspberry ripple ice cream for Zak and Chloe.

'Oh, wow! They look amazing,' she said, spotting the batch of gooey chocolate caramel cupcakes Jasmine had just finished in readiness for collection by the local knitting group. She'd decorated them with huge swirls of caramel buttercream and sprinkled them with miniature chocolate buttons.

'There's one going spare, if you fancy it?'

'Are you kidding? Hand it over!'

In between chomping on her cupcake, Stella had offered more words of reassurance regarding the letter from the Forsters' solicitors which had further calmed Jasmine's concerns. They'd both agreed that a response in the form of a letter from a legal firm would have greater impact than one sent directly from her. It would show the Forsters she was taking their allegations seriously. The conversation had naturally turned to Max, but since she'd seen nothing more of him since Monday evening, there was nothing new to share.

'I reckon he'd have mentioned it if he wasn't staying for long, or at least called at your parents' house,' Stella had said.

'Yeah, that's what I was thinking.' In fact, Jasmine had found herself hoping that her old friend hadn't left town and that she'd have the opportunity for a decent catch-up with him.

The following day, Jasmine made herself an appointment at Cuthbert, Asquith & Co. She'd been disappointed to find the next available slot that fitted in with her work schedule wasn't until twelve thirty on Wednesday of the following week, but told herself at least she was being proactive. She was dealing with the situation in a calm, measured way rather than trying to talk to Bart's parents as she'd done in the past, getting herself wound up as she tried in vain to get them to believe she didn't have anything that belonged to them. Their son had made certain of that.

She was still waiting to hear from the garage with news of her car and whether it could be fixed and, if so, how much it would cost. That particular problem had kept her awake at night. Luckily, Kristina, a colleague at Spick 'n' Sparkle who had one of the cleaning company's cars, was on holiday that week, stretching into the next, and her boss, Alice, on hearing Jasmine's predicament, had added her name to the insurance of the vehicle, saying she could use it while Kristina was away. She'd also generously told her to make full use of the car and not just save it for getting to and from her cleaning jobs. Stella's mother might share the same first name with Bart's mother, but there the similarities ended. The group of friends had often joked that the two women couldn't have been more different if they'd tried, with Alice Hutton being kind and generous while Alice Forster had always been brittle and mean-spirited, particularly so with Jasmine.

. . .

By the time Friday evening arrived, Jasmine was glad of the chance to catch her breath.

The rhythmic beat of a bodhran accompanied by the jaunty lilt of a fiddle floated over the hum of chatter in the crowded bar of the Jolly as the local folk band launched into one of their most popular songs. Customers tapped their feet in time to the music, some singing along. The waiting staff, in their Jolly Sailors' T-shirts, bustled back and forth, ruddy-faced, carrying plates piled high with the landlady's legendary fish and chips, the delicious aroma filling the air and making Jasmine's stomach rumble.

Jasmine blew her fringe off her brow as she settled herself into her seat at the friends' usual table. She was glad of the breeze that was sneaking in through a nearby open window, brushing over her skin and offering welcome relief after the muggy warmth of outside. The heatwave of the last couple of weeks showed no sign of abating and, if anything, the temperatures appeared to be rising. It felt as if the earth had sucked every last drop of the sun's heat and was now throwing it back into the evening air, making it stifling and heavy.

It had been the usual Friday evening race down to the pub for Jasmine since she'd needed to add the final touches to the current birthday cake she'd been preparing. Handling sugar paste wasn't easy in such warm conditions, it made the icing sticky and difficult to mould, hence the extra time it had taken her to complete her latest commission. As usual, her hair felt tacky with the icing sugar that had been floating around her kitchen, though tonight there was a distinct lack of edible glitter and sparkles. It transpired that the boy's birthday cake had been ordered for Zak's new, football-mad friend Connor, and it was due for collection tomorrow morning, as was a viewing of her home. Jasmine hoped the two didn't overlap.

'I gather you've been having a bit of a week of it, flower.' Maggie gave her a sympathetic smile from the other end of the table.

'Yeah, you could say.' Jasmine rolled her eyes. 'Poor old Lark here had to contend with the fallout – really sorry about that, Lark.' Jasmine cringed with embarrassment whenever she remembered that she'd actually sobbed snotty tears into her friend's shoulder. And if that hadn't been toe-curlingly embarrassing enough, it had happened in the street, with people watching. She shuddered at the memory.

'No need to apologise, Jazz.' Lark reached across and squeezed her arm. 'Are the aromatherapy bits and bobs helping?'

'Do you know what? I actually think they are.' Whenever she'd found the stress creeping back, Jasmine had reached for the rollerball filled with essential oil Lark had given her, gliding it over her temples and dabbing it on her wrists. She topped it up with a couple of spritzes of the matching spray – being sure to avoid the kitchen and the birthday cake. And though she didn't want to say it would take more than a room spray or pillow mist to help her sleep well, she had to admit she'd slept better these last couple of nights than she had for a while. Maybe there was something in it after all. Or maybe it was simply because her body had finally given in to the exhaustion that had been threatening to drag her under.

Lark laughed. 'Don't sound so surprised! I knew they would; the crystals will be helping, too.'

'Yeah, why d'you think our Lark here is always so Zen and chilled?' Florrie chuckled.

'It's cos she douses herself in the stuff,' Stella added dryly.

Jasmine couldn't argue with that, though she held back from airing her doubts about the efficacy of the crystals, reluctant to hurt Lark's feelings or offend her.

'I'm looking forward to hearing all the deets of your trip to

Danskelfe Castle and the meeting with Lady Caro,' said Maggie. 'Catch your breath first, though, Jazz, the night is young.'

'Yep, grab yourself a mouthful of this.' Stella passed her a glass of freshly poured Pinot Grigio.

'Thanks, Stells.' Jasmine took a sip then pressed the cold glass to her cheeks. 'Ooh, bliss.' She sighed.

Maggie had sent her friend a text on Tuesday evening, asking how the meeting had gone and, with everything else that had been happening, Jasmine had sent a brief, and hurried, reply, saying she'd fill everyone in on Friday evening. She wasn't sure how much they all knew, or if Lark had shared what had happened on Tuesday afternoon. Though, judging by the occasional concerned glance her pals were sending her way, she suspected she'd said something. Not that Jasmine minded, she knew it would have come from a caring place and not simply to share gossip. They all looked out for one another, as they had since primary school.

And then there was Max to discuss, now they were all together. Of course, Maggie had never met him, but she'd heard them mention him on numerous occasions. Maybe she'd finally get to put the face to the name.

A warm smile lit up Florrie's face. 'I'm not going to spoil Jazz's news, but while we're waiting, all I'll say is that it is *amazing*.' She'd already explained to the rest of the group about having to give Jasmine a lift and the reason for it before Jasmine had arrived, but she hadn't said anything further, declaring it not being her news to share.

'Yeah, it is; it went really well and I'm over the moon. And you should have seen our Florrie here. Anyone would think she was my manager the way she got stuck in promoting me and bigging me up to Lady Caro.' Jasmine giggled, a ripple of excitement rushing through her at the reminder.

'I wanted to make sure her ladyship was fully aware of the

fabulous reputation you've built up with your cakes and how lucky she'd be to have you make them for the castle's weddings.' Florrie turned to the others. 'I also made a point of stressing that Jazz doesn't charge enough.'

'Go, Florrie,' said Maggie, ice cubes clinking as she raised her glass of lemonade. 'We've all been telling you that for ages, Jazz.'

'I know! I hope you've finally listened,' said Stella, the others all agreeing.

'Before I launch into telling you all about it, I'll first apologise to you, Lark, for having to hear it all over again, and to you, Florrie, since you were there and already know the outcome.'

'Happy to hear it again, flower.' Lark beamed at her.

'Same here,' said Florrie.

'Unfortunately, a lot of other, not-so-good stuff's been going on as well, but since it's completely unrelated to the Danskelfe Castle meeting, I'll start with the positive news first and get to that later.' Jasmine went on to recount the details of their visit to the castle and her conversation with Lady Caro, the friends listening intently.

'That's fantastic, Jazz!' Maggie said when she'd finished.

'Sounds to me like it could be the answer to all your juggling problems,' said Stella, the star-shaped diamond earrings she always wore glinting in the light.

'That's what I'm hoping.' Along with calming her worries, Jasmine's chats with Lark and Stella had also freed up some headspace, and, on top of being able to give Lady Caro's brief further consideration, it had also set other ideas racing through her mind. 'Which is why I could really do with running a few things past you all, get your opinion.'

'Fire away,' said Maggie.

Jasmine inhaled deeply and shared her potential plans for giving up at least one of her part-time jobs. 'I reckon I'd still have time to take orders for celebration cakes from other customers, and if I up my prices a bit – not by too much, mind, I don't want to put people off – it should boost my earnings. Though I reckon I should be bringing my wedding cakes more in line with what Lady Caro's going to charge. There's a lot of work involved, and doing the costings for my meeting with her has made me realise what I currently ask doesn't really cover the amount of time they take.'

'It's all sounding good so far, Jazz,' said Stella.

'Actually, that reminds me, I was going to ask about putting in a regular order for some of your tray bakes and cupcakes for us to sell in the tearoom at the bookshop. Would you be okay with that, Jazz?' asked Florrie.

'I'd be more than okay with that, flower. And, naturally, I'd give you mates' rates.'

Florrie shook her head. 'Ed and I have already discussed this in anticipation of you saying that, and we both agree that all deals are off unless we can pay the same as everyone else.'

'But you—'

Florrie held up her palm. 'No buts, Jazz. It's the going rate or nowt.'

'Ooh, I love it when our little Florrie gets all assertive,' said Maggie.

'Yeah, it's definitely a case of "don't mess",' said Stella.

'I'm thinking it'd probably be the cleaning job I'd give up, purely because of the number of Saturday shifts it involves; it's a busy changeover day for the holiday cottages on Spick 'n' Sparkle's books. Though I wouldn't drop your mum in it and leave her short-staffed, Stells. I've been approached by a couple of the mums at school who've asked if I know if any shifts are going. I reckon they'd be okay.' Jasmine had been to their houses to collect her children on several occasions, and could vouch that their homes were immaculate, which would suit Alice Hutton's exacting standards.

'Mum would be chuffed to bits to hear your reason for

leaving is because of your cake decorating business. And she most certainly wouldn't want you to be fretting about finding your replacement.'

'I'd still want to clean for Hilda, though, if your mum would let me. I'd miss her too much if I stopped, plus it's when I drop her shopping round, but regardless of that, she's not keen on change. Poor old soul's still devastated about losing Enid.' Jasmine's gaze fell to the table. 'Come to think of it, so am I. Knocked the stuffing out of both of us.'

Hilda Jenkins and Enid Lambton had been lifelong best friends. In their mid-eighties, the widows were Micklewick Bay born and bred. Both prided themselves on being agile – or "as fit as a lop" as Hilda regularly said, using a Yorkshire variation of "fit as a flea" – and both had a fiercely independent streak. Whereas Hilda had a son and grandchildren who called on her every so often, Enid and her husband had never been blessed with children, and other than a cousin from Lincoln she mentioned with a vague wave of her hand, she had no close living relatives that Jasmine was aware of. As soon as Jasmine got through the door for her weekly cleaning shift, Enid would make a pot of tea and insist the younger woman sat down with her and had a catch up, both of them munching on the homemade shortbread biscuits Enid prided herself on, and sipping tea out of delicate china cups – 'Might as well do it properly, lovey. I always think tea tastes so much better out of china,' she'd say. As Jasmine busied herself tidying and doing the odd bit of ironing, Enid would entertain her with stories of her and Hilda's antics from when they were younger, filling her in on the gossip that had been flying around town in the sixties and seventies. By all accounts they'd been a couple of live wires, full of spirit and fun. Enid had a wickedly sharp sense of humour and a mischievous twinkle in her eye which tickled Jasmine. She'd grown very fond of her elderly friend and found herself looking forward to her shifts there. The feeling was mutual, with Enid watching out of the window, waiting for her young friend's car to arrive. Seeing her peering around the curtains had made Jasmine's heart squeeze with affection for her.

Both ladies had shown an interest in the celebration cakes Jasmine made, encouraging her to consider it as a potential business, and priding themselves on spreading the word. Jasmine knew she'd got a whole tranche of commissions because of them singing her praises to their wide circle of friends, and she was inordinately grateful for their kindness.

It was last winter when Enid had struggled to shake off a virus and ended up in hospital that things had changed. Jasmine had called round for her usual shift to find her elderly friend slumped in her favourite chair, her breathing laboured and her skin waxy. 'Oh, Enid, lovey, you don't look at all well.' She'd taken her hand, shocked at how icy-cold it felt. 'And you're absolutely nithered. You should've rung me as soon as you started to feel poorly, I'd have been here like a shot, brought you some nice warm soup round.' Enid had squeezed her hand and smiled weakly, her once bright eyes now so dimmed it had startled Jasmine. She'd immediately called an ambulance, wishing with all her might for it to arrive quickly. While they'd waited, she'd set to, snuggling Enid up in a couple of blankets and doing all she could to make sure her friend was as comfortable as was possible in the circumstances. When the paramedics arrived, they'd wasted no time in whisking Enid off to Middleton-le-Moors hospital. Sadly, she died of pneumonia a week later, her loss hitting both Hilda and Jasmine hard.

And now she was considering giving up her cleaning job, there was no way Jasmine was going to abandon Hilda, who was slowly working her way through the grieving process by talking about her best friend, tears spilling down the paper-thin skin of her cheeks as she clung onto Jasmine's hands. Just thinking about it brought a lump to Jasmine's throat. She made a mental note to take a bunch of flowers and a couple of homemade cupcakes to her next shift at Hilda's.

'I'm sure Mum'll be fine with that arrangement, Jazz. She knows you and Hilda are close.'

'Yeah, I reckon she will.' Jasmine pushed the shadow of sadness away. Stella's mum had already expressed her concern about how withdrawn Hilda had become. Between them, they'd agreed to keep an eye on her. Hilda adored children and was always glad to see Zak and Chloe when Jasmine had popped in with them after school a couple of times, surreptitiously checking to make sure her friend was doing okay. Hilda had listened as Zak had told her all about his love of football and how he was hoping to be accepted for the Micklewick Lions' junior team. 'By, that sounds "mint", young man,' Hilda had said, picking up on the youngster's term for something that was really good. She'd also listened to Chloe sing, and had even accompanied her on the piano. She'd clasped the little girl's hands, saying, 'You have the voice of an angel, lovey.' Both children had grown fond of the older lady, with Chloe presenting her with a daisy chain she'd made on her last visit which had delighted Hilda no end.

'Right then, onto my other news – unless you fancy a break from hearing me wittering on?' Jasmine felt like she'd been talking for ages without giving her friends a chance to share their news.

'Don't be so daft, of course we want to hear what else has been happening,' said Stella. 'My week's been quite tame so far, so I've got nothing much new to share.'

'What with your work and your private life, I'd never associate the word "tame" with you, Stells,' Maggie said, making them all chuckle.

'That's rum coming from you, Mags. Have you forgotten about last year?' Stella replied. Maggie and Bear's marriage had been tested to the limits by the unexpected arrival of her estranged cousin Robyn who had caused a whirlwind of trouble during her short stay with them. At one point, they'd been worried they'd never be able to get rid of her.

'Ugh! Don't remind me. I still can't help checking over my shoulder, just to make sure she hasn't returned with an evil glint in her eye.' Maggie gave a shudder. 'Anyway, that's enough about her.'

'Too right,' said Florrie. Being the friend closest to Maggie, she and Ed had witnessed much of what had gone on, particularly just before Robyn had left.

'Oh, aye, and I just want to mention that the lasses have brought me up to speed about an unpleasant character called Scraggo and his kids, and your friend called Max,' Maggie told her. 'Bear and me were really sorry to hear Zak and Chloe were having a hard time at school because of them. Bear was totally gobsmacked to hear that family were back in town. And I know I never met them, but I've heard plenty about them, none of it good. At least you've nipped it in the bud at school and Zak and Chloe are okay. It's refreshing to hear the headteacher takes bullying seriously. Anyroad, you know where we are if you need us.'

'Thanks, flower.' Jasmine held on to the hope that the headteacher would keep a close watch on things. She went on to share her news about the letter from Bart's parents, segueing straight into how she needed to find somewhere new to live. Needless to say, these two updates weren't as well received by the friends as the Danskelfe Castle news.

'First off – and I just want to get this out of the way, cos you already know how I feel about that family, particularly Gary flaming Forster – I honestly thought that miserable pair couldn't stoop any lower, but this proves me wrong.' Maggie shook her head in disgust, colour rising in her cheeks. She'd been involved in a road accident caused by Gary Forster when she was pregnant with Lucy and had ended up in hospital. He'd driven off and denied all knowledge, until a witness had come forward. Mercifully, both mother and baby were unharmed. 'In the letter back, you should get old Mr Cuthbert to tell them you'll take legal action if they don't leave you alone and stop hounding you.'

'I agree,' said Florrie. 'Shut them up, once and for all.'

'That's what I've advised her to do,' said Stella.

'As for you having to move house, I've been thinking about it and I reckon it might not be a bad thing in the long run,' said Florrie. 'I mean, your landlord always takes an age to fix anything.'

'True,' said Maggie. 'That combi-boiler is as old as the hills and Bear says the only reason the window frames haven't dropped out is cos you keep painting them, which I don't need to remind you is actually the landlord's job to sort out.'

Jasmine couldn't argue with Bear's assessment. As well as working for his parents at Clifftop Farm, Bear was an odd-job man and was highly regarded in the town. Micklewick Mansions used him to carry out repairs and paint the properties on their books – landlords permitting, of course. But Jasmine's landlord was never keen to dip his hand in his pocket. Instead, he advised her and his other tenants he'd take care of such things himself. Which was something he rarely got around to doing.

'Moving away from the Forsters, slippery landlords and the dreaded Scraggs, and in a bid to keep things light and positive,' Lark chipped in, 'I've got an idea that might solve your accommodation problem and add an extra dimension to your cake baking business, Jazz.'

'Ooh, I'm all ears.' Jasmine was glad to move the conversation away from the things that had given her so much grief that week, but she couldn't begin to think what Lark was going to suggest.

'Me, too,' said Stella.

'So, you know the old bakery on Mariner Street down here in Old Micklewick has just been sold?'

'I'd heard that,' said Florrie. 'And I'd also heard that Dodgy Dick and his cronies were beaten to it, which is always good news.'

'Isn't it just?' said Maggie.

'What about the old bakery?' Jasmine asked.

'Well, if rumours are to be believed, it's supposed to be coming up for rent.'

Jasmine blinked at her, not sure why her friend would think a former bakery would solve her accommodation dilemma, never mind add anything to her business. But Lark was all fired up, which had piqued her interest.

'Go on,' said Stella, leaning forward and resting her chin on her hand.

'I know that look, Jazz, but bear with me,' said Lark, evidently picking up on her friend's doubt.

'You have my full, undivided attention,' Jasmine reassured her.

'Good. So, the property comes with living accommodation – three bedrooms – and a cute little garden area at the back. *And* I've heard a whisper the landlord is keen to rent it to a local small business at an affordable price.' Lark swept her gaze around the table. 'Apparently, it needs quite a bit of updating and the décor in the living quarters is supposed to be a bit on the grim side, but I was thinking, if you found out who the landlord is, then you could get in before anyone else, express an interest, potentially save them having to advertise. And, if you think it'd be any good, you might be able to have some input into the redecoration.'

Jasmine took in her friend's excited expression. Loath as she was to pour cold water over Lark's well-intended suggestion, she felt the need to rein things in a little. 'I know you mentioned something about the price being reasonable, but isn't it still likely to be out of my budget? I mean, with it being a business premises as well as living accommodation, wouldn't we be talking twice the price? And I know rental property is virtually non-existent in Micklewick Bay, so I can see why you'd suggest it, but I'm not really sure why I'd want shop space as well. What would I use it for?'

'That, dear Jazz, is where my idea to expand your business comes in.' Lark reached for her glass of wine and took a sip, her eyes twinkling over the top.

'Ooh, do tell,' Florrie said, leaning in.

'Okay.' Lark set her glass down and flicked her mermaid plait over her shoulder, a wide smile spreading over her face, crinkling her eyes. 'So, the obvious thing as far as I'm concerned is the baking equipment. I know the bakery was small so, though the food mixers and ovens, etc. are all commercial – I'm reliably informed they're still there – they won't be as huge as the equipment some bakeries have, which I think would be perfect for you. They'd be an upgrade in size without being ridiculously large, thus offering the potential to get more cakes made in one go.'

'True,' said Jasmine. Though she still wasn't convinced, she was sufficiently interested to want to hear more.

'And I reckon you could use the shop window to advertise what you offer. You know, prepare some dummy cakes and make an eye-catching display. After all, your cakes speak for themselves, Jazz.'

'Ooh, Ed could help you out there!' said Florrie. 'He could construct a backdrop for you. He loves doing things like that and is full of good ideas.'

'True.' Jasmine nodded.

'On top of that, you could even hold some cake decorating classes; I remember you said you'd been asked if you'd do that loads of times before and you quite liked the idea.' She paused as if trying to read Jasmine's expression. 'Oh, and as far as the accommodation is concerned, I've been told it's ever so cosy and cute, dodgy décor aside. The garden might need a bit of work, but we'd be happy to chip in with the old trowel and fork, wouldn't we, lasses?'

All but Stella agreed. 'I can't say getting down and dirty in the mud's my idea of fun—'

Maggie snorted. 'That's not what we'd heard, Stells.'

'Haha. Very funny.' Fighting a smile, Stella stuck her tongue out at Maggie, making the others giggle. 'What I was going to say before I was so rudely interrupted was that I'd be very happy to assist in my role as supervisor, as well as provide any necessary refreshments.'

'You're all heart, Stells.' Jasmine couldn't help but chuckle along with the others.

'So I'm told.' Stella flashed her a faux angelic smile.

'Imagine how the kids would love it there, Jazz,' Lark continued to enthuse. 'Plus, the potential increase in business would mean you'd definitely be able to give up both your other jobs and work solely from home. In turn, it would mean you'd be around more for the kids which I know is what matters most to you, and it would also help ease your childcare problems. It's a win-win situation.'

Jasmine listened, surprised to find Lark's idea growing on her. There was only one thing left holding her back from being totally sold on it. 'Much as I'm really taken with—'

Lark gently rested her hand on Jasmine's arm. 'I know what you're going to say, but don't let finances hold you back. I've got a really strong feeling about this working for you, Jazz. And you know I wouldn't speak so passionately about something unless I was pretty certain about it. I wouldn't want you to put yourself and the kids in a tricky position. But I've got this unshakeable feeling that this is your time, Jazz.' Her eyes sparkled as she spoke. 'The planets have aligned for you and you're about to shine.'

'About bloomin' time,' said Stella.

'Woohoo! That's what we like to hear for our lovely Jazz.' Maggie gave a happy dance in her seat, Florrie following suit.

'Hang on a minute, you lot, would you just calm your jets? I haven't even looked at the place yet and you've got me moved in, baking cakes and weeding the garden.' Jasmine couldn't help but laugh, her friends' positivity sending her spirits rising.

The week that had started on such an unhappy note, dipping to despair in the middle, now had an almost celebratory feel. *Talk about life being like a roller coaster*, Jasmine thought.

'And lovely as your idea is, Lark, there's a good chance it might never get off the ground. I haven't a clue who the new owner is, or how to get hold of them,' she said.

A mysterious smile played over Lark's mouth. 'Leave it with me. I have a contact who might be able to find out.'

'That would be great, thanks, Lark.' Jasmine found herself suddenly keen to learn more about the old bakery.

'Now then, lasses.' Ando Taylor appeared by their table, standing close to Jasmine, shoving all thoughts of the bakery out of her mind. He was swaying precariously, his half-drunk pint sloshing over his hand. 'Don't sh'poshe you fanshy a shteady little wander back tonight, do you, Jash? Maybe get a bag of chipsh to share,' he slurred. He'd clearly indulged in several pints of Old Micklewick Magic beer that evening.

Jasmine wasn't remotely tempted by Ando's offer. She tipped her head back and looked up at him, noting the large scrape on his cheek. From the way he was swaying – he was almost making her feel seasick – it was a wonder he managed to stay upright. 'I'll be heading home with the lasses, thanks, Ando.'

'Well, you know where to find me if you chanshe your mind.'

Rather than heading back to the bar as he usually did following Jasmine's weekly rejection of his offer, he stood rooted to the spot. Jasmine hoped he wasn't waiting for her to change her mind.

The familiar gravelly tones of Lobster Harry travelled across the bar above the fiddle music. Despite it being warm, he was wearing the Micklewick Bay gansey his wife had knitted for him many years ago, if the number of holes that peppered it were anything to go by. 'Oi, Ando, I haven't forgotten it's your round, laddo.' He waved his empty glass at the younger man, flashing a gap-toothed smile in his weather-beaten face.

'Aye, righto, I'll be over in a shec.' Ando downed the contents of his glass in a single gulp and wiped the back of his hand across his mouth, before staggering his way across the bar, tripping over his own feet and lunging into Lobster Harry who gave him a verbal savaging.

'I wonder how Ando thinks he can walk you home when he can't even manage to make his way across the bar in one piece,' said Stella, watching Ando's performance.

'Good question.' Maggie followed her gaze. 'I reckon it'd be worth watching.'

'Don't even go there.' Jasmine snatched up her glass and sent her friend a warning look.

SIXTEEN
SATURDAY

Jasmine was thankful Connor's birthday cake had been collected before the viewing that morning. Zak had been thrilled when his friend had turned up. He'd arrived with a woman who introduced herself as Sabrina Osborne, elaborating by saying she was "Connor's dad's assistant". From a few things Zak had mentioned, Jasmine got the impression Connor's mum wasn't on the scene and hadn't been for some time. And though she had a friendly disposition, Sabrina, who looked to be in her late twenties or early thirties, with her long, poker-straight curtain of glossy, dark hair and striking blue eyes, not to mention delicate high cheekbones and legs that went on forever, had left Jasmine feeling inferior and distinctly dowdy. Even Sabrina's casual attire of ankle-grazer jeans, chunky brown belt and crisp white shirt, complete with brown leather loafers on her slender feet, managed to look effortlessly stylish. The young woman had an air of authority about her, creating the impression that she was uber organised and efficient. That said, Sabrina was likeable – if not a little cool – and there was something about her that put Jasmine in mind of Stella. She'd found herself wondering if the role of "Connor's dad's assistant" extended to matters of a more personal nature. After all, Sabrina was very attractive, and no doubt turned heads wherever she went.

'Zak's very welcome to come back with us now, if he'd like?' Sabrina had asked with a dazzling smile. Both Zak and Connor had jumped up and down excitedly, begging for Jasmine to say yes, which, of course, she had. It had been good to see Zak so happy after the Scragg drama.

'Oh, and his dad's asked me to double-check it's still okay for him to stay for the sleepover? There are a couple of other lads staying, too.'

'Yes, that's absolutely fine, he's been looking forward to it.' As a rule, Jasmine would need to know the family before agreeing to her son going to a sleepover at their house, but after making enquiries about the family with some of the other mums whose children would be there, too, she'd satisfied herself that all would be okay.

Just then, Jasmine's mobile had started to ring which had prompted Sabrina to declare it was time to leave. She scooped up the cake and headed through the door, the boys bouncing with enthusiasm as they left, Jasmine calling for them to have fun.

An hour later, her heart had plummeted to her feet when she'd answered the door to see Dodgy Dick and his wife Wendy looking back at her, an air of trouble around them. They put her in mind of a couple of black crows with their matching dyed-black hair and funereal clothes. Didn't they know dark colours absorbed heat? As usual, Wendy was bedecked in an array of sparkling jewellery, her face caked in make-up, finished with a slash of red lipstick that was so vivid it practically screamed at you. They seemed to be embracing a generic gangster vibe, not realising it made them look more like caricatures.

'Well, fancy seeing you here.' Dodgy Dick hadn't waited to be invited in, and made to come inside, forcing Jasmine to take a step back, squashing her behind the door as he passed. Wendy had stepped in, her overpowering perfume catching in Jasmine's throat and making her hold her breath.

She hadn't been given the name of the people who were booked for the viewing, and seeing who had arrived, made Jasmine wonder if the omission had been deliberate. And, if so, why?

She'd hated every second of showing the obnoxious couple around. As well as being critical of the condition of the house – something she had to agree with – they'd wandered around, picking up her personal items, sniggering as they'd made derogatory remarks. What was worse, they'd taken their time over it, taking pleasure from her obvious discomfort.

Once they'd gone, she'd puffed out her cheeks, and leant her back against the door, praying they wouldn't ask for a second viewing. Next, she ran around, opening the windows in a bid to release the cloying smell of Wendy's perfume that clung to everything. The little house wasn't big enough to tolerate such a powerful smell.

The bakery had been crazy busy which meant the afternoon had gone quickly. Despite Alice telling her she could use the Spick 'n' Sparkle van whenever she needed, Jasmine still felt uncomfortable about it, so, not wanting to look like she was taking advantage, she'd walked to and from the shop in the square. It wasn't far, but the air was muggy and she was in a lather by the time she got home.

After downing a glass of cold water, she headed upstairs for a cooling shower.

Feeling refreshed, she stepped into a clean pair of utility shorts and T-shirt, then headed into the kids' bedrooms, gathering up clothes for a wash. She stopped in her tracks when she spotted Zak's backpack full of his sleepover things on the floor by his bed. 'Zaky,' she said, using the nickname he'd declared himself to be too old for. He must've been so excited about Connor's party, he'd left without it. Normally, Jasmine was fastidious about making sure her children had everything they would need with them, but she'd been distracted by her phone ringing when they were leaving.

She glanced at her watch, deliberating if she should drop it off. In the end, she decided she should; she didn't want Zak to realise he'd forgotten it when it was time to get ready for bed. And she didn't have to hang around, she could just hand the bag over to Sabrina and bid a hasty retreat. She had a christening cake design to plan, but she could do that when she got back since she had the evening to herself as Chloe was staying at her parents' house for the night after a trip to the cinema in York.

It was years since Jasmine had last been along the track on this side of the cliffs. It was well-worn by dog walkers and precipitous in parts, with the sound of the waves crashing below, the salty tang of seaweed hanging in the air. The views out to sea were spectacular, affording a panoramic view of the bay, reaching right along to Thorncliffe. You could literally see for miles. She headed left and crossed a grassy stretch of land that led to the road and eventually the entrance to Njord's View – so named after Njord, the Viking god of the sea – a welcome breeze gently ruffling her hair. She felt a tingle rush over her skin and she couldn't help but think the area had a magical feel. "Mystical", would be how Lark would no doubt describe it.

'Wow!' She stopped in her tracks, her gaze sweeping over the clean lines of the impressive art deco building that loomed before her, circular turrets sitting at each end. It hadn't looked like this when she'd last set eyes on it. Then, the white-painted walls had been peeling, the metal window frames rusting and weeds had peppered the driveway. The word "unloved" sprang to mind. But now... Now it had benefited from an exquisitely tasteful makeover. Before it was a newly laid gravel drive, upon which sat a gleaming sports car and equally shiny four-wheel drive. Wide, neatly kept lawns stretched out either side. Beyond that, a broad flight of steps led up to a large front door that featured elongated panels. It had been painted a soft blue that matched the sky perfectly. The walls had been painted a chalky white, while the elegant metal-framed windows had been finished in the same blue as the front door, their panes glinting in the sunlight. Everything about it exuded understated style. It was a far cry from her little home that Dodgy Dick and his wife had taken such pleasure in ridiculing earlier that day.

As she drew closer, the sound of young voices reached her ears, laughing and cheering. She detected Zak's in amongst them, full of its usual enthusiasm. The low bark of a dog joined in, making her smile.

With a hint of trepidation, she headed through the large double gates that had been flung back, and made for the front door – she half-wondered if she should look for a tradesman's entrance, which she felt would probably be more fitting for her.

She set Zak's backpack down on the step, and pressed what appeared to be the original doorbell. Standing back, she smoothed her hands over her pixie crop, thankful at least that it was freshly washed and would have no trace of icing sugar or glitter.

A moment later, the door swung open and a tall, broad-shouldered man with dark auburn hair filled the frame. He was wearing an aquamarine linen shirt and navy-blue cotton shorts.

'Max!' Jasmine didn't have time to stop the loud gasp from

escaping her mouth as she tried to make sense of her old friend answering the door of Njord's View. 'What are you doing here?'

'Jingilby!'

She looked on, speechless, as his face broke out into a smile, a twinkle in his hazel eyes that sent her hurtling back over twenty years.

SEVENTEEN

'It's good to see you again.' Max's smile widened.

Her mind raced as she processed the information her eyes were sending to her brain.

'It's good to see—' Before she had the chance to say anything further, he'd scooped her up in a hug and was spinning her round in a cloud of his mossy cologne.

'Argh!' Jasmine gave in to the overwhelming urge to laugh out loud.

'Oh, Jingilby, it really is fantastic to see you. I wanted to give you a hug the other day, but with you taking a bit of a tumble, I thought better of it; didn't want to hurt you,' Max said, his face buried in her neck, making her thankful she'd had a shower. She'd have hated to smell like the hot steak and onion pies that had been popular with customers that day, despite the warm weather. The aroma had a habit of clinging to the bakery staff's clothes and hair, with them complaining it had the unmistakable whiff of sweaty armpits. It wasn't the ideal smell to have lingering on you at the best of times, never mind when you had an unexpected close encounter of the male kind.

When he finally set her down, Max held on to her shoulders, giving her a thorough appraisal.

'Well, that was some welcome,' she said when she'd caught her breath, the scent of his cologne clinging to her clothes.

'Can you blame me? I'm ecstatic to see you, Jingilby. You look fantastic! I thought so the other day when we met,' he said, his eyes roving over her.

'I'm not so sure about that.' She gave a self-conscious giggle.

'It's true! You do.' He beamed down at her, his expression telling her he meant it.

She resisted the urge to ask when he'd last had his eyes tested, which would be her standard reaction to receiving such a compliment, especially since she had Stella's voice ringing loud in her ear from the last time she'd come back with a similar comment, telling her to stop putting herself down.

'Sorry about the other day, you know, with the phone call. I'd been waiting all day for it,' he said.

'No worries at all, I had to get back home.'

Max nodded, still smiling at her.

'You haven't half grown.' Jasmine vocalised the second thought that popped into her head concerning Max. The first was that he was really rather attractive. But she kept that to herself.

'Aye, just a bit. As soon as I hit sixteen, I shot up like some sort of bonkers beanstalk. Thought I was never going to stop at one point. I went that gangly, you'd think I'd been stretched. The growing spurt ground to a halt when I hit six-three.'

'Wow!' Jasmine said, thinking he had the loveliest voice, all rich and deep and velvety. She hadn't noticed it the other day, but then again, her knees had been giving her grief and she'd been overcome with embarrassment for falling over. And wherever he'd been in the last twenty-odd years, he'd still kept his North Yorkshire accent. She wondered if he'd stayed in Harrogate, kept near his grandad.

He clapped his hand to his head. 'What the heck am I thinking, keeping you here on the doorstep? Come inside, let me get you something to drink. I've got a million questions to ask you. The kids are having a whale of a time in the garden, by the way, Sabrina's keeping an eye on them.'

Mention of his PA sent a wave of unease over Jasmine. She couldn't put her finger on it, but though Sabrina had been friendly, there was something about her that had given unspoken warnings. 'Another time, maybe. I should probably be getting back, and I don't want to intrude.'

Max's smile fell. There'd always been something in his eyes that had managed to reach into her heart, even when they were children. She hovered for a moment, battling between going home and staying for a short time, wondering how it would go down with Sabrina. Jasmine didn't want to rock the boat; she had enough going on without dealing with a jealous PA/girlfriend.

'Just so you know, Jingilby, you wouldn't be intruding. I've been hoping to see you again since we bumped into each other. And when Connor said his best friend was called Zak Ingilby, I secretly hoped he'd be related to you. Connor's my son, by the way.'

'Yeah, I realise that now.'

'Somehow, seems fitting they should be friends, don't you think?'

'It does.' She smiled up at him. 'History repeating itself.'

'Aye, that's what I thought. According to Connor, they hit it off straight away. He said Zak was really friendly and made sure to include him in their games.'

Jasmine's heart swelled with love for her son. 'Yeah, he's a good kid, doesn't like to think of anyone being left out or having no one to play with.'

'Sounds just like his mum.'

Jasmine gave an embarrassed laugh, her eyes dropping to the floor.

'Sure I can't tempt you to a quick catch up?' He dipped his head, giving her no choice but to look at him.

Meeting his gaze, her pulse jumped to attention. The pleading look in his eyes took her all the way back to when they were nine years old. How could she possibly refuse? 'Okay then.' She reached for Zak's backpack, but Max got there before her and hooked it over his shoulder.

'Great! Come on.' He guided her into the house, his hand on the small of her back as unexpected butterflies danced a lively jig in her stomach.

'Oh, my days, this is fantastic.' For the second time since she'd arrived, Jasmine gasped. The front door led into a wide entrance hall, a sweeping oak staircase with decorative metal spindles in clean lines at its centre, a woven runner softening its appearance. The walls were painted an eggshell white, their starkness relieved by artfully arranged paintings of scenery, the theme of which was predominantly of the sea and the cliffs of Micklewick Bay; the brooding hulk of Thorncliffe was easy to pick out amongst them.

She followed him into an airy kitchen, the units echoing the pale blue of the front door and window frames. The biggest island she'd ever set eyes on took centre stage. It was topped with light-coloured marble, shot with shades of grey – as were the rest of the units – and added to the light feel of the room. A six-oven Aga sat in what had been a large fireplace, while an all-singing, all-dancing contemporary oven took up position beside it. Alongside the double-fronted American-style fridge stood a glass-doored wine chiller. Jasmine had never seen such a kitchen. Everywhere was flooded with light and, though what she'd seen of the house so far had a distinctly contemporary feel, the atmosphere was warm and welcoming, with personal items dotted about the place, including photos of Connor and Ernest together.

'Make yourself at home, Jingilby.' Max gestured to the high-backed Lloyd Loom-style bar stools, his arm extending to the L-shaped sofa at the other end of the kitchen. 'Tea? Coffee? Hot chocolate – I remember you used to be a huge hot chocolate fan.' He grinned at her as he set Zak's backpack down.

'And I seem to recall I wasn't the only one.'

'Your mum's were the best,' he said fondly.

'Still are.'

'In that case, maybe we should stick to tea. I'd hate my hot chocolate to be a crashing disappointment,' he joked.

'I doubt it would, but tea's good for me, dash of milk, no sugar, thanks.' She headed over to the enormous floor-to-ceiling window on the opposite wall. It overlooked a sweeping lawn where the boys were playing football against a backdrop of the sea. She spotted Zak, running about, the corners of her mouth lifting with a smile. He looked happy and carefree. It was good to see he'd put the trouble of earlier in the week behind him.

'How are they, by the way? Your parents, I mean? I'd been hoping to call in on them as you suggested, but work commitments haven't allowed. I'd love for Connor to meet them; I've told him loads about them, and you.'

Jasmine pulled herself away from the window and made her way over to the island. Pulling out a bar stool she hooked her bag over the back. 'Mum and Dad are good, thanks. It's their ruby wedding anniversary soon, so they're getting excited about that, Mum particularly so.' She wondered how much detail Max had gone into with his son about his past.

'Ruby? How many years is that, then?'

'Would you believe, forty?'

Max gave a low whistle. 'Forty years? That's a heck of a long time.'

'It is. Though Mum jokes it feels more like a hundred and forty.'

That raised a smile from Max. 'Are they having a party to celebrate?'

She shook her head. 'No. They're putting the money a party would cost towards a holiday; they fancy going somewhere sunny rather than holidaying in this country, which is what they usually do. They've had a few unexpected expenses over the last year so they've postponed the break until next year.'

Max listened quietly as he poured the tea, bringing the mugs over to the island. Setting them down, he slid onto the bar stool opposite Jasmine. She took a moment to survey him, her mind running over the hundreds of questions that were piling into her mind. He looked back at her. Though his expression was inscrutable, she wondered if it was the same for him.

'How's Ernest?' she said, breaking the silence – not that it was uncomfortable; she was just a little conscious of it. 'Cute name for a dog, by the way.' She chuckled.

'He's currently having a whale of a time in the garden with the lads. I'm sure he thinks he's one of them.'

He'd seemed to be enjoying himself when Jasmine had been looking out of the window. 'What breed is he?'

'Good question. We know his mother was a black Lab, and from the look of his coat, his dad was evidently something fluffy or long-haired. We rescued him from a shelter over Harrogate way a couple of years ago, but he's the most upbeat little fella considering his past. Absolutely adores Connor.'

'Oh, bless him.' From the expression on Max's face, she could tell the Lab cross had taken up a huge chunk of his heart. 'He seems adorable.'

'He's that all right.' He smiled affectionately. 'Oh, and I must mention that Connor's thrilled with his birthday cake. It's genius. In fact, he says he likes it so much, he doesn't want to cut into it.'

Jasmine laughed. 'Ah, that's sweet, but he really should enjoy it before it goes mouldy and has to be chucked away.'

'I'll tell him you said that.'

After umming and ahhing about whether to do a cake in the theme of a football pitch, with a sugar paste character in a Micklewick Lions football kit, she'd sought Zak's advice and eventually settled on making a cake in the shape of a football shirt in the local team's colours, complete with sugar paste football boots posed on top. Much as Zak had liked the first option, he thought it might be a bit babyish for his ten-year-old friend. Jasmine had appreciated his advice.

'You always enjoyed baking with your mum. I remember the chocolate cookies you used to make.'

'You do?'

'Of course, they were so chocolatey and delicious.'

'That's probably because I used to sneak in extra hot chocolate powder when my mum wasn't looking.'

'That'd explain it then. Don't suppose you still make them, do you?'

'I do actually, when I'm not busy baking cakes, that is.'

'It didn't come as a surprise when I saw you made celebration cakes for a living. Your creative streak was evident when we were kids.'

'A lifetime ago,' Jasmine said wistfully.

'Yeah, a lifetime ago.' Max inhaled deeply and ran a hand over his close-cropped hair, his eyes shining as he looked at her. 'We've got so much catching up to do, Jingilby. I don't know where to start.'

'My mum and dad were so chuffed to hear I'd seen you in town, they'll be even more delighted when I tell them you live here and are not just visiting. They're looking forward to seeing you again, if you've got time to pop in on them.' It suddenly crossed Jasmine's mind that if this was Max's home, and the swanky cars on the drive belonged to him, then his fortunes had clearly changed since he'd left Micklewick Bay. He might have some high-flying business to run and no time for visiting people. Her next thought was to wonder what had brought about such a change in his circumstances.

'Of course I've got time to see your parents! I've been desperate to know how you've all been doing.' He reached for his mug, his expression serious. 'So, Zak's father...? Connor said he... passed away – sorry to hear that, by the way.'

Jasmine huffed out a sigh. 'That's a very long story, and definitely not for right now.' She'd hate for Zak, or any of the children for that matter, to walk in and hear her talking about what had happened. 'All I'll say is that, yes, he's no longer with us. He's been gone seven years now.' She swallowed. Now wasn't the time to let the memories of such a painful time sneak in. 'How about you? Zak mentioned his mum's not around.' She winced inwardly, wishing she'd worded that better, especially with Max's history.

'Yeah, we parted company when Connor was a baby. Being a mother wasn't for her, she said.' He paused, lost in his thoughts for a moment. 'If you're thinking it's a case of history repeating itself, you wouldn't be wrong.'

'Oh, Max, I'm so sorry.' She was taken by the urge to reach out and take his hand but thought better of it, and besides, the island was so vast, she very much doubted she'd be able to reach him from her side of it.

He pushed his mouth into a smile, and it struck Jasmine that there was no trace of the chipped front tooth he'd had when he left town. 'Hey, don't be. Connor and me are doing just fine, we make a great team. And when I said it was history repeating itself, that's not strictly true. I'm not quite as flaky as my dad. I put my lad's needs way, way before my own. Connor's my world. He's brought so much joy into my life, I can't even begin to put it into words. My driving force is to make sure he feels happy and secure and loved.'

Jasmine was blindsided by a bolt of emotion, hitting her with such force it almost took her breath away. Despite all he'd been through as a small boy – the rejection by his mother and distinct lack of care from his father – hearing Max describe his love for his son was incredibly moving. It also struck a chord with her.

'I get that, it's the same for me with my kids, they're everything to me.'

Their eyes met, a mutual understanding exchanged without words.

'Listen, we've got loads of catching up to do, and some of it has the potential to be pretty heavy, so why don't we save that for another day and haul out some happy memories instead?' Max suggested, his tone upbeat. 'We've got shedloads of those.'

'What? You mean like the day you were leaning over the railings on the bottom prom and your ice cream fell right on top of that bald man's head? That sort of thing?'

Max released a deep chuckle that was so full of mischief and mirth, she couldn't help but join in. The memory that they'd regularly fallen about laughing when they were children bloomed in her mind. He'd had an infectious laugh as a little boy, and once he'd started with his throaty giggle that seemed to bubble up from his boots, he'd set her off, the pair of them unable to stop even though their cheeks and sides were aching.

'How could I have forgotten about that? I'll have you know I don't class losing my ice cream in such a way a happy memory. Scarred me for life, actually.' He tried to pull a serious face, but his laughter spluttered through.

'I reckon it's a happier one than it was for the bald fella it landed on.' Jasmine was laughing so hard, she had to wipe tears from her eyes.

'He was so cross his face went purple. We had to scarper. Don't think I've ever run so fast in my life.'

'It's cos he thought you'd done it on purpose.'

'D'you remember the splat sound it made when it made contact with skin?' asked Max, sending them into further hysterics.

The two old friends were bent double with laughter, their shoulders shaking hard when a voice pulled them back down to earth.

'Someone's having fun.'

EIGHTEEN

They turned to see Sabrina standing in the doorway. She was wearing a pair of oversized sunglasses which meant there was no way of telling if her smile reached her eyes. Though, if her tone was anything to go by, Jasmine was sure she detected a note of disapproval.

Uh-oh! She really didn't want to get on the wrong side of Max's PA – or girlfriend, if that was the case – so soon.

'Ah, Sabrina, we were just having a little wander down memory lane.' Traces of amusement still lingered in Max's words. 'Jingilby and I go back a long way.'

'So I see.' Sabrina sauntered in and retrieved a glass from one of the overhead cupboards, setting it down firmly on the worktop before filling it with freshly squeezed orange juice she pulled from the fridge. There was a coolness to her body language that hadn't been apparent when she'd called at Jasmine's house that morning.

'How are the lads doing? D'you reckon they'd like an ice lolly to cool down?' Max asked.

'I think they'd love that. They could do with calming down a bit, too, it's sweltering out there, too hot to be racing around.'

Sabrina pushed her glasses onto her head, apparently reluctant to make eye contact with Jasmine.

'Great, I'll give them a shout.' Max slid off his stool and headed out into the garden, leaving Jasmine feeling suddenly awkward with Sabrina. She racked her brains for something to say, but the PA got there first.

'So, were you just passing and decided to pop in?' Sabrina asked, fixing Jasmine with her cool, blue gaze.

'No, Zak forgot his backpack. I was distracted by my phone ringing when you were leaving so it slipped my mind. I found it when I went to get some washing from his bedroom.'

'Ah. So, you thought you'd drop it off?'

Jasmine shrugged. 'I did, yeah.' Why was she being made to feel that she'd done something wrong? 'I didn't want Zak to fret about not having his stuff.' She was beginning to regret accepting Max's invitation into the house. Much as she was desperate to find out what he'd been doing all these years, she should've suggested a catch up at her home, or her parents'. They would be delighted to see him. That way she would've avoided this uncomfortable exchange.

A loaded silence stretched out. Jasmine wondered if every woman who entered Max's home was given the frosty treatment.

'So, have you worked for Max long?' She regretted the question as soon as it left her mouth, hoping it didn't sound like she was prying or trying to ascertain their relationship.

Sabrina lifted her glass to her mouth and took a slow drink, as if she was giving her answer some careful consideration. 'I've worked for him for the last five years, known him for seven.'

'Right, yeah, that's good. I bet he keeps you busy.' *What are you saying? Why are you talking such drivel, woman? Get a grip! Stop now!*

Sabrina gave a thinly disguised snort accompanied by a small hitch of her eyebrows. 'Oh, he does that all right.'

Jasmine couldn't have been more relieved when half a dozen rosy-cheeked boys bounded into the kitchen, filling the room with their energy and enthusiasm, snuffing out the awkwardness that had started to swamp her. Hot on their heels was Ernest, his ears flapping, tongue lolling, and if his expression was anything to go by, he seemed to be having as much fun as the boys.

Spotting their visitor, Ernest raced over to her, but he was going at such a pace, he skidded straight past her and spun around on the polished marble floor, making everyone howl with laughter. Even Sabrina cracked a smile, albeit small.

With his paws scrabbling to gain purchase, Ernest finally reached Jasmine, pushing his head onto her lap, his fluffy tail wagging at great speed. She looked down at the two amber eyes gazing up at her and her heart melted. 'Hello again, Ernest.' She smoothed her hand over his soft head. 'You having fun?' Ernest's tail wagging upped its speed and he gave a happy whimper. Jasmine gave him a tickle behind the ear.

'You've made a friend for life if you keep doing that,' Max said, folding his arms across his chest as he looked on.

'Don't know about you, Ernest, but I'd be happy with that.' Jasmine giggled at the dog's blissed-out expression.

In the next moment, Sabrina clicked her tongue and called for Ernest. 'Come on, out you get, mister. You can't go pushing yourself onto strangers like that, you know.' She took him by the collar and led him away from Jasmine, and out into the garden. Sliding the large glass door shut, she left Ernest peering in at them, puzzled as to why he'd been banished.

Jasmine wanted to say she was a dog lover and really didn't mind but thought better of it. She had a feeling such a comment wouldn't go down well with Max's PA.

'Hiya, Mum.' Zak appeared beside her. It hadn't escaped Jasmine's attention that his face had fallen as soon as he'd spotted her. 'How come you're here?' he asked.

'Just dropping off your sleepover stuff. You left your backpack in your bedroom.'

'Ah, cool. Thanks.' His expression brightened, lighting up his eyes. 'We've been having a totally mint time and we're going for a swim in the indoor pool after we've had some ice lollies. Connor's got an inflatable dinosaur. Then after that we're gonna watch a movie in the private cinema.'

'Sounds like you're having loads of fun.' Her eyes landed on Connor. She was struck by how much he resembled Max at that age, from his hazel eyes, russet curls and cheeky smile. He even had a crop of freckles that danced over his nose and cheeks, just as his dad used to have. She wondered what part of him resembled his mother.

With the ice lollies devoured, the boys had changed into their swimming shorts and headed to the indoor pool which, Jasmine was informed, was in the basement and next door to the room that housed the cinema. Sabrina accompanied them to keep an eye on things and to make sure they played safely. Jasmine felt instantly at ease once she'd gone. If Max had noticed the atmosphere had lifted, he kept it to himself.

They slipped back into their reminiscences, keeping the topics light, skirting around the less palatable subjects, like Scraggo and Max's father's arrest. They were definitely best left for another day. Apart from the Friday evenings at the Jolly with her friends, she'd forgotten what it was like to switch off and have an impromptu chat like this. It felt good and reminded her of how Max used to be such easy company.

Jasmine's eye caught the large clock on the wall, giving her a jolt. 'Crikey, is that the time? I'm really sorry, I didn't mean to stay so long.' She hoped she hadn't interfered with Max's plans for Connor's birthday or over-stayed her welcome.

'You've hardly been here any time at all. You're welcome to

stay for dinner, if you like?' Was that a hopeful look in Max's eye she detected? She wasn't so sure the same welcome would be extended by Sabrina.

'Sounds lovely, but I'd best get back. I've got another cake to make a start on.' She jumped up, tucking the bar stool under the island. The unfriendly vibes that had radiated from Sabrina had unsettled her a little and she doubted her presence there any longer, never mind joining them for food later on, would go down well. Though things had improved somewhat, after the week she'd had, Jasmine still felt drained and would rather not have to spend her evening negotiating the PA's hostility. 'And I've pulled you away from Connor's party way too much already.'

'You really haven't; he'll be having a much better time without his uncool dad hanging around him and his mates and cracking sad dad jokes.'

'Hardly. But I reckon Zak would prefer it if I went, so I'll head back home.'

'That's a shame, we've still got so much to catch up on. I want to hear all about what you've been up to, hear about your parents, and Jonathan – how's he doing, by the way?' Max shoved his hands into the pockets of his shorts.

'Jonathan's fine.' Mention of her big brother made her smile. 'He's still footie mad, much to Flic, his wife's, frustration. They have their own building firm, live just outside of York in a house Jon built – with their two boys, who are also footie mad.' An idea started circling around her mind.

'Sounds like life's treated him well.'

'It has; he's happy as Larry.' She hooked her bag over her shoulder, fiddling with the zip as she made up her mind whether to share what she'd been thinking.

'That's good to hear. Tell him I was asking after him next time you see him.'

'Will do.' She loitered a moment. 'Listen, this is just a

suggestion, but why don't you and Connor join us at my parents' for lunch tomorrow? Dad's doing a barbecue, there'll be plenty of food to go round.' She recalled how Max always used to get excited by her parents' barbecues. 'Like I said, they'd be over the moon to see you. They often mention you, wondering how you're doing.'

'They do?'

'Of course. They thought a lot about you, Max.' She looked up to see a pair of gentle eyes gazing back at her, faint shadows of the past lingering behind them. 'You turning up with a Max mini-me would absolutely make their day,' she said with a laugh. 'Unless you've got other plans, of course.'

'I'd love to see your parents again, and, if you're sure it'll be okay, tomorrow sounds perfect. We can all have a catch up together.'

'Fab. They still live in the same house, believe it or not. Think you can find your way?' she asked jokingly.

'Jingilby, I could always find my way to your parents' home.' He held her gaze for several long moments.

After refusing his offer of a lift home, Max swept her into a tight hug, kissing her cheek. 'I can't tell you how good it is to see you again, Jingilby.'

Despite not being much of a hugger – her hugs were reserved solely for her children, parents and close friends; she visibly recoiled at the first sign of physical affection from anyone else – Jasmine found herself quite liking how it felt to be wrapped in Max's strong arms.

NINETEEN

Jasmine picked her way along the cliff path, her mind running over what it was about Max's hugs that made them feel so different. Or rather, made *her* feel so different. Not that she'd hugged many men. In fact, she'd started dating Bart Forster when she was sixteen. He'd been her first boyfriend and about as affectionate as a wet fish, but he'd had a brilliant sense of humour which was what she'd found so appealing about him. Whenever the doubts surfaced, particularly when he seemed to prefer spending time feeding money into the slot machines – sometimes *her* money – he always managed to reel her back in by making her laugh and pushing her misgivings away; in the early days, at least. She'd lost count of the number of times she wished she'd listened to her friends, warning her against him. But at least something good had come out of her relationship with him: Zak and Chloe. And she wouldn't change that for the world.

Bart may have been able to make her laugh, but his hugs had never felt anything like the two she'd just had from Max. And neither had Lewis Murry's, the lad she'd briefly dated when she and Bart had broken up for a couple of months. The feelings Max's hugs had triggered were in a different league altogether. Maybe it's because they'd been friends way back and had instantly fallen into their old friendship, she reasoned with herself. Like slipping on a pair of comfy slippers, or a snuggly cardigan; they were always guaranteed to feel good.

As she walked on, she told herself it was the unusually hot weather that was causing her pulse to gallop and her stomach to flip-flop whenever she thought of him, and nothing at all to do with his warm, enveloping hugs. And she'd thought of him pretty much every step of the way so far. What was going on?

Max Grainger had left Micklewick Bay a skinny, scrawny little scrap with wild curls, and had returned a broad-shouldered man with captivating hazel eyes and a voice that could melt chocolate.

Oh, my days!

By the time Jasmine had reached the end of the track, she'd finally worked out what it was about Max's hugs that evoked feelings Bart and Lewis's hadn't: they made her feel safe. Other than her dad, no man had ever made her feel that way before.

How did two brief hugs have the power to do that? she wondered. It didn't make any kind of sense. But she'd surprised herself by thinking she'd quite like some more.

She threw her head back and groaned. 'What is going on with you, Ingilby? You need to get that notion right out of your head. You don't need hugs from any man, never mind Max Grainger, and he certainly doesn't need any from you. The heat's clearly mashed your brain!' She had enough to think about, what with having to find somewhere new to live and chase the garage about her car. It didn't help that the trouble with the Scraggs was never far from her mind. She hadn't mentioned Scraggo's return to Max, not wanting the news to put a cloud over Connor's party.

She upped her pace, arms swinging. She needed to rid herself of this totally out of character madness before she next saw her friends. Their reaction didn't bear thinking about, with all the knowing looks, not-so-discreet nudges, and twitching eyebrows. It was already a given that they'd pin her down and question her relentlessly until they'd squeezed every last minuscule detail out of her. And, worse, she knew however much she denied these weird, new feelings, there'd be no hiding it from Lark, with all her extra sense whatdoyoumacallit going on. Jasmine had a funny feeling her friend already knew, if what she'd been hinting at last night in the pub was anything to go by. But despite her anticipated struggles to get the message across, and whatever it was that was causing chaos inside her, her stance still remained the same: she had neither the time, nor the inclination for a man in her life. Including Max Grainger. *Especially* Max Grainger! End of.

Jasmine finally reached the top prom, the view opening and embracing the beach and cliffs up ahead. The temperature had dropped a little, and she welcomed the cooler breeze that was blowing in from the sea and cutting through the headache-inducing mugginess that had been hanging in the air for much of the day. As she strode along, her mind went over what could have brought Max back to Micklewick Bay. She'd been too lost in thought to notice that overhead, dense gunmetal clouds were gathering, smothering all traces of sunshine. A large drop of rain landed on her cheek, quickly followed by one on her arm.

'Oh!'

Before she knew it, the sky darkened and the raindrops increased in number. A boom of thunder rang out and lightning streaked across the sky. People started rushing about her, diving for cover in the bus stops, taking shelter in their cars if they were lucky enough to be nearby. It didn't take long for numbers to thin and before she knew it, she was alone.

Jasmine upped her pace, her sandals slapping against the wet flagstones. She was so focused on getting back home quickly that she hadn't noticed a car slowing down beside her.

'Well, well, well. I'd know that ginger mop anywhere. I was hoping I'd run into you. Been keeping an eye out for you.'

She turned, starting when she saw a heavily tattooed man looking back at her, a cruel sneer on his skeletal face revealing a missing front tooth while those that remained were at varying stages of decay. Almost every inch of his face had been darkly inked and studded with multiple piercings, including a bull ring through his nose. The dense pattern of tattoos continued over his shaved head, and onto his arm that rested on the open window. A sheen of sweat glistened dangerously over his skin. Whoever he was, he made for an intimidating sight.

Adhering to her policy of not engaging with strangers who tried to strike up conversation, especially those who triggered a warning in her gut, she pushed on, head bowed against the rain, arms hugging her chest. She didn't know him from Adam; he'd clearly mistaken her for someone else.

'Oi! Don't be ignorant. I'm talking to you!' He continued to drive alongside her, revving his car in a pathetic display of machismo.

The rain was coming down harder now, bouncing off the pavement. A crash of thunder ricocheted off the walls of the grand Victorian properties on the other side of the road, lightning illuminating the sky. Jasmine shivered as cold set in.

'I said, I'm talking to you!' His tone suggested her silence was only serving to annoy him.

Reluctant as she was to engage with him, she didn't want to anger him further by ignoring him. 'You must be confusing me with someone else. I've never met you before in my life,' she called across, veering away from his car.

'That's where you're wrong, Jasmine Ingilby.'

Her face fell as a rash of goosebumps erupted over her skin.

TWENTY

How does he know my name? She continued to hurry along, panic pushing her faster. She was desperate to get home, and thankful Zak and Chloe weren't with her. A couple of cars drove by, their tyres swishing through the puddles. She heard the sound of a car door closing nearby and her heart rate accelerated. *Why is the creep following me?*

'Oi! Get here! There's summat I wanna say to you.'

She darted a look in the direction of the voice to see a short, skinny man walking towards her with an exaggerated ape-swagger. Ignoring him, she continued along the path, panic shooting through her as she realised there was no one else around, her heart thumping hard in her chest.

'I said, I wanna word with you.'

Hearing the thud of his shoes as he bore down on her, she went to run, her heart now hurling itself against her ribcage. In the next moment, she felt the grip of his fingers digging into her shoulder. She tried to yank herself away but found herself being pulled back by the soaked fabric of her T-shirt.

Every instinct told Jasmine to fight and scream at the top of her lungs. 'Get off me! Get off me!' she yelled loudly, pinching the fleshy underside of his arm, digging her nails in as hard as she could and twisting the skin.

'Argh!' he yelped.

She yanked herself free, her green eyes ablaze. 'Touch me again and you'll get a kick in the balls! I know how to look after myself. You'll come off worse.' Thunder echoed around them. Jasmine wiped the rain from her eyes, her chest heaving.

'That bloody hurt,' he said, rubbing where her nails had left their mark. 'I could sue you for assault.'

'Don't fancy your chances, buster,' Jasmine said, as she moved away from him. A lightning-quick appraisal told her he was only a couple of inches taller than her and on the puny side. 'Men like you who think it's okay to intimidate women are pathetic and despicable.' She spat the words out, rage coursing through her. 'You should be locked up and the key thrown away.'

Her words must've hit a nerve as, before she knew it, he'd pushed his chest out and started walking towards her. 'That right?'

She felt utterly fearless. He'd picked on the wrong woman. 'Yes! that's right! There's no room for the likes of you in this world anymore.'

He pulled his top lip back in a snigger, showing his mouthful of snaggled, rotten teeth. 'All I wanted was to have a word. That's not unreasonable. What was I supposed to do if you wouldn't listen? You didn't give me any choice, did ya?' The ape-swagger was in full swing and his voice had taken on a sinister tone.

'I don't know who you are, you can have nothing to say to me. So you'd better keep away!'

'That's where you're wrong, Jasmine Ingilby. We do know each other.' He smirked, drawing closer, his eyes mean and hard. 'It's got back to me that you and your brats have been causing trouble for my kids. And I'm seriously brassed off about it. You need to back off running up to school and telling tales to the teachers like you and your pathetic friends used to do for me when we were there. You won't get away with it this time.'

'What?' *No! This was Jason Scragg?* Had he been deliberately driving around looking for her to get this message across? Fear that things weren't as under control with the Scragg children as she'd hoped pushed to the forefront of her mind. She was half aware of the pounding of feet nearby as Scraggo moved closer.

'Jingilby! Are you okay?' In the next moment, Max was standing beside her, his arm sliding across her shoulders. 'What's going on?'

'Who the hell...?' Jason Scragg stepped back, glancing up at Max, his callous sneer replaced by a look of alarm.

'I could ask you the same thing, and why you're bothering my friend.' Rain splashed up from the pavement.

'Keep your hair on. And anyroad, it's nowt to do with you, I was just having a word, that's all. Nowt to get het up about.'

'Didn't look like nowt to me, looked like you were making a nuisance of yourself.' Max towered over Scraggo, his eyes hardened in a way that took Jasmine by surprise.

'Aye, well, you were mistaken.' Scraggo backed away. 'I'm off now.'

They watched as he scuttled over to his car, all trace of the ape-swagger gone.

'What was that all about?' Max asked, looking down at Jasmine, his shirt drenched.

'I'm afraid that was Jason Scragg – I daresay you remember him.' She watched Max's reaction, his eyes betraying his feelings as realisation dawned.

'He's a hard one to forget,' he said coolly, watching the car screech away. 'He didn't hurt you, did he?'

Jasmine shook her head. 'It was the other way round. And I

left him in no doubt that I wouldn't hesitate to fight back if he gave me any crap.'

'Still fearless, then, Jingilby?' He drew her closer to him, smoothing his hand over the top of her arm, oblivious to the rain.

'You'd better believe it.' She was aware of her body pressed against his, the warmth he was generating seeping through her saturated clothing.

'That's good to hear,' he said, grinning down at her, his eyes soft.

'I hate to say it, but he's landed back in town, has two kids the same age as Zak and Chloe – Connor, too,' she added reluctantly, knowing how it would worry Max. 'They haven't been here long but already they've made their mark at school.'

'Which can only be bad news.'

'I know. It wasn't pleasant at first, but I feel confident that school has got it under control. The headteacher's brilliant, won't tolerate bullying. She's fully aware of the situation.' She glanced up at him. 'She's nothing like Old Troutface.'

'I'd be hard to be worse.'

Jasmine was struck by a thought. 'How come you're here?' she asked, looking up at him. With the adrenalin that had been pumping through her only moments ago now draining away, she was suddenly aware of how cold she felt. She was soaked right through to her underwear and her clothes were clinging to her skin. She started shivering uncontrollably.

'I saw it had started to rain and I remembered you didn't have a coat, thought you might need a lift.'

She glanced over to the shiny vehicle she'd seen parked on the gravel at his house. 'But I'm absolutely drenched, I'll leave a soggy puddle in your car,' she said through chattering teeth.

'You think I'm bothered about that kind of thing?' he asked, as thunder reverberated around them. 'Come on, let's get out of this crazy weather.'

Lightning lit up the sky again, illuminating the grey storm clouds that were angrily tumbling over one another. Max took Jasmine's hand and they raced over to the car, her feet squelching in her sandals. He opened the door for her and she jumped in gratefully.

'Ugh! I feel liked a drowned rat!' She ran her hand over her hair that was plastered to her head. She was sure she must look a sight.

'Well, you're the prettiest drowned rat I've ever seen.'

'No one's ever said that to me before.' They both burst out laughing at that. If there was a compliment in there, Jasmine chose to ignore it.

'Right then, Jingilby, let's get you home. It's Rosemary Terrace, isn't it?'

'That's right, the less salubrious part of town.'

He looked across at her but didn't say anything.

With the wipers swishing frantically back and forth on the windscreen, she guided him along the streets to her home, thinking she'd never been in a car as fancy as this one. The seats – which had taken her completely by surprise by growing warm – were plush leather. 'I make no apologies if I start steaming,' she joked. The dashboard had a variety of screens that she thought were more akin to an aircraft's cockpit. It was a far cry from the ancient little banger she drove – when it was working, of course. And then there was his mossy cologne that lingered. She inhaled deeply, her senses sitting up and taking notice.

'Now, don't be shocked by my home. I dare say it's probably half the size of your garden shed,' she said as they pulled up outside it.

'Size isn't everything.'

She gave him a sideways look, catching his eye. 'Bet you say that to all the girls,' she quipped, and they both burst out laughing.

'I can't believe I just said that.' Max clapped his hand to his forehead. 'I just meant something doesn't have to be big to be... Ugh!'

Jasmine watched him squirm, her eyebrows quirking in amusement. 'I get your point. Now, would you like to come in for a cuppa, or do you need to get back to the party?'

As grateful as she was for the lift and thought it only polite to invite Max in, she really wanted to make a start on planning her next cake or it was going to be another late night. She didn't even want to think about the pile of ironing that would be waiting for her.

'Much as I'd love to, I'm aware you've got things to do, and I should probably be heading back to Connor and his mates. I could drop Zak off in the morning, if you like? Or whenever suits, he's welcome to stay with us as long as he fancies. I know Connor would love that. I could maybe grab a cup of tea then, do a bit more catching up, if you've got time?'

'Sounds good.' With the rain drumming on the roof of the car, Jasmine became suddenly acutely aware of her close proximity to Max. From her seat, the gold flashes in his hazel eyes were more noticeable, as were the freckles he'd evidently hung on to from boyhood. She felt a flutter in her stomach and was sure she could hear her heart thumping inside her chest. She hoped he couldn't hear it, too. That would be mortifying! She found herself being torn between wanting to spend more time with him, and wanting him to leave. Fear of the unfamiliar feelings he'd triggered had unsettled her. She needed to regain an element of control, put them in order and get back to normal. *Max Grainger is an old friend, you're pleased he's back, happy he's doing well for himself. That's all it is, nothing more.*

'Tell you what, we could always go to my parents' house straight from here, if you like?' she said. 'Say, midday?'

'Won't the weather mean the barbecue's cancelled?'

'My mum'll do a roast if it's still raining; she'll be keeping a close eye on the forecast, she likes to be organised.'

'I remember,' Max said fondly. 'I'm really looking forward to seeing her and Uncle Steve again. And I'm not saying your mum's Sunday roasts are the reason I came back to Micklewick Bay, but they were pretty legendary!'

'I can't wait to see their faces when they realise who you are.' They both smiled at that, Jasmine wondering if Max would tell her what had brought him back to the town. 'Oh, and Ernest's welcome, too.'

'You sure?'

'I'm positive.'

'You're moving, or is that for next door?' He nodded towards the For Sale sign.

'No, it's advertising mine,' she said wearily. 'The landlord's decided he wants to sell up. He reckons property round here has suddenly become very desirable. Given me a bit of a headache to be honest; rental properties like this are hard to come by. I've already had one of the town's most unsavoury businessmen sniffing round it. You might know him: Dick Swales, a.k.a. Dodgy Dick.'

'Hmm. I know of him.' Max paused for a moment, looking thoughtful. 'I can imagine Victorian terraces like yours have retained a lot of their original features. They'll be perfect for first-time buyers who have a bit of money in their pocket.'

'I s'pose so.' *Lucky them.*

After a couple of minutes' small talk, she unclicked her seat belt. 'Right, I'd best go, but thanks for the lift and helping me see Scraggo off.'

'Hey, you had it all under control, you didn't need any help from me.' Max raised his hands, chuckling.

'That may be so, but I appreciate the moral support all the same.' Stella had seen to it that the group of friends had all attended self-defence classes. Her line of work as a criminal barrister had made her aware that there were some decidedly unpleasant characters out there, and she'd told her friends she wanted to make sure they could all defend themselves if necessary. Jasmine had enjoyed the empowering feeling it had given her, not that she'd ever had to put it to use. After her encounter with Jason Scragg, it made her glad to have it under her belt.

She went to open the door, but struggled to find the handle. 'How the bloomin' 'eck do I get out? It's like some kind of mental agility test.' She laughed.

'It's just here. S'cuse me.' Max leant across as Jasmine pushed herself back into her seat, the skin of his arm brushing against hers.

'Oh!' His touch had sent an unexpected bolt of electricity shooting through her, briefly knocking her off kilter. She cleared her throat. 'So, that's where the handle is,' she said, adopting a casual tone.

Their eyes met as he went to move back. Jasmine could feel the colour rise in her cheeks and dropped her gaze to her hands.

'Well, um... thanks again for the lift.'

'No problem.'

'I'll see you tomorrow.'

'You will, indeed.' Max smiled, giving a happy sigh. 'I know I keep saying it, but it really has been great to see you again, Jingilby. You and your family have never been far from my thoughts ever since I left.' He leant across and kissed her cheek. 'See you tomorrow.'

'Yeah, see you tomorrow.'

How she'd managed the short walk across the pavement and into her house, Jasmine would never know. Her legs felt like they could buckle under her at any minute as she kicked off her sodden sandals and made her way down the hall to the kitchen. What was going on with her? Why was Max Grainger, her friend of over twenty years ago, making her feel all unnecessary after suddenly bursting back into her life? It made no sense.

And it wasn't just that, but the feelings that were currently swirling around her, she'd switched them off years ago, swearing to herself she was never going to let another man in, that she wasn't going to expose herself to hurt and heartache again. She'd built her walls so high, she could barely see over them. Which was just the way she liked it. It had been just her and the kids for the last seven years, and that was how it was going to stay.

She released a frustrated groan as she headed upstairs to get changed out of her wet clothes. She wasn't ready to head down that route; she had too many other things to occupy her thoughts.

The Scraggo incident, for example. The reminder of her unexpected confrontation with her former nemesis had a sobering effect. She quickly made up her mind to alert the staff at school about what had happened, the threats he'd made. She wasn't going to allow his bullying ways to intimidate her, and nor was she going to tolerate his children targeting Zak and Chloe because of the history between her and their father. He and they needed to get the message as soon as possible.

TWENTY-ONE

Sunday morning dawned bright and clear with a cerulean sky washed clear of the rain and storm clouds of the previous evening. The sun was shining brightly and the birds were singing. Jasmine had just finished hanging a load of washing on the line in the small backyard when she heard the sound of a car pulling up outside.

Moments later, Zak burst through the door, Connor close behind. Both were wearing their Micklewick Lions football strip.

'Mum! Mum! Are Connor and Max really coming for a barbecue with us at Grandma and Grandad's?' Zak asked excitedly.

'Hi, Zak. Hi, Connor.' Jasmine smiled at the two boys. 'Yes, they really are.' Jasmine smoothed her hand over her son's head. She resisted the urge to kiss him, not wanting to make him feel self-conscious.

'Awesome!' said Zak.

'Mint!' said Connor.

'Connor's dad has a really cool car. He said I can drive it when I'm old enough.'

'Oh, wow! That's kind of him.'

'I know!'

'Hi, Jingilby.'

Jasmine's attention was drawn to the doorway to see Max standing there, Zak's backpack in his hand, aviator sunglasses pushed back onto his head. He was looking casually stylish in a striped short-sleeved shirt and chinos, a pair of leather trainers on his feet. The smile he gave made her heart give an unexpected flutter.

'Hi, Max.' She smiled back at him.

'Are the plans for today still on?' he asked. Jasmine was sure she detected a hopeful gleam in his eye.

'Very much so. I've been reliably informed by my mum that it's full steam ahead for the barbecue.'

'Great.'

'I still haven't told them about you and Connor, though, I want to keep it as a surprise for them.'

'I hardly slept a wink for thinking about today,' he said. 'It has something of a monumental feel to it, almost like returning to your roots, if that doesn't sound too melodramatic.'

'It doesn't at all, I can totally get where you're coming from.' She held back from adding that the last few weeks before he'd left so suddenly had been a heck of a build-up for a young child. She'd leave it to Max to bring that up when he was ready.

'No Ernest?' she asked.

'He's still in the car. I thought I'd better double-check he was still welcome to go to your parents'. Ernest and barbecues are a deadly combination.'

'It'll be the Labrador in him. And, honestly, he'll definitely be welcome at my parents'. He's got bags of personality, they'll love him.'

'Let's hope he treats them to his full charm offensive then.'

It hadn't crossed her mind to invite Sabrina. She felt a twinge of guilt at that. Though, in fairness, as far as she was concerned, Sabrina was Max's PA and hadn't been introduced as anything more, so no one would expect the invitation to be extended to her. It hadn't been intended as a snub. And Jasmine had a feeling Sabrina wouldn't enjoy such a get-together anyway, especially if it was filled with chats about shared memories of which she had no involvement or knowledge. She'd brace herself for an extra frosty reaction the next time their paths crossed.

The smoky tang of a barbecue filled the air as they all headed down the path of number eight Arkleby Terrace. The two boys headed in first, dashing through to the back garden, leaving Jasmine – whose hands were full with a large homemade strawberry cheesecake covered in foil – and Max with Ernest on a tight lead. Jasmine noted Max give his old home nothing more than a cursory glance. She understood why, it being a place of unhappy memories for him, unlike her parents' house.

'Are you sure your mum and dad won't mind having two unexpected mouths to feed, not to mention me turning up with a rather lively hound?' Max asked, looking uncertain as they stepped into the kitchen.

'I'm positive. Stop fretting, they'll be overjoyed to see you.' Jasmine slid the cheesecake into the fridge so it wouldn't melt before they were ready to tuck into it.

Just then, Chloe skipped into the hallway, her strawberry-blonde hair in a long plait down her back, her face shiny with sunblock. 'Hi, Mummy.' She wrapped her arms around Jasmine's middle, peeking shyly at Max before switching her gaze to Ernest whose tail was wagging hard.

'Hello, sweetheart, did you have fun last night?' Jasmine kissed the top of her daughter's head, which felt warm from her playing in the sun.

'Yes, thank you. The film was really good, but Grandad fell

asleep and started snoring. It was so loud it made people laugh.' She covered her mouth with her hand and giggled.

'Not again! What's your grandad like, Chlo?'

'I know.' Chloe stole another look at Max.

'Hi there, Chloe.' Max smiled and raised his hand in a small wave. Ernest whimpered, eager to make friends.

'Hello.' She leant into her mum and whispered, 'Who's that?'

'This is Connor's dad. He's a friend of mine from way back when I was your age and even younger.'

'Oh, okay. And now Connor's a friend of Zak's.'

'That's right.' Jasmine loved how accepting young children could be.

'I like your dog,' said Chloe. 'What's he called?'

'He's called Ernest, and I think he likes you, too, he's keen to say hello.' Max let Ernest's lead out a little so he could reach Chloe. 'He's a big fan of tummy tickles and ear ruffles. Oh, and watch him with your ice creams. I'm afraid he's been known to steal them given half a chance.'

Chloe giggled at that. 'Hi, Ernest.' She let him sniff her hand before giving his ears a quick scratch. Jasmine looked on, smiling.

'Come on, let's go through and see Grandma and Grandad.' Jasmine guided Chloe through to the kitchen, Max and Ernest following. Turning to Max, she said, 'I can't wait to see their faces.'

The back garden was bathed in sunshine, with the flowerbeds a riot of colour, and the small lawn area neatly trimmed. A football net sat at the furthest end. The picnic table had already been set, and cheery music played from the speakers next to the barbecue where Jasmine's dad was poised ready to take charge in his role as head chef. Her mum had a plate piled with raw burgers and sausages in her hand as she chatted to Zak and Connor.

'Hi there, folks,' Jasmine said, in a bid to get her parents' attention.

'Hello, lovey. Tell you what, I aren't half glad that rain stopped. I thought I was going to have to—' Her mum turned, her face a picture of confusion as she took in the tall man standing next to her daughter, the large dog on the end of a lead. 'Oh, hello there,' she said, addressing the stranger, her eyes flicking back to Jasmine who could only imagine as to the questions currently racing through her mum's mind, and she found herself having to stifle a giggle.

Her dad pulled his gaze away from setting out the barbecue utensils. 'Ey up, who've we got here, then?'

'Mummy's got a new friend,' announced Chloe.

'Has she now?' said Heather.

'And he's got a dog called Ernest.' Chloe treated Ernest to a scratch between his ears.

'Mum, Dad, I've got a surprise for you,' said Jasmine.

'You do?' Heather said, confusion clearly putting her at a loss for words. She set the plate down on the food preparation table next to Steve.

Jasmine couldn't help but laugh. They were completely thrown by the concept of her bringing a man to their home, but, she supposed, it had been a while.

'You remember little Max Grainger, don't you?' she said.

Heather glanced from Jasmine to Max, then to her husband, before settling on Jasmine again. 'Aye, course I do. Why?'

Jasmine stood aside. 'Max is here, Mum. This is Max. He's moved back to Micklewick Bay. He's Connor's dad.'

'Hi, Auntie Heather, Uncle Steve.' Max gave an apprehensive smile. 'It's good to see you. I hope you don't mind us gate-crashing your barbecue.'

The uncertainty in his voice tugged at Jasmine's heart-strings. She watched as her parents' expressions morphed from utter shock to unbridled delight as this new set of circumstances sank in.

'Well, I never,' said Steve, dropping his barbecue tongs.

'Max? Little Max Grainger? Oh, my goodness! I can't believe it!' Heather clapped her hands to her face. 'Oh, lovey, come here.'

She hurried over to Max, sweeping him into her embrace, kissing his cheek, just as she'd done when he was a small boy, tears trickling down her face. 'What a wonderful surprise! It's so fantastic to see you, my love.' Keen to be part of the welcome, Ernest nudged at her legs, his tail swishing from side to side.

The three children looked on, giggling before turning their attention to the small paddling pool Steve had filled earlier for them to have a splash about if they got too hot.

Max dropped Ernest's lead and returned Heather's hugs with equal warmth, bending to wrap his arms around her. 'It's so good to see you, Auntie Heather. I've been wanting to come and see you for a long time.' His voice cracked. 'I wanted to thank you and Uncle Steve for always being so kind to me.' Ernest trotted over to the children, jumping straight into the paddling pool and making them hoot with laughter.

'Get away with you, there's no need to thank us, but it isn't half grand to see you, sweetheart. Now, let me look at you.' She took a step back, taking his hands in hers as she surveyed him. 'My goodness, it's hard to believe you've grown so tall, you were always such a little scrap of a lad. And I'd recognise those twinkly eyes anywhere. Steve, see what a fine-looking young man our little Max has grown into.'

'Max, welcome back.' From the way her dad was beaming, anyone would be forgiven for thinking he'd won the lottery. 'By 'eck, it isn't half good to see you, lad. You've made our bloomin' day.' Steve hugged him close, patting him soundly on the back, his eyes dancing with happiness.

Jasmine looked on. It was a scene she never thought she'd

ever witness: Max Grainger returning to her parents' home, all grown up with no trace of the skinny little boy he used to be. Both she and her parents had assumed they'd never see Max again, that he'd be swallowed up by a new life, with new friends over in Harrogate, and forget all about them. Their greatest wish for him was that he would be happy and feel settled with his grandfather. It felt good to know that had evidently been the case.

'It'll be just like old days,' said Heather, through happy tears. 'You always used to love it when your Uncle Steve got the barbecue going.'

'I remember.' Max smiled fondly at her, his eyes damp. 'All of my happy memories as a child are of being here, with all of you, and hanging around with Jingilby.'

'Oh, aye, I remember that nickname you had for our Jasmine.' Steve chuckled. 'She used to go mad if anyone else ever dared use it. "Only Max is allowed to call me that," she'd say.'

'Really?' Max said. 'I had no idea.' He looked over at Jasmine.

'Oh, aye, your Uncle Steve's right. The pair of you were very close. We always used to say there was a special bond between you.' Heather reached for the nearby kitchen roll, pulled off a square and dabbed at her eyes.

Thanks for that, Mum and Dad! Jasmine hoped Max wouldn't notice her blushes, but judging by the way he was scrutinising her, she suspected the chance of that was slim. She was relieved when her mum spoke.

'Right, we have a load of catching up to do, so I suggest you get yourself comfy, lovey. Our Jasmine can fetch you a drink and then you can tell us all about what you've been doing right from when you left here that day, sobbing your little heart out, up to the day you moved back to Micklewick Bay.'

'Aye, I reckon the food can wait a bit longer, while we give

Max our full attention. I'll pacify the kids with an ice pop each,' said Steve, before heading in the direction of the kitchen.

Sitting in the shade, a glass of shandy in his hand, Max's chest expanded as he drew in a deep breath. Jasmine and her parents looked on. She felt a thrum of anxiety reverberating around her, preparing herself for what she was about to hear. She'd always hoped Max's new life had been a happy one, that the hard times he'd been through had been left behind in Micklewick Bay. She really hoped she wasn't going to hear something to the contrary.

TWENTY-TWO

'That day I left Micklewick Bay, I thought my heart was actually going to break, it felt like a real, physical pain. I'll never forget it as long as I live. My life had been turned upside down and I was being taken to a place I didn't know, leaving the people I loved, people who'd been the only constant in my life. You and Uncle Steve were like parents to me, Jingilby and Jonathan like siblings and I loved you all.'

A sob escaped Heather's mouth. 'Oh, sweetheart.' She reached over and squeezed Max's hand. Jasmine felt her eyes blur with tears and she quickly blinked them away. In the background the three children were chattering away happily, sitting on the grass and enjoying their ice pops, oblivious to the contents of the conversation going on at the opposite end of the garden.

'On top of that, I didn't know what was going to happen with my dad. I know he hadn't been the best father, but he was still my dad at the end of the day and I was worried for him. The journey to Harrogate seemed to take forever; I'd never spent so long in a car. You probably know better than me, but, up to that point, I hadn't had much contact with my grandfather, and it felt like a stranger was taking me to the opposite side of the world, away from everything and everyone I knew.'

'Please tell me he was kind to you, lovey,' Heather said.

'He was.' Max nodded. 'He was very patient with me actually, did all he could to help me settle. Looking back now, I can see he must've been lonely. My grandma had died a few years earlier – she was only in her fifties – and I could tell how much he missed her from the way he spoke about her. He was actually a really lovely man, I've no idea why my father turned out the way he did. I hasten to add, I'm not telling you all this for you to pity me, it's just with you saying you wanted to know everything that happened from me leaving here...'

'We know that, lad,' Steve reassured him, his voice gruff with emotion. 'You carry on.'

The three listened as Max told them how his introduction to a new school hadn't been anywhere near as terrifying as he'd expected. His grandfather had kitted him out in not just a new uniform, but he'd also got rid of his small collection of shabby clothes. He made sure his grandson showered every day and that his mass of curls were regularly trimmed, combed and clean. His home was warm and he was well-fed and the days of going back to an empty house, not knowing if he was going to be on his own overnight, were a thing of the past. Max had been relieved that the stigma of coming from a dysfunctional home where there was very little care, hadn't followed him to Harrogate. At school there, he wasn't picked on or called names for having dirty clothes and he'd been thrilled to find that he made friends easily.

'I'm not surprised, lovey, you always were a friendly, likeable little lad,' said Heather, her smiles making a return. 'Always full of fun; a little ray of sunshine despite what you had going on at home.'

'I made some good mates there, but there was never anyone

that matched the friendship I had with you, Jingilby.' He lifted his gaze and smiled at her, making her heart squeeze.

Max went on to say he'd been surprised to find how quickly he'd managed to put what had happened with his father behind him. 'Which I suppose was down to my grandfather and his care.' He'd enjoyed his time at school, where he'd thrived and developed a passion for learning. From what Jasmine could glean, it was clear he'd been popular and it gladdened her heart to know that he'd made lots of friends, that he'd no longer been an outcast amongst his peers.

It would seem his enthusiastic nature and innate zest for life had returned, and there'd been no looking back.

His grandfather had nurtured and guided him with a quiet patience, particularly whenever Max had shown an interest in a subject or hobby. And, just as he'd enjoyed helping Jasmine's dad with little jobs, it had been so with his grandfather. Jimmy Grainger had started giving his grandson small tasks in order to earn his weekly pocket money, which Max had squirrelled away, taking pleasure in seeing his savings grow. It had quickly led to Max thinking up other ways he could add to his junior savings account. His first dabble into "entrepreneurship", as his grandad had called it, was to offer his car washing services for their neighbours and other residents in the area. His sunny disposition combined with him leaving their cars gleaming meant Max was often given a bonus for his efforts. It was the same with the path clearing service he'd added to the list of jobs he offered. On top of that, he had a paper round which added to his weekly earnings and was pleased to find his savings soon totted up, even more so when he got a weekend job at a local garden centre, taking on extra shifts during his school holidays.

It meant he was able to pay his way through university, where he'd taken a business degree, which had given him a great sense of achievement, and a taste of what could be done if you put your mind to it. 'The best thing was seeing the look on my grandad's face on graduation day.'

'I can imagine,' said Heather. 'He must've been as pleased as punch.'

Max continued, explaining that it was during his time at university, at the age of nineteen, that he'd set up his first proper "grown-up" business, importing and selling artisanal mugs and cups online. He'd sold the brand name after three years, making his first tidy profit, which he'd put towards the purchase of a floundering local homewares business for which he'd paid peanuts. With a strong vision for the future direction of the store, he'd commissioned new branding, invested in better quality stock and streamlined the range. He'd looked closely at their competitors, analysing the strategies they'd used that had contributed to their success, and applied them to his own business. And he hadn't been afraid to try out new things in a bid to keep one step ahead, which appeared to be something he'd developed a flair for. On top of this, Max had upped the standard of the store's marketing. He'd also enlisted the skills of a photographer friend to take high-quality photos for the company's slick new website. As well as increasing their online presence, he'd worked hard to build bonds with social media influencers which had paid dividends. Having turned that business around and improved its fortunes, he'd sold that, making himself a sizeable profit.

It was during this time Max had employed his first member of staff. Marketing executive Danielle Clarke – or Danni, as she preferred to be called – not only had impressive credentials in her field, but she was also bubbly and friendly. With her short, blonde hair and large brown eyes, she was incredibly pretty, too. Danni was a couple of years older than Max, and seemed level-headed and stable which was something he'd found appealing. It hadn't taken long before their professional relationship had spilled over into their personal lives and they'd started dating.

All had been going well until six months later, Danni had found herself pregnant, which had sent her into a tailspin. She'd yelled at him that she'd never wanted children, that her career would be ruined, that her life was over. Though the news had been just as much of a shock to Max – after all, they'd only known one another a short time and were living in the moment, having never discussed future plans for their relationship – he'd managed to calm her down and assure her that everything would be okay, telling her they were in it together, that he'd support her in any way she needed.

He heaved a sigh. 'I hadn't realised it at the time, but I think I was looking to recreate my own little family unit.'

'No one could blame you for that, lovey,' Heather said.

'It was very naïve of me, though. We hardly knew each other, we didn't even live together. The relationship went downhill quickly after that, and was pretty much non-existent by the time Connor was born.'

Jasmine saw hurt flicker in Max's eyes as he explained how she'd turned up at his office one day and coolly handed the baby over to him, saying she couldn't do it any longer. That motherhood wasn't for her. Declaring that she and Max wanted different things from life. That Connor would be better off without her. Despite Max pleading with her to stay and talk, she'd walked out without a backwards glance.

At the age of twenty-four, he'd found himself in the role of a single parent.

Jasmine felt her mouth fall open but was too stunned to close it. Her first thought was to wonder if Danni had suffered from post-natal depression, but Max went on to clarify that hadn't been the case. She'd simply had no plans to be a mother. Her career and freedom came first, and giving birth to Connor hadn't changed her views in the slightest.

Jasmine's heart went out to both Connor and Max. She'd

thought she'd had it tough after Bart died, but at least she'd had the support of her parents.

He told them how Danni had popped back into his life occasionally over the last ten years, usually asking for money to get her out of a hole. In each of those times, she'd never asked to see Connor, coolly rejecting Max's pleas, saying it would "only confuse the boy". 'This is the longest I've gone without hearing from her.'

Jasmine wanted to ask how he'd explained Danni's absence to his son, but held back in case Connor overheard. From what she'd seen of grown-up Max so far, she felt he'd have handled it in a way that would cause his son the least hurt.

'That must've been hard after what happened with your mother,' Heather said, her voice soft. 'But looking at that little lad over there, anyone can see you've done a grand job of him, Max, you should be proud of yourself.'

'Aye, from what I've seen, he's a proper chip off the old block, isn't he?' Steve chuckled. 'And he's the spit of you when you were that age, what with those dark copper curls. He's even got your twinkle in his eyes.'

Max smiled, twisting round to see Connor taking turns to kick a football into a net with Zak and Chloe. The three of them were getting on like a house on fire. 'I do my best. He's a great kid.'

'Sounds like your life's been a bit of a whirlwind since you went to uni.' Jasmine batted a wasp away. It would seem she wasn't the only one to have been dealing with a load of chaos over the last ten years. It didn't stop her wondering if there'd been any other women in his life. Her thoughts segued to Sabrina, wondering how she slotted into it.

'What did you do after you sold your homeware company?' asked Steve. 'After what you've been telling us, I can't imagine you sitting still for long.'

Max swirled the dregs of shandy in his glass. 'I'd had my eye on another couple of businesses that hadn't been doing too well and were looking to be bought out. After a good think about what I could do to improve them, I bought them using the profit I'd made from the sale of the previous business.'

'Wow, Max! You evidently have a flair for this sort of thing.' Heather beamed as proudly as if he was her own son.

'Who'd have thought, little Max Grainger a high-flying business entrepreneur,' said Jasmine's dad. 'Good for you, lad. I can't think of anyone more deserving of success than you.'

'That's kind, Uncle Steve, but I think luck's had a lot to do with it.'

'Rubbish!' said Heather. 'Credit where credit's due, it'll be down to good business acumen and a sharp brain.'

Jasmine caught Max's eye and the two shared a smile. Her mum had always been as protective and supportive of him as she'd been of her and Jonathan. It warmed Jasmine's heart to know nothing had changed there. And from the look in Max's eyes, he felt the same.

'And have you still got these businesses?' asked Steve.

'No, I sold them eighteen months ago – I daresay you can see a pattern forming.' He grinned. 'The profits I made allowed me to buy a small chain of shops, as well as a few properties here in Micklewick Bay.'

'Here?' Jasmine couldn't hide her surprise. 'Have you been in town all this time?'

'No.' Max shook his head. 'Connor and I were living on the outskirts of Middleton-le-Moors.'

'Oh, right.' Jasmine allowed this information to sink in. Surely he must've returned here on several occasions to view the properties he'd bought?

'And do we know the chain of shops you bought – and do you still have them?' Steve stretched his legs out, chuckling.

'I still have them, and don't have any plans to sell – for the foreseeable future at least. The chain's Campion's of York, the flagship store is in Middleton-le-Moors.'

'Campion's of York?' Jasmine asked in disbelief. Max had achieved all this? There was no wonder he could afford his fancy pad on the cliffs.

'Ooh, I'd heard the one in Middleton had been recently refurbished. It's lovely by all accounts, I've been meaning to have a trip over there. There used to be a little store here, too, you know. S'just used for storage these days.' Heather fanned herself with a magazine she'd been reading earlier. 'Don't tell me you own that as well?'

'I'm afraid I do, and I've got plans to reopen it in time for Christmas.'

'You're a right business tycoon, Max lad,' said Steve.

'So, I'm guessing you know of my friend Maggie Marsay?' Jasmine asked. Last year her friend had been approached by the Campion's buyer Emma Bramley to supply the store with signature handmade bears, as well as designing a new logo for the company which had thrilled Maggie no end. Though Jasmine recalled her saying she'd never actually met the owner, with all her dealings being through Emma, adding an air of intrigue to the proceedings. The thought that it was a small world ran through her mind.

'Maggie, of course. Why? Is she a friend of yours?' asked Max. 'The first time I saw one of her bears, I knew I wanted her to design a range for the store.'

'She's one of my best friends, along with Florrie Appleton, Stella Hutton and Lark Harker. Remember them?'

A wide smile creased the corners of Max's eyes. 'Of course. It'd be great to see them again. Is Stella still kickass?'

Heather snorted with laughter. 'Just a bit. Mind, she's all loved-up now, so she's calmed down a bit in the fella department. She's a lovely lass, they all are, actually.'

'When you mentioned you bought up some other property

in the town, you didn't actually include the Micklewick Majestic Hotel, did you?' asked Steve.

From the tone of his voice, Jasmine could tell her dad was only half-joking.

'I did actually, Uncle Steve. It needs a lot doing to it to restore it to its former glory, which is what I intend to do. I reckon it's going to keep me busy for a while.'

'I can imagine, it's stood empty for years,' said Heather.

'So I gather. I'm going to brief the same architect I used to convert the old warehouse, Fitzgilbert's Landing. He's very forward-thinking. He had some fantastic suggestions and solutions for there. I'm hoping it'll be the same for the hotel.'

'That's Stella's bloke, isn't it, Jasmine?' Steve asked.

'It is, it's Alex! Stella actually bought one of the apartments in Fitzgilbert's Landing, it's the one opposite his.' Jasmine laughed in disbelief.

'Blimey, talk about a load of coincidences,' said Heather. 'What other properties have you snapped up, Max?'

He was prevented from answering when a loud shriek pierced the air followed by Chloe shouting, 'Mummy! Mummy!'

Jasmine leapt to her feet and rushed over to her daughter who was holding her hand out, tears streaming down her cheeks. Zak and Connor looked on in concern.

'Oh, goodness me!' Heather's hand went to her chest. 'Whatever's happened?' She pushed herself up and began making her way over to her granddaughter.

'What's up, Chlo?' her brother asked.

'It's hurting, Mummy! Make it stop!' she sobbed.

'What's happened, lovey?' Jasmine examined Chloe's rapidly reddening finger. Closer inspection revealed a bee sting protruding from the side of her finger. 'Oh, little love.' She turned to her mum. 'Can you bring some tweezers? Chloe's been stung.'

The revelation made Chloe howl even louder.

'I'll grab the medical box.' Steve rushed into the kitchen and pulled the tub from the cupboard.

'Is she okay? Is there anything I can do?' Max was beside Jasmine in a flash, his expression soft with concern. His arm brushed against hers, the soft hairs sending a tingle rushing over her skin. She stole a look up at him, to see a pair of gentle eyes looking back at her, triggering a flutter in her stomach.

Once the drama of the bee sting and Chloe's finger had subsided and the little girl's smiles had returned, the boys had declared themselves to be "absolutely starving". Steve added more fuel to the barbecue and before long the smoky aroma of grilled sausages and burgers was wafting around the garden.

Beckoned over by his son, Max joined the kids to show off his "keepy-uppy" skills with a football, which didn't look easy with Ernest trying to get the ball. 'Your Uncle Jonathan taught me how to do this when I was a little lad,' Max said. The information seemed to go down well with all the children.

Jasmine observed Max's easy relationship with his son, so far removed from the one he'd had with his own father. She wondered what had happened to Bazza Grainger. No one had heard anything of him after he went to prison. Max had done well not to absorb even the slightest trace of his father's toxic personality, nor display any bitterness or resentment as a consequence of his unhappy childhood, and being failed by both parents. But then, he always did have a positive outlook, even at a young age.

Moving on from "keepy-uppy", the children had talked Max into joining them taking shots at the basketball hoop on the side wall of the house. Little Chloe hadn't managed to score once on account of being so small. Sensing her disappointment, Max had lifted her onto his shoulders and bounded towards the hoop so she could drop the ball through it. Chloe's squeals of laughter had bounced around the garden along with Ernest who was having enormous fun.

'Oi, that's cheating,' called Steve, laughter in his voice.

Setting Chloe down, Max flopped onto the grass. 'I'm exhausted,' he said, stretching out and throwing his arms wide. In a matter of seconds, the three children had piled on top of him, laughing as Max jokingly shouted for help. Ernest joined the fun, rolling on the ground beside them, his legs kicking out every which way. Heather and Jasmine were laughing so hard, tears were rolling down their cheeks.

When the hilarity had finally calmed down, Jasmine sat back in her seat, savouring the warmth and surprising herself with how she'd been able to relax – bee sting drama aside. Usually, her mind would be full of everything she needed to do, reminding herself to be sure she transferred those thoughts to her "to-do" list. If she'd been at home, she'd have been feeding clothes into the washing machine, catching up on housework, changing the beds, ironing uniforms and working on her latest cake, whether it be sketching out a design, crafting elements or baking the cake itself. Every minute was usually spoken for. But today, after all that had gone on over the last week, she'd listened to her body and allowed herself to relax. Her gaze went to Max, who was now chatting to Connor and Zak about the Micklewick Lions. A thought floated into her mind, and she found herself asking if she'd have been quite so willing to switch off like this if Max hadn't been there. She pulled herself up sharp, hastily telling herself she didn't want to know the answer to that. Why was she even thinking it?

'Have you sampled the delights of The Cellar yet, Max? It's a micro-brewery in town. It's very popular.' Her dad's voice cut through Jasmine's thoughts.

'Not yet, but I must admit it looks very appealing. The signage is great; grabs your interest straight away.'

'You should get our Jasmine to take you there,' said Heather, oblivious to the stern look coming from her daughter's direction.

'I'd like that.' Max switched his gaze to Jasmine who quickly changed her expression. 'It'd give you a chance to tell me what you've been up to since I left. I feel I've dominated the conversation so far.'

'Give over, lad, we were all keen to know what had happened to you. It's been awful not knowing all these years.'

Jasmine went to speak, but Heather jumped in. 'Tell you what, why don't the pair of you have a wander down there now? Your dad and me'll look after the kids, if you're okay with that, Max?'

'I'm good with that, as long as you're sure,' said Max.

''Course I'm sure. We've stocked the freezer with ice creams for them.' She turned to Jasmine. 'And before you say it, I'll slather a load of sunblock on them.'

'Cool! Ice cream! Have you got any of those with raspberry sauce, Grandma? They're my absolute favourites,' said Zak.

'Mine too,' said Connor, matching Zak's enthusiasm.

'Sure do, lads.' She directed her gaze at Jasmine, hitching her eyebrows at her daughter. 'Well? Are you going to take your dad and me up on our offer, or not?'

'I... um...' Her mum's suggestion had taken Jasmine completely by surprise but the hopeful look in Max's eyes pulled at her insides. After hearing what he'd been through, there was no way she could refuse. 'Okay, why not?'

TWENTY-THREE

'Your parents are exactly as I remember them,' Max said as they turned out of the gate and onto the footpath of Arkleby Terrace. 'It's been so good to see them again.'

'I knew they'd be ecstatic to see you, and Connor too. The look on their faces was priceless.'

'So many memories came flooding back of playing in their back garden, and how they made me feel like one of the family,' he said fondly. 'You all did, even Jonathan.'

'You pretty much were one of the family.'

'Do you remember the swing your dad made from an old tyre fixed to the end of a rope? He'd suspended it from the branch of a tree that my memory tells me was overhanging from the house at the back. I'd forgotten all about that until today. I used to love swinging on it.'

'Yeah, me too. It suffered a sad demise when Jonathan was swinging on it a bit too vigorously and the branch snapped. Got a nasty bump on his head for his trouble. Mum gave Dad a right earbashing for not checking it was safe before we used it.'

'Poor Uncle Steve.' They looked at each other and laughed.

Despite her smiles, something had been troubling Jasmine

all afternoon, and she couldn't hold it in for much longer. She needed to know; she didn't want any gossip to start up about her, especially for the kids.

'Can I ask you something?'

'Sure, ask away,' Max said.

'Where does Sabrina fit into your life?' She pulled a face. 'Sorry, I didn't mean that to sound as direct as it came out. What I do mean is, what's her role, and should I have invited her to my parents' with you and Connor? She introduced herself as your PA, but I kind of get the impression she's a bit more than that.' Jasmine winced again. Her words had sounded so much better in her head. She didn't want Max to think she was checking to see if they were an item, or that she was prying.

'Sabrina and I aren't together, if that's what you mean? She works for me, that's all.' He looked across at her, but she couldn't meet his gaze.

'Phew! At least I won't have offended her, then.' Jasmine felt unexpectedly bright at hearing this news.

'Not at all. She doesn't live with us, she has her own place in town – one of the little terraces I bought and did up near Fitzgilbert's Landing. I hung on to a couple of them for rental purposes.'

'Oh, yeah, I know the ones.' Up until the terrace in question and Fitzgilbert's Landing had been renovated, that part of town had been run-down and best avoided, especially after dark, with many of the properties being boarded up. Max's refurbishments had given the area a change of fortune and the houses had become suddenly more appealing and much sought-after. It was a far cry from her little home on Rosemary Terrace.

'So, as you've rightly assumed, Sabrina is more than your average PA, she helps look after Connor, too – it's all in her contract, and was in the description when she applied for the job. I'm not taking advantage of her, and she's more than happy with the arrangements. I do have a PA based at my office in

Middleton-le-Moors, who's solely dedicated to my work life. Sabrina liaises with her.'

'Oh, right.' Max was clearly unaware that Sabrina would rather be more than simply a member of staff, not that Jasmine was going to say anything.

Before long, they'd turned onto Endeavour Road and were standing outside The Cellar. Max held the door open for Jasmine and they both stepped inside, their shoes tapping over the wide, wooden floorboards.

'Wow! This place is fantastic.' Max surveyed the room, his eyes roving over the exposed brick walls and rustic-chic furniture that included a huddle of semi-circular booths with padded leather seats. The room was illuminated by a range of statement lighting, while candles in lanterns created a more intimate effect on the tables. The décor had been described as "contemporary saloon" in a write-up in a local magazine that had heaped praise on the hostelry. At the far end of the room was a highly polished oak bar, set with a row of gleaming beer pumps advertising The Cellar's own beers. Bill, one of the bar's co-owners, was busy at the coffee machine frothing milk, while Pim, his husband and business partner, was pulling a pint of Micklewick Mischief and chatting to the customer he was serving. A carefully chosen playlist of indie rock infused with a hint of folk music mingled with the hum of gentle chatter.

'Hello there,' said a smiley-faced member of staff who swept by, carrying a tray of drinks as they made their way to the bar. He was wearing the micro-brewery's signature uniform of waistcoat, white shirt and long apron, tied at the waist and trimmed with The Cellar's logo.

Reaching the bar, they didn't have to wait long to be served.

'Hi there, Jasmine,' Pim said in his lilting Dutch accent. 'I see you have a friend with you.' His eyes twinkled at her as he pushed his chin-length, Nordic-blond hair off his face. His expression told her exactly what he was thinking.

Ignoring it, she said, 'Hi, Pim, this is Max, he's an old friend of mine. He's recently moved back to Micklewick Bay. Max, this is Pim, you recall I mentioned he was Stella's half-brother. He and Bill over there are The Cellar's owners.'

Max extended his hand across the bar. 'Hi, Pim, pleased to meet you.'

'Good to meet you, too, Max.' When he'd shaken Max's hand, Pim turned to Bill who'd just finished serving the customer with the coffee. 'Hey, Bill, come say hi to Jasmine's friend. He's called Max and they go back a long way.' He gave Jasmine an impish grin.

Bill appeared before them, an amused smile on his face. Unlike Pim, Bill was short with a small build and wore a neatly trimmed beard. Both were dressed in The Cellar uniform though their waistcoats were a different fabric to the rest of the staff. 'Hi, Jazz. Hi, Max.' From the glint in his eye, Jasmine could see he was thinking along the same lines as his husband.

'You've got an amazing place. I'll look forward to spending many happy hours here,' said Max, sounding suitably impressed.

'And we'll look forward to seeing you both here, too,' said Bill, adding extra emphasis to the word "both".

'Right then, what cool, alcohol-free drinks can you recommend?' Jasmine was eager to steer the conversation away from the route Bill appeared keen for it to take.

'Our virgin mojitos have been a big hit today,' said Pimm.

'Sounds perfect,' said Jasmine.

Armed with an alcohol-free mojito, jam-packed with a profusion of fresh mint, Jasmine led Max to a table for two in a corner by the window, hoping he hadn't seen the cheeky wink Pim had given her as they'd picked up their drinks. She took the seat that meant she'd have her back to the room, which she hoped would minimise any attention on herself. She could understand why seeing her having a drink with a man would raise interest amongst those that knew her, but it was something she could do without right now. She didn't want to have to fend off a barrage of questions when she had so many other things going on in her life.

Max settled himself in his seat, retrieved his mobile phone from the back pocket of his trousers and slid it onto the table, then took a long slug of his alcohol-free beer – his choice of drink had raised eyebrows with Bill and Pim, who prided themselves on their in-house beers, until he'd explained he was driving.

'So, Jingilby, are you okay to tell me what's been going on in your life since I last saw you? From what I can gather, you haven't had an easy time of it. What happened with Bart?'

Jasmine swallowed and girded herself, ready to head back to a time in her life that was littered with difficulties, recriminations and sorrow.

TWENTY-FOUR

Jasmine was fifteen years old when she first met Bart Forster. He'd moved to Micklewick Bay with his family and was placed in Jasmine's registration class at the local secondary school where he quickly established himself as the class clown, apparently thriving on making people laugh. He wasn't out-of-the-way good-looking and was on the short side, but Jasmine had been instantly attracted to his sense of humour, as had lots of the girls in their year.

She was sixteen when he finally asked her out, and she'd been ecstatic, having fancied him for ages. 'Omigod! Omigod! Bart Forster's only gone and asked if I'll go out with him,' she'd said to her friends in the school dinner queue. 'He wants to take me to the school disco next Friday!' All but Stella had been happy for her. 'Just watch him, Jazz. A lass in my maths class went out with him and she said he kept borrowing money off her but never paid her back. She ended up dumping him.'

But Jasmine had been so blinded by her youthful feelings, she'd blithely ignored Stella's advice.

It was something she was to bitterly regret.

The pair continued to date on and off and their relationship could only be described as stormy. Just when Jasmine vowed she was done with him forever, Bart would manage to draw her in with his jokey ways, making her laugh, despite the fact she was infuriated with him. Her parents issued various warnings, as did big brother Jonathan who had no time for Bart, describing him as a "bum who wastes all his money at the local amusements".

In turn, Bart's parents had thoroughly disapproved of Jasmine, declaring her not good enough for him and further stating in their superior manner that she was from the "rough part of town".

At the age of twenty, they moved in together, renting a tiny flat above a shop just off Victoria Square, which didn't go down well with either family. A couple of years later, Bart inherited a small sum of money from his maternal grandmother which he put towards the deposit on a house. Rather than getting a mortgage with Jasmine, Alice and Gary Forster had talked their son into taking one out in his own name, and encouraging him to ask Jasmine to pay rent which would help him afford the mortgage repayments. Their argument was that he was the one who'd be putting down a chunk of money and not Jasmine. Little did they know that the reason Bart's girlfriend didn't have a chunk of money to match their son's was because he'd been slowly eating his way through what she'd earnt from her weekend job, along with the savings she'd had.

Jasmine chose to ignore the alarm bells going off in her head, and the warnings that it all felt wrong. Instead, she managed to convince herself that it would still be "their" home. It was somewhat telling that she didn't share this fact with her parents, knowing what they'd have to say. They'd never explicitly said they didn't like Bart, instead they'd issued subtle warnings, which Jasmine had taken little notice of.

With a distinct lack of motivation, Bart spent the next couple of years drifting from job to job with a half-hearted approach to each one. Jasmine had felt like she was on a piece of elastic, just as she was pulling away from him, trying to break free, he'd turn on the charm or make her laugh, pulling her back to him. It turned out that Jasmine didn't just contribute to the mortgage with her rent, but she'd ended up giving Bart the money to cover the full amount of the monthly repayment.

Unable to tolerate any more, she'd made up her mind to leave him when the unthinkable happened, and Jasmine discovered she was pregnant. Bart had been angry, but it was nothing compared to the rage vented on her by his parents. Accusations flew and fingers were pointed, with them screaming at her that she'd deliberately got herself pregnant so she could trap Bart into fatherhood. They'd relished telling Jasmine that she wasn't the sort of girl they'd hoped their son would settle down with, never mind start a family. Heather and Steve hadn't been overjoyed to hear the news either, but it was more to do with concerns about what kind of father Bart would make, and if he would hang around and support their daughter.

Things came to a head when Gary Forster turned up on the doorstep of the Ingilby's home. Without waiting to be invited, he pushed his way in to discuss what could be done about the "nightmare of a situation" his son had found himself trapped in.

Heather, who'd been the only one home, had listened as he'd raged on, her anger brewing with every word he uttered. When he'd finally finished, she'd let rip and wiped the floor with him, leaving him in no doubt about what she and Steve thought of his son. 'Do you really think we want our Jasmine to be tied to a waster like your lad? She's the one who's trapped, not Bart! He couldn't keep a job if he tried, he's bone idle and hasn't got an ounce of motivation in his body! The only thing he has any enthusiasm for is gambling, and we know for a fact he scrounges money off our daughter to feed his habit. What's he going to do when he has to take a bit of responsibility when the baby gets here? I can't see him manning up, can you?' After saying her piece, she'd told Gary Forster to sling his hook and never darken their doors again.

Despite the animosity between the two families, Jasmine decided to stay with Bart, clinging onto the hope that they could make a go of their relationship for the sake of their baby. She'd even told herself being parents might bring them closer. Those thoughts were galvanised when Bart surprised her with a solitaire diamond engagement ring, saying it had been passed to him from his grandmother and that she would've wanted it to go to Jasmine. Jasmine wasn't so sure his parents would agree and when she'd put the question to him, he'd brushed it off with the skill of a politician, such that she didn't realise he hadn't given her a proper answer.

When Zak was born, Bart surprised them all further. He seemed overjoyed at becoming a father, and couldn't have been more attentive, filling Jasmine with hope that their relationship would work. He'd even talked about setting a date for them to get married the following year. But that was all it had been, just talk.

The reality was, with Bart saying he was unable to find a job, Jasmine had gone back to work sooner than she'd planned, leaving him at home looking after Zak who, despite his parents' niggly relationship, proved to be a sunny baby with the most adorable chubby cheeks Jasmine had ever set eyes on. She adored her son with a passion she hadn't expected and was prepared to do all it took to make sure he was happy. She threw herself into trying to make her relationship with Bart work, despite her growing misgivings about the amount of time he was spending on his laptop. He'd dismiss her concerns, telling her to stop nagging, that he was job hunting, but her worries had been confirmed when she'd returned home from work unexpectedly one day and found his laptop open on a gambling website. His excuse that it had been "accidental" hadn't washed with her and a blazing row had ensued.

It was when she was expecting Chloe that things took an unexpectedly sinister turn. Jasmine found herself answering the door to unsavoury characters demanding the money Bart allegedly owed them, and issuing threats if he failed to deliver. One day, she'd arrived home to find a particularly sinister-looking man sitting on the sofa in their living room, eating a packet of crisps he'd helped himself to while waiting for Bart. An air of danger emanated from him that sent goosebumps springing up all over her skin, and the hairs on the back of her neck standing up on end, though she did her best not to show it. She had no idea how he'd got in, and he'd only left once he was satisfied Jasmine would get the message to Bart that if his debts weren't settled by the weekend, then unpleasant things would start to happen. He'd picked up a vase on the nearby table as he left, dropping it on the floor in the hall where it smashed into hundreds of tiny pieces. As soon as he'd gone, she rushed to the bathroom where she was violently sick. She was only glad Zak was with her parents at the time.

Jasmine had still been shaking when Bart returned home.

Once she'd relayed the threatening message to him, it was the first time he hadn't tried to laugh it off or make a joke of it. Instead, his face had paled and fear had filled his eyes, which had unnerved her.

'This can never happen again, Bart! I could've had Zak with me! He would've been terrified. Whatever it is you're doing, you need to stop, or that's it, I'm leaving and taking Zak with me.'

'I'm really sorry, Jazz. I promise I'll get it sorted. But I think I'm gonna need that engagement ring, see what I can get for it at the pawn shop in Lingthorpe.' He'd at least had the good grace to look sheepish, but Jasmine had been more than happy to hand it over if it meant the menacing thug wouldn't come round again. It still hadn't stopped her heart from hammering whenever she put the key in the door for fear of what could be awaiting her behind it.

It was when she was checking the pockets of Bart's jeans before putting them into the washing machine that she found a handful of expensive-looking jewellery, including a pair of sapphire and diamond earrings and a diamond necklace stuffed inside. When she'd questioned him about them, he'd grown defensive, eventually becoming verbally abusive and accusing her of spying on him and snooping through his things.

'Please tell me you haven't stolen them,' she'd cried. She'd never had Bart down as a thief, but she didn't know what else to think.

'Of course I'm not!' he'd yelled back. 'How could you even think that?' He'd stormed out, slamming the door behind him.

Six weeks later, Bart was found dead.

'According to the policeman who knocked on the door to break the news, Bart's car had skidded on a sharp bend, before coming off the road and careering down the cliffside over by Clifftop Cottage not far from where Maggie lives.' Even after all this time, it still felt surreal to her.

Max ran his hand around the back of his neck, momentarily lost for words. 'Jeez, Jingilby, I don't know what to say. Sounds like you've been to hell and back.'

Jasmine blew out a deep breath and sat back in her seat. She lifted her gaze to Max. 'It's years since I talked about it, sounds even more like something from a soap opera this far on.'

'Do you think it was a genuine accident? Or do you think someone else was involved; I only ask because of what you said about the people making threats about him not paying his debts.'

'You've no idea how many times that's crossed my mind, or maybe that he even deliberately drove off the cliff.' She paused, lost in her own thoughts for a moment. She'd overheard the whispers at Bart's funeral, that his car going over the cliffside wasn't an accident. That he'd been driven off the road by the people he owed money to, but she'd brushed it off as spiteful gossip, telling herself it was the people who thrived on drama who were spreading the rumours. She decided to keep that to herself for now. 'In all honesty, I could never see him hurting himself, though I guess we'll never know the truth.'

'Wow, Jingilby, you haven't half been through it,' Max said. 'No one would know it from looking at you, though. You give off serious "don't mess" vibes.'

'Is there any wonder when I've had gangster-type apes turning up at my home? Took me a long time to get over that.' Just thinking about it had sent adrenalin racing around her. 'I honestly have no idea how I let myself get so caught up in all of Bart's crap. It's not like me. I mean, I knew I was unhappy, and I knew he was making a mug of me but, for some bonkers reason, I chose to ignore it and stay with him, kidding myself the whole time he'd change. I'm usually a strong person, my own person, but it was as if I'd lost myself for a while.'

'You're not the first woman to have done that, and I daresay you won't be the last so don't beat yourself up over it.'

'And that's the reason I've stayed single. I swore I'd never let another man in my life again after that. It's just me and the kids all the way.'

He reached for her hand, smoothing his fingers over her knuckles. 'Seems we're both a little battle-scarred by our past, Jingilby.'

'Yeah, seems we are.' She caught his eye and smiled. 'Unfortunately, it's still not over yet.'

'In what way? You look like you're doing okay to me.'

'Thanks.' She found herself thinking that Max's comment mattered to her, and it brought a smile to her face. 'I'd say just think of me as a swan, gliding gracefully over the water, but whose feet are going like the clappers beneath the surface, but I'm not exactly what you'd call swan-like and elegant. Anyway, I'm waffling. So, I got a letter from a solicitor acting on behalf of Bart's parents last week, listing the jewellery I found in his pocket one time, including the engagement ring he gave me but took back and pawned. They're demanding I hand it back or they'll take legal action.'

'What?'

'I've lost count of the times I've told them I don't have any of it, but they won't let it drop. The last time I saw the stuff from his pocket was when I handed it to Bart, I just assumed he'd pawned those, too.'

Max rubbed his hand across his jaw, perplexed. 'But why are they continuing to hound you after all this time?'

'If you met them, you'd realise. They're two of the nastiest people I've ever known and only seem happy when they're making other people's lives miserable. I know they've lost a son, and I can't even begin to imagine what that must feel like; it's bound to affect you forever. But anyone will tell you they were like that before Bart died. Fuelled by bitterness.'

'What a horrible way to live your life.'

'I haven't told you the worst of it.' She took a sip of her drink through the straw, the sprigs of mint tickling her nose. 'They refuse to have anything to do with Zak and Chloe, always have; wouldn't even acknowledge them when they were born. They told Bart it was to show how disapproving they were that I was their mother. I'd honestly expected them to change after Bart died. In fact, I'd anticipated them getting full-on over Zak and Chloe, and causing problems that way, but if anything, they withdrew even further.'

'You've got to be kidding me.' Expressions of outrage and disbelief ran across Max's face. 'What kind of people are they?' He raised his palm. 'Actually, you don't need to answer that, I already know.'

'At first, I thought it was awful. I felt hurt for my kids, but now I realise it's probably for the best. I dread to think what sort of poison they'd be whispering in their ears if they had any contact. And I doubt Zak and Chloe would like going to their house. On the couple of occasions I was allowed in, the atmosphere used to be so tense and stifling. I couldn't wait to get away. Bart told me he felt the same way.'

Max sat up straight in his seat, his face serious. 'Have you responded to the letter? Would you like me to get my solicitors onto it? They're pretty hot on stuff like this – they could put something together to make sure the Forsters back off.'

Jasmine shook her head. Though she was touched by his offer, she wanted to deal with this herself. 'I've got an appointment with Cuthbert, Asquith & Co next week, but thanks anyway.'

They were interrupted by Bill arriving at their table, a perfectly balanced tray of drinks on his arm, his crisp, clean cologne wafting around them. 'Sorry to interrupt, but Pim and I thought you two could do with a little drinky refresh, and these little beauties are on the house.' He set down a repeat of their first order along with a small bowl of snacks. 'Enjoy, guys.' His gaze snagged on Jasmine and he treated her to a loaded smile as he swept away.

'What a decent bloke.' Max reached for his fresh bottle of alcohol-free beer, drops of condensation beading the glass. 'I'll definitely be back. This place has a great atmosphere, very chilled.'

'Yeah, him and Pim have worked hard to build up a good client rapport. They often have special nights on here, you know, a live band. Last year, they held an auction to raise funds for a family whose daughter needed some pioneering treatment that's only available in the States. Folk were only too happy to support it.'

A round of cheering rang out at one of the nearby booths,

followed by an out of tune chorus of "Happy Birthday". Jasmine and Max looked on, smiling, as Pim carried an elaborate cocktail, trimmed with a sparkler, carefully setting it down on the table in front of the birthday girl. That done, he grinned over at them, giving a thumbs up, to which Jasmine replied with a jokey roll of her eyes.

'So, the house you're living in, the one that's for sale, I assume it isn't the one you shared with Bart?' Max said, picking up the conversation once more.

'You assume right. As I said, the one I lived in with Bart was in his name.' Jasmine took a fortifying breath. 'After he died, everything went to his parents. Bart and I never married – though loads of people used to think of us that way, probably cos we'd been together for so long. When his estate was finally sorted, I got a letter from the Forsters telling me that Zak and I had to leave the house, as they now owned it.'

'Seriously?'

'Seriously.' Jasmine nodded.

At eight months pregnant, she'd found herself looking for a new home for herself and Zak, and her unborn baby. Her parents had told her she was welcome to move back in with them, but Jasmine was used to her independence and didn't think it would be fair on them to have a toddler and a newborn baby suddenly descend upon them, shattering their peace.

'Anyroad, I managed to find the place we're in now, and made it as homely as possible. Moving there was the most settled I'd felt for ages, and the best thing was, Zak seemed to thrive.'

Max sank back in his seat. 'Between us we've had some testing experiences, Jingilby, but I think we're similar in that we try to pull the positive out of a negative situation. With all we've been through, I'd like to think it's made us stronger, more compassionate people.'

'Hmm. Maybe. Though I actually feel it hardened me. I feel

like I've surrounded myself in an impervious shell that only my kids can get through. Can't see that ever changing.'

'I'm not so sure. You've got a big heart, it wouldn't be right to keep it locked away.'

She met Max's gaze, conscious of his eyes searching hers. He smiled and a flurry of butterflies took flight in her stomach.

TWENTY-FIVE

A succession of pings pulled Max's attention away from Jasmine. 'Someone's keen. Sorry, Jingilby, I'd better check who it is just in case it's urgent.' He scooped up his phone and tapped the screen.

Jasmine took the opportunity to survey him unobserved. With his head tipped forward, her eyes roved over his hair, noting it was cropped close, but still long enough to give a hint of his curls. Her gaze dropped to his shoulders, broad and strong, a far cry from the skinny, undernourished frame he had as a young boy. Her eyes slid to his arms – she already knew what it felt like to have those wrapped around her. She felt the heat of a blush creeping up her face at the reminder. Before she knew it, she'd released a wistful sigh, making Max's head jerk up.

'Apologies, that was really rude of me. Turns out it was nothing important.' He set his phone down.

'No, not at all, it's fine. I was just...' From the corner of her eye, she became aware of someone watching her. She glanced over to the bar to see Bill and Pim smiling broadly. Bill waved and Pim gave her another thumbs up, his eyebrows dancing mischievously.

No points for guessing what those two are thinking. Jasmine couldn't help but laugh, shaking her head.

'What's up?' Max followed her line of sight. 'Ahh.' He chuckled and returned Bill's thumbs up.

It occurred to Jasmine that, after filling him in on her time with Bart and the situation with his parents in one massive splurge, Max might have formed the impression she was a right old self-pitying misery guts. She felt the need to rectify that straight away, and make sure he knew she was a generally cheerful person.

'Max, can I just clarify something?'

''Course. What is it?'

'I'm conscious that what I've just told you makes it sound like my life has been one long doom and gloom session, but it hasn't been that way at all. I'm told I'm quite an upbeat person – granted, I can be a bit feisty at times.'

His mouth twitched at that, making her smile.

'Anyroad, I feel lucky in so many ways. I've got the most supportive family. My parents are amazing, and it goes without saying that I love my kids to bits and feel incredibly blessed to have them. On top of that, I've got the best group of friends anyone could ever wish for. And now, with the Lady Caro and Danskelfe Castle wedding cake contract, it looks as though I'll have my dream job, too.' Saying it out loud reminded Jasmine she had much to be thankful for. 'And it wasn't all bad with Bart, we did have some good times. I wouldn't have stuck with him otherwise.'

She hoped she hadn't overdone it, and made everything sound too saccharine sweet, but she didn't want to add to her tales of woe telling him how much of a struggle it had been since Bart's death, scrimping and saving so Zak and Chloe wouldn't have to go without – and she certainly didn't want his pity, that would be unbearable. Her parents were a great help as far as childcare was concerned; there was no way she'd be able to manage her jobs without them. Though, her pride made sure she drew a line as far as financial help was concerned, which wasn't hard since she'd always been fiercely independent, even as a child. It was in her DNA. It was important to her that she didn't accept handouts, and not just because Bart's parents had accused her of only being with him because of his money – they refused to accept that he didn't have a bean. Their words still rankled to this day.

But it wasn't just that. She knew her mum and dad didn't have much spare cash to splash around, especially now they were saving for a special anniversary holiday. And she held back from telling Max that taking time out and chilling like this wasn't the norm for her on a Sunday – not least being on her own in male company. That was unheard of and without a shadow of a doubt it would set tongues wagging! But she had to admit, it did feel rather nice. More than nice. Max was easy company and, weird as it felt, it was almost as if he hadn't been away for all these years, that their bond had remained as strong as ever, ready to be picked up on his return. And then there were the other feelings he was stirring inside her…

Forty-five minutes later, they were having a steady walk back through town, Max telling her of his plans for the new Campion's store there in Micklewick Bay. He'd threaded her arm through his and Jasmine found herself quite liking how it felt, marvelling at how natural and easy everything seemed with him.

'Will you be stocking Maggie's bears at the Campion's store here?' she asked.

'Of course. Em Bramley, who's my buyer for the stores, is about to give Maggie a call.'

'Mags will be thrilled. Hopefully you'll get to meet her soon.'

They were pulled out of their conversation with a start thanks to the loud beeping of a car horn.

'Flippin' 'eck! Who's that?' she said, looking up to see a car slowing down, the driver and front seat passenger wearing wide smiles and waving enthusiastically.

Though her heart sank, she forced a smile and waved back. Her heart plummeted further still when the driver pulled up beside them and wound his window down.

'Ey up, lass, it's grand to see you out and about on this fine sunny day.' It was local author and poet, Jack Playforth. He was squinting against the bright sunshine that was picking out the silver strands in his salt and pepper hair. Beside him in the passenger seat was fellow author, Jenna Johnstone.

'Hi there, pet,' Jenna said in her sing-song Geordie accent. She and Jack had been dating since last year, with Jenna eventually moving in with Jack at his little cottage in Old Micklewick. 'Who's your friend?' she asked, her eyes sparkling with interest.

Jasmine eased her arm from Max's. 'Hi, folks, this is Max Grainger, he's an old friend who's recently moved back to town.' She could almost hear the cogs of their minds cranking away as she continued with the introductions.

'Pleased to meet you both,' Max said in his friendly manner.

'Aye, likewise,' said Jack. 'We're just heading over to Florrie and Ed's place to have a bit of a chat, get ourselves up to speed about the preparations for the book festival.'

'A book festival?' Max said.

'Aye, it's a new venture for the town,' said Jack in his gravelly North Yorkshire tones. 'Jen and me have combined our ideas with Florrie and Ed's and intend to make it an annual event, offering a variety of workshops and author Q&As to tempt as many folk as we can.'

'That's right,' Jenna chipped in. 'Our ideas just seem to keep on growing. We'd originally hoped to hold it over the summer, but the timings didn't work out, so we've plumped for early September instead.'

'Sounds great. I'm an avid reader myself – love a gritty psych thriller.' Max looked genuinely interested. 'Let me know if there's anything I can help with. I'd be happy to get stuck in.'

'You could end up regretting those words, lad.' Jack gave a throaty chuckle. 'Anyroad, it's been nice to meet you, but we'd best be off.'

With the goodbyes out of the way, Jasmine wondered how long it would take for word to reach her friends about her being seen in town looking all cosy with a mystery man. She'd have to send a group text to them later, explaining it before their minds went into overdrive, especially with Jack and Jenna heading straight to Florrie's. This was going to take some explaining next Friday night at the Jolly.

The first thing Jasmine did when she got home and had a quiet minute to herself was to send a group text to Florrie, Stella, Maggie and Lark. It didn't take long for gossip to fly its way around town, setting the Micklewick Bay rumour-mill grinding away in earnest, and she wanted to act quickly, before her friends got overexcited about her being seen in town with Max.

> Hiya lasses, got some news! Long story short, ran into Max Grainger again and we had a catch up at The Cellar earlier today. Before you get yourselves excited, we're JUST FRIENDS!!!!
> xx

It didn't take long for a flurry of replies to land, the first one being from Florrie.

> Hi Jazz, so I hear!! looking forward to hearing all about it!! Fxx

'Yes, I can imagine Jack and Jenna had plenty to say after they saw us,' Jasmine said quietly to herself.

Next, she tapped on Stella's message.

> Hi Jazz, I get the feeling there's more to this "catch up" than your innocent message would suggest. Be prepared for a very thorough cross-examination when I next see you!! Sxx

'Yikes!' Like all of their group of friends at one time or another, Jasmine had sat in the public gallery at York Crown Court and observed Stella in action as counsel for the prosecution. The words fierce, intimidating and brutal had come to mind. Jasmine would anticipate her interrogation over Max with a feeling of utter dread.

Maggie's reply made her laugh, at least, with its array of shock faced emojis.

> Jazz Ingilby have I understood your message correctly? Are you telling us you've been in the company of a MAN?!? ALONE?!? WAHHH?!!!? xxx

Lark's message was exactly as Jasmine would have expected, brimming with warmth and peppered with a selection of heart emojis.

> Oh, flower! I'm so happy for you and Max. I remember him as always being so lovely. I hope the years have been kind to him and he's found the happiness he deserves. Can't wait to hear all about it xxx

From the content of the messages, her friends clearly had

high hopes on the romantic front as far as Max Grainger's return was concerned. She'd need to set them straight on that score, before they got too carried away and had her married off. Her next thought was that they were going to get one heck of a shock when they set eyes on him after all this time.

That night in bed, with the glow of the outside streetlight casting shadows around her tiny bedroom, Jasmine carried out a sweep of her mind, a ritual she went through almost every night before she could settle down and go to sleep. She'd work her way through her worries along with the events of the day, turning them over and over until she'd examined them from every angle. She'd been so worn out recently, she usually didn't get beyond the first item on her agenda before her eyes got heavy and she gave herself up to slumber that beckoned. But there had been so much going on over the last few days that by the time she'd got to bed, her worries had taken on a life of their own, keeping her awake, no matter how exhausted she felt.

After segueing from the letter sent by the Forsters' solicitor, to house-hunting, to Scraggo – that particular worry had sent unease prickling over her skin; she hoped she'd heard the last from him – her thoughts settled on Max. It didn't take long for her to realise what it was that made her feel so at ease with him and as if he'd never been away. It was his eyes with their gentleness, and that unique way he had of looking at you, as if he could see right into your soul, just as they did when he was a small boy.

She'd felt an instant reconnection between the two of them that had deepened over the course of the day. And now, in the quiet of the night, Jasmine found it unnerved her. She gnawed on her bottom lip, hoping she hadn't given him the wrong impression. Much as she'd enjoyed catching up with Max and being in his company, it couldn't be anything more than that.

She'd need to set boundaries, make sure he was aware of them, but do it nicely, with none of the usual Jasmine bluntness and sass. The last thing she wanted was for people to get the wrong impression and think they were an item, and worse, for word to get back to their children. That would be confusing for Zak and Chloe, not to mention potentially unsettling. For Connor, too, no doubt. 'There's no room for a man in your life, Jazz,' she reminded herself quietly. 'You need to stick to your guns, it's just you and the kids.'

She rolled over and plumped up her pillows, another thought pinging into her mind, giving her a jolt. Was *she* the one reading too much into everything and worrying unnecessarily? What if Max simply saw her as the friend he used to have and was just happy to have caught up with her again, picking up where they left off? Nothing more.

She puffed out a sigh. That would be way, way easier, she told herself as she closed her eyes.

And who are you trying to kid, Jasmine Ingilby?

TWENTY-SIX

Monday morning proved to be an even more frantic dash around than usual at Rosemary Terrace, with Jasmine and the children being late to leave the house thanks to Zak misplacing his football boots. He'd found them stuffed under his bed where he'd left them after getting back from his grandparents the previous day – die-hard Micklewick Lions supporters, he and Connor had worn the team's football strip on the Sunday, too. It was unlike Jasmine not to check the kids had everything ready for school the following day, but it had completely slipped her mind. But then, her Sunday had been more than a little out of the ordinary.

With no news from the garage about her car, she was grateful for the use of the Spick 'n' Sparkle van rather than the three of them having to walk – or rather, run – up to school. But with her colleague returning later this week, she'd have to chase the garage, see if they could speed things up a bit.

She hadn't told Zak and Chloe about her unpleasant encounter with Jason Scragg over the weekend, not wanting to worry them, but she'd gently reminded them that if there was any trouble from Bruce or Nina Scragg, then they were to discreetly inform a teacher.

It was while she was scrubbing the shower of one of the Spick 'n' Sparkle clients that a text landed from Micklewick Mansions. She pulled off her cleaning gloves and retrieved her phone from her pocket, her expression clouding over. 'Not again!' she said, as she read the message informing her they'd organised a viewing of her home for later that morning. She jabbed at the screen until she found the call icon, pressing it.

It didn't come as a shock to Jasmine that Don Carswell was unable to take her call.

'Look, I know it's not your fault, but for future reference, a bit more notice would be nice,' she said to the young receptionist. 'I know I'm only a tenant, but I'd prefer to be in when strangers are wandering around my home. So, in future, I'd be grateful if you could call me in advance, that way we could at least have the chance to arrange a viewing for a mutually convenient time. I wouldn't even mind showing whoever it is around myself.'

'I'm really sorry, Miss Ingilby, I completely understand, and we do have a note of this on our file, but the prospective buyer was insistent they look around first thing this morning. They seemed pretty keen, so we didn't like to put them off. If it helps at all, they looked very respectable, and Mr Carswell will be accompanying them. Are you okay with that?' the receptionist asked.

'I suppose I'll have to be.' The young girl sounded sweet, making Jasmine instantly regret her snappy tone. 'Sorry I bit your head off. Like I said, I appreciate it's not your fault, but if you could just bear it in mind for any future viewings.'

With the call ended, Jasmine sat on the floor, her shoulders slumped as her irritation leached away. She was going to have to increase her efforts on the house-hunting front. She might have to give Lark's suggestion of the old bakery further consideration.

The idea had been growing on her, especially with it having a garden for the kids, though she'd put it to the back of her mind on the grounds that it wasn't even available to rent yet and there was no way of contacting the owner. It wasn't just that, she hadn't wanted to build her hopes up; she had a feeling it would be out of her budget anyway. She could only hope some new rental properties had appeared since the last time she'd scoured the internet.

It hadn't all been bad news that morning. A call to the garage revealed that her car should be ready for collection by the end of the day. The cost was eye-watering, but at least last Thursday had been payday, so she'd be able to afford it – just. Jasmine was thankful she didn't have the headache of searching for a cheap run-around on top of looking for a new home. She very much doubted that would have been within her budget.

The following morning, Jasmine was relieved to find a conveniently located parking space directly outside one of the grand Victorian houses on the top prom. It had been split up into luxury apartments, one of which belonged to Hilda Jenkins whose home she was about to clean. She was lifting her cleaning equipment out of the van when an inexplicable wriggle of unease slithered up her spine. She turned cautiously to see Jason Scragg standing beside her, a threatening look in his eyes. His unexpected presence made her gasp, and he smirked. She noticed an elderly lady, walking her dog, eyed him warily as she gave him a wide berth. Jasmine couldn't blame her.

'I've just had a phone call from that flaming school, complaining about my kids.' From the tone of his voice Jasmine guessed it hadn't been a friendly phone call.

'And?' She set her jaw. Not for one minute did she want him to think she was intimidated by him.

'And I reckon it's got summat to do with you and your goody-goody brats.'

'I can assure you, you're mistaken there, which means I've got nothing more to say to you. So, if you wouldn't mind moving out of the way so I can get past...'

'Or what?' He stood directly in her path, pushing his puny chest out and performing more of the ape-like posturing she'd witnessed on Saturday. Jasmine felt a giggle rise up inside her. She swallowed it down, telling herself it would only serve to antagonise him. She just wanted him to go. Hilda would be expecting her. She'd have the kettle on and a plate of biscuits set out, and Jasmine didn't want to make her worry or wonder where she was.

'Or you're going to make me late for my shift.' She deliberately kept her tone indifferent.

He sniggered and her stomach churned at his breath that caught in her nose. She couldn't recall the last time she'd smelt anything so foul.

She took a step forward, hoping he'd move aside, but instead he inched closer. She felt her heart start pumping fast, sending a surge of adrenalin racing around her body; she could really do without this right now but there was no way she was going to back down.

'Not scared, are you, Ingilby?'

Jasmine didn't flinch. Instead, she held his gaze, trying not to inhale the revolting stench that emanated from him. 'You know, I always think people like you must feel inadequate or inferior in some way. I mean, why else would you behave like this? I actually feel sorry for you that you haven't moved on from being the toxic little bully you were at primary school. You're no different, are you?' She battled the urge to take hold of the bull ring in his nose and lead him out of the way. 'And, in answer to your question, no, I'm not scared.' The emotion currently raging around her was anger that men like him thought they could get away with this sort of behaviour, thinking it was okay to intimidate women.

His top lip curled into a snarl, revealing his row of rotten teeth. 'Think you're dead good, don't you, Ingilby? But I reckon it's time someone taught you a lesson or two, put you in your place, like.'

'You're pathetic.'

He took a step forward, sticking his chest out further, centimetres separating them. Jasmine was just about to bring her knee up when a voice stopped her.

'If you know what's good for you, Scragg, you'd move out of the way right now.' Before Jasmine had a chance to think, Max was standing beside her, glowering down at Scraggo.

'Oh, aye, or what?' Scraggo turned, tipping his head back so he could make eye contact with the person addressing him. 'You again! Make a habit of poking your nose in where it's not wanted, do you?' He made a show of swaggering on the spot, unaware of how ridiculous he looked. 'And who are you, anyroad?'

'Don't you recognise me, Scragg?' At almost a foot taller than Jason Scragg, Max towered over him.

'No, should I?' Scraggo faltered and he started inching away.

'Oh, I think you should.' Max regarded him with utter disdain. 'I'm Max Grainger, remember me? I remember you. Hard to forget really, with your nasty little campaign to make my life a living hell when we were at school.'

Scraggo flinched. 'I don't know what you're talking about. You've got me confused with someone else. I've never bullied no one, me.'

Max stepped towards Scraggo, his eyes boring into him. 'There's no confusion. You picked on me mercilessly. And what was that less-than-charming nickname you gave me? Oh, yeah, "Rubbish", that was it.'

'It was just a daft joke. I didn't mean owt by it.'

'So you do remember. Thought you would.'

'Aye, well, I was just messing around.'

'"Just messing around", a "daft joke". Hmm.' Max appeared to consider that for a moment. 'Didn't feel much like a joke at the time, or that you were messing around. And when you tipped the contents of a rubbish bin over me in front of everyone after school, or stuffed my new coat down the toilet after covering it in paint, were you just joking then, too? It didn't feel very funny from my perspective.'

Oh, Max, thought Jasmine, the reminder of what he'd been through triggering an ache in her heart. She hoped facing such awful memories wasn't too painful for him.

'I–I– 'Course I was, what else would it've been?' Scraggo swallowed audibly, clearly unnerved by Max's calmly intimidating demeanour. 'Come on, surely you can have a laugh about it all now, mate. We were just kids.' He gave an uncertain laugh.

'I'm not your mate. Never was, never will be.'

What goes around, comes around. This is what Lark would call karma. Jasmine looked on, transfixed by this version of Max.

'I don't know what you're making all the fuss about, looks like you've done all right for yourself.' Scraggo looked Max up and down, taking in his neatly barbered hair and expensively cut clothes.

'Oh, I have. Done more than all right, actually. But I've worked damned hard for it. Looking at you, I doubt very much you'd know what a day's work feels like.'

'Oi, just watch what you're saying.' Scraggo's anger resurfaced, and he puffed his chest out once more. Max had clearly hit a nerve.

'Trust me, I'm being very considered about what I'm saying, and let me tell you this, if you go within an inch of Jasmine, or your kids give hers any more crap, then I'll see to it that the police are informed about your nasty little drug dealing set-up, and how you've been stalking and intimidating a woman. I'll tell them how I've witnessed it and make sure—'

'Aye, and so will I, you nasty piece of work.' The three of them were startled to see Hilda standing outside the gate to her building. Her outfit of a light-blue cardigan over a summer dress in a cheerful, floral print was at odds with the upturned sweeping brush she was brandishing. 'And if you don't clear off and leave our Jasmine alone, I'll take this to you, you scrawny little thug!' She waved the brush at him. 'And don't be fooled, I know how to use it! You have no idea who you're messing with.'

Jasmine briefly locked eyes with Max, a flash of humour fleeting across his face. She was torn between wanting to rush over and hug her elderly friend, and bursting out laughing. Scraggo saved her from having to make a decision as Hilda briskly headed towards him.

'I don't want owt to do with any of you.' He jabbed a finger in their direction. 'Just keep out of my way.'

'*What?*' Jasmine looked at him, incredulous. As if she'd want anything to do with him.

The three of them watched as he turned on his heel and strutted off, his ape-swagger in full swing.

Jasmine glanced between Max and Hilda. Despite the tense situation, she couldn't help but smile at her brush-wielding friend.

'You okay, Jingilby?' Max rested his hand on her shoulder.

Jasmine nodded. 'I am now he's gone.'

'Well, my goodness, what a start to the day that was.' Hilda lowered her sweeping brush and peered at Jasmine through her large-framed glasses. 'Are you sure you're all right, lovey?'

'I'm fine, thanks, Hilda,' said Jasmine. 'And I'm very grateful for you coming to my assistance, but you really should be careful of people like that.'

'I agree, you shouldn't approach the likes of him, you never know what could happen,' said Max.

Hilda harrumphed. Though she only scraped five feet in height, she appeared even more petite with Max standing beside her. 'Aye, well, I probably wouldn't have done that if you weren't there.' Her eyes wandered up to his face, her brows hitched in interest. 'And who's this knight in shining armour, then?'

'I'm Max.' He held out his hand. 'Not so sure about the knight in shining armour bit, though,' he said.

Hilda slipped her hand into his. 'And I'm Hilda Jenkins.' She turned to Jasmine. 'Ooh, your young man's got a lovely handshake, strong but not overpowering. *Very manly.*'

Max laughed. 'Delighted to meet you, Mrs Jenkins.'

'It's Hilda to you, Max.' Her eyes shone as she gave a coquettish giggle.

'In that case, I'm delighted to meet you, *Hilda,*' he said.

Charmer! 'Max isn't my young man, he's an old *friend.*' Jasmine gave Hilda a look to emphasise the point, and Hilda returned one that said, '*And who are you trying to kid, young lady?*'

'Well, I don't know about you, but I think I need a cup of tea after all that excitement.' Hilda made to head back to her home. 'And I expect you to join us, Max, you've earnt yourself one and some of my special homemade shortbread biscuits, what with you being all chivalrous and seeing off that obnoxious individual.'

'You had me at homemade shortbread, Hilda, I'd be delighted to join you.' Max treated her to one of his heart-melting smiles. 'And you're giving me way too much credit for getting rid of "that obnoxious individual". I think between you and Jingilby, you had him quaking in his boots. I just seized the opportunity to remind him of what he did all those years ago. Call it closure.'

'Well, I hope you got it, lovey,' Hilda said kindly, patting him on the arm.

'I sure did.'

Jasmine wasn't sure whether or not she was glad Max helped carry her cleaning equipment into Hilda's apartment. Granted, it saved her making two journeys, but on the other hand, she wasn't sure how she felt about the whole "damsel needing the help of a man" scenario that seemed to be the case whenever Max showed up and intervened in an altercation she'd been having with Scraggo. She was used to being independent as far as things like that were concerned, used to sticking up for herself. She'd never felt the need for anyone to do it for her before, and she didn't now. But it was Max, and she told herself he wouldn't have been able to stand by and watch without stepping in. It would have been the same if the tables had been turned. After all, she'd done just that when they were children and Scraggo had picked on Max. And as far as helping carry her stuff into Hilda's house, she'd have done the same for him. *Stop overthinking, woman!*

'Jasmine and I always start our Tuesday mornings with a cuppa, don't we, lovey?' Hilda padded over the carpet, armed with an extra cup and saucer she'd fetched from the kitchen, setting it down on the small table in the high-ceilinged living room.

Despite its classic Victorian proportions, the room was cosy and welcoming thanks to Hilda's comfy furnishings. Pictures of family were dotted about the space along with a couple of her much-missed friend, Enid.

'We do, we put the world to rights.' Jasmine was glad her elderly friend hadn't taken long in the kitchen. Her head had been swimming with the Scraggo incident, and she hadn't known what to say to Max. She didn't feel it was right to discuss what had happened all those years ago in front of Hilda in case it made him feel uncomfortable. Though, in fairness, he'd appeared lost in his own thoughts as he'd gazed silently out of the large Victorian window and onto the view of Thorncliffe and the sea. She wondered what had been running through his mind, hoping the interaction with Scraggo hadn't resurrected painful memories.

'Can't think of a better way to start the day than with a cup of tea and a good old chat.' Max turned, a smile fixed to his face. 'That's a grand view you've got of the cliffs and the sea, Hilda.'

'Aye, 'tis that. It's one I never tire of, lovey. Seems to look different every day. And I like to sit in that seat just by you there, and watch the world go by. Anyroad, young man, come over here, make yourself comfortable. You can tell me all about yourself and how you know our lovely Jasmine while she pours the tea.'

'It's little Max Grainger, Hilda. Surely you remember him?' Jasmine said, the teapot poised in her hand. 'He lived over the road from us when I was a kid.'

Hilda leant towards Max, who was sitting in the chair opposite, and studied his face for what felt like an age. Max sat unflinching throughout, a hint of a smile on his lips.

'Oh, my goodness!' Hilda clapped her hands to her face. 'It is you!'

'Yep, Hilda, it is me.' Max grinned.

Well, I never, little Max Grainger. It isn't half lovely to see you, sweetheart. Mind, you're not so little now, are you?' She gave a delighted chuckle. 'So, what's brought you back to Micklewick Bay, and do you intend to stay?'

Jasmine added a dash of milk to the three cups of tea – it had somehow stuck in her mind that when he'd made them both tea at his house, he'd added just a splash to his own mug then.

Max sat back and breathed deeply. 'I'd always planned to return, but wanted the time to be right. And, yes, I intend to stay. My son, Connor, has settled in well at the local school so there's no way I'd uproot him.'

'You have a son?'

'I do.'

'And is your wife here, too?'

'I'm not married, it's just Connor and me.'

'Ahh, I see,' said Hilda. You could almost hear the cogs of her brain whirring. She picked up the plate of shortbread, offering Max a piece. 'You must try some, Max.'

'Thank you, Hilda, it looks delicious.' He took a square and bit into it, the elderly lady watching his reaction closely as he chewed. 'Mmm. Oh, wow, Hilda! This is sublime! It's so buttery with the perfect amount of crunch. I can honestly say, I've never tasted better shortbread.'

Hilda couldn't have looked more thrilled if she'd tried. A huge smile lit up her face and she clapped her hands together. 'That's very kind, Max. I knew you'd like it.' She lowered her voice. 'It's a secret family recipe.'

'Well, I'll tell you what, I wish I was a part of your family, Hilda, with a recipe as excellent as this one.' With the square finished, he leant forward, his hand hovering over the plate of shortbread. 'May I?'

'Of course, sweetheart. You dive in, a big lad like you needs filling up.'

Jasmine watched the interaction, touched by Max's kindness. She knew this would make Hilda's day and she'd be talking about it, singing Max's praises for weeks afterwards.

'In fact, you're welcome to call in for a cup of tea and some shortbread any time. I don't go out much, and when I do, it isn't far. It'd be lovely to see you. I've got one of them mobile telephone things, so if you remind me to give you my number before you leave, you can just give me a little tinkle if you fancy popping in, make sure I'm home. Not that I go far, mind,' she said. 'Ooh, and you could bring your son, too.'

'That's very kind, Hilda, I'd like that.'

'You're honoured, Max,' said Jasmine. 'Hilda doesn't share her shortbread with just anyone, you know.'

Hilda started to chuckle, waving her hand in front of her face. 'I've just remembered something your mum told me, Jasmine.'

'You have?'

Hilda nodded, still chuckling. From the mischievous gleam in her eyes, Jasmine had a feeling she wasn't going to like what she was about to hear next.

'Come on, Hilda, don't keep us dangling,' Max said, laughing himself.

Hilda patted her chest, her laughter finally subsiding. 'It's something you said, Max, just before you left with your grandad. Mind, it was such a long time ago, you'll have to excuse me if I don't get the words in exactly the right order.'

Jasmine groaned inwardly, her heart plummeting all the way to the black trainers she wore for work. She gave Max a sideways look, noting his smile had fallen and he was squirming in his seat. It would appear that he remembered, too.

Hilda!

'It was when you were walking down the path with your grandad, and you turned round and said something like. "Jasmine, I'm gonna make my millions, get a big, fast car and drive all the way back to Micklewick Bay so I can marry you."' Hilda pressed her hand to her mouth, her giggles resurfacing. 'I always thought that was so sweet.'

An awkward silence hung in the air for what felt like forever, Jasmine racking her brains for something to say that was totally unrelated to Hilda's bombshell. Of course, Jasmine had remembered it. In fact, she'd been thankful her parents hadn't brought it up on Sunday when Max had joined them for the barbecue – or since, for that matter. Though she was going to have a serious word with her mum about sharing it with Hilda. She'd sworn both her parents to secrecy at the time, making them promise they wouldn't tell anyone else what Max had said. Jasmine took a sip of her tea, taking sanctuary behind the cup and willing Hilda to change the subject.

'I remember,' said Max, keeping his tone light. 'And it was Jingilby, not Jasmine.'

'Jingilby? Oh, yes, of course, silly me. Now you mention it, I can recall Heather telling me you always used to call her Jingilby, and Jasmine would only allow you to use the nickname, no one else.'

Two dots of colour blazed on Jasmine's cheeks. Much as she tried to resist, she felt the pull of Max's gaze. Her eyes met his, the look she saw there setting her insides dancing in a way she hadn't expected.

'So, is that why you're here, then, Max?' Hilda asked, undeterred. 'Have you made your millions and got yourself a fancy, fast car?'

Jasmine pinned her elderly friend with a warning glare. Unfazed, Hilda merely smiled sweetly as she awaited Max's response.

Max laughed, clearly amused by Hilda's mischief-making. 'Well, I'm doing okay for myself, and I suppose I've got a nice enough car, but as far as—'

'Actually, Max, before I forget, Zak wanted me to ask if it's okay for Connor to come for his tea one night soon.' It was the first thing that sprang into Jasmine's mind to send the conversation in a different direction.

'Er, yeah, I know he'd love that.'

'What were you going to say before Jasmine interrupted, Max?' asked Hilda.

Jeez, Hilda! Talk about persistent. Jasmine ploughed on, ignoring Hilda's question. 'Great! I'll check my calendar and we can fix a day. Oh, and how come you were driving along the top prom this morning? I thought you said your office was in

Middleton-le-Moors.' She always gabbled when she was nervous or uncomfortable.

'Ooh, Middleton-le-Moors is a lovely little place, full of fancy shops. Not that I've been for a while,' said Hilda.

Despite her discomfort, it struck Jasmine that she hadn't seen Hilda so perky or her cheeks so rosy since before Enid had passed away. And though she would've preferred it if Hilda hadn't reminded them of Max's parting words, seeing her friend looking brighter, took the edge off her irritation.

'It is a nice spot,' said Max. 'I'll be heading over there later this morning. And, in answer to your question, Jingilby, the reason I was driving along the prom was because I was on my way to Old Micklewick. I've just bought the old bakery on Mariner Street. I'm meeting a builder there in' – he checked his watch – 'about ten minutes.'

'Oh, right.' *The old bakery? So Max is the mystery new owner.* She wasn't sure what to think about this information. Would she feel comfortable having Max as her landlord, or would it put her off enquiring if it would be available to rent? There was no doubting it would add another dimension to their friendship. That aside, apart from Campion's of York, he didn't appear to have hung on to any of his other businesses, which means he'd more than likely bought the old bakery to do up and sell, and therefore, have no plans to rent it out. Which would rule it out as a contender in the hunt for a new home anyway.

Jasmine felt an unexpected pang of disappointment, but remained quiet. She'd keep Lark's suggestion to herself.

Max took a final sip of his tea before setting his cup and saucer down on the table. 'Well, Hilda, thank you for the tea and the delicious shortbread, but I'd best be heading off. I don't want to be late for my appointment.'

'Of course, lovey, but don't forget, you're very welcome to call in any time, though you might prefer a Tuesday morning when our Jasmine's here.' Hilda gave him a conspiratorial smile.

'I'll bear that in mind.' He pushed himself up, flicking a look at Jasmine who quickly busied herself gathering up the cups and saucers, deliberately avoiding meeting his eye. 'It's been a pleasure to meet you, Hilda, and I'll be sure to call in again soon.' He bent and delivered a kiss to the older lady's cheek which seemed to delight her no end.

'See you later, Jingilby.'

Jasmine jumped to her feet, tray in hand – setting the china and teaspoons clinking and clattering – putting some distance between herself and Max, just in case he was minded to kiss her, too. She wasn't ready for such gestures in front of Hilda. 'Yep, see you, Max. I'll be in touch about Connor coming round.'

'Sure.' He gave her an uncertain smile before turning to the older lady. 'I'll see myself out, Hilda – and don't forget what we said about not confronting thugs like Jason Scragg. Otherwise, have a good day, both of you.'

As soon as the front door clicked shut, it was clear that Hilda wasn't done with her matchmaking.

'Well, isn't that a turn up for the books?' she said, bustling with excitement.

'Hmm.' Jasmine deliberately avoided asking her friend to elaborate, knowing full well it would lead to comments and questions she wasn't inclined to answer. She decided it was best to guide Hilda's thoughts down a different route. 'Looks like someone else is crazy about your shortbread, Hilda.'

'It does, doesn't it?' Hilda clasped her hands together, her face animated. 'And if I'm not mistaken, it's not the only thing young Max is crazy about.'

Here we go! 'I'd best get cracking, or I'll be late to my next job.' Jasmine sent Hilda a gentle warning look. 'I'll just take this tray through to the kitchen.'

'There's no point ignoring it, lovey. I can see you like him, too. And it would be such a shame not to act on your feelings.' She cupped Jasmine's face in her hand. 'And if anyone deserves some happiness with a lovely young man, it's you, flower.'

TWENTY-SEVEN

'I know what you're thinking, young Jasmine. But I always say everything happens for a reason, and exactly when the time is right. And I reckon that's why Max is back now. Some greater force is at play.'

Jasmine's copper eyebrows knitted together. 'Have you been talking to Lark recently by any chance, Hilda?'

Hilda chuckled. 'No, but we both know she'd tell you something similar.'

Jasmine sighed. 'You're not wrong there.' How could this be happening? Max had only come back into her life less than two weeks ago!

Setting the tray back down on the table, she flopped into the chair. It was clearly pointless hiding her feelings from Hilda. Before she knew it, the words were tumbling out. 'But he's only just come back. It's hardly any time at all. And it's been twenty-five years since he last lived in Micklewick Bay. That's a lifetime ago. Couldn't my emotions be confused?' It certainly felt as if they were. 'Don't you think I could just be confusing being really happy to see him again, knowing life has been kind to him, with something else? Something... more... Ugh!' She rubbed her hands over her face. 'I mean, I'm so happy things have turned out well for him after everything he went through.'

'Aye, so am I, bless him. And he's grown into such a lovely young man.' Hilda eased herself onto the sofa and took Jasmine's hand. 'Now, listen, lovey, if what I've witnessed today is anything to go by, I don't think your emotions are confused about anything in the slightest. And it's exactly the same with Max. I saw the way he was looking at you, there was no mistaking it. It was just how my Joe used to look at me when we first met. Used to make my heart all of a flutter, he did,' she said, smiling wistfully. 'We'd only been courting six weeks when he proposed. We both knew right from the start we'd found "the one". And we never had a day's regret.'

'Ahh, Hilda. I'm so sorry you didn't get longer with him.' Jasmine squeezed her friend's hand. Hilda had been widowed for over ten years now, and she regularly told Jasmine that not a day went by when she didn't miss Joe.

'Aye, me too, sweetheart, me too.' She patted the top of Jasmine's hand. 'But getting back to you, don't you think it's time you had a bit of romance in your life?'

Jasmine gave another sigh. There were so many reasons why that wasn't an option. 'It's not that simple, I mean, there's so much to consider before I'd even think about having a... well, getting involved in a...' Why was she finding it so hard to use the word "relationship"? She gathered her thoughts back together. 'First of all, I'd never want to do anything that would confuse or upset Zak and Chloe; they're my priority in everything. We both know things don't always work out the way we hope they might.' Jasmine wasn't just thinking about her time with Bart; what Max had told her about Danni, his ex, came to mind. He'd already hinted that his relationship with Connor's mum had made him wary. That made two of them, which wasn't a great starting point, if Hilda was right about his feelings for her.

'You shouldn't let what happened with Bart put the dampeners on any future relationships before they've even got started, flower.'

Jasmine went to speak, but Hilda beat her to it. 'And I don't just mean how things ended, which, of course, was very sad, but let me put it this way, you'd known Bart for years before you moved in with him, hadn't you?'

'I had, yeah.' Jasmine wondered where Hilda was going with this.

'Well, at the risk of sounding blunt, which, at my age, is something I reckon I can get away with.' She softened her words with a smile. 'You and Bart didn't seem that well suited, and it was no secret that your relationship was a rocky one. Enid and me regularly discussed it; we were both worried for you. He was a nice enough lad, but he'd been spoilt rotten by his parents, indulging him and letting him have his own way. And I can tell you this, the day you moved in with him was the day you lost that cheeky sparkle of yours.'

'Wow. I had no idea people knew what was going on.' She thought she'd hidden their problems well with her supposedly well-honed act that everything in the garden was rosy. Turns out the only person she'd been fooling was herself.

'It's a small town, lovey, you know how fast gossip travels round here. And besides, folk aren't daft. Everyone could see how you were running yourself ragged while he spent his days at the amusements or hanging out at the bookies over in Lingthorpe. Your hard-earnt wages ran through his fingers like water and he didn't seem to have any qualms about it. I know he had a good sense of humour, and could be the life and soul of the party when the mood took him, but he ended up owing money to some really bad folk, the sort you wouldn't want to get on the wrong side of. That wasn't fair on you and Zak and little Chloe who hadn't even been born then.'

Jasmine blew out her cheeks. She hadn't been expecting this today. She closed her eyes, hoping Hilda wasn't going to remind her of the whispers that had been stealing around the church at Bart's funeral. It still occasionally crept into her mind after all this time. For the first few years she'd lived in fear of "debt collectors" turning up at her home, but as time had gone on, and she hadn't been troubled by anyone, she'd gradually allowed herself to let go of that particular spectre. She'd accepted she'd never know the truth, had made a kind of peace with it. She preferred it that way, for Zak and Chloe if nothing else. And it had meant she could move on and forge a new life for herself and her children.

'He had an addiction, I pushed him to get help, but he was in denial, even at the end, he kept telling me he had it all under control, which he clearly hadn't.' Jasmine's eyes lowered to her hand, still cradled by Hilda's. She felt her throat tighten. 'I must've looked like a right mug.'

'Oh, lovey, no one thought that. Folk in this town hold you in very high esteem, they're always singing your praises, saying what a wonderful mother you are, how hard you work. Uhh! And don't get me onto your cakes.' Hilda smiled, rolling her eyes, feigning exasperation which raised a smile from Jasmine. 'Anyone would think you were a local celebrity the way they go on about you.'

Jasmine gave a weak smile. Did people really think of her that way?

'His parents blamed me for everything, even his gambling. They still do.'

'That's just their grief talking, they need someone to point the finger at. Try not to take it to heart.'

'I wish it was that easy.' Jasmine told her about the letter from the Forsters' solicitors.

Hilda tutted, a frown furrowing her brow. 'They need to let go now. They're hurting themselves more than anyone else. I hope Mr Cuthbert's going to point them in the direction of the pawn shop over at Lingthorpe. From what I've heard, their son was a regular there. I daresay their records'll prove that.'

Jasmine hadn't thought about the shop having records. 'Good point. I'll mention that to Mr Cuthbert tomorrow.'

'You do that, lovey. But Bart and the Forsters aside, and getting back to what we were talking about before, what I'm trying to say is, when you get a chance at happiness, don't push it away. You deserve it more than anyone I know. Give love a chance, sweetheart. And give Max a chance, it doesn't matter if he hasn't been back long. If those feelings are there, they'll be genuine. Don't be frightened to have what me and my Joe had, it's the most wonderful thing.'

Jasmine lifted her gaze and was met with a kind smile. It had been surprisingly good to get it all out, to hold her concerns up to the light and examine them through someone else's eyes. She smiled back, feeling suddenly lighter as Hilda's advice sank in. 'Remind me how we got onto all of that?'

Hilda gave a hearty chuckle, patting Jasmine's knee. 'I reckon it's because love is in the air for you, young lady.'

Love! A nervous thrill tingled its way through Jasmine. She wondered what Florrie and the rest of the lasses would have to say about that.

TWENTY-EIGHT

Jasmine had worked through lunchtime at Hilda's, busily catching up with her cleaning session. Her friend, satisfied she'd got her point across about Max, had moved on to quizzing Jasmine about her trip to Danskelfe Castle and her meeting with Lady Caro. She'd been thrilled to hear about the wedding cake offer. 'I'll be keeping my Tuesday mornings with you though, Hilda. I look forward to them, and not just because of your delicious shortbread, I promise,' Jasmine teased, sending her friend a quick grin. And though Hilda had protested, telling her she should focus on her new venture, the look in her eyes told a different story, which made Jasmine glad of her decision.

'Right, that's me done,' she'd said, pulling her household gloves off and stuffing them in her caddy of cleaning equipment. 'If you let me have your shopping list, I'll just nip to the supermarket for you.'

'Are you sure you've got time?' Hilda had asked.

''Course I have. I'll be quick as a flash. Mind, if you spot Jason Scragg while I'm out, you've got to promise me you won't tackle him again, or ever again for that matter.' Jasmine feared

Scraggo wouldn't back down quite so easily if Hilda confronted him by herself.

'Cross my heart, lovey.'

'Good.'

It was while she was in the supermarket car park that Jasmine had rung the school, explaining what Scraggo had said about them being in touch with him. She'd breathed a sigh of relief when Charlotte, the headteacher's PA, had reassured her it had nothing to do with Zak and Chloe. Instead, Bruce Scragg had targeted another child, and the parents had lodged an official complaint with the governing body. His behaviour had warranted instant expulsion, while his sister, Nina, had been suspended for bringing a vape into school. 'You can rest assured both Zak and Chloe are fine, and they weren't involved in any of it,' Charlotte had said.

Jasmine only hoped that this turn of events would mean the Scraggs would move to another town, not that she wanted to inflict their nastiness onto anyone else, but, with her history with Scraggo, she thought it highly unlikely that they'd manage an easy co-existence in Micklewick Bay.

On her return home that afternoon, Jasmine was dismayed to find a Sale Agreed sticker plastered over the For Sale sign outside her home. It added a new urgency to her house-hunting plans. She rushed into the kitchen, filled the kettle and fired up her laptop. She should be getting on with her latest cake, but knew she wouldn't be able to settle until she'd had a quick check online to see if any new rental properties had become available.

A quick search threw up a small house on Ox Row which was on the other side of town. The street had a dubious reputation and, worse, from what she'd heard, it wasn't far from where the Scraggs lived. Added to that, the houses were even smaller than the ones on Rosemary Terrace, if that was possible. She chewed at the corner of her mouth, wondering whether to book a viewing. The only other property that had been remotely suitable was on Lavender Terrace, a couple of streets away from where she was currently living, but it was overpriced, pushing it out of her budget by a considerable amount. She expected it wouldn't get snapped up as quickly as the other properties.

She was scrolling through the properties one last time, just to make sure she hadn't missed anything, when a semi-detached house on Wilkinthorpe Road, not far from where her parents lived, caught her eye. Her hopes lifted. It was a new listing since the last time she'd checked. And, if she wasn't mistaken, the layout looked pretty much the same as her childhood home. Like number eight Arkleby Terrace, it was a former authority house. The accompanying photos showed a neatly kept lawn which was divided by a short footpath that led to the front door, while a generously proportioned garden stretched out at the back. An image of Zak and Chloe playing there filled her mind.

According to the details, the property had three reasonably sized bedrooms, a newly fitted kitchen and bathroom, as well as a new central heating and hot water boiler. *Bliss!* It was also double-glazed. The property had clearly undergone a renovation with a view to renting it out. Her heart thudded with excitement. It would be perfect for her and the kids. Telling herself not to get her hopes up, Jasmine stole a cautious glance at the monthly rental figure. Disappointment flooded through her. Though it wasn't unreasonably priced, it was too much of a stretch for her budget, and much as everything about it was ideal, she didn't want to have sleepless nights, worrying about how she was going to pay the rent every month. 'You're just going to have to put it out of your mind,' she said flatly, closing the page.

Putting her disappointment behind her, Jasmine called the letting agents and booked a viewing at the Ox Row property for

Thursday lunchtime. Hopefully, something more suitable would come up in the meantime.

Jasmine was elbow-deep in washing-up, the kitchen filled with the aroma of the fruit cake that was baking in the oven, when there was a knock at her door, startling her out of her thoughts. She dried her hands and headed down the hallway, hoping it wasn't going to be a viewing she hadn't been warned about, quickly discounting that as she remembered the Sale Agreed sign. She flung open the door and her heart leapt to attention.

'Max, hi. Come in.' She couldn't have stopped the wide smile that spread across her face if she tried. He looked handsome in his jeans and crisp shirt.

'Hiya, Jingilby, it's not a bad time, is it?' He took off his sunglasses and bent to kiss her cheek, sending butterflies tumbling around inside her.

'Not at all, I was just washing up, can't say I'm gutted at having that interrupted.' She grinned at him.

'No, I wouldn't be either.' He chuckled as he followed her into the kitchen. 'Mmm. Something smells delicious.'

'That would be the fruit cake that's been baking slowly in the oven for the last half hour. It's for a christening at the weekend.'

'Lucky guests who'll get to sample a slice.'

'There was actually some leftover mix which I put into a smaller tin. If you play your cards right, I'll let you have some when it's ready.'

'In that case, I'll be on my best behaviour.'

'D'you have time for a cuppa?' She glanced up at him, noting he seemed even taller in such a small space.

'Love one, thanks.'

'Great.' Hilda's advice about Max had never been far from her thoughts since she'd got home, and now he was standing in front of her, she found herself feeling suddenly nervous. Pulling herself together, she invited Max to sit down as she busied herself filling the kettle and throwing teabags into the pot, all the while aware of his eyes on her.

'So, to what do I owe this pleasure?' she asked, after a few minutes' small talk, hoping she sounded normal and not at all like a giddy schoolgirl who had a crush on the popular boy at school, which was exactly how she felt right now.

'I wanted to tell you, before you heard it from anyone else, that I've—'

Jasmine's heart froze but she plastered a smile on her face as she anticipated what he was about to share. 'Let me guess, you and Sabrina have finally given in to your feelings for one another? Can't say I blame you, and you do make a great couple.' If that was what he was going to say, then at least she hadn't made a fool of herself and let him know she liked him. She was going to bury her feelings, make sure he was none the wiser. She busied herself pouring the tea, taking the time to compose herself.

'What?' Max looked at her in disbelief. 'No! That's not what I was—'

A loud banging at the door sliced off his words, making Jasmine start such that the tea missed the mug and went all over the table instead. 'Oh, my God, who's that?'

'Someone who's very keen to get your attention by the sound of things.' Max ran his hand over his hair impatiently.

Setting the teapot down, Jasmine rushed to the door, eager to find out what was so urgent. Her hackles prickled when she found herself faced with Dodgy Dick and Wendy.

'What are you doing here?' she asked, unable to hide her displeasure.

'What sort of welcome's that?' Dodgy Dick smirked, sending Jasmine's irritation rising.

'How rude,' said Wendy, as the pair of them pushed their way in.

'Excuse me, but what do you think you're doing?' said Jasmine, her hand on her hip. 'You can't just barge your way in here like you own the place.'

'We've booked another viewing, that's what we're doing. We needed another look at the place before we put in our offer,' Dodgy Dick called over his shoulder on his way to the kitchen. Wendy followed, sweeping past in a cloud of her cloying perfume.

'Now hang on a minute. I haven't been told about any of this.' Jasmine closed the front door and hurried after them. 'I was on the phone to the estate agents an hour and a half ago and no one mentioned anything about viewings, least of all one today.'

'That's nowt to do with us, blame that Don Carswell, he doesn't know his head from his ar—' Dodgy Dick's expression darkened when he saw Max sitting at the table. 'What's he doing here?'

'He's a guest, not that it's any of your business, And *he's* welcome.' Jasmine couldn't believe the nerve of the man. As soon as she could get rid of him and his wife, she was going to get on to Micklewick Mansions and give that Don Carswell a right royal earbashing.

Max got to his feet. 'Did I hear you say you'd come for another viewing?' He loomed over the slippery businessman.

'Aye, you did. Not that it's owt to do with you.'

'That's where you're wrong.'

'How d'you work that one out, then?' Dodgy Dick sniggered. He turned to his wife. 'Got a right smart alec here, love.'

'That's just what I was thinking.' She gave a derisory sniff as she looked Max up and down.

'I think you'll find you're wasting your time here. I put an offer in on this place this morning and it was accepted straight away.'

'What? No one's told me about it,' Dodgy Dick spluttered angrily.

'I suggest you take that up with Don Carswell,' Max said, calmly.

'Too right I will. Useless moron that he is.'

Jasmine blinked, slowly processing what she'd just heard. *Max was going to buy this place?* Why would he do that?

She watched in a daze as he ushered a grumbling Dodgy Dick and Wendy out of the house.

'Is it true?' she asked when he came back into the kitchen.

'It is, it's what I'd come to tell you. I wanted to stop you worrying about having to find somewhere new to live.'

'Right.' She absently picked up a cloth and wiped the spilt tea from the table. She wasn't sure how she felt about this information.

'But if you've set your heart on leaving, I've got a couple of other properties, if you'd rather have a look at those instead? You never know, they might be more suitable.'

She rinsed the cloth, turning to meet his gaze, pushing her mouth into a smile. She didn't want to appear ungrateful or rude, especially when his intentions came from a good place. 'No, that's fine. I'd rather not disrupt the kids if possible. I'd like to stay, if that's okay?'

'Yeah, of course, whatever you feel's best for the three of you.' He let out a sigh, clearly relieved. 'Just as soon as the sale goes through, I'll look into getting the windows replaced and deal with whatever else needs doing; just make a list and I'll get onto it straight away.'

Jasmine nodded, not liking the feeling that was creeping over her.

TWENTY-NINE
WEDNESDAY

A feeling of apprehension gripped Jasmine as she perched on the edge of her seat in the waiting room of Cuthbert, Asquith & Co. It wasn't helped by the awkward atmosphere that pervaded the air. The only sound was the sonorous ticking of the large clock on the wall and the tapping of fingers on a keyboard. With everything else that had been going on recently, she'd put the Forsters' accusations to the back of her mind until this morning. She just hoped Mr Cuthbert would believe her when she told him she didn't have any of the things the Forsters' solicitors had listed in their letter.

The phone on the receptionist's desk rang out, splicing through the uncomfortable quiet of the room. Jasmine and the two other waiting clients turned towards it.

Moments later the receptionist peered over at Jasmine. 'Miss Ingilby, Mr Cuthbert's ready for you. His office is on the first floor. If you take a left at the top of the stairs, it's the door at the end.'

'Okay, thank you.'

Arriving outside a door bearing a brass plate with Mr Cuthbert's name in a cursive hand, Jasmine gave a tentative knock, her heart hammering.

'Come in,' said a well-spoken voice.

Jasmine stepped into the room to see the solicitor sitting behind a large partners' desk, his thinning grey hair swept back over his head, his half-moon glasses perched on the end of his nose. The shelves of legal books that occupied the full length of the wall behind him and the dark wood panelling gave the room an old-fashioned and formal air.

'Good afternoon, Miss Ingilby, please take a seat.'

'Thank you.' She gave a nervous smile.

'So, thank you for coming.' He leant forward, threading his fingers together. 'I expect you're here about the letter.' He smiled kindly at her.

Jasmine cleared her throat, wondering how he already knew about the Forsters' communication to her, she hadn't mentioned it when she'd made the appointment. 'Er... yes, that's right. I was hoping you'd be able to advise me what to do.'

'Advise you what to do?' He arched a bushy, grey eyebrow.

'Yes, if you wouldn't mind, that is.' She swallowed, noting his slightly baffled expression. She hoped she didn't sound stupid. 'I've told them so many times, I don't have the things they've listed, but they don't believe me. And when I got the letter, with them threatening legal action, I thought I should make an appointment with you so you could reply on my behalf, if that's okay.'

Mr Cuthbert rubbed a hand over his chin. 'You're here about a letter from the Forsters?'

'Yes, it arrived last week.' She reached into her bag and retrieved the envelope. Straightening out the letter, she handed it over to him. 'This is it.'

He read it quietly, his expressive eyebrows rising up and down.

'I honestly don't have any of it. I've lost count of the number of times I've told them. The last time I saw any of the jewellery, Bart had it. He told me he needed to pawn it. That was over seven years ago and, as far as I'm aware, he never bought them back. My friend, Stella, she's a lawyer – you probably know of her – and she suggested I get you to send a reply to them on my behalf. Do you think the pawn shop in Lingthorpe will still have copies of receipts of whatever records they keep?' Though she was aware she was gabbling, Jasmine just wanted to get all the information out. She continued, telling him of Bart's debts and the unsavoury characters he'd got himself involved with.

Mr Cuthbert listened quietly, scribbling down notes with a fountain pen. 'I see. It must have been a dreadful time for you, Miss Ingilby.' He set his pen down on the table and steepled his fingers together. 'I think the first thing we should do is contact the pawnbrokers and ask them if they have any documents or receipts relating to Bart and the items listed in the Forsters' letter. If so, we'll request that they send copies. That way you'll have irrefutable proof that their son pawned the items and the pawnbroker, in turn, sold them on. I'll ensure that a letter goes out in the post today. We'll just have to hope they've still held on to the documents.'

'Thank you,' she said, relief rushing through her that Mr Cuthbert not only believed her, but that he also thought there was a chance they could show the Forsters physical proof that she didn't have any of those things.

Mr Cuthbert cleared his throat. 'When I saw your name in my diary, I assumed you'd made an appointment to discuss the other matter.'

'Other matter?' The relief of moments ago was elbowed out of the way as a fresh surge of adrenalin started pumping through her veins. What else could there be? Not more from the Forsters, surely?

'Yes, the letter I sent you regarding Mrs Enid Lambton.'

'What letter? I haven't received anything from you.' *Please don't let it be more hassle!*

Mr Cuthbert picked up a file from his desk, pulling out the correspondence. 'Apologies, Miss Ingilby, I'm afraid I'm what you'd call old school, and I prefer pen and paper to computers, hence the file.'

'No need to apologise, I'm the same.'

After a moment's flicking through the typed sheets of A4, the solicitor's face brightened. 'Ah, here it is. Yes, from the date on our copy of the letter, you should have received it last week.'

'Last week?' A thought pinged into her mind: the letters she'd scooped up and stuffed into her bag on the day she'd stomped down to the estate agents after the For Sale sign had appeared on her house. She'd read them, sitting on a bench on the top prom. Bizarrely, it was the day the Forsters' letter had arrived. 'One second.' She unzipped her bag and after a brief rummage pulled out a crumpled envelope. 'I think I might've found it.'

'Ah, so you have.' The solicitor's face brightened. He watched as she slid her finger under the flap of the envelope to reveal a letter bearing Cuthbert, Asquith & Co's letterhead.

'Looks like this is it.'

'In that case, my dear, I'll give you a moment to read it.'

The letter was short and to the point, Jasmine's face morphing from confusion to disbelief as she read.

'But... but... Surely, this can't be right? I mean... I...'

'I can assure you, it's right, Miss Ingilby. And, like the letter says, as soon as you instruct us as to your preferred way of receiving payment, we'll get onto it right away.'

THIRTY

Jasmine had left the solicitor's office in a daze, wondering when the roller coaster that her life had become was going to slow down or preferably stop so she could get off and find somewhere quiet where she could gather her thoughts. She needed time to absorb this latest piece of information, but her head was so full of other things, she was struggling to find a space for it.

She glanced at her watch, then over at The Happy Harte's Bookshop. The bakery, where she was due to start her shift in just over half an hour, was two doors down. She could do with talking this new development over with Florrie before then; her friend had found herself in a similar situation a few years ago, though on a slightly larger scale.

A moment later, the bell above the bookshop door jangled noisily as Jasmine stepped inside, the inimitable smell of books rushing at her.

'Hi, Jasmine.' Leah, the young assistant, beamed at her from the counter where a small display of stationery and bookmarks had been artfully arranged.

'Hi.' Jasmine smiled back.

Gerty, the bookshop's resident Labrador, heaved herself out of her bed by the counter and trotted over to greet Jasmine.

'Hello there, Gerty.' She bent and smoothed her hand over the Labrador's velvety head.

'Jazz! Great to see you.'

Jasmine followed the direction of the voice to see Florrie peering around a bookshelf, a clutch of paperbacks in her hand.

'Hi, Florrie, don't suppose you've got a minute? I could do with running something past you.'

"Course, I was going to take my lunchbreak just after I'd put these on the shelves. Give me two ticks, we can head through to the back.'

Jasmine gazed around the bookshop while Florrie finished her task. The salvaged staircase they'd had fitted had totally transformed the space, its ornate ironwork spindles and the rich patina of the handrail adding character. It led to the newly created tearoom located in the converted living quarters. Florrie and Ed were thrilled with it.

'Right, that's that done,' said Florrie, emerging from the romance section. 'Come on, I'll pop the kettle on and you can tell me what's on your mind.'

Arriving at the tiny kitchen, Florrie didn't waste a moment. 'So, is this about Max?' Her eyes sparkled behind her tortoiseshell glasses.

Her question took Jasmine by surprise. 'Well, it wasn't, but maybe it could be.'

'I see, I think.' Florrie laughed as she reached for a couple of mugs. 'Park your bum, missus, and tell me all about it.'

'I'll start with my original reason for being here.' Jasmine pulled out a chair at the small table. 'You know I had an appointment at Cuthbert, Asquith & Co today?'

'Yes, it's this afternoon, isn't it?'

'It was at half-twelve, I've just come from there.'

'Oh.' Florrie's hand froze over the tea caddy. 'Sorry, Jazz, I thought it was later. How did it go?'

'No worries, and it went well as far as the Forsters are concerned. Mr Cuthbert was really nice actually, suggested contacting the pawnbrokers where Bart was a regular.'

'Why do I get the feeling there's a but?'

'It's not really a *but* as such. While I was there, he brought up something else that took me completely by surprise.'

'Right,' Florrie said, drawing out the word.

She listened as Jasmine explained about the misplaced correspondence, clamping her hand over her mouth when Jasmine told her how Enid Lambton, the elderly lady she used to clean for, had bequeathed her a sum of money.

'You're joking? Enid, Hilda's friend?'

'I'm not joking at all. Look.' Jasmine fished out the letter, handing it over to her friend. 'It just doesn't seem right, somehow. Makes me feel like I've done something a bit dodgy.' Jasmine gave a shudder. 'I'm not so sure I should accept it.'

Florrie handed the letter back to Jasmine, fixing her with a sympathetic look. 'Listen, flower, I totally understand, it was the same for me when Mr H willed me a share in this place. I nearly didn't take it for the reasons you've just stated.'

'That's why I'd appreciate your advice. I'd hate for people to think I only did her shopping and called on her just so she'd leave me something in her will. It'd honestly never crossed my mind. It's the sort of thing that makes me feel I shouldn't accept it.'

'I'll tell you what made me accept what Mr H had bequeathed to me,' said Florrie. 'It was being told that it was what Mr H had wanted, that he hadn't made the decision lightly, that he'd given it considerable thought. And if I refused it, then I'd be going against his wishes.'

Jasmine nodded. 'I remember you saying you'd been told that at the time.'

'Enid thought a lot about you, Jazz, she used to come in here to get her books, telling us all about how kind-hearted you were, and how she used to look forward to your shifts, plus all the other times you called in to check on her, grab her some shopping, or drop a cake in for her. You brightened her days, and she's chosen to remember you in her will to show you how much it meant to her.'

Jasmine hadn't thought of it like that, she hadn't given herself much of a chance to think of it at all really.

'Do you honestly think that's why she did it?'

''Course I do. There's no other reason – and before you say it, no, I definitely don't think she thought of you as a "charity case".' Florrie gave Jasmine a pointed look. 'You need to stop overthinking, and accept Enid's gift, just as I did with Mr H's. End of, the lasses would tell you the same.' She gave a wide smile. 'Anyroad, change of subject, how's things with you and Max? Tell all.'

'Firstly, there is no me and Max.' She gave Florrie a stern look. 'But it would seem he's going to be my new landlord, unless I find somewhere else to live, that is.'

Florrie's eyebrows knitted together. 'Max is going to be your landlord?'

'Yup.' Jasmine rolled her eyes. 'He's been buying up a load of property in the town and he's put an offer in on my house and it's been accepted.'

'Okay.' Florrie rubbed her fingertips over her brow. 'There's clearly a lot for us to catch up on, but that aside, how do you feel about him owning your home?'

'I feel a bit niggled to be honest. Almost like I have to be grateful to him, which isn't a nice feeling actually. My head's all over the place with everything.'

'Hardly surprising considering the last couple of weeks you've had.' Florrie handed Jasmine a mug of tea before sitting down in the chair opposite.

'How did you find out?'

As well as giving Florrie a highly abridged version of what had happened since she'd first seen Max, telling her she'd explain it all in more detail on Friday at the Jolly when the rest of the group were there, Jasmine relayed what had happened earlier that day. She kept out the matter of her feelings for her old friend; there was no point in sharing that now. Though the reminder of Dodgy Dick and his wife had made her blood boil all over again.

Florrie took a sip of her tea, contemplating what she'd just heard. 'I can see that Max means well, but I can understand why it would make you feel uncomfortable. I reckon I'd be the same if I were in your shoes.'

Jasmine sighed. It felt good to know she wasn't the only one who felt that way, that she wasn't overreacting.

Florrie sat up straight. 'Actually, you do realise you have a solution, don't you?'

'Do I?'

'That little nest egg Enid left you, would you consider putting it towards the rent of a more expensive property?'

Jasmine took a moment to consider Florrie's suggestion. She hadn't even got as far as thinking about what she'd do with the money if she kept it. The house on Wilkinthorpe Road popped into her mind, making her feel suddenly brighter. 'You know, that's not a bad idea. Has anyone ever told you you're a genius, Florrie?'

'Not nearly often enough.' They both hooted with laughter at that.

'Yikes! Have you seen the time?' Jasmine glanced at the clock and got to her feet, downing the dregs of her tea. 'I'll be late for work at this rate.'

'Just as well you don't have far to go.' Florrie giggled, scooping up the mugs and popping them into the sink.

'True. Thanks for listening to me moaning, and for your fab

advice, flower. If I don't see you before, I'll see you at the Jolly on Friday.'

'You're welcome. And I'll look forward to hearing all about Max and the stuff you didn't share today.'

Don't go there! 'Don't build your hopes up, there's nowt to tell.'

'Then why is your body language telling a different story?'

Jasmine shook her head. 'You're seeing things. Anyroad, I'm off, see ya.'

She dashed out of the bookshop before her friend could say anything further, calling a goodbye to Leah and Gerty as she went.

THIRTY-ONE
THURSDAY

It had been a crazy busy day, starting off with a one-bedroom flat that needed a deep clean after a particularly scruffy tenant had vacated. Thankfully, the landlord had forewarned Alice at Spick 'n' Sparkle and she'd sent Nuala, another one of her cleaners, along with Jasmine. The two women had been appalled by what had greeted them. 'How can anyone live like this?' Jasmine had said when they'd peered into the bathroom.

Three hours later, the flat was gleaming, and Jasmine and Nuala were glowing with the satisfaction of a job well done, as well as feeling utterly shattered.

Jasmine barely had time to go home and get changed before it was time to head to the viewing at Ox Row. After her conversation with Florrie about putting some of Enid's bequest towards the rent of a better home, Jasmine had considered cancelling today's viewing, but she'd thought better of it, just in case, since she still hadn't made up her mind about accepting the money.

Her heart sank as soon as she turned into the street. It had been a while since she'd ventured into this part of town and from what she could see it had gone downhill if the graffiti and houses with boarded-up windows were anything to go by.

The interior of the tiny house was worse than she'd expected. The whole place reeked of stale cigarette smoke, and the décor was basic at best. The hot tap at the kitchen sink dripped and there were holes in the lino on the floor. And if she wasn't mistaken, Jasmine was sure there were mouse droppings on the worktops. She wondered what Lady Caro would think of having her wedding cakes baked in such a grimy place.

She turned to the landlord. 'Actually, I think I've seen enough.' She didn't need to view upstairs to know that she couldn't bring Zak and Chloe to live here.

She'd need to get something sorted sooner rather than later, especially since the niggle about Max being her landlord had mushroomed. She only hoped she didn't bump into him since she didn't want to say something she'd regret. It would be best for all concerned if she found somewhere new to live. That way, if Max was only buying the property to help her, rather than it being a house he'd like to have in his property portfolio, then he still had time to withdraw his offer.

Jasmine was glad when her shift at the bakery came to an end. Usually, she enjoyed her job there, and the banter between the rest of the staff, but the deep clean at the flat that morning had left her feeling more worn out than usual. Of course, the lack of sleep didn't help, and it seemed that each day brought something new to occupy her mind and fret over.

'S'just me,' Jasmine called as she opened the door of her parents' home. She followed the sound of voices to the kitchen, stopping in her tracks when she saw Max sitting at the kitchen table, cradling a mug of tea in his hands. She felt a pulse of attraction, that quickly gave way to irritation. She could've kicked herself for not spotting his car outside, alerting her to his presence and allowing her to prepare herself. It wasn't lost on her how twenty-five years ago, she wouldn't have batted an eyelid to see him looking so comfortable in her home.

'Hello there, lovey, how's your day been?' Judging by the cheerful note in her mum's voice, she was inordinately happy to have Max there.

'Hiya, Jingilby.' Max's smile reached up and made his eyes shine.

'Hi.' Jasmine did her best to muster up a smile, cursing her knees that had decided to go wobbly at his smile.

'Your dad's just getting changed out of his work stuff. He should be down in a minute,' her mum said, oblivious to her daughter's mood.

'How are the kids? No problems with school?' she asked, peering out of the window. Her heart filled with happiness as she watched Zak and Chloe tearing about the garden with Connor and Ernest. It was difficult to say who was having the most fun.

'They're all fine, having a whale of a time out there by all accounts.'

'That's good to hear.' Aware that she was avoiding meeting Max's eye, she headed over to the door and popped her head out, the scent of freshly cut grass floating under her nose. 'Hiya, kiddiewinkles, having fun?'

A chorus of 'Hi, Mum,' mixed with, 'Hi, Jasmine,' rang out. Chloe ran over to her, her pigtails flying out behind her, Ernest not far behind. She flung her arms around her mum's middle while Ernest nudged at her legs, his tail wagging happily as he looked up at her.

'You okay, little love?' Jasmine smoothed a hand over her daughter's hair, following up with a kiss.

'Yep.' Chloe nodded, gazing up at her. 'We've been having an awesome time with Ernest. He's brilliant at dribbling the football. Zak says he should go to footie school with him and Connor in the summer.' She covered her mouth with her hand and giggled at that.

'I reckon the daft hound would be in his element there, wouldn't you, buddy?' Max said, as Ernest trotted over to him for an ear ruffle.

'Now then, flower, had a good day?' Jasmine turned to see her dad making his way across the kitchen.

'Hi, Dad, it's been busy. How about you?'

'Can't grumble.' He flashed her a smile, his teeth looking extra white against his sun-kissed skin. 'Are you stopping for your tea?'

'Um—' Her mind went to the christening cake she'd yet to cover in marzipan.

Before she could reply, her mum jumped in. 'Max and Connor are staying, you might as well, too. I've made a massive quiche and some potato and chive salad so there's plenty to go round.'

'*Please*, can we stay, Mum? We're having the best time. *Please*.' Chloe's pleading look was all it took.

'Okay then, thanks, Mum, that'd be really nice.' Jasmine was known for not being able to hide her feelings, but for the sake of the kids and her parents she was going to have to keep a lid on her annoyance with Max. It wasn't going to be easy.

Happy with her mum's answer, Chloe skipped off into the garden. Ernest scrambled to his feet, his claws clicking over the floor as he followed her.

'Looks like you could do with this, lovey.' Heather pushed a mug of tea into Jasmine's hands. 'Go and sit yourself down, you look worn out.'

'Thanks, Mum, I'm shattered.'

'You okay, Jingilby?' Max asked, his eyes roving her face. 'Is there anything I can do to help?'

'I'm fine, thanks. This cuppa should put me right.' His

comment made her bristle and she didn't like herself for it. She knew he was trying to be kind. She just wished he'd stop or transfer his help elsewhere.

Max nodded, though he didn't look totally convinced. It crossed Jasmine's mind she probably looked as drained as she felt.

'Actually, now you're here, Uncle Steve, I've got something for you and Auntie Heather.' Max reached down to a backpack by his seat.

'Oh?' Heather closed the fridge door, chives in hand.

'Why have you got something for us, lad?' Steve asked.

'Jingilby mentioned you're celebrating a special wedding anniversary this year, and are planning a trip away.' Max glanced between them.

'Aye, that's right,' said Steve. 'Mind, we won't be going away till next year on account of us having a few unexpected expenses recently.'

'It'll give us longer to look forward to it,' Heather said with a chuckle.

Jasmine fixed her gaze on Max, wondering where he was going with this.

'Well, you might be able to go away a little earlier than you thought. This is for both of you.' He got to his feet and handed a large white envelope to Heather.

'Whatever's this?' she asked, her face pink from the warmth of the potatoes boiling on the hob nearby. Steve moved beside her.

'Open it and see.' Max gave a mysterious smile.

Jasmine watched as her mum opened the envelope and pulled out a ruby wedding anniversary card.

'Are you sure we should've opened it now? It isn't our anniversary for a good while yet,' Heather said, puzzled.

'Yes, you definitely should open it now,' said Max.

As Heather opened the card, a smaller envelope fell out onto the floor. 'Oops.'

'Ey up, what's this, then?' Steve bent to pick it up, handing it back to his wife.

Heather reached into the envelope and pulled out what appeared to be a voucher. 'What's... I don't understand.' Her face was wreathed in confusion. She glanced up at Max who was smiling down at her.

'It's an airline voucher for you to use to book return flights for you and Uncle Steve. I have a little villa in Sorrento which you're very welcome to use – I don't want anything for it. It's tucked away from the busy part of town, but it's within easy access of some great restaurants.' He was watching them closely, his expression uncertain. 'Of course, you don't have to go there, it's entirely up to you—'

'Oh, Max, lovey, I don't know what to say.' Heather's eyes brimmed with tears. 'This is way too generous, isn't it, Steve?'

Jasmine's gaze flicked to her dad, observing his reaction. Her parents were proud people – a trait she was regularly told she'd inherited – and she wasn't so sure Max's gift would be well received by her father. She felt her annoyance stir.

'I'm gobsmacked, lad. I don't know what we've done to deserve such a gift.'

Jasmine was shocked to see her dad as choked up as her mum. It set a little niggle working away at her.

'It's just to say thank you for looking out for me when I was younger,' Max said. 'You've no idea what your care and kindness meant to me. It's something I understand more now I'm older.'

'Ah, it was the least we could do, sweetheart, and there's no need for thanks.' Heather smiled through her tears. 'You always were a kind-hearted little boy, but this is too much.'

'It isn't at all. Please accept the tickets,' Max said firmly.

Jasmine leapt to her feet, anger propelling her. She'd heard enough. She opened her mouth before putting her brain in gear. 'Don't you think it's enough that you've made yourself my landlord without coming here, lording it over my parents like some sort of flash git? You haven't even been back five minutes and you're buying up the town or acting like some sort of benefactor to people. You're no better than Dodgy Dick!' Her eyes glittered angrily.

'Jasmine! That's a horrible thing to say!' Despite the rage pumping through her, Jasmine could see her mum was mortified.

'That's enough, Jasmine,' her dad said, sternly. He looked equally stunned by her outburst. 'Don't be so unkind.'

'Well, you two might be happy to bow and scrape and be beholden to him, but there's no way I am.' She grabbed her bag, pushed through them and made for the door. Spinning on her heel, she glared at Max. 'And for your information, I'll have left the house on Rosemary Terrace before you've completed on it, so don't feel obliged to buy it on my account.'

Max said nothing, but seeing the hurt in his eyes, it was as if someone had reached in and ripped Jasmine's heart out before throwing it to the ground and stamping on it.

'I'll come back later for the kids, I've got a cake to get ready for the weekend.' With that, she bolted for the door, slamming it shut.

Tears blurred her vision as she drove away and by the time she'd reached Rosemary Terrace her anger had subsided and she felt utterly ashamed of herself. Once inside, she threw herself onto the sofa and put her head in her hands. 'What have I done?'

As she busied herself, smoothing marzipan over the fruit cake, all Jasmine could see was Max's face, his wounded expression. She'd seen it before, many years ago, when they were children and he was being picked on. And she hated herself for making him feel that way.

She hardly dared show her face at her parents when she went to collect Zak and Chloe later. They looked at her in disbelief, their expressions betraying their disappointment in her.

'I'm really sorry.' She hovered in the doorway of the kitchen, uncertain if she was welcome to join them. She could hear Zak and Chloe who were still playing in the garden, but Max, Connor and Ernest had gone, much to her relief.

'It's not us you should be apologising to, it's Max. He tried to hide it, but it was very obvious he was upset,' said her mum. 'It actually reminded me of how he was as a little lad, pretending everything was okay when it very clearly wasn't. I'm ashamed of you, Jasmine.'

'I'm ashamed of myself. I'm really sorry, Mum.' Jasmine's heart clenched. She didn't want to be someone who made him feel like that.

'It was totally uncalled for and unkind. I expected better of you, Jasmine. You had no right to speak to Max like that in our house.' She couldn't remember the last time she'd seen her dad look so cross.

'I don't know what came over me, all I can say in my defence is that I've been having a stressful time and I think it must've caught up with me.' Even to her ears, her explanation sounded woefully inadequate.

'It's still no excuse to take it out on Max, you should've kept that temper of yours under control. You need to apologise to him first thing in the morning when the kids have gone to school; I don't want them getting wind of what you said.' Heather started gathering bits together on the worktop, as she seethed quietly, annoyance radiating from her. 'I saved some quiche and salad for you. You can have it at home. Steve, can you give the kids a shout, tell them their mum's here?'

It bothered Jasmine that she was being dismissed by her mum, but all the same, she knew she deserved it.

She was going to have to work out what to say to Max in the morning, and only hope he'd find it in him to forgive her. She fought against calling at his house for fear Connor overheard and got upset. She'd just have to wait.

THIRTY-TWO
FRIDAY

If Jasmine thought she'd been sleeping badly over recent weeks, then last night's insomnia had reached a whole new level. Max's hurt expression had been the first thing she'd thought about as soon as she'd opened her eyes, sending regret prickling over her skin. What the heck had made her lash out so cruelly? And to Max, of all people. It was so unlike her, and worse, she hadn't meant a word of it.

He'd occupied her thoughts all day, the pain in his eyes haunting her through her cleaning shift, and into the afternoon while she was working on the christening cake. It hadn't given her a moment's peace, not that she thought she deserved it. She'd called his mobile as soon as she'd dropped Zak and Chloe off at school, but each time it had rung out and gone to voicemail. She'd eventually left a message, apologising and asking him to call back, but so far there'd been an agonising radio silence. She told herself he was probably in meetings, or too busy to take calls, but deep down, Jasmine knew that he was avoiding her. And she couldn't blame him.

By the time it came for her to get ready for her night out at the Jolly with her friends, she felt uncharacteristically glum.

She'd much rather hide under the duvet than slap a smile on her face and go out and enjoy herself. She felt she didn't deserve to have a nice time after what she'd said to Max. The only good thing to come out of the day so far was that she'd been able to book an appointment to have a look around the Wilkinthorpe Road property that had caught her eye. She'd been relieved to learn it was still available and hadn't been snapped up straight away.

When seven o'clock arrived, it wasn't Eloise, the sixteen-year-old babysitter, who was making her late for once, it was Connie Jamieson, the woman from Lingthorpe, who was supposed to have collected the christening cake an hour ago. Jasmine supposed she could have left Eloise to do the handover, but she preferred to do it in person. She liked to make sure her clients were happy with their order, and provide them with any instructions where necessary.

With an exasperated huff, Jasmine picked up her phone in readiness to call Connie, when a text pinged through from the woman in question, telling her she'd been held up and would collect the cake first thing in the morning. 'Could've told me sooner,' Jasmine muttered to herself as she fired off a reply in a more cheerful tone than she was feeling, saying that would be fine.

Since she'd already had a text from Florrie advising her she was running late, and would meet her down at the Jolly, Jasmine popped her head around the door of the living room where Zak and Chloe were laughing at something on the television, along with Eloise. 'Right, I'm heading out now. Be good, monsters, and go to bed when Eloise tells you to, okay?'

'Yes, Mummy. Have a lovely time.' Chloe ran over for a kiss; Jasmine knew better than to trouble her son for one, especially in front of Eloise. Though, seeing him looking so relaxed and happy made it good to know the kids hadn't picked up on her internal anguish.

Jasmine headed across the bar of the Jolly, a sense of doom in her chest. As she expected, the pub was busy and she had to squeeze her way to the usual table, but even the lively chatter and the folk band's toe-tapping tune failed to raise her spirits as it usually did as soon as she arrived. And nor did the aroma of Mandy's fish and chips have their usual effect, kick-starting her appetite. She'd barely eaten all day, her insides were too churned up to face food. She'd had to force down a couple of slices of toast before she left the house, not wanting her glass of wine to land on an empty stomach, but that had been as palatable as a sheet of sandpaper and had stuck in her throat.

'Now then, Jazz.' Maggie's warm smile dropped as soon as she took in Jasmine's lacklustre demeanour. 'What's up, flower?'

'Oh, Jazz, what's happened? Your aura's not right.' Lark smoothed a hand down Jasmine's arm. 'Is the essential oil blend not helping? I can give you something else if you like?'

'I think my problems are a bit too big for your roller balls and pillow sprays, unfortunately, Lark,' Jasmine said flatly.

'I thought your appointment with old Cuthbert went well.' Stella frowned as she poured a glass of Pinot Grigio and slid it across the table to Jasmine.

'It's not that – and you're right, Stells, it did go well. As for the essential oil blend, Lark, I've pretty much used up all of the pillow mist and I carry the roller ball thingy everywhere.'

'What have I missed?' Florrie appeared, her face flushed with rushing as she slipped into the settle alongside Stella.

'Nothing, our Jazz was just about to tell us why she's got a face like a wet weekend,' said Maggie.

'Why, what's happened?' asked Florrie, looking closely at Jasmine.

'Ugh!' Jasmine put her head in her hands. 'Where do I start?'

They all listened as Jasmine brought them up to date with everything that had gone on that week, including Max's offer on her home and Edith's bequest, but she'd struggled to look any of them in the eye as she told them of her outburst on Max. Lark had gasped which had made Jasmine squirm and added to her guilt.

'Oh, Jazz, that's so not like you,' Maggie said. She was wearing an expression of disbelief that tore at Jasmine's insides.

'Neither can I.' She covered her face with her hands. 'Believe me when I say I feel absolutely dreadful about it. If I could take those bloody awful words back, I would in a heartbeat. The look of hurt in his eyes has plagued me ever since I said those horrible things.'

'Listen, flower, I think you've beaten yourself up enough. You need to try to get hold of him again tomorrow, and if he still refuses to answer his phone or return your calls, then, if I were you, I'd go to his house, see him face to face and tell him how sorry you are, clear the air. Once he sees you, he'll be in no doubt that you mean it.' Stella always favoured a direct, no-nonsense approach.

'You've been under a lot of stress recently, Jazz, running on adrenalin. Something was bound to give,' Lark said soothingly.

'Yeah, s'just a shame poor old Max was in the firing line and not someone like Scraggo,' said Jasmine.

'Now that would've been worth seeing.' Florrie gave a wicked chuckle, setting them all off. Even Jasmine found herself laughing.

Jasmine was standing at the bar, waiting to order a bottle of wine, and doing her best to avoid being spotted by Ando Taylor. She'd noted he was having a noisy conversation with Lobster

Harry and handful of other local fishermen and she was trying to keep out of his eye line.

She felt a tap on her shoulder and turned. It took her a couple of seconds to realise that the pinched face looking back at her belonged to Sabrina. She was looking effortlessly stylish again, wearing a linen halter-neck dress, and her hair fixed in a messy up-do, a pair of silver dangly earrings completing the look.

'Sabrina, hi.' Jasmine gave a hesitant smile, noting the look of hostility in the other woman's eyes.

'Have you got a minute?' Sabrina made no attempt to return Jasmine's smile.

'Er, yeah.' The last thing she needed to deal with was a jealous wannabe-girlfriend.

She followed Sabrina outside and over to the sea wall where it was quiet, just the sound of the waves rushing to the shore and a solitary seagull overhead, cawing as it headed towards the cliffs.

Stay focused! 'Look, if you've brought me out here to warn me off Max, you're wasting your time. I can tell you quite categorically that he's not interested in me and I'm not interested in him. So he's yours.' Jasmine gave a defeated shrug just as the vintage streetlights flickered into life.

'What?' Sabrina looked at her as if she'd lost the plot.

'Sorry if I'm speaking out of turn, or if you—'

'You think I'm interested in Max in *that* way?' The breeze blew tendrils of hair across her face and she swept them away with her fingers.

'Aren't you?' There'd been no doubting the side-eye Sabrina had treated Jasmine to on her visit to Max's house.

'*No!*' Sabrina shook her head so hard, her earrings jangled loudly. 'I can't believe you think I'd come to warn you off. Max is my boss, and though our relationship is relaxed, it's purely professional. And not just that, but I'm engaged to someone else. We're getting married next year.'

'Oh.' *How could I have got it so wrong?* 'So what are you wanting to talk to me about, then?'

'I wanted to tell you to treat Max with care. He hasn't gone into a great deal of detail, but I do know he was really looking forward to catching up with you and your family after all this time. And I could tell by the way he was when you called up at the house that he likes you. A lot.' Sabrina stopped talking as a couple walked by, waiting until they were out of earshot. 'I'm not sure what's happened between you, but he's been distracted all day. I haven't seen him subdued like this before and I can't help feeling it's got something to do with you.'

Guilt tore at Jasmine's insides as Sabrina continued.

'Max has a big heart and he's just crying out for someone to love. He's a good guy, and one of the kindest, most generous people I've ever met and he deserves to find someone who's his equal in that respect. What I'm trying to say, is don't hurt him, because if you do, I fear he'll never trust again.'

Not waiting for an answer, Sabrina flounced off back inside the Jolly, leaving Jasmine contemplating her words.

'Where've you been, Jazz?' asked Florrie, when Jasmine finally arrived back at the table, bottle of wine in hand.

'I was beginning to think you'd taken Ando up on his offer of a walk back to his place for a couple of pickled eggs and a pint of gut rot,' Stella said dryly.

The look Jasmine shot her made them all hoot with laughter.

'I've been having a wild old time, with Max's PA, who's just treated me to a lecture about how I should treat Max.'

'What? What gives her the right to speak like that to you?' Maggie snatched up her glass of fizzy orange juice, looking put-out on Jasmine's behalf. 'And, more importantly, why is it any of her business?'

'It wasn't said nastily, more that she wanted to get her point across,' Jasmine explained.

'Sounds like she was overstepping the mark to me,' said Stella.

'Maybe she was a bit.' But she'd given Jasmine pause for thought, which had galvanised her plans to speak to Max as soon as possible tomorrow.

THIRTY-THREE
SATURDAY

Despite calling Max's number several times first thing on Saturday morning, Jasmine still hadn't managed to speak to him. She'd been up early, stress depriving her of sleep, and had baked a batch of his childhood favourite double-chocolate cookies to give him as a peace offering. She'd even taken the bull by the horns and driven to his house, armed with the cookies, as Stella had suggested, only to find no one home.

It was torture!

She returned to Rosemary Terrace and set about making the two dozen cupcakes ordered by the local history group since one of their members was celebrating a special birthday that week.

The highlight of the day was the viewing of the Wilkinthorpe Road property which had turned out to be everything Jasmine had hoped. She'd viewed it on her own, leaving Zak and Chloe with her parents, not wanting to unsettle them if the property didn't work out. As she'd suspected, the house had been refurbished in readiness for the rental market, and from what she could see it appeared to have been done to a high standard. It was light-years ahead of her current home and, much as she would love to sign on the dotted line immediately, she was going to give it some careful consideration over the weekend, telling the letting agent she'd get back to them on Monday. Jasmine didn't take decisions of this kind lightly and didn't want to rush into something as important as somewhere to live.

When she'd returned to her parents' house afterwards, Jasmine was relieved to find the awkwardness after how she'd spoken to Max had gone. She'd apologised again, and listened as her mum had gently reminded her that she wasn't the person Jasmine should be apologising to. 'I know, Mum, I've been trying to get hold of him. I won't settle until I speak to him,' she said. Her mum had come back with, 'Well, keep trying.'

Jasmine was ironing in the kitchen when her phone pinged heralding the arrival of a text. She set the iron down and reached for her phone to see the text was from Florrie.

> Hi all, apologies for the short notice, but Ed and I are having a BBQ tomorrow here at Samphire Cottage. 12 noon-ish. We're keen to make the most of the sunshine while it lasts!! Would love it if you could all join us. Fxx

Jasmine smiled. A barbecue at Florrie and Ed's always made for a good do. It was just a shame Max was playing it cool with her, she was sure her friends wouldn't mind if she'd invited him along to meet everyone. It would've been the perfect occasion to do it, when they were all feeling relaxed. *Too late for that now, Jasmine.*

THIRTY-FOUR
SUNDAY

With the last load of washing hung on the line in their poky backyard, Jasmine scooped up the tin of caramel brownies she'd baked that morning and whose indulgent chocolatey aroma still permeated the whole house, and grabbed her keys.

'Zak, Chloe, time to go,' she called up the stairs.

Seconds later Zak thundered down from his bedroom, almost crashing into his mum when he reached the bottom.

'Go steady, Zak, these brownies nearly ended up on the floor.'

He pulled a mock horrified face, making her laugh just as Chloe appeared and skipped her way towards her. 'I'd still eat 'em,' he said.

'I don't doubt that for a second.'

The little garden at Samphire Cottage was a cheery suntrap, the flowerbeds spilling over with brightly coloured blooms. Bunting in pastel shades was festooned along the walls and around the shed, while a floral cloth was thrown over the trestle table that was groaning with food. Smoke from the barbecue swirled around on the light whisper of a breeze, tormenting Gerty.

Stella and Alex were already there, as were Lark and Nate, with the two men chatting to Ed at the barbecue. They all called over their hellos to Jasmine and the kids.

'Maggie and Bear are running late, baby Lucy's having a nap and since she was up most of the night, they don't like to disturb her,' explained Florrie.

'Don't blame them. I can remember those times, hopefully Mags'll grab some sleep while she's got the chance,' said Jasmine.

'What can I get you to drink, Jazz?' asked Florrie. She was looking cool in her mint-green knee-length sundress.

'Ooh, I think I'll have a have a glass of cider, thanks.'

'Kids, how about you? We've got some ice pops in the freezer if you fancy one of those each.'

Florrie's suggestion was enthusiastically received by Zak and Chloe who followed her into the kitchen.

Jasmine headed over to the table and made a space for the tin of brownies.

'Now then, Jazz, please tell me that contains something delicious baked by you,' said Stella, looking coolly sophisticated as always in her cream linen knee-length dress that showed off her long, coltish legs. Her straight, blonde hair was swept back in a loose ponytail while dark sunglasses shielded her eyes. She had a glass of what Jasmine guessed was a spritzer in her hand. Stella invariably had prep to do for her cases on a Sunday, so limited her alcohol intake.

'Caramel brownies today,' said Jasmine.

'Ooh, heavenly,' said Lark, whose silver-threaded fine cotton dress created the illusion she was shimmering in the sunlight. Her wavy blonde locks were woven into two plaits and arranged on top of her head in a bid to keep her cool.

'So, how's things?' asked Stella. She and Lark were sitting on all-weather chairs in the small, paved area of the garden.

'Things seem to have calmed down over the weekend. Touch wood.' Jasmine tapped her head before flopping into one of the empty seats. 'The viewing went well yesterday, so I'm just having a think about that. I told the agent I'd ge—'

'Who's *that*?' said Stella, sitting up straight and cutting Jasmine off.

'Who?' said Jasmine.

'Who? The drop-dead gorgeous bloke standing next to Florrie, that's who!'

'Ooh, he is very attractive,' said Lark.

Jasmine followed their gaze. 'Oh, my days. What's Max doing here?' Her thoughts went into overdrive and she didn't know which one to tackle first.

Stella and Lark exchanged confused looks.

'That's Max?' said Stella.

'I can't believe it!' Lark sounded as stunned as Stella.

'Yep, it's him,' said Jasmine as Zak and Chloe ran by on their way to greet Connor. This wasn't the way she'd expected to introduce Max after all these years.

'That must be his son, he's the double of Max when he was that kind of age,' said Stella.

'Isn't he just?' agreed Lark.

'Yes, Connor's his son,' said Jasmine, her heart going like the clappers. 'And the Labrador crossed with something fluffy that Gerty's currently making eyes at is Ernest who's a real sweetheart.'

'Ah, he looks it too.' Lark looked over at the two Labradors and smiled.

'It would seem love is in the air,' said Stella, a hint of mischief in her voice.

'Don't start,' said Jasmine. She swallowed nervously as Florrie headed towards them, Max following up behind. Stella had hit the nail on the head, he was drop-dead gorgeous. He made her wayward heart flutter. *Time to put your big girl panties on and face what he has to say to you.*

'Hi, Max.' She smiled up at him, and was relieved when he smiled back.

In her role as host, Florrie dealt with the introductions in her usual friendly manner. 'Max, you remember Stella and Lark, don't you? They'll have grown a bit since you last saw them.'

'Of course I remember, it's great to see you both again.'

'It's great to see you too, Max.' Stella took off her sunglasses, giving him a full appraisal before getting to her feet and giving him a hug. 'And you've definitely grown! I'd never have recognised you.'

He gave a deep laugh. 'And you've barely changed.'

'Yep, still a lanky-legs.' Stella chuckled. She'd always been tall for her age and worn her blonde hair long.

'Max, welcome back to Micklewick Bay, I was thrilled to hear you'd returned.' Lark enveloped him in one of her fragrant embraces.

'Thanks, Lark, I'm thrilled to be back.'

Feeling it would look unfriendly if she was the only one to remain in her seat, Jasmine got to her feet. Max turned to her, an uncertain look in his eye.

She reached up and wrapped her arms around him just as Stella and Lark had done, inhaling the clean fragrance of his cologne. 'It's good to see you, Max. I've been trying to get in touch.' He slid his arms around her.

'Work's been busy.' It tore at her insides that his voice was so flat because of her. She hugged him tight in a most un-Jasmine-like way.

'Not too busy for a chat later, I hope,' she whispered.

When she eventually released him, she asked, 'So how come you're here?'

'I reckon he followed the smell of the barbecue,' Ed called over.

Max laughed, the twinkle in his eyes reappearing and gladdening Jasmine's heart.

'Connor was after a book, so I took him to The Happy Hartes Bookshop and got chatting to the friendly young woman at the till, who turned out to be Florrie. She mentioned the barbecue and said we – including Ernest – were invited. Talking of my wayward hound, I'd better check he hasn't been helping himself to food on the sly.'

A quick glance around revealed him to be sitting beside Gerty, the pair of them observing the barbecue with great interest and much drooling.

Max chuckled. 'Seems he's got himself a new lady friend.'

'Reckon he's not the only one,' said Stella, sotto voce.

Jasmine shot her a look for her trouble.

They'd waited as long as they could for Maggie and Bear to arrive before serving the food, but a further text from Bear told them that baby Lucy was still fast asleep and now Maggie had crashed out such that he couldn't wake her. He'd given them the go-ahead to start without them. Soon, everyone was tucking into plump sausages and burgers and piling their plates with salad and couscous, all the while quizzing Max about what he'd been up to since he'd left Micklewick Bay. He, in turn, caught up with what the others had been doing, listening with interest.

Zak, Connor and Chloe sat away from the grown-ups, sneaking bits of sausage to the dogs and giggling mischievously.

'It's so cool you're all still such good friends,' Max said.

'Aye we've been together through thick and thin,' said Jasmine.

'We certainly have,' agreed Lark.

'Tell you what, I don't know about Ernest, but Gerty's

looking like she could do with a bit of a leg stretch. With it being so hot earlier, she didn't get a chance for one. It's cooled down a fair bit now. I don't suppose you'd mind taking her for a quick run on the beach, would you, Jazz?' Florrie announced out of the blue. 'Just while I get some of this cleared away.'

A quick run on the beach? Had her friend lost her marbles? Jasmine shot Florrie a look; she couldn't have been more transparent if she'd tried.

'I reckon you're right, Florrie, Ernest's overdue a walk,' said Max. 'Fancy joining me, Jingilby?'

Jasmine could feel several pairs of eyes boring into her like laser beams.

'Yeah, why not?' It would give them the perfect opportunity to have a chat and for Jasmine to apologise.

Jasmine and Max took a left out of the gate at Samphire Cottage, the dogs on the end of their leads, trotting along at a jaunty pace, a welcome breeze drifting in from the sea. It wasn't long before they'd reached the top prom.

'Get the feeling we've been set up?' Max asked, smiling.

'Er, just a bit.' She laughed. In the next moment her expression turned serious. She couldn't keep it in any longer, it had been churning around inside her ever since he'd arrived at Florrie and Ed's. 'Listen, Max, I want to say how sorry I am for the way I spoke to you at my parents' house the other day. It was horrible of me, you're the last person I'd want to upset. I'm not trying to excuse myself, I take full responsibility for what I said, but all I can say is it's been a stressful couple of weeks and I lashed out.' She turned her head to him. 'I'm really sorry, Max.'

'Of course I accept your apology, Jingilby. I'm not going to say your words didn't hurt, because they did. I'd never want to make anyone feel I was "lording it over them" as you described it. And if I gave that impression, then I should apologise for that.'

'You didn't, Max, it's me. I've got this thing about people

helping me financially, thinking of me as a charity case. My parents and my friends are always pulling me up about it, saying I'm stubborn. It's a legacy from my time with Bart, I think, but it seems to have taken root so deeply, it's hard to shift. And I still get his parents accusing me of being a gold-digger. Those horrible things I said to you was more about me, than it was about you.'

'You need to stop being so hard on yourself, Jingilby, and let your family and friends help you.'

That's easier said than done.

'I can remember your mum saying how you were so independent when we were younger, how you always liked to do things for yourself, didn't like help. How you'd save up for things you really wanted. I wanted to be like you.'

'You did?'

'Yeah. Then when I got to be an adult, and became aware of just how bad my family situation had been as a child, I promised myself that if I had any children of my own, they were going to feel nothing but loved and cared for and valued.'

'From what I've seen of Connor, I'd say you've achieved that. He seems a happy well-grounded kid.'

Max turned to her and smiled. 'Thanks. And you've done a pretty awesome job with your two, but they're even luckier than Connor cos they've got an endless supply of cakes on tap.' Jasmine laughed out loud at that.

'That reminds me, I've got a tin of double-chocolate biscuits at home for you. I'd made them hoping you'd forgive me for my ridiculous outburst.'

'Are they made from the same recipe you used when we were kids?'

'They are.'

'In that case, you're forgiven.'

'Thanks.' Jasmine chuckled, feeling a weight lift off her shoulders.

Soon, they found themselves on the beach, golden sand stretched out before them. They freed Gerty and Ernest from their leads, and watched them race down to the sea, leaping over the waves with abandon. Seagulls wheeled above before dipping and diving into the water.

'D'you get the impression those two are enjoying themselves?' asked Jasmine, chuckling.

'Just a little bit.' Max watched the dogs splashing around in the water, chasing one another. His chest heaved with a sigh. 'You know, the reason I wanted to help with your house situation and why I got the flight vouchers for your mum and dad was because it was a way of saying thank you for all you did for me when I was a little lad. I was made to feel like part of a family and I've cherished those memories. I don't think you realise what you and your family meant to me. It wasn't just about the warm meals and the clean clothes, it was the feeling that someone actually cared, that I actually mattered to you all – Jonathan's included in that.'

'Oh, Max.' Jasmine's voice came out in a whisper.

'I'm not telling you this to make you feel sorry for me – that's the last thing I want. I just need you to understand the reason behind my actions. I wasn't trying to be a flash git. I'd hate anyone to think that of me.'

'I know you weren't.'

'It wasn't till I got older that I realised just how much your parents did for me, handing down Jonathan's clothes, mending mine. And you, Jingilby, you're the best friend I've ever had. No one has ever come close. The way you used to stick up for me, how you stood up to Scraggo and risked being suspended from school or risked getting a thumping from him. I used to think you were awesome.'

Jasmine sniffed and wiped her eyes. 'Me? Awesome?'

'Yeah.' He nudged her with his shoulder, making her smile.

'And then when you arrived at my house with Zak's sleepover stuff, I realised you were actually still pretty awesome.'

'Didn't take long for me to make you change your mind, though, did it?'

'I didn't change my mind. If anything, it made me realise I had to be a bit more careful and sensitive about the way I approach things.' Max stopped walking, turning to face her, his shirt fluttering in the breeze. 'But I realised I'd started to develop different feelings for you. Strong feelings. And the speed they arrived took me by surprise. In fact, at the risk of making you run very quickly in the opposite direction, I felt something that first day at my house, but I put it down to the fact that we'd been such close friends when we were kids; a connection we'd never lost.' His eyes searched hers, making her heart perform somersaults. It was time to open her heart.

'It was the same for me,' Jasmine said. 'I felt it that first day too and it threw me into a right old tailspin.'

'So, now we've established we both feel the same way, what do you think we should do about it?' The look he was giving her made her insides turn to jelly.

'I don't know.' She couldn't tear her eyes away from his, sparks dancing in the air around them. 'I'm a bit scared, Max,' she whispered.

'Don't be, Jingilby, it's me. There's nothing to be scared of.'

'Are you sure?' Jasmine's heart was galloping, her emotions flying around inside her. She suddenly recalled how good it had felt to be in his arms; she'd felt safe.

'I'm sure. I don't think we should ignore these feelings.'

'Neither do I.' She felt a shiver of anticipation rush through her.

'I'm so glad you said that.' He gave one of his heart-melting smiles.

'But where do we start? I mean, it's been so long since I've been on a date, I'm out of practice. I feel like a girl on her first date with her first boyfriend.'

'Well then, let me give you your first kiss.' He leant forward, cupped her head in his hand and tentatively pressed his lips to hers, his kiss slowly deepening, the sound of waves in the background slowly fading away.

The touch of Max's lips on hers was intoxicating. She slid her arms up around his neck and pulled him close, never wanting this moment to end.

When they finally pulled apart, he rested his forehead against hers. 'I don't know about you, but I think that was a pretty good place to start.'

'It was the best.' Euphoria flooded Jasmine's chest.

'Do you think we should try it again, see if we can make any improvements?'

'Well, they say practice makes perfect.' Jasmine's eyes twinkled at him as her heart soared with happiness.

EPILOGUE
NOVEMBER

The last four months had been a total whirlwind for Jasmine. The wedding planning service offered by Lady Caro and her team at Danskelfe Castle had been well received. As had the option of the smaller, more intimate ceremonies, with couples thrilled to find a castle wedding within their budget. As a consequence, the newly available dates were being eagerly snapped up and Lady Caro had taken great delight in informing Jasmine that they were fully booked for the next eighteen months. Furthermore, of the couples who hadn't gone down the wedding-planner package route, many had ordered their wedding cake independently from Jasmine thanks to Lady Caro's generous promotion of her designs.

Indeed, Jasmine was still basking in the glow of a wedding cake she'd made for well-known social media influencer Demi Constantine-Powell who hailed from the city of York, and whose brief had been for "six tiers of glorious English country cottage garden in cake form". It had been Jasmine's most elaborate design to date, and one that had taken the most time, but she'd enjoyed every minute of its creation. As expected of someone in her line of work, Demi had shared her wedding photos on all of her social media channels which had created a huge clamour of interest, with a particular image of the elaborate wedding cake going viral overnight.

That had been a real "pinch me" moment for Jasmine.

Unsurprisingly, this interest had generated a whole tranche of publicity for her and the Danskelfe Castle weddings, resulting in a busy diary for both parties.

Jasmine had been thrilled to find that her dream of dedicating her time solely to creating celebration cakes had become a reality, and far sooner than she'd anticipated too. This was, in part, down to her taking on board Lady Caro's advice that the prices she charged should reflect the amount of work involved in her beautiful creations. It had seen a dramatic rise in her profits. That, and the orders from Lady Caro, meant that she'd been able to hand in her notice at the bakery and Spick 'n' Sparkle. However, Jasmine was true to her word, and still hung on to her weekly cleaning session at Hilda's, where her friend had delighted in hearing all of Jasmine's cake decorating news and, in turn, Jasmine had taken great pleasure from her weekly catch-ups with her friend.

That wasn't the only change recent months had seen for Jasmine and her two children. In early July, they'd moved out of the tiny house on Rosemary Terrace and into the property on Wilkinthorpe Road. Jasmine had been thrilled and relieved in equal measure to see that Zak and Chloe had settled quickly, playing out in the generous-sized garden at every opportunity. Connor had been a regular visitor, he and Zak spending endless hours practising kicking a football into the net she'd set out at the bottom of the back garden. Chloe's friendship with Sophie had gone from strength to strength too, and the little girls spent many happy hours playing in the Wendy house Jasmine had picked up for a song on the Micklewick Bay online selling site.

Her children were thriving, and it brought Jasmine a great sense of joy.

But it wasn't just Connor and Sophie who were regular visitors to the house on Wilkinthorpe Road. After their first kiss on the beach, Max had asked Jasmine if she'd consider letting him take her out on a date. After the riot of emotions that had exploded inside her when his lips had touched hers, she'd found herself unable to refuse. If Max was prepared to put his trust in love after all he'd been through, then she should do the same.

She hadn't had a moment's regret.

If only her friends would stop teasing her, then everything in her life would be perfect. A recent Friday night at the Jolly had been particularly excruciating.

'It's so good to see you all glowing and happy, Jazz,' Lark said, beaming.

'It so is,' Maggie agreed. 'Never thought we'd see the day, mind.'

'Yeah, love suits you, flower. It's making you sparkle,' Florrie chipped in, causing Jasmine to roll her eyes, while her face took on a beetroot hue. She was still uncomfortable talking about her relationship with Max, not to mention how he was affecting her.

'I reckon it's not just love we can attribute to that particular type of glow and sparkle.' Stella chuckled wickedly into her glass.

'Trust our Stells to lower the tone,' Maggie said, laughing. 'Mind, I reckon she could have a point.'

'Yes, but whatever Jazz is doing with Max, it's all wrapped up in love, isn't it?' Lark said, deepening Jasmine's blushes and making her cringe. 'You can see it a mile off, they're so loved up.'

'Yeah, you two are so meant to be together,' said Florrie.

'Argh! Will you lot stop with the torture! You're making my bloomin' toes curl with it all! And since when have I said anything about the "L" word, or anything else for that matter?' Jasmine covered her scarlet face with her hands. Though she kept it to herself, she knew Lark was right. She recalled her mum saying that as a little boy, Max had been easy to love. Which was exactly how Jasmine felt right now. Before she knew what was happening, she'd found herself falling head over heels in love with the kind, considerate and gentle man he'd become. And though the intensity scared her a little, she'd found herself unable to stop herself. There was something about his smiles and the way they made his eyes twinkle that made everything seem right.

The other two matters that had been a cause for concern earlier in June had finally been put to bed much to her relief.

It was early August when it reached Jasmine's ears that the police had been showing a keen interest in Jason Scragg, with one of their vehicles being regularly parked up outside his house. It had added weight to the rumours circulating around Micklewick Bay linking him to a spate of burglaries. Not long after, the unscrupulous family had packed up and left town, disappearing under a shadow of suspicion. Jasmine had been inordinately relieved, knowing that her children could enjoy their summer holidays and go back to school without the worry of having to face the Scragg children.

As for the Forsters and their relentless hounding of her, Mr Cuthbert had seen to it that their latest campaign of harassment was ceased. By a stroke of luck, the pawnbroker in Lingthorpe still had copies of his transactions with Bart and had provided Cuthbert, Asquith & Co with copies of the same. It proved, irrefutably, that Bart had pawned the jewellery and never returned to buy any of it back. Instead, the items had been sold on to other customers.

In his letter to the Forsters, Mr Cuthbert had not only imparted this information, but also advised that unless they stopped making a nuisance of themselves, the firm would be forced to take further action, starting with a cease and desist letter on her behalf. So far, Jasmine was relieved to find that the response had been met with radio silence. She was optimistic that's how it would remain.

And now, standing there on the beach with Max's arm wrapped around her, waves crashing against the shore and sending spray into the air while the autumn wind nipped at her face, a feeling of utter contentment washed over Jasmine. She looked on, smiling, as Zak, Chloe and Connor, along with the hapless Ernest, tore about, kicking up sand, their laughter and cries of delight, joined by the occasional happy bark, whipped up by the breeze. She'd never imagined it was possible to feel this level of happiness; was unaware it even existed. For so many years, stress and tension had ensured her body was on a permanent state of high alert, but she'd been pleasantly surprised to find herself absorbing Max's calm, relaxed approach to life, letting her anxiety drift away. If anyone had told her this was possible, she would never have believed them.

Jasmine inhaled a lungful of salty air, releasing it in a sigh as she rested her head on Max's chest.

'You okay, Jingilby?' he asked.

She looked up to see his gentle hazel eyes gazing down at her, triggering a now-familiar flurry of butterflies looping the loop in her stomach.

'More than okay.' She smiled up at him, oblivious to the harsh cries of the seagulls that screeched overhead.

'Good.' He pulled her close and pressed his lips against hers.

'Mmm.' Her heart dissolved into a delicious molten puddle.

After their initial tentative kisses on that very spot way back in June, the couple had agreed to take things slowly, not wanting to unsettle the three children if things didn't work out.

As cheesy as she thought it sounded, everything about being with Max felt right. Even from the start, the ever-cynical Jasmine had found that any feelings of doubt on her part had been overridden by the unspoken acceptance that she and Max were meant to be together.

Thought you didn't do love and mush and happy-ever-afters, Jasmine Ingilby, she'd said to herself one night gazing over at Max as he'd slept contentedly beside her when he'd stayed over one night. But one look in his eyes, and the brush of his lips against hers told her that she very definitely did.

She'd never dared to believe she could ever feel such happiness or know what being properly in love felt like. But being with Max had allowed her to experience all of that and more. He made her feel safe and loved, which had taken some getting used to, but now she'd reached the point where she allowed herself to enjoy it.

The sound of the children's laughter growing closer pulled her out of her thoughts.

'Hey, Mum, is it true that Max told you he was going to come back to Micklewick Bay in a fast car and ask you to marry him?' Zak asked, mischief dancing in his eyes.

'Did anyone ever tell you you're a right little squirt?' Embarrassment sent a blush creeping up Jasmine's neck and flooding her cheeks.

Max let out a roar of laughter.

'Yep, you, loads of times.' Zak gave her an impish grin that melted her heart.

'My dad told me he said that when he was about nine before he left for Harrogate with his grandad,' said Connor, wearing an equally mischievous smile.

'Is that why you've come back, Max?' Chloe asked, swiping her hair off her face as she gave him an enquiring look. 'And would that mean you'd be mine and Zak's daddy as well as Connor's?'

'That would be *so* cool!' said Zak.

'You'd be a dead mint brother,' said Connor, both boys beaming broadly at one another.

'Hey, what about me and Mummy?' Chloe said, hands on hips.

'You'd both be dead mint, too, especially if we got to eat loads of your mum's cakes,' said Connor.

'Aren't you forgetting someone rather important?' asked Max, feigning a serious expression.

'Who?' the three children chorused.

Max shifted his gaze to Ernest, who was looking up at him expectantly, a ball at his feet, his fluffy tail swishing across the sand. 'This fella, of course.' He bent, picking up the ball and threw it as hard as he could, Ernest and the three children racing after it with whoops of delight.

'Thanks for that,' said Jasmine, her face still burning. 'I love him to bits, but Zak can be a right little rascal sometimes.'

'He's a good kid; they all are.'

Max stood thoughtful for a moment before turning to her. 'Jingilby.' He rested his hands on her shoulders, gazing deep into her eyes, making her heart thud faster. In the next moment he let out a hoot of laughter. 'Your face! Don't worry, I'm not going to get down on one knee in front of the kids.'

'Phew!' From the myriad emotions that were currently flying around her, Jasmine wasn't sure what to think. Surely that wasn't a hint of disappointment sitting in her stomach?

'What I was going to say was that I may not have consciously come back here to ask you to marry me – and it's way too soon to think about now, we're both cautious people and rightly so – but it's not something I'd rule out next year.' He cupped her face in his hands, rubbing circles on her cheeks with his thumbs. 'How d'you think you'd feel about that?'

Jasmine swallowed. How *did* she feel about that? 'I... I feel the same as you.' In fact, she'd been shocked to find herself, on several occasions, thinking of a long-term future that featured the two of them and their blended family, and it had made her heart fill with joy.

'I wish I'd come back sooner, Jingilby.'

'You came back when the time was right.'

'I did. And, talking of timing being right, I reckon it's time I did this.' He lowered his head and whispered, 'I love you, Jingilby,' before pressing his lips against hers, all soft and warm.

If they hadn't been so lost in the moment, they'd have heard their children cheering.

A LETTER FROM THE AUTHOR

Huge thanks for choosing to pick up *Cupcakes and Kisses in Micklewick Bay*. I hope you were hooked on the latest instalment of the Micklewick Bay series. If you'd like to hear about my new releases with Storm Publishing, you can sign up right here:

www.stormpublishing.co/eliza-j-scott

If you'd like to join other readers in hearing all about my new releases and bonus content, you can sign up for my newsletter!

www.elizajscott.com

If you enjoyed this book and could spare a few moments to leave a review, that would be hugely appreciated. It doesn't have to be long, just a few words would do, but for us authors it can make all the difference in encouraging readers to discover our books for the first time. Thank you so much. If you click on the link below it will take you right there.

I'm thrilled to have been able to tell Jasmine's story, not least because I was desperate for her to get the happy-ever-after she so deserves. She's a big-hearted character who I really admire, with her love for her children, strong work ethic and the way nothing (usually) fazes her. And despite having a tough few years, not to mention being pulled in so many different directions, she still managed to hang on to her sense of humour, which can't have been easy. It doesn't help that she lets her pride get in the way at times. But with having so many challenges land on her at once, it was only a matter of time before something had to give.

As for Max, life's certainly given him a few bumps and bruises along the way but, he's managed to come out smiling. After his difficult start in life, I wanted him to return strong and successful, proving to the world that he wasn't going to let his past define him or his future. And let's not forget, he had a certain promise to fulfil...

The idea of Max promising Jasmine that he'd return to Micklewick Bay and marry her actually came from somewhere close to home: my parents-in-law. It was one I've always wanted to include in a story so I was thrilled when I got to use it for Max and Jasmine.

My in-laws grew up in a small community, with my father-in-law being a few years older than his future wife. Unbeknown to him, she'd developed a schoolgirl crush on him – she told me she was very taken by his dark curls! Apparently, she used to tell her friends: 'I'm going to marry that lad when I grow up.' It was only when she was old enough to go to the local weekend dances that he finally noticed her and, by all accounts, he fell head over heels in love with the beautiful young woman she'd blossomed into. Before long, he proposed and they were married in the local church. It makes me smile to tell you that they had a long and happy marriage. Sadly, they're no longer with us, but my heart squeezes whenever I think of that story.

Writing another instalment in the Micklewick Bay series has been the perfect excuse to take lots of trips to the stunning towns and villages that line the North Yorkshire Coast. As I've mentioned in previous books, Micklewick Bay is an amalgamation of all these places. Saltburn-by-the-Sea is the inspiration for the "new" part of town with its beautiful Victorian architecture and looming Huntcliff which features as Thorncliffe in my series. Old Micklewick, the huddle of houses where the town has its origins, is based on the characterful fishing villages of Staithes, Runswick Bay, and Robin Hood's Bay. While Whitby, with its mix of new and old houses and streets – or "gates" as many of them are known – also deserves a mention. I never tire of visiting any of these beautiful places.

- facebook.com/elizajscottauthor
- instagram.com/elizajscott
- bookbub.com/authors/eliza-j-scott
- bsky.app/profile/elizajscott.bsky.social

ACKNOWLEDGEMENTS

Here's where I get to say thank you to everyone who's helped, in one way or another, to bring this book together for publication. I'm going to start with the man at the top, Oliver Rhodes. A great big thank you for setting up Storm Publishing, Oliver! I'm thrilled to be a Stormie! Next up is Kathryn Taussig for giving me an "in" and introducing me to my lovely editor, Kate Gilby-Smith. Kate is not only insightful, inspiring, and a joy to work with, she's also incredibly kind. I suffered from quite unpleasant back pain whilst writing Jasmine's story, which made it difficult to concentrate and even more difficult to sit at my desk and write. When I told Kate of this, she was enormously supportive and patient and allowed me the time I needed to finish the book. Huge, heartfelt thanks, Kate! (I've since invested in a new desk which has helped ease my back troubles enormously!)

I also owe a great big thank you to the rest of the wonderful team at Storm, including the eagle-eyed Editorial Operations Director, Alex Begley, and Editorial Assistant, Naomi Knox (huge congratulations on your recent promotion, Naomi!), for their fabulous formatting skills and for patiently putting up with my final tweaks. Huge apologies, and thank you! Thanks is also owed to Elke Desanghere and Anna McKerrow in the marketing and publicity team. Thank you for all you do in promoting my books. Big thanks to Chris Lucraft for his techy wizardry skills. It's all way over my head, Chris, but thank you so much for everything you've done and continue to do with the Micklewick Bay books and getting them into the hands of new readers! As I write this, *The Little Bookshop by the Sea* is at #11 in the Amazon Kindle UK charts and #2 in Amazon Prime Reading UK, which is a real "pinch me" moment. Thank you also to copyeditor, Shirley Khan, and proofreader, Amanda Rutter, for their part in the editing process and giving Jasmine's story the pre-publication polish it needed. And thank you also to super-talented book cover designer, Rose Cooper, for creating yet another stunning cover for the Micklewick Bay series.

Once again, huge thanks to the awesome Rachel Gilbey of Rachel's Random Resources for organising another wonderful blog tour with all her usual organisational flair. Thank you so much, Rachel! I continue to be in awe of your organisational skills!

Next up I get to say a massive thank you to all the wonderful book bloggers for taking part in the *Cupcakes and Kisses in Micklewick Bay* blog tour. I'm enormously grateful to you all for giving up your time to read and review my books, not to mention sharing your reviews on social media as well as your amazing blogs.

As ever, my two fabulous author friends, Jessica Redland and Sharon Booth, must get a mention. They're two of the kindest, most generous-spirited people I know and their friendship means a huge amount to me (they're also amazing authors!). We share a fondness for warm cheese scones and I always look forward to our catch-ups – not just because of the said cheese scones!

My long-suffering family also deserve a shout-out, for putting up with me locking myself away in my writing room for long periods of time, particularly when a deadline is looming – I've had some scary sessions with this book, I can tell you. I owe them an extra thank you for all their patience and endless supply of cups of tea when my back was at its worst. I think the discomfort might have made me a bit grumpy, so big apologies there. I love you with all my heart.

As ever, I'd like to send out a thank you to the beautiful towns and villages listed above for providing me with so much inspiration for the Micklewick Bay series. The North Yorkshire Coast really is full of stunning places. If you've never been before, I can highly recommend you take a trip there – the delicious fish and chips and ice cream are an added bonus. Thanks also to the locals for always extending a friendly welcome.

Finally, I'd like to thank you, the reader, for choosing to pick up and read my book. It still feels surreal that my childhood dream of becoming a writer has actually come true, and that people take the trouble to read what I've written is truly humbling. I'm not sure I'll ever get used to it, but I'm enormously grateful. Thank you so much!

Much love,

Eliza xxx

Printed in Dunstable, United Kingdom